SAILING INTO TROUBLE

BY

ANNA ST. JUDE

This book is dedicated to all the authors who have colored my world with their imaginations.
Thank you, I am forever grateful.

CASE FILE: GEORGIA

ONE

As John Colby concentrated on driving the black king cab pickup through the heavy mid-morning traffic, his younger brother Alex eagerly turned to their business partner in the back seat.

"What do you know about this woman, Nick?"

"Nothing, Alex," Nick Duffy sighed heavily, lounging with his legs stretched across the seat and his handsome features twisted into a grimace; irritated by Alex's unflagging enthusiasm almost as much as his mother's last minute phone call begging him to do her a favor. "I've never met her; I never heard my mother mention her before she called last night and asked me to show her '*dear friend Georgia*' some interesting places. I tried to get out of it, but you can't say no to my mother."

"Don't worry about it, Nick. I'm sure she's a nice old lady and we can show her around for a few days since we're not busy right now." John consoled him, turning into the airport.

"That reminds me, guys; remember we're *boat salesmen*!" Nick ordered, sitting up suddenly alert.

"Boat salesmen?" John laughed scornfully, shooting him a quick look.

"We sell boats! Got it?" Nick declared belligerently as John continued laughing and Alex looked bewildered.

"Why are we boat salesmen?" His puzzled expression cleared as he suddenly realized why. "Why don't you just tell your mother we're private investigators, Nick?"

"She'd worry, Alex. She likes to worry; she worries about me being a boat salesman. She'd call me every night to check on me if she knew I was a private investigator!"

John tried not to laugh at his friend as they got out. "What did you say this woman's name is?"

"Georgia Lorman. She's coming in on Western, gate three," Nick morosely followed them, muttering under his breath; chauffeuring an old woman around was not his idea of a good time.

*   *   *   *

Inside the airport, a young woman in her early twenties stood against the wall watching a mime entertain the waiting passengers and reached for her camera with a smile. The mime moved as she tried to focus on him, quickly clicking the button. He moved once again as she refocused and two figures partially obscured the mime.

"Drat!" she moaned in exasperation, trying again. After several more attempts to capture the mime on camera, her attention was drawn to a small Oriental man sitting in the chair in front of the mime. She absently snapped a picture, moving toward the chair. The man was slumped in his seat with his head resting on his chest; he appeared ill. She barely noticed the man bending over him. "Is anything wrong with Mr. Togee?" she asked in concern.

The stranger straightened up and walked rapidly away saying gruffly, "I'll get a doctor." The young woman gave his retreating back a cursory glance before turning to the sitting man.

"Mr. Togee," she called, gently shaking his shoulder. There was no reaction so she tugged at his suit coat and stared wide-eyed at the protruding knife. She shrieked as a hand touched her shoulder and turned in speechless horror with her hand over her heart, to see a security man.

"Is anything—" he stopped, seeing the knife and quickly spoke into his radio.

John and Alex idly watched the people, milling around trying to find their luggage, while waiting for Nick to come back. John was staring intently over Alex's head at a group of people in the distance when Nick rejoined them.

"Her plane would land a half hour early!" He sighed in annoyance.

"I wonder what's happening over there," John wondered aloud, noticing the group included several policemen.

"Who cares? Let's just find our old lady and get out of here," Nick replied brusquely, pulling him along.

The young woman was sitting on the far side of the gawking crowd when a police officer came up to her, "You can go now, Miss.

We've got your statement and your address. If we have any more questions we'll contact you; thank-you for your cooperation."

She shrugged and smiled slightly, "I'm sorry I can't be more help. I didn't see anything. Poor Mr. Togee, he seemed such a nice man on the plane. Who would want to murder him?"

"We don't know yet, Miss," the policeman murmured as he left.

She picked up her bag and immediately spotted Nick standing with two handsome blond men; one very tan and muscular, at least six feet four inches tall, the other man was younger and thinner, about five foot eight, she guessed as the three men checked out the terminal, vainly trying to spot a lost woman. Nick was just as tan but more heavily muscled, although not as tall as his blond friend. He was impatiently running his hand through his dark wavy hair as she walked up behind him and tapped his shoulder.

"Hi, Nick."

Nick turned to see a pale, tired-looking, petite young woman smiling at him. Her blonde hair hung limply and she wore shapeless baggy clothes.

"Do I know you?" he stared in confusion as John and Alex turned around.

"Georgia Lorman." She held out her hand which Nick automatically shook.

"*You're* Georgia?" John demanded in surprise, staring over Nick's shoulder.

"Yeah, what did you expect; a little old lady?" she asked sarcastically.

"Yes." Alex, always honest, piped up.

"How'd you know who I was?" Nick asked suspiciously, still confused by the unexpected.

"I've seen your picture a thousand times. Can we leave?" she asked abruptly.

"Oh, sure," John picked up her travel bag. "Is this all your luggage?"

"Dream on." she replied sharply. "I haven't had a chance to pick up my luggage yet," she walked away quickly, leaving them to follow her; staring at one another in surprise at her manner which was strangely authoritarian and not at all friendly. Nick ran to catch up to her.

"How'd you meet my mother?" he questioned curiously.

"At Karate class," she replied absently, searching her purse for her luggage tickets so she missed his mouth dropping open. When they stopped at the luggage rack, she pointed out two bags which Alex and John grabbed as Nick continued staring incredulously.

"*My* mother takes Karate?"

"She's the instructor," she informed him in surprise; leading the way out of the airport. Nick stood stock still, a look of total shock on his face, staring after her until John grabbed him by the arm, propelling him after Alex and Georgia.

"A Karate instructor?" he repeated dazedly.

"That's what she said, Nick." John replied cheerfully, grinning broadly.

Alex walked in front with Georgia showing her the way to the truck. They piled in with Georgia sitting up front.

"I'm staying at the Coco Palms, do you know where that is?"

"We thought we'd take you to the boat and then to dinner." John glanced over as he started the truck.

"A boat!" Georgia wailed in horror. "God, no!" She refused, turning to look at them. "I'm looking forward to laying down on something that doesn't move or make any noise. You know what I mean?" her eyes begged them to understand. John looked in the rear view mirror meeting the glance of the other two.

"No," they replied in unison making Georgia laugh softly.

"You guys are very nice to pick me up," she turned to Nick. "I'm sure your mother asked you to show me around and I do appreciate it really," she said sincerely, putting her hand on John's arm and leaning forward. "But I feel like a rag doll. Tuesday morning I flew from Miami to Alaska. On Wednesday, I flew back to Miami. This morning I had to go to the office before I flew here. I really don't know whether I'm coming or going. I haven't slept in two days."

"Why didn't you sleep on the plane?" Alex wondered.

"I hate flying *because* I can't sleep on planes," She explained as John parked at the hotel. "And if that's not bad enough; the guy I sat next to on the plane got murdered while I was waiting for you at the airport. It was awful," she wailed as she hopped out.

"Murdered?" All three men demanded in unison.

"That's why the police were there."

"How did he—" Nick was interested but stopped himself, almost forgetting his secret.

"Someone stabbed him. I didn't even see it happen! No one did! It's really creepy that someone can get killed like that," she shivered as they handed her bags to the waiting bellhop. She checked in and turned to them. "Thanks so much, guys." The men said goodbye and turned to leave. "Oh, Alex?" He turned back. "What time would I have to be ready, tonight?"

He looked confused for just a moment before replying, "About seven thirty."

She smiled, "If the offer is still available, I think I'll take you up on it. I'm feeling better already; after a couple hours of sleep, I'll be fine."

Alex grinned with pleasure, "That's great! I'll pick you up at seven thirty. It's formal dress, of course."

"Ok. Bye." Georgia nodded and got on the elevator with the bellhop. As the doors closed, John and Nick turned to Alex.

"What was that all about, little brother?" John asked Alex with a puzzled frown.

Alex grinned, "I asked her to the Robotics Convention Ball tonight." He explained as they got in the truck to head home.

"When did you do that?" Nick asked in amazement since Alex was normally very shy with women.

"When we were walking to the truck, she asked me about Quark; she said she was very interested in computer robots." As they headed away from the hotel in heavy traffic, Nick looked very perplexed as Alex continued, "I wasn't planning to go but I just decided to ask her. You know it's very formal and by invitation only. I'm—"

"Alex, how does she know about Quark?" Nick interrupted impatiently.

Alex stared without understanding. Quark was Alex's very unique computer robot which had an all-terrain vehicle bottom, six different robot arms in the middle and a ventriloquist dummy head with a mouth that moved when he 'spoke' and blue LED eyes that flashed. Alex couldn't comprehend anyone *not* knowing about him.

"I'm sure she's read about him. I am very well known in computer circles, you know," he replied pompously.

"Maybe your mother told her, Nick." John ignored his brother's idea.

"I never told her." Nick replied deep in thought as John looked at him questioningly.

"Maybe you did and just forgot?" He suggested.

"No, I've never mentioned Alex to her," Nick said positively.

"We've been working together for four years and you've never mentioned me to your mother?" he demanded indignantly.

"I can't, Alex. You're too famous! You're always in the papers and magazines. If she connects you to me, I'd be in big trouble when you tell people you work for the On Board Detective Agency," he explained hastily, hoping to soothe his hurt feelings.

Alex still looked troubled as they parked at Wally's Marina 54. They silently boarded the Baby, their very large, very impressive boat. Nick and John threw themselves down on the soft chairs under the awning as Alex continued into the main cabin. They lived on board as well as using it as their office. The beautiful ship always impressed their clients. It had been customized on an opulent scale by the previous owner, a rich drug dealer before the DEA had confiscated it at the end of one of their cases. They had also discovered many hidden secret compartments on board; even after four years they still occasionally came across a new one. Alex absently crossed the slightly messy but extremely luxurious main cabin on his way down to the next level, putting his hands on the grab bars they had installed, to swing himself down the steep ladder-like steps without touching any of them except the top one. He went into the spare room where Quark was waiting and threw himself down on the bed, still feeling slightly insulted. He had thought of himself as one of the guys until Nick had said that.

The three of them shared ownership of the boat, the truck, three motorcycles and an Army surplus helicopter even though Nick and John had known each other for over ten years and he had just come into the circle four years ago.

They lived outside the mainstream rat race very happily even though most people thought them insane just because they never knew if the bills would be paid at the end of each month. Alex had enjoyed every minute of his time with them. Nick and John supplied the brute force and the detective skills needed while Alex used his computer genius to uncover every little piece of information possible. He looked up to see John standing in the doorway.

"Don't take it personally, Alex." He advised his younger brother. "You know how secretive Nick can be. You're just too famous!" he reminded him truthfully. Alex was a computer genius who was called in to assist with all sorts of top level, high profile cases in businesses and governments; usually resulting in news coverage.

"It's not like she doesn't know you exist, Alex." Nick chimed in, coming into the room. "She knows you're John's brother and you occasionally stay here with us."

"Occasionally?" Alex yelped, making Nick grimace and hang his head. "Well, she'll know I live here now, won't she?" he demanded spitefully. He grinned, knowing by Nick's shocked expression that he hadn't realized Georgia would tell his mother all about her vacation.

"Damn!" Nick jumped to his feet and left the room. Alex felt better and got to work on his computer. John patted Alex's shoulder with a shake of his head and followed Nick.

TWO

"Alex is still up." Nick commented in surprise, seeing all the lights on as he and John returned late that night.

"What time is it anyway?" John yawned.

"2:10." Nick looked at his watch as they entered the main room to find it empty with every light on. They heard laughter coming from Alex's room and exchanged an amused look. "The good doctor is busy," Nick smirked. He put his hands on the bars, about to descend the steps when Alex appeared at the foot of the steep stairwell.

"Oh, hi guys," he called cheerfully, still in his tuxedo. John and Nick wore dress shirts and slacks. Alex's back blocked their view of Georgia as she came upstairs with him holding her arm, helping her up the steep steps. He moved out of the way as she reached the top and Nick and John stared in astonishment; the ugly duckling of the afternoon had been transformed.

Georgia was the picture of beauty and refinement. The lank hair was now shining and piled on her small and shapely head. She wore glittering jewelry in her ears, hair and around her neck and wrists. The pale tired face has been replaced by white skin highlighted with very subtle makeup. The shapeless clothes had been exchanged for a strapless white dress clinging to a perfect figure. John and Nick openly gaped at her.

"Oh, hi!" she gave them a brilliant smile.

"Hi," they both chorused at a loss for words.

Alex sat at the breakfast counter as John absently sat on the corner seat and was the first to recover. Nick stood on the other side of the room, staring at Georgia as if he had never seen her.

"I knew you lived on a boat, Nick but your mother didn't tell me it was a drop dead gorgeous yacht!" she grinned.

"It's a three-mast schooner, actually." Alex informed her. "It's a custom designed, one hundred foot ship with a draft of—"

"Relax, Alex, she's not buying it." John interrupted with a poke of his elbow while gazing at Georgia.

"Your business must be making money hand over fist to afford this boat!" she smiled at Alex.

"Actually, we couldn't have afforded it at all if Uncle Sam hadn't confiscated it in a drug raid!" John brought her attention back to him.

"What do you mean?"

"I had just arrived here and I helped them crack a big drug ring. We got a hefty reward from the government and we pooled all our resources and bought the Baby." Alex interrupted proudly. "It was dirt cheap but it still took every penny we had."

"Why would they sell it so cheaply?" Georgia asked, looking around, obviously impressed.

"Because it's a huge boat and it was costing them a fortune to maintain." John replied drily. "She needs an especially deep berth."

"Why did you name it Baby?" she asked curiously.

"That was her name, you never rename a ship; it's bad luck." Nick put in tersely, frowning at her as Georgia looked around the large open main cabin leading into the dining area where they were sitting. It had a separate table area but they were sitting at a counter where she could look down a short hall into the small galley. Alex had been showing her the four large opulent staterooms. There were also four tiny crew cabins, which weren't being used. The outside deck had a large awning covering half the deck.

"I'm very impressed!" Georgia smiled. "But I have to be going." She said softly to Alex.

"Did you have a nice time?" John asked curiously, looking from her to Alex.

"Oh, yes!" she gushed, suddenly full of energy and very animated, "We had a fabulous time! I love to dance. Alex told me the funniest stories about everyone there." she giggled. "He was just showing me Quark. He's fabulous!"

"Quark!" Nick shouted, abruptly coming to life, making everyone turn to him in surprise. "How did you know about Alex and Quark?" he demanded staring at Georgia intently.

"Your mother told me," she looked at him, obviously confused.

"She doesn't know about them," he denied, shaking his head vehemently.

Georgia slowly smiled broadly, "Yes, she does, Nick."

"How could she know?" Nick questioned uncertainly as she tried hard not to laugh.

"She didn't believe your story about being a boat salesman. So she hired a detective to follow you," she laughed at Nick's shocked expression.

John laughed out loud, "You never could lie to her, Nick."

"You're telling me." Nick agreed ruefully. "How long has she known?"

"Oh, about four years now," Georgia smiled, "Your mother is something else, Nick. I'm going to miss her."

"Miss her?" Alex quizzed.

"I just moved about two weeks ago; to New Orleans for my job," Georgia nodded her head ruefully. Alex suddenly perked up.

"New Orleans? Do you know a friend of mine—"

"Alex!" Nick interrupted, shaking his head and saying his name through clenched teeth. Georgia was looking behind her at the clock and missed his actions. She moved to stand behind John as she turned towards them.

"I actually only know one person in New Orleans; she's an old friend of mine, but I doubt you know her, Alex." she laughed lightly. "She's a high priced hooker called Miss Pearl."

John and Nick looked stunned as Alex replied cheerfully, "That's my friend! What a small world it is. Are you a hooker, too?" John was too far away so Nick slapped the back of Alex's head as Georgia laughed.

"No, we went to school together in Pennsylvania. Every year about six of us get together in New Orleans for a reunion. Sally was voted most likely to succeed. She says she's going to retire soon and write a book about all her men." Suddenly Georgia gave a gasp and cried, "Oh, my God! You're the Professor!" She stared at Alex with a big grin. She put her hand over her mouth trying to stifle a laugh. "We wait all year to hear Sally's stories about her—clients." She stumbled slightly before the last word. "Alex, you're going to be the first chapter," she smiled broadly at him. John and Nick exchanged worried glances but Alex was eager to hear more.

"What did she say about me?"

"She said you were *'Fractal cool'* if you understand what that means. She never explained that one." Georgia murmured more to herself than Alex. John and Nick tried to hide grins knowing it was Alex's favorite phrase for something that thrilled him.

"Alex thought she was pretty *'Fractal cool'* too, didn't you, Alex?" Nick teased. Alex had met her on the beach and had no clue what her profession was. She had simply liked his honesty and open admiration of her.

Alex grinned broadly, "What else did she say?"

"Well—," Georgia hesitated, raising one eyebrow. She came around next to John, putting one knee on the seat beside him saying, "Excuse me." and leaned across him to whisper in Alex's ear while supporting herself with one hand leaning on the table, cupping the other around her mouth. John quickly moved his hand off the table only to find it in close proximity to her inviting derriere. He took a deep breath while averting his eyes and ran the hand through his hair before catching sight of Nick engrossed with the view of her cleavage, staring stupidly. Nick received a hard kick on the shin under the counter and jerked his eyes to John in surprise. Nick glanced back at her face close to Alex's before Georgia stood up suddenly. Alex smiled in delight. Georgia looked at him with an expression of disdain, "Alex, I'm surprised at you!" But before he could reply, she added in a husky voice with a sexy look, "and intrigued!" She laughed lightly. "I think it's time I went home," she said breaking the spell.

John and Nick both jumped to their feet, "We'll take her home, Alex; you must be tired."

"I'll go with you, guys."

"Oh, good," Nick replied sarcastically, thinking it was very unfair since Alex had already had so much time alone with this lovely woman. John held her hand going down the ramp and lifted her off the ramp after pointing out that it was on wheels and might move.

"Thank you." she smiled.

Nick adroitly pushed him out of the way to escort her up the marina ramp and helped her into the truck, getting in beside her, leaving Alex in the back by himself. John gave Nick a dirty look over Georgia's head as he got in the driver's seat.

"You look very lovely tonight." John told her sincerely. She looked pleased and thanked him.

Nick claimed her attention, "What would you like to do tomorrow?"

She looked surprised, "Oh, I don't really know, I didn't make any plans."

"How would you like a helicopter ride?" he suggested with a smile.

"I'd love a ride in Dolly," she replied, shocking him because she knew the name of their helicopter. Georgia laughed in delight, "She was a very thorough detective," she teased.

"She?" The three men chorused in disbelief.

"She." Georgia nodded, looking very pleased with herself. "That was my idea," she gloated. She shrieked as the car behind rammed them and grabbed Nick's leg as the car did it's best to run them off the road.

"Hang on!" John shouted as the truck careened wildly from side to side, trying to avoid a head on collision with cars coming from the other direction. Georgia gave a small, very frightened shriek as they narrowly missed hitting a tractor trailer head on. She had her left hand against the dashboard. Nick had his left arm around her shoulders and hung onto the door with his right. As they narrowly avoid hitting a pole, Georgia tightened her grip on his leg. Nick momentarily forgot their danger as his face contorted in pain.

"My leg!" he shouted. "Stop pinching me!" She released the inside of his thigh to place both hands against the dashboard.

"He's trying to kill us!" she shouted.

"Oh, I don't think so." Alex stated calmly. "There are much more efficient ways to kill someone. I think he wants us to stop."

John grinned, "Good idea, Professor," he slammed on the brakes, at the same time yanking the wheel as hard as he could, making the truck spin in a circle. When it stopped, it was headed in the other direction. John hit the gas and took off back the way they had come. Their antagonist continued speeding in the opposite direction. John turned this way and that for several miles to be sure they had lost their pursuer before he slowed his speed. "Anyone get a plate?"

"There weren't any plates. It was a black BMW® with tinted windows," Alex replied sadly.

"Are you alright?" Nick nervously asked Georgia, who hadn't said a word.

"Just swell," she answered sarcastically, turning her head to stare directly at Nick. "Are there a lot of people who want to kill you?" she asked curiously.

"Only a couple," John replied cheerfully. "All in a day's work for us," he shrugged.

After they let Georgia out at her hotel, Alex mused reflectively, "I wonder what she'll tell your mother?" Nick made a sour face, rolling his eyes as John laughed out loud.

THREE

The next morning Georgia got out of the truck with John, staring at the huge military helicopter. "Why is it purple and yellow?" she asked Alex, who was there to greet her.

"Because the paint was free." he shrugged.

Nick came from around the other side, eyeing her appreciatively; enjoying the cute short set that showed off her fabulous figure.

"Hey, Georgia!" he greeted her cheerfully. "Are you recovered from last night's excitement?" She turned her attention from the helicopter to him.

"You call someone trying to kill you; *excitement*?" she demanded incredulously. All three guys shrugged.

"Well, yes." Nick admitted sheepishly.

"Well, this trip better not be *exciting*." she warned as Nick laughed it off. "Where did you get hold of a military helicopter anyway?" she asked curiously.

"Army surplus, it's a Chinook CH46. John and I flew these babies when we were in the army," he paused then said, "You can ride up top with me."

"Can I really?" her eyes shone with excitement. "How do I get up there?" She asked staring up puzzled. John took her around to the other side and helped her climb up to the navigator's seat, standing below her enjoying the view until Alex poked him in the ribs. He looked chastised by Alex's disgusted look as they climbed into the bay of the helicopter. They put on helmets so they could talk to one another while flying.

Georgia busily snapped pictures as Nick narrated with occasional comments from John and Alex. Nick noticed her examining her camera looking puzzled.

"What's the matter?"

"Oh, um, it's just that I'd swear I had thirty-six exposure film in here; but it's only twenty-four." Nick shrugged not understanding why it's important.

"So, maybe, you made a mistake" he reasoned as she dug in her camera bag. She held up an empty film box triumphantly.

"No. See, it's a thirty-six exposure." she held it up and shook her head. "The weirdest things have been happening in the last two days. Last night, when I got back to my room, I'd swear someone had been in my room but nothing was taken."

"It was probably the maid," John suggested calmly.

"After midnight?" she questioned skeptically. There was a noticeable pause, "And maybe, I just imagined it, right?" she snapped sarcastically, looking at Nick. Her attention was caught by a helicopter heading towards them. "Why is he heading right towards us?" she demanded nervously.

"Hey, Nick, there's a helicopter coming straight for us," Alex piped up.

"No kidding?" Nick rolled his eyes.

Georgia screamed as the helicopter opened fire on them. John and Alex fell back from the open bay doors. Nick took evasive action while John and Alex broke out rifles from a locked box in the bay and returned fire at the pursuing helicopter. A battle ensued with the two helicopters chasing and firing at one another. Georgia had her eyes tightly closed, clutching the seatbelts until her knuckles were white. Suddenly the attacking helicopter veered off and Nick let it go.

"Why are you letting them get away?" John yelled furiously.

"We're low on fuel. We have to land." Nick replied bitterly, hating having to let them go. He radioed the tower, informing them of the actions of the helicopter and giving them the identification numbers and telling them of their flight plan change. John angrily shook the gun after the departing helicopter.

"Georgia, are you alright?" Alex asked in concern.

Nick looked over when there was no answer. Her head was down with her eyes tightly shut as she clutched the straps in a death grip. Nick reached over and tapped her arm but got no response.

In a few minutes, they landed at the private airfield they used. Nick was still in the pilot seat on one side of Georgia while John stood on the outside ladder on her other side.

"Georgia, you can let go now," he assured her, trying to pry her hands loose.

"Not till we're on the ground!" she refused fiercely. John and Nick exchanged glances.

"We're on the ground, Georgia!" John reassured her, trying not to laugh. "Open your eyes, you'll see." One blue eye opened suspiciously then the other eye. John pointed through the windshield. "Look, there's Alex standing on the ground." Georgia looked at Alex cautiously as he waved. She looked at John and nodded.

"Okay, now let go of the seat belts," Nick urged.

"I can't!" she wailed in desperation.

They finally managed to pry her hands free and she groaned and stretched her fingers. They unbuckled her and John helped her down the steps. Nick waited at the bottom for them and swung her off the last step onto the ground.

"See, that wasn't so bad, nobody got hurt," Alex tried to console her. She remained silent, shaking the hand of each one in turn.

"Thank you very much for the *excitement,* gentleman." she said before walking away. They watched her walk away with their mouths hanging open for a few minutes before running to catch up with her.

"Wait, where are you going?" John demanded incredulously.

"I'm going back to my hotel," she replied quietly.

"We'll take you there." Alex assured her.

"Oh, no, you won't!" she refused emphatically. She stopped abruptly and turned, "I'm sure you're all very nice men, even though people *are* trying to kill you. But if I never see you guys again, it would be too soon!" she explained. She turned and walked quickly away, leaving them staring after her.

"I think she's upset." Alex volunteered. John and Nick exchanged a 'Do you believe he said that?' look.

"I think we'd better let her go and give her a few hours to calm down." Nick stated.

"Yeah, that'll give us time to find out who's trying to kill us." John agreed, walking back to the truck, occasionally looking behind them at the disappearing figure of Georgia.

FOUR

Georgia walked up to the hotel desk, wearing a beach robe and carrying a bag.

"How was the beach?" the desk clerk smiled as he retrieved the key.

"It was perfect! I couldn't ask for a better day," she smiled and walked away.

"Oh, Miss Lorman," the clerk called after her; Georgia turned.

"Yes?" she walked back to the desk.

"Did you have film in to be developed?"

Georgia stared blankly, "No, I didn't. Why do you ask?"

"Someone broke in and destroyed everything! Exposed all the negatives, burnt all the photos." The clerk told her in shocked tones; they both shook their heads.

"Why would anyone do that?" Georgia asked unable to understand the motive for such behavior.

"For kicks, I guess," the desk clerk replied before turning to the next customer asking, "Did you have any film in for developing?"

Nick, Alex and John arrived in the lobby to see Georgia speaking to the desk clerk. She was at the elevators when she heard her name being called once more. She turned casually and was at once horrified to see them standing there.

She pointed an accusing finger at them, "Get away from me!" She ordered loudly.

"Georgia, listen," Alex pleaded.

"No! Go away!" she demanded. The elevator opened behind her and she stepped in saying, "Stay away from me. Every time I'm with you, someone tries to kill me!" The elevator doors closed on a small crowd staring at Nick, John and Alex.

A security guard came hurrying over, "Gentlemen, you'll have to leave."

"Yeah, yeah," Nick shook the man's hand off his arm and they headed for the exit.

"You'd think we had the plague," John grumbled, back on the sidewalk.

"We'll have to give her more time, guys." Alex said; never afraid to state the obvious.

"Yeah? We'll give her a week," John sniped. He suddenly noticed Nick wasn't with them and turned to see Nick staring at the ground some distance behind them. "Nick, what are you doing?" he called. Nick looked up from his study of the ground.

"Did you hear what she said?" he asked John.

"Loud and clear, buddy. The whole lobby heard her," John replied angrily.

Nick shook his head, "She said '*someone tries to kill me*'. What if she's right?"

Alex jumped in excitedly as they hurried back to the hotel. "We've been on the wrong track! Someone wants to kill her, not us!"

"Of course!" John agreed but grabbed Nick's arm halting him. "But why? Who would want to hurt Georgia?"

"Let's go ask her." Nick replied and reentered the hotel. They warily walked across the lobby, keeping an eye out for the security man.

Georgia struggled with two men in her hotel room; one of whom had a needle. She screamed again as John and Nick kicked the door in and rushed in. The men threw Georgia at them and rushed out of the room. John and Nick ran after the men, leaving Alex to help Georgia up from the floor where she had fallen.

"Alex, those men are after *me*!" she cried tearfully, not able to fully comprehend what had just happened.

"Did they say why?" Alex questioned gently, leading her to the couch shaking her head.

"They kept asking me about some pictures." she replied, confused. Suddenly, she grabbed Alex's arm shouting, "Togee! Togee!" Alex was startled and left behind as Georgia ran out of the room, snatching her purse from a chair as she hollered, "Come on!" He caught up with her as the elevator doors opened on Nick and John arguing.

"I can't believe you let them get away!" Nick accused to John.

"I didn't let them get away! There were too many people around for a shooting match, you know." John replied defensively.

He startled as Alex and Georgia rushed in, hitting the lobby button. "Alex! What's going on? Where are we going?" he demanded as they descended.

"I have no idea," Alex replied truthfully as the doors opened and Georgia rushed out. They followed her through the lobby to the street at a run. She continued her headlong rush up the street, making several turns. They were all panting when she finally stopped and entered a shop.

"Will someone please tell me what's going on?" Nick complained breathlessly as Georgia handed the girl behind the counter a slip of paper. She gave Georgia an envelope of developed pictures which she tore open, looking through them rapidly.

"Hey, that's ten fifty, Miss." the girl objected, holding out her hand. John hurriedly gave her money.

"I'm surprised you don't use a digital camera, Georgia." Alex mused following his own train of thought.

"I usually do, Alex. But I dropped it four days ago and I haven't had time to get it fixed. So I had to use my old film cartridge camera." she answered absently, looking through the three packages of photos.

"If you told us what you're looking for, we could help you look." John snapped edgily.

"This!" she shouted triumphantly, handing John three photos. In the first one, a man with a knife in his hand was standing over a napping Mr. Togee. The second picture showed the man with his hand still on the knife in Mr. Togee. The third picture clearly showed the man's face as he turned to look around. Alex and Nick looked at the pictures over her shoulder as she showed them to John. Nick looked at Georgia in astonishment.

"You see a murder and you don't tell anyone?" he asked incredulously but she shook her head.

"I didn't *see* it. I was trying to get a picture of the mime. Look." She pointed to the background of the pictures. "But the camera was on auto focus and it took pictures of the foreground."

"Well, whoever that is," John pointed to the murderer, "knows these pictures exist and he knows about you."

Georgia put the three photos in her purse, "We have to get these pictures to the police." She noticed the camera shop girl listening with interest.

The bell on the door rang as it opened and all eyes turned to see a man enter. He's nicely dressed in a dark three piece suit and a gun.

"I'll take all of them," he said pleasantly; no one moves. "Give them to me," he demanded. Nick reached to take the envelopes from Georgia who whipped them behind her back.

"Georgia, give them to him!" he ordered angrily.

"No," she flatly refused.

"Don't play games, Georgia," John ordered angrily. "He's got a gun."

"There's five of us and only one of him. He can't shoot all of us at once," she insisted.

"Are you crazy, woman?" Nick demanded incredulously.

"Are you volunteering to be shot, Miss Lorman?" the gunman asked sarcastically.

"If I must, whoever you are." she replied calmly. "You'll kill us all anyway." The man gave her a small nasty smile.

"Georgia, give him the pictures!" Alex pleaded.

"Here, Alex, you give them to him," she tossed the envelopes over Nick and John's heads to Alex who promptly dropped them. The man with the gun was momentarily distracted, swerving his gun over towards Alex. Georgia tackled him around the knees as Nick and John both grabbed for the gun. A shot was fired into the ceiling and the four of them fell together to the floor, knocking over a display.

"Wow, this is great!" the awed cashier shouted, leaning over the counter to watch.

Alex grabbed the phone to call the police. Georgia sat up, taking her camera out of her purse.

"Smile," she said brightly. John and Nick posed with a smile for the picture. The anonymous gunman struggled but he was well pinned by the two men.

FIVE

"I like her," John grinned as the men relaxed on Baby's deck.

"Forget it, John," Nick replied vehemently. "She's a crazy woman! She says no to a man pointing a gun at her."

"But it worked, Nick," Alex defended her.

The conversation was interrupted by Georgia's appearance from inside the boat. She seated herself comfortably.

"Have we all recovered from our '*excitement*'?" she smiled looking very pleased with herself. "Your mother was very upset, Nick."

His mouth dropped open as he sat bolt upright, "You told my mother?"

Georgia nodded, "She's taking the next plane out—" she stared over the rim of her glass as he leaped out of the chair and ran into the cabin.

"His mother is coming here?" Alex questioned confused.

Georgia looked at him from the corner of her eye, "No," she stated non-chalantly.

"But you said—" Alex broke off as he and John stared perplexed.

She grinned wickedly, "I lied." The two men couldn't help laughing but she suddenly sobered, "I still wish I knew why he killed Mr. Togee," she said sadly.

"He was a diamond courier," Alex replied calmly. "I hacked into the police files." He shrugged at her questioning look.

"Mr. Togee?" she questioned in amazement. He had seemed such a quiet little mouse of a man; she couldn't imagine him doing such a dangerous job. She shook her head and leaned back enjoying the sun. "I'm going to miss this boat when I go to New Orleans."

"I've been thinking of taking a trip to New Orleans," Alex said pensively, thinking how much he enjoyed the last time.

John looked at Georgia. "It does sound good," he agreed hopefully but she didn't respond; turning to Nick as he came out of the main cabin. She couldn't help grinning as he gave her a sour look.

"You're a riot," he snapped, throwing himself into a chair near her as she giggled. John and Alex grinned while Nick tried very hard not to grin.

CASE FILE: KARINA

ONE

On a beautiful sunny California day Alex, John and Nick were being watched while they relaxed on the deck of the Baby. A man hidden in the hills across the street from the marina swept the area around the boat with binoculars. He stopped his scan of the area abruptly as he saw someone else watching the boat through binoculars. The second binocular man was lying flat on the rooftop of a store on the same side of the street as the marina. The man in the hills reported his finding into his walkie-talkie.

That night in a run-down neighborhood many miles away, a figure left an apartment house wearing a dark raincoat with the hood up and walked down the alley at a good pace keeping her head down. She glanced nervously behind as another figure followed her, making no attempt to conceal himself. She turned the next corner quickly. Her pursuer sped up but just as suddenly stopped abruptly as two dark shadows detached themselves from the wall to block his path. Large, mean, rough looking men stared at one another. The woman heard the sounds of fighting as she continued to walk rapidly away. She hailed a taxi on the main street and alighted from her taxi in a much nicer neighborhood. As she turned to walk down the street a little way, a second car pulled to the curb. A well-dressed man got out and followed. She entered a building quickly without looking behind her. The man attempted to follow her only to be stopped by two burly bouncers.

"Sorry, Mac, Ladies Night Only," the larger man told him bluntly, pointing to a sign. The man noticed the neon sign for the first time. **ALL MALE REVUE**. He stepped back looking irritated, knowing she had gotten away. He made a call as he melted into the crowd wandering the streets.

*   *   *   *

John was napping on one of the lounge chairs when Alex ran up the boarding ramp.

"Hi, Alex," he opened one eye and murmured drowsily. Alex sat on the foot of the chair staring unhappily at his brother. It was so unusual to see Alex upset over anything, John sat up.

"What's up, Brain?" he asked in concern, using a nickname from their childhood.

"I have been to every store in town and no one has a 386 micro-processor," he stated mournfully. "Dooley says they stopped making them in 1993," he added for John's benefit.

"Then why do you want one? Don't they make something better now?"

"No, no, the output configuration of the 386 micro-processor would be perfect for this application!" Alex objected. He sighed once more, "Dooley says I'll have to go to a third world country where they recycle our old computer parts."

"Uh huh," John muttered, not the least impressed with Alex's computer geek friend Dooley. Dooley worked at the local geek tech store and got Alex parts at the best prices. In John's opinion, they came up with a lot of hair-brained schemes. He closed his eyes, "Why don't you advertise for an old computer that has that part in it?" He suggested lazily.

Alex jumped up, eager once more. "That's a great idea, John!" He was walking away when John called.

"Alex!" John reached under his chair and held out a manila envelope, "A young lady left this for you."

Alex's ears perked up, "A young lady?" He repeated happily reaching for the envelope. "I don't know what a young lady would be writing me about—" he opened the envelope and suddenly became very still; inside was a picture of Alex wearing a devil costume. He looked slightly younger in the picture. Alex stood staring at the picture as if turned to stone. John shaded his eyes, looking up at Alex curiously.

"What's wrong, Alex?" he sat up to peer at the picture. "Why Alex, you little devil," he laughed, teasing him gently. "What's it say on the back?" he asked noticing the writing from his vantage point.

Alex snapped out of his reverie, "The back?" He repeated stupidly, turning the picture over. 'Meet Elgin Park, 4:00 PM, General Grant Statue, Come alone, Tell no one' Alex read it silently. "John, what did this woman look like?" he tried to sound casual but his heart raced.

"Young, blonde, pretty." John replied, trying to read the writing since Alex didn't tell him what it said.

"How young?" he quizzed his brother, very serious now.

"About eighteen."

Alex was immediately disappointed.

"I've seen her around here before. I think she works for a message service, come to think of it," John informed him, watching him closely. Alex walked away to stand at the rail, looking out on the bay.

John followed him, "What's going on, Alex? What does this mean?" He pointed to the picture in Alex's hand. Alex hastily put the picture in his shirt pocket.

Alex put his hand up and adjusted his sunglasses, "It's nothing, John." He turned away then turned back. "What time is it?" John, who never wore a watch, picked up Alex's wrist and showed him the time. "Oh, yeah," Alex muttered lamely.

"Why do you want to know what time it is? Got a heavy date?" John quizzed sarcastically.

"What?" Alex was startled and alarmed, "Oh, no! Of course not, John." He denied vehemently, "I've got to go."

"You just got back," John reminded him. "Where are you going now?"

"Um, I'm just going to take a walk in the park," Alex stammered; he was a terrible liar.

"That sounds great! I'll go with you," John replied cheerfully, needling him even more.

"No! You can't!" Alex cried, desperate to get away.

"Why not?" John was open and friendly and determined to find out what Alex was up to.

"You just can't!" he shouted, completely flustered now. "Sometimes a guy just has to be alone!" He yelled, running off the boat.

John jogged beside him up the ramp leading out of the marina, "Alex, why are you being so mysterious?"

Alex gave John a hard shove, "Back off! Just leave me alone!" He ordered sharply; shocking John.

"Sure, Alex; whatever you want." John backed away with a casual shrug. He leaned against the railing, watching Alex walk rapidly away. Alex put a hand to his head walking to his motorcycle, strapped on his helmet and rode off. John waited until he was almost out of sight.

*   *   *   *

Alex walked up to the statue of a man on a horse, idly wondering how many statues of General Grant there were in the country. He walked around the statue pretending to examine it from all sides. A few feet away from the statue were large, dense bushes almost three quarters of the way around. There was no one to be seen in any direction as he leaned back against the base looking at his watch; ten minutes to four.

John walked slowly across the grass looking for Alex. When he spotted him, he ducked behind a tree as a woman dressed in a dark raincoat with the hood up appeared suddenly from the back of the statue. She touched Alex's arm from behind and he turned suddenly, his face lighting up.

"Karina?" Alex stared in confusion into the face of a stranger.

"Don't move!" a masculine voice ordered as Alex felt a gun shoved into his back.

"What's going on here?" a very confused Alex demanded. John left his tree and jumped the man with the gun. They were rolling around on the ground, fighting for control of the gun when other men arrived. One man pointed his weapon at Alex and another one cocked his gun near John's ear. John looked up startled and grudgingly released his opponent as the man, holding the gun on Alex, flipped open a badge.

"CIA." John muttered irritably, shooting a dark glance at Alex before looking around for the woman who was nowhere to be seen.

"Don't tell them anything, John," Alex warned as they were handcuffed.

"How can I tell them anything when I don't have the foggiest idea of what's going on?" John complained loudly as he was pushed into a car.

TWO

It was dark as the slight figure boarded the boat and slipped into the main cabin.

*   *   *   *

Nick boarded the Baby and saw a flashlight moving around in the main cabin. He looked around and picked up a hammer he had neglected to put away, after fixing some of the rigging earlier, lying conveniently on the nearest deck chair. He silently entered the cabin and switched on the light; startled to see a small, thin woman dressed in black. The woman reacted instantly, kicking him in the stomach and fleeing off the boat. Nick picked himself up and ran after her in a flash. As she reached the top of the marina ramp, she stopped, hanging onto the chain link fence and sinking to her knees, gasping for breath. Nick came up behind her slowly, puzzled and wary.

"Please, don't hurt me," she begged in a hoarse whisper with a heavy accent.

He made a quick decision and reached out to help her to her feet, "I'm not going to hurt you. Let me help you back to the boat." He supported her as she moved slowly down the ramp, leaning heavily against him, still struggling to breathe. Neither one spoke as they both looked around nervously several times.

*   *   *   *

"Alex, you have to tell me why I just spent six hours being questioned by the CIA!" John demanded testily.

"I told you a thousand times, *I don't know*!" Alex responded equally annoyed.

"Why don't I believe you?" John grumbled. "Wait till Nick hears this," he muttered as they boarded the Baby. They entered the main cabin to see Nick putting the phone down.

"Where the hell have you two been?" he demanded angrily. "Alex, you have a very strange visitor," Nick didn't wait for an answer to his question as he pointed down the stairs. Alex leaped down the ladder steps without a word and Nick looked at John, "What's going on?"

John threw himself on the couch petulantly, "Don't ask me! I don't know anything! Just ask the CIA!" He was explaining the events of the afternoon when Alex ran back into the room.

"Guys, we have to put out to sea. Go to this location," he ordered urgently, handing Nick a piece of paper as they both stared in amazement, and turned to leave.

"No! Wait, Alex!" John shouted.

"Why?" Alex looked at them, "Guys, I need your help. This is more important than anything we've ever done. I'm asking you to trust me." They stared at a man they didn't even recognize; gone was easygoing, head in the clouds Alex. The man speaking to them was tense and driven, utterly serious.

"Okay, Alex," Nick agreed first and Alex gave him a grateful glance before leaping back down the ladder. The two men exchanged a glance, "Why do I feel as if we just entered the twilight zone?"

"You and me both, buddy," John agreed. They jumped to their feet to get the boat ready for departure.

The Baby had a covered wheelhouse, accessible by double sided outside entrances, which sat forward of the main sail and was slightly higher than the main cabin but under the main sail to give the pilot an unobstructed three hundred sixty degree view. Nick was usually the captain on the helicopter and John was the usual captain on the ship although they could both sail and fly. Baby had powerful engines which came in handy when she wasn't under sail.

"Something weird is going on here, Nick," John worried as they met back on the top deck. Nick nodded silently but pulled John into the wheelhouse, shutting the doors, making John give him a quizzical look.

"I've been feeling like we're being watched," Nick explained in a low voice.

"I'm not sure Alex can handle this," John lowered his voice, moving closer to Nick. "Who's his visitor?"

"A foreign woman; she wouldn't say anything to me. She doesn't look at all well, but she wouldn't let me call a doctor," Nick shrugged as John headed the boat out of the marina and into the bay.

*   *   *   *

Alex returned to his stateroom, sitting on the edge of the king size bed and picked up the hand of the woman lying on top of the covers.

"Karina," he called very softly; his face transformed as he gazed at the beautiful woman with long, dark curly hair. She had very pale skin and delicate features; the skin of her face was stretched tightly across very high Russian cheekbones. There were large dark circles under her eyes and the hand Alex was holding was thin with long, incredibly delicate fingers and very cold. He rubbed it gently with a worried frown; she was obviously seriously ill. Her eyelids fluttered and she stared sightlessly at Alex for a moment then smiled gently as she recognized him once more.

"It is so good to see you, my darling Alex," she whispered.

"What's wrong, Karina?" he asked sadly, touching her face reverently.

She gave a small laugh that had no humor in it, "What's not wrong, Alex?" She turned her head away for an instant before looking at him tenderly, "I did not want to put you into danger, Alex. I just wanted to see you one more time."

"I'm glad you found me no matter what happens," he replied holding tightly to her hand. Her use of the words 'one more time' had sent chills through him. "We're on our way to the coordinates you gave me," he told her unnecessarily as they could both feel the sway of the boat and hear the creaking as she skimmed through the sea. "What's out there?" he asked curiously.

"Absolutely nothing," she grinned broadly. "Just another false trail like the park," she sighed softly.

"Why do you need all these false trails? Who's after you?" he asked in concern.

"Very dangerous people, Alex," she reached for him, grasping his shirt fearfully. She fell back on the bed as the effort exhausted her. "Promise me, you won't get killed! Promise me," she begged urgently.

"No, of course not," he tried to soothe her. "Nick and John will help—"

"No, you mustn't tell them anything! The less they know the longer they'll live," she breathed heavily as she reached for his hand, "Six months ago, Miroslav was assassinated."

"I'm sorry to hear that, Karina. I know you loved him." Alex said softly, looking away.

She nodded, biting her lip, "It is worse than that, Alexi," unconsciously calling him by her pet name for him, "an informer had found out about his part in the underground rebellion; so he was killed. I smuggled the children out of the country and went into hiding. I just arrived in this country last week. I was to give a micro dot to someone in the Defense Department; a General Dalton, then I was going to be free to say goodbye to you." She paused; even talking exhausted her, "My informant, the one who set up the trade, got a message to me. Dalton plans to sell the micro dot back to the Russians for two million dollars."

"Two million? Wow! What's on the microdot?" Alex asked curiously.

"Military secrets, a new offensive weapon. Gary didn't meet me at the airport. My contacts in this country tell me he is dead. You have been under surveillance for two days, Alex. I asked Gary to find you for me; Dalton tortured it out of him before he killed him, I'm sure but my men have been watching you, we arranged the meet at the park to draw everyone away from the boat so I could board."

"Well, it worked. Dalton has the CIA looking for you. He's accusing you of stealing U.S. secrets." Alex informed her.

She nodded slowly, "The Russians are also looking for me. That's why we're here at sea. A Swedish trawler will pass by here shortly. I want them to think I left on it."

"Oh, I see," Alex nodded.

Karina took his hand placing a ring in his palm, "I'm returning this to you, Alex. Don't take it off and think of me."

"My college ring!" Alex slipped it on his finger remembering all those years ago when he had given it to Karina. He was shocked by her pallor, "Are you alright darling?" He was afraid, "You need a doctor."

"No, Alex, doctors can not help me. Just let me sleep; I'll be fine in a little while," she dropped off to sleep, leaving Alex deeply concerned as he gently placed the quilt over her.

He slowly went upstairs, deeply absorbed in his thoughts and sat at the table across from John and Nick, who waited impatiently for him to speak. When he didn't say anything, they exchanged a worried glance.

Nick sighed, "How's your friend, Alex?"

"She's sleeping now," Alex answered mechanically.

Nick nodded, "She doesn't look too good, Alex. Maybe—"

Alex put up his hand to stop him, "She's exhausted, Nick. She's been in hiding for six months trying to get out of her country."

"What country is that?" John asked pointedly.

"Russia."

"How did I know he was going to say that?" Nick looked at John.

"Alex?" John called quietly, waiting for Alex to look directly at him.

"Yes, John?"

"Why are we hiding a Russian spy on our boat?" John asked pleasantly.

"And how does she know you?" Nick added for good measure.

Alex got up, pacing in agitation, "She's not a Russian *spy*." he refuted angrily. He sighed deeply and sat back down, running a hand through his shaggy blond hair. His manner again changed; he wasn't light-hearted, happy go lucky Alex anymore. John was surprised; he seemed suddenly more mature than both of them.

"I met Karina nine years ago in Washington D.C. at a Science convention," he looked at his brother. "You remember when I went there?"

John shook his head. Alex had been a child-genius; while his three brothers had followed the normal development, Alex had graduated from high school at ten. He had earned his first degree in computer science at twelve, the second in robotics at thirteen. He had two master's degrees by fifteen and two doctorates by the time he was eighteen. He had been away from home since he was ten; traveling the country and the world while his family had stayed at home. Hasty visits and phone calls had been the only contact with his brothers.

No one had been more surprised than John when Alex had shown up in Bridgeton out of the blue. He said he was there on vacation but they had found out he was desperately unhappy, living and working in his academic world. He had stayed with them and decided to make the change permanent after helping them crack the biggest case John and Nick had ever worked on. They had spent the reward money on Baby and the helicopter and the On Board Detective Agency came into being. Alex had rarely spoken of his life before joining them. John was again at this moment, reminded how much of a stranger his own brother was. All this passed through John's mind as Alex sighed and began to explain.

"I fell in love with her the moment I saw her. She loved me, too," he sounded amazed. "But she was married and had two very young children," he paused lost in thought.

"How old was she, Alex?" Nick asked.

"She was twenty-six. She was with her husband who was there on international business. State department business; he was very highly placed in the Russian Government," again he paused; it was painful to remember this time in his life.

"So, you had an affair?" Nick questioned hesitantly.

"No, of course not!" Alex denied, deeply offended. "She loved her husband, Miroslav. It didn't seem right to either one of us. We just—" he closed his eyes remembering the good times, "spent every moment we could together. Taking walks, canoeing, mostly talking and knowing that at the end of two months we would say goodbye and never see each other again." The pain of parting was reflected in Alex's voice, "It was a spring I'll never forget. I don't regret a moment. I was never happier than the time I spent with her." Alex spoke forcefully as he opened his eyes to glare at them.

Nick touched his arm, "I'm sorry, Alex."

Alex shook his head, "Don't be, Nick. I'd do it all again in a minute." He stopped speaking to look at the table. "But now she needs my help," he looked at them. "And I need your help, but I can't tell you why. The less you know the better. I can tell you the CIA is after her because a crooked general is using them and the Russians are after her because she's a leader in the underground."

"What underground, Alex?" Nick questioned curiously.

"The Russian Underground against Oppression."

"I didn't know there was one?" John said.

"Aren't they a little late?" Nick asked confused. "The USSR no longer exists."

"There is still oppression," Alex informed them coldly. "And there will always be people like Karina and Miroslav who give their lives to fight oppression."

"Can you tell us why we're out here in the middle of nowhere, just bobbing like a cork?" John asked a trifle sarcastically.

Alex got up, "If anyone asks, you never saw or heard of Karina. When you're tortured, tell them we brought her out here and she got on a Swedish trawler. Now I think we'd better get some sleep." 'In-command-Alex' told them and abruptly left.

Nick stared at John, "*When* we're tortured?" He repeated unhappily.

THREE

The three men sat on deck in the bright sunshine. John looked impatiently at the clock on the wall and turned to Nick.

"You think she's ever going to wake up?" he whispered.

"Maybe we should go check on her?" Nick asked in a normal tone of voice, looking hopefully at Alex. Alex stared towards the horizon, completely oblivious to them as well as their hints; the ring Karina gave him glinted on his finger. Karina startled all of them by suddenly appearing in the doorway.

"Karina!" Alex leaped up, running to her.

She smiled and for a moment, they were the only two people in the world staring into each other's eyes. She offered her hand to Alex and he helped her out onto the rolling deck as Nick vacated his lounge chair to take her arm and sit her down.

"I'll get you some lunch," Alex patted her shoulder.

"Oh, no, Alex," she reached up to stop him but he was already gone. She turned her head to find John and Nick staring intently and lowered her gaze. "You are good friends to my Alex," she spoke gently without raising her head. "I am glad he has such friends," she suddenly raised her head to stare intently at them. "You must take care of him," she urged. She stared at John. "I have not met you. You are very like my Alex," she murmured, slightly puzzled. They shared almost the exact same handsome face topped with very pale blond hair and bright blue eyes. Alex was obviously younger, an impression heightened by his boyishly slight build and shaggy mop of hair. Alex was also much shorter and paler than the tall, broad shouldered, very tan John.

"I'm his brother John," John replied grimly. "You're putting him in danger."

She met the challenge in his voice, looking back calmly, "I am afraid so." She sighed, "I did not mean to."

"What can we do?" Nick asked bluntly.

"Do you know how to fish?" she asked startling them both.

"Yes." Nick answered slowly, very puzzled.

"Then go fish."

"What are we fishing for?" John asked, not sure what she wanted them to do.

Karina looked confused by his confusion, "The fishies." She patiently explained, making a wiggling fish motion with her hand and then pointing at the water.

John tried to clarify it one more time as Nick sat back with a disgusted snort.

"You want us to fish?"

"The more fish the better."

"What do fish have to do with this?" Nick asked exasperated.

"Nothing," she smiled in delight and shrugged, apparently enjoying their bewilderment.

They glanced at each other as Alex came out of the galley with a tray of food and Nick got up, motioning to John who followed suit. Karina and Alex didn't notice their departure.

"I don't like this, John. She's doing her best to keep us out of whatever is going on. It's very suspicious!" Nick complained.

"Maybe not, Nick. She doesn't trust us. If her story is true, she's got every reason not to," he looked over his shoulder at Alex and Karina; their heads were close together as they smiled and talked.

"I don't like not knowing what's going on." Nick grumbled. "How does she expect us to protect Alex without knowing anything?"

"She's so worried about Alex," John commented, concerned. "What's going to happen to her?"

Nick handed him a fishing reel, "Go fish." he muttered drily.

Karina sipped orange juice as she eyed Alex sadly with an air of enduring patience, looking towards the completion of her goal. Alex sat across from her not meeting her eyes. She put her hand under his chin, turning his face to her, raising her eyebrows inquisitively. He placed his hand over hers on his face.

"You're not staying this time, either. Are you?" he murmured sadly.

"I cannot," she looked him squarely in the eye.

"Let me come with you; anywhere you go," Alex begged impulsively. She suddenly looked away to hide her tears. He fiddled nervously with his glass and his sunglasses. "I— I understand. I thought— Well, I still love you. Just like last time," he explained, looking down at his hands.

She laughed, shaking her head at him, "Alex, I too still love you. Just like last time." She put her hand in his. "You cannot know how many times I have thought of you and— what might have been," she picked his hand up, kissing it and putting it against her cheek. "Do you know why I stayed with Miroslav?"

"No, I didn't want to think about him at all," Alex said in a hard voice.

"I told him, I had fallen in love with you. I told him I was thinking of not going home with him. He was very deeply upset; he told me how much he loved me and begged me to stay with him," she closed her eyes, biting her lip. "I told him I needed him to understand and give me the space to decide," she stopped, looking out over the water.

"What did he do?" Alex asked, needing to know.

"Just that; I spent every minute of every day with another man and when I returned, he was open, friendly and supportive. He told me he would fight to change my mind if I decided to stay with you but otherwise he was wonderful," her voice softened considerably. "I couldn't hurt someone who loved me so much, Alex," she looked at him with tears in her eyes. "I would never have seen my children again," she wiped away a tear that had fallen. "I have been happy, Alex. But always I thought of you." She put a hand to her head. "I think I have had enough sun, Alex, please help me back to my room." She needed his arm around her waist to stand and enter the cabin. She was so weak, he carried her down the stairs; by the time she was back in bed, Alex was quite alarmed at how terribly pale and exhausted she looked.

"Karina."

She put a hand limply on his arm, "Come wake me in an hour." She was asleep before he reached the door which he left open.

Alex came to sit beside her at the end of the hour, lightly touching her shoulder. Her eyes opened very suddenly as if she had been waiting for him.

"There is a reason I cannot stay, my love," she said abruptly. "I'll be dead very shortly." She watched him with sad eyes.

"We won't let them kill you, Karina," he protested.

"There is no 'them', Alexi. When we met all those years ago, I was in this country with my husband for leukemia treatments. Every morning I would go to the hospital for a treatment and then meet you; being with you got me through the pain."

"You never told me," Alex whispered horrified.

"I wanted our time to be perfect. And it was!" she whispered, her face glowing. "But now it is too late. When I die, I want you to bury me at sea. When you return to Bridgeton, you will tell the Russians these sea coordinates and they will assume I left on the Swedish trawler. You tell the American agents, I was never here. Don't tell John or Nick I am dying; they will make you take me back. You understand how important this is? Take the ring I gave you to someone in the defense department you can trust. Maybe Boorfield—" she was talking to herself and frowning. Alex took off the ring, looking at it in amazement. "There is a microdot under the stone," she explained. "I think Boorfield is your best bet but check him out carefully. I really am sorry, Alex, I left Russia to come say goodbye to you. This information just fell into my hands. I only wanted to see you again, to touch you one more time. Now I've put your life and friends in danger. If it wasn't this important, I wouldn't ask you," she pleaded with him to understand.

Alex kissed her gently, "I understand, Karina. I'll do it for you gladly!" He pulled her to him urgently but gently. "Seeing you again is worth dying for," he whispered in her ear.

"Hey— oh!" Nick stood in the open doorway but quickly turned away. "Dinner is ready. We're having fish!" he said loudly as he disappeared. He heard Karina's delighted laugh.

She grinned at Alex, "I want nothing." There was a slight pause. "Maybe some milk?" she reconsidered.

"I'm not hungry either," Alex replied, content to just sit and look at her.

"You go eat," she commanded sternly. "You are too thin." He reluctantly left.

Nick returned carrying a glass of milk. "Alex, said you only wanted milk?" he questioned curiously.

Karina smiled and struggled to sit up. Nick put the glass on the floor and helped prop her up on one elbow. She took the milk, sipping it and tilting her head inquisitively.

"Yes?"

"We care a lot about, Alex." Nick replied staring intently.

"I know you do," she agreed taking small sips of the cold milk.

"We don't want him used, even by an old— friend," he chose the word carefully.

"I am not using him," she assured him solemnly.

"You have an awful lot of secrets," he retorted bluntly.

She smiled, "I have no secrets from Alex."

Nick had one more question, "How long are we going to be fishing and where are you going?" He asked still suspicious.

"Not long and soon you will know," she replied cryptically.

"I'd like to know now," Nick insisted stubbornly.

"All things come to those who wait," she smiled, teasing him gently.

"You're not going to tell me, are you?" he guessed.

"It's important that I don't," she said with a little apologetic shrug of her thin shoulders.

He didn't feel consoled as he stood up, "You haven't eaten anything since you came on board."

"I'm on a diet," she laughed. He reluctantly left.

FOUR

It was dark and silent on the boat as Nick and John slept. Alex slept on the bed next to Karina who lifted her hand to pull aside the curtain, letting the moonlight flood into the room. She looked at the clock, midnight.

"Alex" she called softly but he woke instantly. "I want to see the moonlight on the water, Alex," she could barely speak. "Can you carry me to the deck?"

He got up and came around to her. He helped her stand, wrapping a blanket around her before he picked her up. He was appalled how light she was. He easily carried her up to the deck. He sat in a lounge chair still holding her in his arms. They remained silent for many minutes gazing out at the brilliantly lit water.

"It's so lovely," she barely breathed the words in his ear.

"Yes." He replied never taking his eyes from her face.

"Whenever we were hiding from the guards or police or troops, in cold attics and cellars for hour and days, I would think of our two months together. It kept me sane. It kept me going."

"Where are your children?" Alex asked suddenly.

"In a neutral country with new identities; they are safe, guarded by good friends. I've said goodbye to them," she cried softly. "I won't see them grow up." Suddenly she looked at him. "Have you been happy, Alex?"

He reflected for a moment before answering. "Yes, I have been happy. I've thought about you a lot. I remember what you said when you left." She looked puzzled. "Look to the future." He reminded her.

"I'm glad, Alex. I want you to be happy; I want you to find a Miroslav, someone who loves you wholeheartedly and generously," she urged.

"I don't know, Karina. I compare every woman I meet with you and no one stands up," he shook his head sorrowfully.

"Someday, Alex, you'll find her," she looked out over the ocean. "Somewhere, sometime we're going to meet again, my darling. We will be together then, I promise you," she said fiercely as he looked down into her eyes and kissed her. "I am so happy to be here in your arms," she sighed. "It is like heaven."

"I love you, darling Karina," he held her so tightly he was afraid she might break. They kissed.

"Look to the future, my Alexi," she whispered softly. She rested her head against his chest, completely exhausted once more. Alex gently tightened his arms around her. He rested his chin on the top of her head looking at the moon on the ocean, blinking back tears.

Alex was suddenly aware of waking up. "Karina," he whispered. She felt very heavy and he moved his arm gently. Her head fell back limply, following the curve of his arm; alarmed he felt for her pulse. "Karina," he whispered in despair, laying his head on her shoulder.

*   *   *   *

A bump woke Nick. He listened wonderingly and heard another bump. He got up to look into the hall. John opened his door and stared at Nick.

"Is that you making that noise?" John asked grumpily. Nick shook his head; listening for more sounds. Alex came up the ladder from the hold carrying a sand bag and dumped it on the floor before disappearing back into the hold. John and Nick stared, unable to comprehend anything this strange at three am when he appeared with a third sand bag.

"Alex, what the hell are you doing?" Nick demanded irritably.

Alex picked up a sand bag, "Help me with these, will you?" he asked mechanically. The two men exchanged a glance and sighed. They each picked up a sand bag and reluctantly followed Alex up on deck.

"Alex, *why* are we carrying sand bags at three in the morning?" John asked in exasperation as they walked through the main cabin.

"I have to bury Karina," Alex replied emotionlessly. John and Nick stopped dead, staring at one another in alarm.

"She's dead?" Nick asked, appalled.

John slumped against the doorframe, "A dead Russian spy is worse than a live one," he moaned.

They ran after Alex who was out on deck. Nick grabbed Alex's arm as he knelt beside Karina's body wrapped in a sheet.

"Alex, you can't do this!" Nick remonstrated but Alex ignored them, continuing to tie the sandbags to a rope and wrap it around her body.

"You can't just get rid of her body!" John insisted, trying to take the rope from him.

Alex grabbed it back, roughly shoving him aside. "This is the way she wanted it, guys. She asked me to bury her at sea and I'm going to," he replied fiercely.

Nick sighed and began to help, "I don't believe I'm doing this," he muttered angrily. He looked at Alex, "What did she die from?" he asked suspiciously.

"Leukemia," Alex replied in a hard, tight voice.

John put his hand on Alex's shoulder, "We're sorry, Alex."

Alex looked away, "It's all right. But—" He faltered. "We have to look towards the future now."

*   *   *   *

It was daylight when Nick and John jumped off the boat to tie up to the dock. Alex came out on deck looking tousled but dressed.

John looked up, "Did you get any sleep?"

"A little," he said grimly, leaning on the rail watching them. He looked up as several men came down the marina ramp onto the dock. The man in the center of the group waved a hand over his head and the men quickly boarded the Baby, rudely shoving Alex aside.

"Hey!" John hastily finished his tie down and ran up the boarding ramp with Nick following close behind. "Dalton, what's the big idea?"

Dalton waved a search warrant under his nose, "Where have you guys been?"

Nick sauntered over, "Fishing. Did they make a law against that, too?" He baited the General.

"What's the deal, here? You tell us to stay out of the way so we take a little fishing trip and you come search us!" John asked in innocent indignation.

"Since when do Generals get this involved?" Alex questioned earnestly. "Who is this woman? And why do you want her so badly?"

"I told you; she's a dangerous Russian spy," Dalton informed him nastily. He turned as one of the men came out of the cabin shaking his head.

"Nothing, General; fishing tackle and fish mostly."

The General grimaced, "Watch your step, punks! We'll be keeping a sharp eye on you." He threatened but left with his men following.

"Punks! Punks?" Nick shouted indignantly. "Did he call us punks? Where'd they dig this guy up anyway?"

John looked at Alex, "Well, little brother, what do we do now?" he asked sarcastically.

"We wait for the next set; the *really* dangerous ones," Alex replied grimly, going into the cabin to eat.

"Just great," Nick whispered to John with heavy sarcasm before following Alex inside. Nick had that creepy feeling of being watched again.

* * * *

"No fish!" Nick said emphatically as they walked down the main street in the bright light of midday discussing lunch choices. "I'm sick to death of fish."

"Alright!" John agreed calmly. "What *do* you want?"

Alex walked slightly behind them, deep in thought, as they passed an alley; hands reached out to grab him, pulling him swiftly into the alley. He only made a small grunt before disappearing from view.

"What did you say, Alex?" Nick turned his head. "Alex? Alex!"

The two men ran back to the alley where four huge husky men were waiting to grab them; after a brief useless struggle, they were neatly handcuffed and pushed into a van.

Inside an abandoned building a half hour later, they were hanging upside down five feet apart with their hands still cuffed behind them.

"This is great!" John grumbled, vainly trying to stop himself from turning in circles.

"Where have I seen this trick before?" Alex mused thoughtfully.

"The late, late show, Alex," Nick grumbled sarcastically. "Yow!" He yelled in pain as the lash of a whip left a bloody mark on his bare arm as an older man came into his line of vision. "What's the big idea?" Nick challenged.

"Why are we here?" John was next to feel the whip but he was braced for it and grit his teeth and whistled. "That little sucker smarts," he quipped.

"I think you know exactly why we are here." their nameless tormentor replied silkily, with only a slight accent. "What did she give you?"

"Who?" Nick asked innocently.

Alex felt the lash and gave a small shriek. "You know, you'd get better contact with that if you moved—"

"Alex!" John and Nick both shouted.

"Oh, right!" he fell silent about improving your whipping techniques.

"Where is it?" their captor hit Nick harder.

"Arggh," he gasped, struggling against his bonds. "She didn't give us anything!" he yelled. He was hit again, "Nothing!" he repeated. Once more, he was hit harder across the back, drawing more blood.

"She didn't give us anything!" John yelled. "We're telling you the truth, she—" he jerked his head back as the lash curled around his neck.

"You will be dead within the hour in this position." the man informed them quite cheerfully. "It won't be an easy death unless you tell me what I want to know."

"Tell me what you want to hear and I'll say it," Nick retorted nastily. "This guy must be left over from the war," he told John, catching each other's eye as they slowly turned.

"What rock did they find you under?" John asked seriously as he turned past Mr. X.

The man wrapped the leather whip around his throat. John made choking sounds as he tried to jerk his body away.

"Alright, alright!" Alex cried out. "Let him go and I'll tell you everything." The man smiled in satisfaction and released John who began coughing and gulping air. "We're private investigators. She hired us to take her out to sea." Alex explained in a rush as Mr. X grabbed hold to keep him from spinning.

"And?" he prompted as Alex stopped.

"And nothing," Nick interrupted nastily.

"When we got up the next morning, the woman and our scuba gear were gone," Alex said trying to shrug his shoulders.

"Hmm," their tormentor was silent, contemplating. "What were your coordinates?" he demanded sharply. John answered in a strained voice. Mr. X disappeared as suddenly as he appeared.

After several minutes of useless struggling and turning, they heard shouting and shots outside the building. General Dalton walked in; staring at them contentedly.

"Your Russian friends are quick; two got away, one is dead," he walked slowly around them. "They were leaving as we arrived," he stopped, gazing at them once more.

"Get us down, General!" Nick demanded sourly.

He clicked his tongue, "The young are so impatient!" He nodded to his men and one of them left and returned with a ladder. He cut the ropes; letting them fall painfully to the ground. They sat up stiffly, still handcuffed and glaring malevolently at the General who smiled smugly.

"You were following us! You saw them kidnap us!" John accused in a rasping voice and began coughing again.

The General smiled nastily, "Well, now I know you did have her on the boat." He said raising his eyebrows.

"We did not! We were lying to them," Alex snapped in disgust. "Uncuff us!"

"Maybe later, Genius; bring them," he ordered his men as he walked out.

They resisted as much as possible.

"Are we under arrest, General?" Nick shouted, dragging his feet and trying to pull away from the guard.

"On what charges?" Alex shouted after the man.

They kicked and struggled but were eventually shoved into a windowless van and driven to a two story cinderblock building where they were placed in three identical cubicles still handcuffed. Nick had to be tied to the chair and each one in turn was hooked to a polygraph machine.

"What is your name?"

"I don't know," Nick answered sullenly.

"You're not cooperating, Mr. Duffy," the interrogator lectured.

"Really?" Nick asked in surprise.

"You could be here for a very long time."

Nick sighed in resignation.

Two hours later, the three men were still handcuffed but back together, sitting in a room with Dalton and the polygraph man with three armed guards in the room. Nick sported a black eye.

"Well?" Dalton asked the man irritably. "What are the results?"

"Everything *he* says is a lie," he replied irritably, pointing to Nick who grinned. "Including his correct name and age; I think he's a pathological liar," the man added in disgust.

"Hey, yo, give me a break," Nick protested cheerfully.

"Blondie is lying about the woman but on every question, not just the trick ones," again the man shook his head in disgust. He walked behind Alex who looked bored and scornful. "This is the only one who has reliable test results," the technician paused. "He's scared to death but truthful; says she hired them to take her out to sea. She pulled a gun on them and left in a boat. She paid them a thousand dollars which she deposited in their account yesterday."

"Left? Damn!" Dalton shouted, pounding the table. "She must have met her contact at sea. These bozos were a blind!"

"Which you fell for," the technician reminded him superciliously.

Dalton gave him a dirty look and abruptly left. The tech followed him out as the guards prodded the men to their feet and out of the room. They were being led, still in cuffs, down the halls when Alex broke away to run awkwardly in the opposite direction to accost a man.

"Major Boorfield, I must speak to you. General Dalton is a traitor," Alex blurted out as the guard grabbed him. The major raised his brows sardonically as the guard dragged Alex away.

"Dalton collecting misfits again?" he queried the guard.

"Yes sir, sorry sir," the guard apologized, angrily pulling a protesting Alex away.

"No, Major, you must listen to me!" Alex yelled as Major Boorfield rapidly walked away.

*   *   *   *

It was late evening when they boarded the Baby, tired and sore.

"Alex, how could you fool a lie detector?" Nick questioned, obviously impressed.

"I tried a little self-hypnosis this morning instead of sleeping. I hypnotized myself into believing it really happened that way," Alex explained quietly.

"Uh huh," John said doubtfully. "At least it worked." He entered the main cabin and switched on the light.

"Oh no, not again," Nick cried in exasperation as two men faced them with automatic rifles. "What is this?" Nick asked aggressively. "Who do you guys work for?"

"Whoever pays," the tall, heavy-set black man told him. "Turn around; you're going for a ride and don't get cute." They turned, resigned and disgusted.

"Don't you guys ever give up?" Alex protested as they were hustled into a black limo. When they reached the highway, five identical black limos fell into line with them, making Nick and John exchange a worried look.

"Get on the floor" Rifle man ordered.

They piled on one another uncomfortably as the cars began to weave in and out before suddenly splitting off in five different directions at a major interchange. Two of the cars turned completely around, returning the way they had come. Two men in a red sedan quickly decided which car to follow but they were not happy.

Night had fallen when they got out of the car in the desert and were prodded by their friend with the rifle into a small cave. Inside, a campfire flickered and the guard stayed by the opening still covering them with the rifle as a shadow came forward into the small circle of light.

"Major Boorfield!" Alex was pleasantly surprised; John and Nick were astonished.

"Sit down, gentlemen," their host indicated flat rocks and empty sand. They settled themselves stiffly. "I'm intrigued, Mr. Colby. Do you wish to explain your earlier statement?"

"Where's Dalton?" John interjected, putting his hand on Alex's arm; suspecting a trap.

"Safely back in Bridgeton," the major patted a radio phone kit sitting on the ground by his leg and looked towards the guard at the door. "I didn't use any of our men. Tell me, Mr. Colby, what do you know of Dalton's activities?"

"Only that he planned to sell the information back to the Russians for two million dollars and he's already killed one man," Alex answered calmly.

"How do you figure into this?" the major looked at Alex puzzled.

"Karina was an old friend. We helped her escape."

The major nodded, "Then you have no proof, either." He stated sadly, rubbing his head and suddenly looking very tired.

"What if we were to get you some?" John offered. The major narrowed his eyes but looked mildly interested.

"How?" He questioned; not really expecting much.

"We call him; tell him we have whatever it is he's looking for and make him a deal to split the profit with us." John suggested.

"If you had it, why would you split it with him?" Major Boorfield objected.

"Because we know he'll kill us if we don't," Nick added.

"It would be a breach of security if I tell you what it is," the major raised another point.

"So, don't tell us! He already thinks we have it. He'll set up the meet with the Russians with very little persuasion." Alex replied confidently.

Boorfield stared uncertainly, "Why do you say that?"

"He's greedy," Alex made it a statement. "He can't afford to pass up the opportunity to get his hands on two million dollars. He can easily kill us afterward."

"Who else would buy this?" Nick asked.

"There's an agent for the Chinese hanging around," Boorfield said quietly.

Nick nodded, "We'll tell Dalton; this was a meet with the Chinese. The thought of competition will clinch the deal."

The major smiled for the first time, "It's a shame you two didn't make the Army a career." He stared morosely into the fire. "It's completely out of the question, of course; the Pentagon working with outsiders," he shook his head.

Alex stood up suddenly, "Then I guess it's a good thing we're working on our own and you were just astute enough to have us followed."

"If you get any packages from Speedy Cleaners, you'll know what to do with it, of course," Boorfield said cryptically as they parted; understanding one another completely.

FIVE

"Ok, guys. The phone is bugged, that's it." Alex informed them after setting Quark to do a twenty-four hour check for electronic surveillance as soon as they got back to the ship.

"John Colby to speak to General Dalton." John placed the call to the base and put it on speaker phone. They waited for several minutes before they heard Dalton.

"What do you want, Colby?" he barked.

"A trade, General," he said calmly then paused. "We've made contact with a buyer. The Chinese will give us a million for it. We'll sell it to you for the same amount."

"Why would you do that?" the general asked after a long pause.

"Safety, General," Nick cut in. "We know you're still tailing us. We make the sale; you bust it and kill us. You report that unfortunately, it's lost in the struggle; then you sell it to the Russians as you planned."

"You see, General, this way, we keep an eye on you. You can't play the hero at our expense," John added. There was silence on the other end for several minutes.

"Of course, if you don't want to, we'll take our chances with the Chinese," Alex said firmly.

"No, that won't be necessary—" the General replied hastily.

"Good," Nick took over the conversation. "You set up the deal with the Russians and we'll meet you there."

"Don't try any tricks, Dalton. Or you'll never see your precious microdot again," Alex snapped harshly and hung up. The two men stared at him speculatively.

"You've known all along what they were looking for?" Nick asked bitterly.

"Of course," Alex said curtly and left the room. They all tried to get some sleep.

*   *   *   *

John came in, from an early morning check of the perimeter, carrying a brown paper package to see Nick hanging up the phone.

"That was Dalton. It's today at two o'clock, on the base, Hangar 8. He'll leave passes at the gate."

"On the base?" Alex asked incredulously, coming upstairs.

"The man has guts," John agreed.

"It makes it easy for the General," Nick replied. "But I'm surprised the Russians went for it." He watched curiously as John unwrapped the package.

"You sent your shirt to the cleaners?" John questioned Nick who looked at his familiar striped shirt in confusion.

"*I* didn't," he denied, shaking his head and putting down his coffee to reach for the shirt. "This is weird. This has to be the package from *you know who*; but a shirt?"

Alex sat Quark on top of the shirt and grabbed the lap top. "Analysis," he commanded, frowning at the screen. "It's a transmitter," he said after several minutes. "They can hear every word."

"From a shirt?" John asked in disbelief. "How?"

"Very thin glass filaments sewn into the seams. The cuff buttons are batteries. The top button is the microphone. This is *fractal cool*!" Even Alex was awed.

"I just hope it works," Nick grumbled. "I guess this means I get to wear it?" he questioned, taking it from Alex as if it might break.

They drove onto the base easily enough and went straight to the hangar. The huge hangar doors were closed as they got out of the truck and warily entered the side door. The building was in darkness but the lights came on as they closed the door. General Dalton stood a few feet away pointing a gun at them. Three crewmen worked on the plane behind him, ignoring the General's activities.

"Right on time, gentlemen," he said pleasantly. He snapped his fingers and one of the crewmen came to frisk them.

"Unarmed, no wires," he told the General and moved away.

"Good. Good," the general said pleased, holding out his hand, "the microdot please."

John shook his head, "We give it to the Russians, General."

"The Russians." The three detectives exchanged a startled look as the three crewmen came over as the General indicated them with a wave of his hand.

"The microdot," The shortest Russian held out his hand.

"The money," Nick responded. Two of the men went to a stack of nearby barrels, bringing out two briefcases from behind them. They opened the cases for inspection and then snapped them shut.

"Whew!" Alex whistled seeing all the money.

One of the Russian agents again held out his hand silently.

"Put down the gun, General," Nick insisted. "You're not going to shoot us the minute we give it to you."

The General hesitated but grudgingly complied as John and Nick looked at Alex. He put a hand on John's shoulder to steady himself and took off his shoe. He handed an envelope to the Russian as Nick and the General each reached for a briefcase. The Russian opened the envelope carefully and looked up sharply; enraged. A grating sound startled them as the hangar doors began to open.

"Stay where you are!" a voice commanded.

Alex threw himself on top of the gun to prevent the General from getting it. The Russians tried to leave by the side door which was opened for them by armed men. They surrendered. The General ran to the plane only to stop as bullets jumped at his feet. Boorfield came up to the three detectives.

"How did you know they were the real Russians?" he asked skeptically.

"They had two million dollars," all three answered simultaneously as two armed military men came and took the money. An older man came up to the group as they sadly watched the money leave.

"Good work, Boorfield— three Russian agents and a traitor; not a bad day's work." Although his words were praise, he spoke dolefully.

Boorfield smiled slightly, "Thank you, sir. But I wish we knew where that microdot is."

The three detectives watched with puzzled faces, wondering who the man was. He wasn't in uniform. Boorfield noticed them staring and performed introductions.

"Adam Kaylor, Under Secretary of Defense, Pentagon."

The dour man gratefully shook their hands and Boorfield added his thanks.

"I'll send someone to collect that shirt." He said casually as they turned to walk away.

"Major Boorfield," Alex said his name quietly; both men turned.

"Yes?" Boorfield asked quizzically.

"I'd like the ring back." He took it off and handed it to him. "It's under the stone."

Four men stared with their mouths open.

"You had it all the time?" John demanded indignantly.

*   *   *   *

Back on the boat, they entered the cabin to see almost a dozen roses lying spread over the table on green ferns. An envelope lay on top and Nick picked it up.

"It's for you, Alex," he said quietly, holding it out.

"Read it for me," Alex asked, his eyes glued on the roses.

Nick opened it and read it aloud, "There is no way to thank you for all you have given me, my darling Alexi." Nick paused a moment before saying the unfamiliar name. "A rose for every year since we met and the tenth because—"

"You must always look towards the future." Alex finished it as he picked up one rose. Nick turned the card over.

"But don't forget the past," Nick finished softly looking at Alex. John stood beside his brother with his arm around his shoulder. Alex gently put the rose back on the table.

"I won't ever forget you, Karina," he promised with a bittersweet smile.

CASE FILE: SHELLEY

ONE

It was early morning and the marina was very quiet. The fishing boats had long since departed since the summer sun rose several hours ago. A lone seagull perched on the rail of the Baby. An indistinct shape under a pink blanket lay on one of the lounge chairs under the awning. John came from the cabin, yawning and stood facing out to sea. Another typically beautiful California day, he thought stretching his arms and turned to see a small face peering at him from under the blanket. He returned the stare in silent astonishment as Nick came down the ladder from the roof deck of the main cabin. He walked over and picked the blanket up.

"What's this?" Nick startled as the girl screamed and jumped back, hastily dropping the blanket.

"Don't do that!" They both yelled at one another in shocked surprise. The girl rolled her eyes as she sat up shaking her head before turning to John.

"Is this the On Board Detective Agency?" she asked nervously looking from one man to the other.

"Yes, it is. I'm John Colby. That's my business partner, Nick Duffy."

"Hey, guys, I found a—" Alex stopped in midsentence as he came out of the cabin and saw the girl. "Oh, hello."

"This is our other partner, Alex Colby." John introduced him as the three men looked at the young woman speculatively.

"Shelley Hal." she said hesitantly.

"What can we do for you, Miss Hal?" Nick asked curiously.

Shelley clutched her blanket around her as she tried to sit up straighter and pull it around her shoulders like a cape; they caught a glimpse of short, frilly pj's, reminding them that they were barefooted and bare-chested wearing only the cutoff sweat shorts they wore to bed. She was a pretty brunette in her early twenties who didn't answer right away; looking out over the moored boats and then back to them. They glanced at one another, becoming more curious by the minute but gave her time to answer.

"I want you to protect me."

"From who?" John asked gently.

"A ghost." she said with a little shrug.

"A ghost?" Nick couldn't help smiling as he questioned dubiously.

She gave him a small smile in return, "Of course, it's a person but he wants me to think he's a ghost."

"What's he done?" Alex asked.

"Well, for the past few days, I've heard voices in my apartment but no one is there. Things have gone missing and then turned up in strange places. The lights and my alarm clock go off and on in the middle of the night. The TV and the stereo turn themselves off and on." she paused as the guys exchanged glances, not yet ready to make a comment. "Two nights ago, I rented a guard dog. I didn't hear a peep out of him all night and in the morning, he was missing!"

"No kidding!" Alex whistled.

"The company wants me to pay for him!" she exclaimed, outraged.

"Why are you in your pajamas?" John broke in, unable to restrain his curiosity any longer.

She took a deep breath, "Last night, I was asleep when I felt a cold breeze on my face. I opened my eyes and the whole room was glowing red! At the foot of my bed, was this large black shape that spoke to me in a deep voice. '*Give it to me. I will have it. It is mine.*' It moved around the bed towards me. I screamed and asked what he wanted. He said '*Your soul.*" I was absolutely paralyzed; I just couldn't move! Until he plunged an eight inch dagger into the pillow beside me; that's when I jumped out of bed, I was halfway across the room in one bound! I ran out of the house; there was something that looked like red paint on the staircase wall. As I reached the front door; it opened for me! I ran out and just kept running till I couldn't go any further. I remembered seeing your ad on the internet and came here." She breathed heavily; frightened by the memory of last night.

"You poor girl!" Alex consoled her, sitting beside her on the lounge chair and putting his arm around her shoulders.

"Where do you live?" Nick asked sticking to business.

"7th and Westmont," she shivered slightly.

"You walked five miles in your pajamas and bare feet?" John asked incredulously.

"Yes, and I have the cuts to prove it," she stuck one foot out from the blanket so they could see it was still bleeding slightly in several places.

"Why didn't you call the police?" John asked curiously.

"Oh, sure, call the cops and tell them there's a monster in my bedroom!" She snapped. "I don't want to look like a fool, thank you!"

"Why didn't you go to an agency closer to you?" Nick asked.

"Because I've heard of *you*," she turned to Alex. "You're some kind of electronic genius, right?" Alex nodded, obviously pleased. "Well, I figure you're the man I need. This guy must be using hundreds of dollars' worth of electronics equipment."

Nick was impressed with her courage, "You sound so calm and rational. Why did you let this guy get to you?"

Her eyes opened wide in protest, "Sure, I can be rational now in the light of day with three guys around me! You try being rational when you're alone at two in the morning, with a man who can come and go in your apartment whenever he wishes, throwing knives at you." She cried indignantly.

"I see your point." Nick agreed with a small smile.

"How'd you like some breakfast and then we'll go to your apartment with you and check it out?" Alex asked cheerfully.

"Sounds good to me."

Nick offered a hand to help her to her feet. Alex got her a robe so she could be more comfortable while eating.

*   *   *   *

They got out of the truck in front of a large old house that had been proportioned into apartments. They started forward but Shelley hung back.

"I'm not going in there." She stared fearfully at the men standing on the steps, half turned towards her.

"Don't worry, Shelley, we'll protect you." Alex quickly reassured her. He carried several pieces of electronic gear.

She shook her head, "No, no, I just can't go in." She gave them an embarrassed smile. "I'll just wait out here for you."

"I'll stay with you," Alex volunteered immediately.

"You're the one who knows how to use the equipment, Alex." Nick reminded, rolling his eyes. "I'll stay with her."

"No, you all go. What could happen to me in broad daylight in plain sight?" Shelley waved her arm around her. "Just bring me some clothes to put on, okay?"

"Ok, we'll be right back," John replied.

They entered slowly; looking around carefully. Shelley stood looking at her feet pensively. She raised her head to stare at the house. Suddenly, she stiffened, her eyes widened and a small moan escaped from her lips.

*   *   *   *

"Where the hell did she go?" Nick demanded angrily as they walked down the marina ramp to the dock.

"Where *could* she go; dressed like that?" John questioned.

"Without anyone seeing her, no less." Alex added, walking up the ramp to the Baby. "The police were no help. They think we're crazy."

"And we didn't even tell them the whole story," Nick added bitterly, entering the cabin and helping themselves to coffee as they sat around the table.

"Maybe someone is playing a joke on us?" Alex mused.

"It's definitely a possibility," Nick agreed.

John was about to answer Alex when he heard a soft sound like a moan. "Did you hear that?" He asked the other two.

"Hear what?" Nick demanded.

John shook his head, not certain what he had heard, "Something."

They all listened intently but heard nothing.

"You're hearing things, John." Nick teased.

"There it is again." John jumped up and leaped down the stairwell, going into his room.

Nick looked at Alex as he got up to follow John, "Did you hear anything?"

Alex shook his head but they found John standing beside his bed, mystified. They joined him staring in disbelief at Shelley; sound asleep under her pink blanket.

"There's something weird going on here, guys," Alex whispered. "How'd she beat us back here? She didn't walk this time and she had no money."

Nick and John just shrugged as Shelley stirred and stretched. She yawned and slowly opened her eyes; blinking in surprise to see three men staring down at her. She sat up suddenly, looking around in confusion as John sat on the edge of the bed.

"How'd you get here?" he asked pleasantly.

"Where am I?"

"You're on our boat, the Baby." Nick replied calmly.

Shelley nodded slowly, "And who the hell are you?"

John stared blankly as Nick and Alex exchanged concerned glances.

"What do you mean who are we? You met us three hours ago!" Nick replied aggressively. "What kind of game are you playing?"

"I'm not playing any game," she retorted. "I don't like this any more than you do. Now get out of here!" She ordered.

"This is my room, lady!" John retorted sharply.

"Fine, I'll leave! Where are my clothes?" she stood up angrily, looking around the room.

"Stop!" Alex insisted; putting a hand on her shoulder and making her sit back on the bed while moving John and Nick back. "Nobody is leaving before we get to the bottom of this! We didn't bring you here but I'll get you some clothes." He ran from the room, leaving them staring at one another silently. "Here." He was back in a moment, handing her a shirt and pants. They left her alone to dress.

Shelley appeared in the main cabin in a baggy shirt and pants cuffed several times. She sat down silently at the table, refusing coffee. Her attention was caught by a folded newspaper on the table and she stared in disbelief at the date.

"Thursday?" she shouted, glaring at them suspiciously. "What happened to Wednesday?" She demanded, absently rubbing the back of her neck.

"You really don't remember anything?" John questioned, she shook her head slowly, deeply confused.

"About coming here this morning, telling us that fantastic story and then disappearing?" Alex added eagerly.

"What story?"

"Wait!" Nick shushed them all. "Do you remember standing outside your apartment this morning?" She concentrated, searching her memory but shook her head in defeat.

"No."

"Ok," Nick relaxed back against the chair. "This morning you came to us and asked us to protect you from a ghost."

"A ghost!" she laughed.

"You said you knew it was a man but he wanted you to think it was a ghost." Nick continued.

"You said you wanted an electronics expert to go over your house, so we went with you." Alex informed her.

"What did you find?" Shelley asked eagerly.

"Absolutely nothing," John shook his head in disgust.

"Except you were gone when we got outside again," Nick told her.

Shelley slowly nodded her head. "One of us is crazy. And it's not going to be me," she stated positively and walked out the door.

"Hey! Wait!" Nick yelled as they scrambled after her.

They almost ran into her just outside the cabin door, staring open mouthed at a seagull perched on the rail. They crowded behind her, staring in confusion.

"What's the matter?" Alex asked curiously.

She pointed at the bird and demanded calmly, "Shoot that bird." Alex stared stupefied. Nick turned away with a hand to his head as she grabbed John by the arm. "That bird is wired! It's been following me for days. That's how it all started."

"I've always thought one seagull looked like another," Alex mused, looking thoughtfully at the bird.

"Get that bird!" she shouted, practically jumping up and down.

Alex ducked back inside the cabin. Nick leaned against the ladder to the top deck with his arms crossed over his chest, disgusted with the whole thing. Shelley stared intently at the bird until it suddenly flew off.

"Follow that bird!" she screamed and tried to run off the boat.

John grabbed her around the waist with both hands as she went up the steps, "It's crazy to think a bird is following you." He said gently, trying not to smile. She opened her mouth to protest angrily but was interrupted by Alex's return.

"She's right, guys. That bird was wearing an electronic tracking device."

The two men stared with their mouths open.

"You're kidding me," Nick asked clearly unbelieving.

"Why?" John's question was more practical.

"And you let it go!" She spit out accusingly, turning to them angrily. She turned to run off the boat once more but John again grabbed her around the waist.

"We can't follow a bird!" he yelled, exasperated by her single minded determination.

"Then what *do* we do, Mr. Big Shot Detective?" she demanded furiously, pushing him away.

"Guys, guys!" Alex interceded. "Let's talk about this calmly." Shelley shushed him with an impatient wave of her hand.

"How can I be calm? Somebody's throwing daggers at me and you tell me there's no sign of anything. I want to see it myself!"

"Fine! We'll go back to your apartment right now and you can see for yourself." Nick replied defensively.

"Fine!" she agreed equally defensively. She rubbed the back of her neck again, a look of irritation crossing her face. "Why is my neck killing me?" she complained.

"Let me see," Alex offered and gazed at the nape of her neck; just below the hairline, was a small puncture mark and a slight swelling. "Looks like a bee sting."

She nodded slowly, "I do remember a sting when I was standing by the truck." She said as a hazy memory returned.

"Or maybe someone stuck her with a needle and drugged her," John whispered to Nick as they walked up the marina ramp to the truck. Nick nodded silently. They got in the truck and drove once again to the apartment house.

*   *   *   *

They walked up the path together and Shelley stopped in surprise as they reached the porch.

"You guys left my door open?" she demanded indignantly.

"Of course not," Alex assured her blithely, not realizing the implication as Nick and John each took one of Shelley's arms and pulled her backwards between them so she was now standing behind them.

"Hey!" she cried more startled than upset.

"Sh! We go first," they entered cautiously with Alex and Shelley following closely behind.

"Oh my God!" Shelley cried out, staring in disbelief. The apartment had been trashed. Shelley stood stock still with her mouth open and Alex stayed with her as Nick and John moved through the downstairs. Suddenly, Shelley leaped up the curved staircase.

"Shelley!" Nick yelled her name sharply in a commanding tone. She stopped dead; turning to him shocked as he strode across the room and grabbed her wrist. "Get off those stairs," he ordered, pulling her down towards him.

"Ow!" she yelped and stumbled down the steps, falling against him.

"Nick, why are you acting like this?" John asked in amazement as he ran over.

Shelley sat on the floor with Alex kneeling beside her, "Ow, something cut my ankle." A thin red line appeared across her ankle. A quick examination of the stairs revealed a thin wire strung across the middle step. She shook her head in amazement, "I could have killed myself on that last night."

"Why didn't you?" Alex asked. Three pair of startled eyes looked at him. "I meant, maybe it wasn't there," he hastened to explain.

Shelley shrugged, struggling to her feet. "I think I jumped down half the stairs last night." She suddenly looked at Nick. "Why did you yell like that? You scared me half to death!"

Nick replied grimly, "We've got a real psycho on our hands. You know that dog you hired?" Shelley nodded mutely. "His head's in your freezer." She recoiled in horror.

"Yuck!" she grimaced. "A sicko is after me," she stated in a slightly dazed voice.

"Alex, you stay here with Shelley. We'll check out the upstairs," John ordered.

"Right, guys." Alex agreed.

They went upstairs leaving Alex ministering to Shelley's ankle. Nick came back in a few minutes with bandages.

"There's a real mess up there. I'll call the police."

"Can I go up there now? I need some clothes."

"Yes, it's safe. John's still up there." Nick replied while waiting to be connected.

Shelley ran upstairs; anxious to be out of the house as soon as possible. She stopped in shock when she got to her bedroom; bright red paint dripped from one wall and a large mirror was smashed. She surveyed the damage and heard a sound behind her, whirling around.

"Oh," her relief was evident as John came from the attic.

"That's how he got in. Window was unlocked up there."

She stared in amazement, "How'd you get that door open? It's been stuck ever since I moved in here."

"It was open. There's a bolt on the inside; that's probably his work. What are you doing up here?" He was tense and wary.

"Getting some clothes," she replied, opening the closet. She shrieked and jumped on John as dozens of rats streamed out. John jumped on the bed in a single leap with her clinging to him. Nick ran upstairs, leaping straight up with one foot on each side of the wall as the rats poured down the stairs, squealing and out the open front door.

"What the hell!" They heard him mutter. "John?"

John came out carrying Shelley in his arms; she was crying with her face pressed tightly against his neck.

"I'm taking her out to the truck. Grab some clothes for her and her purse." He ordered, passing Nick on the way down.

Nick followed him halfway down, "Okay. Where'd those rats come from?"

"The closet in her room," John replied, going out the door.

Nick looked upstairs with a grim expression, "I checked that closet!"

TWO

Back on the boat, Shelley leaned against the counter in the main cabin dining area watching John talking on the phone.

"Feeling better?" Alex asked solicitously, coming upstairs.

"A little, Alex; safer, anyway but I won't feel good until this is solved."

Nick tapped one finger on the table, "And you have no idea who's doing this?"

Shelley shrugged pacing the room, "Not a clue." She turned, suddenly plopping down in a chair. "I didn't know anyone hated me this much." She stared at the table despondently as John hung up and patted her shoulder. "It's scary."

"It's probably got nothing to do with you," Nick replied consolingly. "He's a wacko."

"Well, we know one thing about him," Alex stated so positively everyone turned inquisitively to him. "He can train seagulls," he shrugged apologetically.

"No one can train a seagull to follow someone," Nick argued disparagingly.

"Well, if they can train goldfish to do tricks, I don't see why not, Nick," Alex argued back. Again, everyone stared blankly.

"What?" John asked totally confused by the conversation.

"I read it in a scientific journal, John, really. They're doing amazing things these days—"

"Wait, never mind, I don't want to know!" he cut Alex off.

Shelley was clearly on edge and jumped to her feet, "Have you got anything to eat?"

"Go check out the fridge," Alex pointed to the narrow hall between the counters.

"Thanks!" she went into the galley.

"Guys, we don't have a clue," John said as soon as she left. "That was the police on the phone. They didn't turn up a single fingerprint!" A thud came from the galley but only John turned his head.

"She says she can't think of anyone who wants to hurt her," Nick reminded them.

"Or why anyone would go to all this trouble." Alex added.

"Hey, Shelley, what are you doing?" John called out curiously. When there was no answer, they ran to the galley. Shelley sat on the floor in front of the fridge staring vacantly into space. Nick knelt in front of her putting his hands on her shoulders and tried to get her attention but she continued to stare vacantly through him. He looked up at the other two.

"What the hell happened? She's in shock," he pulled her to her feet. She stood quietly, staring off into the distance.

Alex took charge, "Put her to bed. We need to keep her warm and quiet with a constant companion. I'll stay with her." Nick helped Alex get her to the guest room.

Nick leaped upstairs back to the galley, "Find anything?"

John nodded grimly, swinging the refrigerator door open silently and Nick flinched in surprise as a man's head on a platter stared back at him.

"Oh my God! No wonder she's in shock! John, we have to put a stop to this!"

"I'm going to put out to sea," John ran out of the main cabin.

A little while later, Nick joined John in the wheelhouse. "It's not real; just a clay mask. I just checked on Shelley; she's still just staring." Nick sighed heavily, looking out over the ocean.

"This is bizarre," John shook his head grimly. "What does this guy want?" He gazed at the setting sun. "To scare her to death?" he guessed.

"It's been tried before," Nick shrugged. "I wonder if she's worth any money."

"What can we do?" John asked helplessly.

"Protect her," Nick said positively. "I checked the boat; there aren't any more nasty surprises, no stowaways. Quark says there aren't any electronic listening devices or trackers." Nick suddenly made a sour face.

"Unless they're on the hull," they both said at once.

"I'll check it out." Nick sighed and went to get his scuba gear.

*   *   *   *

The three men sat in the room with Shelley. John sat beside her, holding her hand.

"Shelley," he called softly and she slowly turned her head to him. "We're out to sea. There isn't another boat near us for miles and no one knows where we are. That face was just a mask; it wasn't real," he paused, uncertain what else to say.

"It looks like my father," she said quietly, displaying no emotion.

"It looks like your father?" John repeated uncertainly as Shelley nodded slowly as if seeing him for the first time.

"Exactly like him," she said a little more firmly.

"Then maybe this has to do with your father. Who is he?" Nick asked.

"What does he do?" Alex questioned.

"His name is Harold," Shelley struggled to sit up, suddenly more alert. "He hunts for treasure."

"Treasure? You said treasure?" John repeated.

"Mm," she nodded, pushing her hair away from her face. "He investigates old stories, myths and legends and decides if there's any truth to them. He's very good."

"Does he have any enemies?" Alex asked.

"Oh, tons," she answered matter-of-factly. "But I don't know anyone who would go to all this trouble towards me."

"Where's your father now?" Nick asked.

"With the Incas," she said quietly. "But I know something's wrong. He always sends a telegram twice a month. I haven't heard from him in three months."

"And you haven't done anything about it?" Nick demanded accusingly.

"Of course, I've done something!" she retorted angrily. "I hired a private investigator to go down and find him. Almost a month ago, I haven't heard from him either."

"What's he after there?" John asked. "And who would be his competition?"

"No one on this trip; it was only for knowledge, to find their history. The Incas are his passion. It's been fourteen years since he was there. He was asked to come by an archeologist who knew about his previous work. There's no money in this deal," she shrugged.

Nick spoke after a long thoughtful pause, "I think we should go back and look into this."

"Right now, I think we should all go to bed," Alex said sensibly.

"I'm not sleeping alone!" Shelley cried, looking around the room which had twin beds with matching covers and walls covered with shelves. There were two desktop counters at the foot of the beds and every surface was covered with electronic gadgets or wires. It was the guest room, but everyone had fallen into the habit of calling it Quark's room since Alex referred to it that way all the time. The little robot was sitting on the floor; his bright blue LED eyes blinking.

"Alright, I'll stay here with you," John volunteered, throwing himself down on the other twin bed. "Alex, get that thin— Quark out of here. I think he scares Shelley," he ordered, having noticed Shelley giving the robot fearful glances from time to time. It had taken he and Nick months to get used the robot following Alex and them around the boat constantly.

"Could— could you get me something to eat?" Shelley asked hesitantly. "I'm afraid to—"

"I'll be right back with something," Alex promised.

Nick patted her hand, "I'll sleep on the couch in the main room, keeping guard."

She gave them a small grateful smile, "I'm sorry to be such a big baby." She apologized, "But I'm really spooked."

Everyone settled down for the night.

*   *   *   *

The boat was silent except for the natural creaking. Shelley slept making small sounds in her dreams. A shadow darker than the darkness reached out towards her.

Shelley sat up screaming hysterically making John sit bolt upright, turning on the light in one motion.

"What?" he went to the hysterical girl, trying to put his arm around her shoulders but she pushed him away angrily.

"No!" she shouted. "This is it! I'm leaving!" she yelled, scooting off the end of the bed.

"You can't leave, we're at sea!" he reminded her, grabbing her wrist.

"Let me go!" she screamed, struggling to get away.

"Shelley, calm down. You're alright. There's nothing here," John sat on the edge of the bed with his right arm around her waist and right arm. He gripped her left upper arm with his left hand. Shelley sat on his leg, still struggling to get away.

"I'm leaving! He's everywhere!" she cried hysterically.

They both looked up as the bedroom door was flung open as Alex and Nick came in. Alex had his arm around Nick who staggered badly as Alex helped him sit on the opposite bed. Nick fell backward with a groan. Shelley and John stared; frozen in position.

"What happened to you?" John asked curiously.

"Someone stuck a needle in my neck!" Nick growled angrily.

"You mean there *was* someone here?" John demanded not wanting to believe it.

Shelley started struggling again, "I told you! He said he wanted everything that was his! He said I belonged to him! He touched my face! It was the touch of the dead!" Shelley yelled, finally giving up trying to get away.

Alex bent to touch the rug under his bare feet, "It's wet."

"He must have used scuba equipment because I didn't hear a boat," Nick stopped groaning to tell them but continued holding his head. "One minute he wasn't there, the next he was sticking a needle in my neck! Wait till I get my hands on him!" he muttered darkly.

"How the hell did he find us?" John yelled, frustrated and angry; feeling helpless and not liking it a bit.

"That damn bird! I told you to shoot it," Shelley said accusingly. "Let me go," she ordered calmly. John released her and she began to pace. "These things just don't happen to me!" she pretended to stare out the port hole into the darkness beyond but Nick was lying below her on the bed and saw her wipe tears from her eyes.

He jumped to his feet to put his arm protectively around her, "It's alright, Shelley. He hasn't hurt you. We're gonna get him; I promise."

"We'll get him, Shelley," Alex reassured her putting an arm around her too.

"It better be soon, Alex," she whispered turning to him. "Because I can't take much more of this."

THREE

They returned to the marina by mid-morning so Alex could connect to the internet and set Quark to work finding out as much information as they could on Harold Hal. He also investigated trained seagulls without telling anyone and found an animal trainer who e-mailed Alex that he had recently trained a seagull for a man. The lead ended there because the man had paid in cash and had given no name.

When they returned from another fruitless visit to the local police station, Alex suggested a sail. They went for a sail to relieve the tension and keep Shelley's mind off her troubles. The sun was setting as Nick and John tied up the boat. Shelley and Alex stood on the dock trying to untangle a rope.

"No, no, Alex," she said pulling the rope the opposite way.

"Miss Hal?"

She gave a small shriek, jumping behind Alex as Nick and John rushed over.

"Can we help you?" Nick aggressively asked the stranger, making the mousy little man shift his weight and clear his throat nervously at this reaction. He glanced away from their unfriendly stares.

"I'm Dan Sherlman. I— I wish to speak to Miss Shelley Hal." he stammered.

"Why?" four voices demanded suspiciously.

He nervously cleared his throat and continued, "We've been trying to contact you for days, Miss Hal. Of course, I don't know what's in it; Mr. Norman took care of all the details you see—"

Shelley came from behind Alex as the little man started rambling, "Mr. Norman? You're from Crassler Associates?"

Sherlman blinked several times, "Yes, yes. Didn't I say that? I got this address from the police."

Shelley interrupted him again before he went off on another tangent, "Why are you looking for me?"

Sherlman looked at her in some confusion. "You— you don't know about your father's death?" he stammered once more.

"Oh!" she cried out in distress, turning her back to them. Alex was the only one near enough to touch her and he put his hand gently on her shoulder.

"Mr. Tortelli sent you a telegram. He was sure your father was dead," Sherlman explained sadly.

Shelley turned suddenly, startling the poor man, "Where's Tortelli? I want to talk to him." She insisted angrily.

"He's dead. A cave in," Sherlman answered clearly uneasy.

Nick suddenly looked around suspiciously, "Let's go inside." He hustled everyone back on board and into the main cabin, whispering to Alex, "Have Quark do a check see if we're being bugged by long range scanners." Alex nodded and disappeared down the stairway.

Everyone was seated around the table when he returned shaking his head and mouthing 'negative' at the detectives while Mr. Sherlman was reading the will.

"Mr. Hal named Jorge Morgast as his executor and your guardian until you are twenty-five years old."

"What?" Shelley interrupted aghast. "When did he write this will?" she asked clearly puzzled, reaching for the document, "Let me see that."

"What's wrong, Shelley?" Alex asked.

"There's no way my father would name Morgast his executor," she looked up from the document. "The man's been dead for thirteen years!"

"This is all very irregular!" Mr. Sherlman complained.

"Does Mr. Norman remember my father making this will?"

"Well Miss Hal, I can't really say. Mr. Norman was a victim of a hit and run accident last week." Mr. Sherlman explained apologetically. He could see this new information upset Shelley again. Nick took the will out of Shelley's unresisting grasp. He examined it minutely and handed it to John.

"Does that name look like it's been changed?" he asked.

John examined it in the light from one of the large windows that circled the room, "Possibly, but if it was, it's been done by an expert."

"Probably License Louie," Alex added, taking a turn perusing the document. The other two nodded knowingly.

"There is no way it could have been tampered with in our office, young man," Mr. Sherlman spluttered.

Alex cut him off, "Have you found Mr. Morgast yet?"

"No, we haven't been able to but—"

"Shelley, you ok?" Nick interrupted Sherlman.

She stared into space and appeared not to have heard him. He touched her arm lightly, snapping out of her reverie. Suddenly she was full of energy, whipping the will away from a startled Alex, folding it and handing it back to Mr. Sherlman as she stood and ushered him unceremoniously out of the room. "Thank you so very much for coming here, Mr. Sherlman. I'll be in to sign all the papers later this week," she shook his hand vigorously and literally pushed the poor man down the ramp.

"What was that all about?" Nick wondered when Sherlman was out of hearing.

"It's Morgast," she said confidently.

"Shelley, you just said he was dead," John objected.

"Well, obviously he's not," She insisted defiantly.

"Maybe it's his ghost." Nick quipped sarcastically; this was getting too bizarre for him. Shelley ignored him and Alex gave him a dirty look. Nick shrugged and sighed, "Okay. Tell me why a man who's supposed to be dead comes back to bother you?"

Shelley leaned against the edge of the table, "How about a million dollars?" she asked smugly; her remark was met with stunned silence.

Alex excitedly shook his finger at her, "I get it! If he's the executor and you're insane, he can do anything he wants with the money!"

"Wait a minute, you two," John broke in. "What makes you think it's Morgast? The man hasn't been seen or heard from for thirteen years. Anyone could be using his name as a cover." Nick nodded in agreement.

"Well, number one, the last time I saw Morgast I was ten years old; he took me by the hand and told me '*You're my beautiful girl.*' I never liked him so I told him I was Daddy's girl! He grabbed my face and told me in a voice that frightened me, '*You belong to me. You're mine.*' I just ran from the room and hid until he left."

"Well, I'm sure you were very scared—" Nick began.

"No! That's what he said last night! That I belonged to him; I was his. And—" she spoke quickly, cutting off a question from Alex. "Number two, Morgast's body was never found."

Nick put his hand up to his head as if in pain, "Why didn't you tell us that before?"

"So, it could be Morgast," John mused.

They sat down to plan strategy as Alex disappeared downstairs and returned almost immediately, going to Shelley. "I want you to wear this," he buckled something on her wrist.

Shelley felt confused looking down at a silver bracelet with large stones all around. "Um, thanks, Alex. But it's not really my style," she began hesitantly.

"It's a tracking device." He laughed at her expression.

She smiled then quickly frowned, "I guess I'm the bait, then." she said with a quiver in her voice. "Would it be okay if I just put it my pocket?" Alex nodded.

"Well, of course he's going to come after you, Shelley but he has to go through us first, don't forget," John comforted her. Shelley didn't feel comforted at the thought of other people being in danger, too. He frightened her further by taking the lid off the cookie jar on the shelf behind him and pulling out a gun. He unwrapped the holster; putting it on without noticing her horrified stare.

"Yeah, don't worry; nothing is going to happen!" Nick took a gun out of the drawer in the table. As he put the holster on, the lights went out. Shelley screamed, grabbing hold of Nick beside her. Nick grabbed her arm, shoving her under the table as she heard a grunt and a thud nearby.

"Damn!" Nick cursed angrily before Shelley heard another thud. She fainted when the third body hit the floor.

*   *   *   *

It was dark when Shelley woke to find herself tied to a chair, back to back with Nick who was still unconscious.

"Nick! Nick, you've got to wake up!" Shelley called loudly, shaking herself from side to side as much as she could to jostle him.

"Ah geez! He got me with another needle!" Nick moaned drowsily, upset with himself. "That man walks like a cat." he complained, blinking and shaking his head to clear the fog. "Where the hell are we?"

"In a warehouse," she sighed. "I recognize this place. My father owns it."

"Where's our devious little friend? Did you see him?" Nick asked. Shelley remained silent. "Shelley?"

"He— he's wearing a mask." she answered very quietly.

"These ropes are really tight!" Nick complained, straining to get free.

"I know! You're rubbing them against my skin!" she yelled belligerently.

"Well, excuse me for trying to get away!" he griped, looking around their prison. They were surrounded by piles of boxes. He lowered his voice, "Do you still have Alex's bracelet?"

"Yes. Will they be able to find us for sure?" she questioned nervously.

"As soon as they wake up," he replied ruefully.

Suddenly a powerful light blinded them, shining directly in their eyes as a tall man with a limp and a long black cape walked to Shelley. He stared at her, reaching out to stroke her face. She turned her head away as far as possible.

"Why haven't you killed me?" she demanded making Nick gasp.

"Kill you? My darling daughter, why would I kill you? I want us to be together. With the treasure of the Incas, of course," he added with a laugh, staring at her expectantly.

"If I'm such a wonderful friend, why am I tied up?"

"That is regrettable, dearest. You have been exposed to the treachery of that man. I must decontaminate you. I will be ready soon." he left as silently as he had appeared.

The light remained on, blinding them and seriously limiting their vision. Shelley started struggling fiercely against the ropes.

"Hey, hey! Watch the skin!" Nick complained loudly.

"Shut up! I'm not sticking around to be *decontaminated*."

"Shelley, stop it! You're only rubbing off our skin!" Nick begged. She desisted reluctantly, breathing heavily. "Why does this nut call you daughter? What happened with this Inca business?" Nick asked to keep both their minds off the next move their captor might make.

"Morgast was dating my mother at the time she met my father. She broke up with Morgast but she couldn't get rid of him; even after she married my father, he hung around. She felt sorry for him. She made my father take him on several expeditions even though he hated Morgast's guts." She shook her head and sighed. "He was weird even then. He'd disappear every now and then for a couple of years. When I was ten, my father was trying to locate the legendary crown of one of the Inca ruler's. Morgast showed up two days before they left for an expedition. He went with them on a disastrous trip; two of the carriers were killed, their food supply was spoiled. My mother was taken ill and she— she died before they could get her to a doctor. Morgast blamed my father for her death. He kept saying my father had murdered her.

They got into a fist fight and Morgast fell into a bottomless pit. Father reburied the crown, came home and never went back. He didn't go on another trip for four years."

"Sh!" Nick hissed.

She turned her head towards him, "What do you mean, sh? You—" she stopped as he shushed her again, straining to hear. Shelley looked around, noticing something in the light. "Nick, this place is filled with dynamite!" she squeaked, unable to speak in a normal voice. She jumped as a voice spoke close to her ear.

"Of course, we need it to conquer the caves." Morgast explained; cutting Shelley's ropes and pulling her out of the chair, gripping her upper arm tightly. He had taken off his mask and Shelley stared in horror; one side of his face was curiously flattened and the skin was very rough and lumpy. He noticed her stare. "The monster did that." he told her curtly. "Where is it?" he suddenly demanded. Shelley kicked him hard in the shin making him release her and howl in pain. She ran away into the dark. "Stop!" he yelled. "Or I will shoot your friend." He leveled the gun at Nick's head. Shelley stopped and turned, knowing he couldn't really see her because he was facing the light and she stood behind it.

"You're going to kill him anyway, just like you killed Norman and Tortelli!" she yelled.

"Yes." he admitted cheerfully. "But you won't have to see and hear me blow his brains out." Shelley slowly moved toward the circle of light but remained out of reach.

"Where is it?" he asked eagerly.

"Where is what?" she asked truly confused.

"The map. Harold made a map, where he hid the treasure in the cave. I need that map."

"I'll tell you what, Morgast. I'll give you the map if you let him go." Morgast shook his head with a nasty smile. Shelley shrugged, "You'll never get the treasure otherwise."

Morgast cut Nick loose and snarled; "Get out of here."

"No." Nick refused to budge.

Morgast angrily picked up a stick of dynamite from the closest box and lit it.

"Drop it, Morgast!" John called out suddenly from the surrounding darkness.

Morgast spun and fired toward the sound. Nick pulled Shelley to the ground, covering her with his body. Morgast jumped behind his pile of dynamite and threw the lit stick in the direction of John's voice. There was an explosion and a wall of fire now separated John and Alex from Shelley and Nick.

"Nick! Shelley!" John called loudly over the roar of the flames.

"John, Alex, just get out!" Nick yelled to the brothers. "If that fire reaches that pile of dynamite, we're all goners." he whispered to Shelley as they crawled along the floor.

"Come this way." she crawled towards the outside wall. They pulled boxes out of the way until a nervous and mystified Nick saw a doggie door. With a little help from Shelley, who got out easily, Nick made it through. They ran around the building to see John and Alex outside the front of the building. They were running away from the building when an explosion knocked them off their feet. They turned to see the warehouse engulfed in flames even as sirens could be heard coming rapidly towards them.

FOUR

The three men leaned against one of the engines as Shelley sat on the runner. It was completely dark now with fire engines and police cars everywhere.

"I wish you'd let us take you home, Shelley." Alex said for the hundredth time.

Shelley stubbornly shook her head, "No, not until they find his body. It won't be over until his body is found." She insisted adamantly as the men exchanged glances and looked away.

"I should have known you'd be involved in this." A voice said suddenly out of the darkness.

"Oh no!" John moaned, turning away.

"Just what this night needs." Nick complained, sitting beside Shelley.

"Where have you been Officer Duncan? The fun's been over for hours." Alex chided.

"So, you've taken up arson?" Duncan ignored them and continued his accusations. "Setting buildings on fire with dynamite, no less! I can't wait till the owner slaps you with a lawsuit. You'll have to hock everything you own." he finished gleefully.

Shelley stood up facing him. "Is there no law and order in this town, Officer? Someone rips my home apart, threatens my life, kidnaps me and there you stand; threatening the three men who saved my life. I believe I'll sue the police department for negligence." she spoke very calmly.

"Who is this bimbo?" Duncan asked derisively.

"I'm the owner of this building!" she replied smugly. "Who are you? I'd like to report you to your supervisor." Duncan furiously turned hastily away.

"Don't worry about him, Shelley. He's always been an ass, ever since John and I met him in the army." Nick said cheerfully.

Alex suddenly shouted, pointing toward the building. "They found something!"

They ran past Duncan to the stretcher being wheeled out of the building.

"Is he dead?" Shelley questioned anxiously.

"Smoke inhalation. The fire never touched him." the man responded dolefully.

Nick lifted the sheet for quick look. "It's him." He looked at Shelley. "It's over."

She fainted but John caught her before she hit the ground and picked her up.

*   *   *   *

Shelley was sitting on the main deck of the boat sunning herself when the detectives came down the marina ramp.

"Hi Shelley!" they chorused as they boarded Baby.

"Hello, guys." She called, cheerful and full of energy.

"How are you feeling?" Alex asked as she gave them hugs.

"Tons better, but still a little jumpy, I'm afraid." she said with a self-conscious laugh.

"It'll take time." Nick took her hand as she smiled gratefully, nodding.

"Oh! I almost forgot; I came to pay you." she handed them a check.

"And we have something for you." John disappeared into the cabin.

"Did you find a new apartment?" Nick asked.

"Yes, I did. It's very nice. I got a nice big dog, too."

John poked his head out of the cabin, "Ready?"

Nick put his hands over her eyes, "Hold out your hands."

"This better be a good surprise." Shelley nervously put out both hands. John put a small metal cage in her hands. She opened her eyes quickly to see a seagull staring at her.

"That bird!" she laughed in amazement.

"Just an ordinary bird now, without his transmitter," Alex assured her.

"Since he follows you anyway, you might as well see if you can take care of him." Nick said as John handed her a black book.

"These are Tortelli's notes. Morgast told him everything one night when they were drinking. Morgast killed him the next day when he went to check out the cave."

"I thought so." Shelley nodded, sitting on the lounge chair, putting the bird cage on the deck beside her. She closed her eyes basking in the warm sun.

"What's the treasure?" John asked curiously.

"A red uncut diamond, over two thousand carats." she replied without opening her eyes.

"Wow!" Alex whistled very impressed.

"And you have the map from your father?" Nick asked incredulously.

"No." she laughed. "Father had the map tattooed on his scalp."

"Why?" John asked confused.

"He couldn't bring himself to destroy it but he never wanted to see it again."

"So, the treasure is lost?" Nick mourned.

"Unless the man who tattooed it on his head remembers," Alex mused out loud.

"Alex, that map is only of the inside of the cave. You don't even know where the cave is." Shelley chided him.

"Oh!" he said crestfallen as they laughed.

Shelley suddenly sobered. "Too many people have already died because of that stone. That's why the Inca's buried it, too!" she shivered. "I wouldn't want it."

"Let's just stick to being detectives, guys." Alex said.

"Who wants lunch?" Nick asked going into the cabin.

CASE FILE: BO

ONE

Lt. Wylan sat in his office staring morosely at a newspaper's graphic headline; 12 DEAD— POISONED BY PSYCHO when a uniformed officer came in, handing him a release form. Lt. Wylan signed it and handed it back, staring dolefully.

"Think you can handle a mass murderer by yourself, Robinson?" he asked scornfully.

"I think so, sir. I just won't eat anything for a while," Robinson replied cheerfully as he left.

Officer Robinson entered the Juvenile Hall and spoke to a harassed looking young woman at the desk, "Picking up Benjamin, D. for a court date."

The woman jerked her head to the left, barely looking at him as she reached for the phone which rang once more. "Waiting for you at the end of the hall," she tossed him a key. "Make sure you return it!" She ordered sharply, covering the mouthpiece of the phone.

Officer Robinson walked down the short hall to unlock the door of a small cell like room. He opened the door to see an older teenage girl dancing to music only she could hear. She spun around and noticed him; her whole manner changed abruptly as if a mask was put on. She stood still; staring sullenly from under her bangs as he stood in the doorway.

"Judge wants to see you kid. Put on some bracelets and we'll go," he spoke jovially. She made no move toward him so he walked towards her and snapped a cuff on one wrist.

"Ow, you pinched me!" she cried, pushing him back with her free hand, annoyed.

"Sorry," he apologized abruptly. "I didn't think they were that tight." He clasped the next one a little more loosely and led her from the room tossing the key back to the desk clerk in passing. "See ya!" he quipped, ever cheerful.

The girl tripped on the top step as they climbed the stairs in the almost empty courthouse. Robinson stepped back to get his balance and support her, leaving him one step below her.

"You okay?" he asked perfunctorily but instead of answering him, she abruptly pulled her arm out of his grasp and gave him a hard kick to the knee while giving his shoulder a shove with both hands; he fell down the stairs with an angry yell. The girl quickly took off, running down a second set of stairs, stopping at the bottom to clasp the open cuff on the opposite wrist then slide them both up to the elbow where they were hidden by her sleeve. She walked through the outside door as the alarms went off and was quickly lost in the crowd on the street.

*   *   *   *

The girl sat at a library table frowning over a large book on the table in front of her. She was small and thin with badly cut, poker straight brunette hair with bangs hanging in her face. She cradled her head with her arm and glanced up to see Alex staring at the double handcuff on her arm.

"What are you looking at Geek?" she hissed challengingly but Alex's curiosity blocked any notice of her insulting tone or words.

"I was noticing your, uh, bracelets. They're rather unique," he said frankly.

"A souvenir," she smiled sarcastically. "Swiped 'em from a cop when he wasn't looking," she gloated.

"You teenagers." He shook his head with a laugh. "What's your name?" he asked, always ready to be friendly.

"Bo," she said after a short pause while studying him intently.

"Alex Colby," he held out his hand. She shook his hand, smiling for the first time; the punk attitude was totally gone. They started discussing the book she was reading.

*   *   *   *

Alex and Bo walked down the street looking into shops. Bo carried a small grocery bag open at the top and glanced around nervously at each window as they stopped. Alex noticed at the second window.

"What's up, Bo?" he asked with an attitude of easy friendliness. They had met several times since the meeting in the library last week.

"Ever get the feeling you're being watched?"

"Yes, I do." he replied positively but didn't tell her that he had been followed several times because of the nature of his business.

"Well, I've had that feeling for a while." she replied uneasily and kept walking.

"Oh, it's probably nothing— hey, look at this!" he interrupted himself to show her a window with the latest electronic equipment in it.

She smiled at his enthusiasm and willingly looked into the window but suddenly noticed a face behind her reflected in the window for a fleeting second; she whirled quickly but there was no one directly behind her, just a stream of quickly moving people. She stared nervously down the street at several retreating backs. Alex hadn't noticed and they continued walking down the street.

Bo was very impressed when they arrived at the marina and Alex led her to the most impressive boat she'd ever seen. She saw the name Baby on the bow and noted the luxurious lounge chairs and table under the awning which covered almost half the deck behind the cabin. There was even a television mounted on the outside of the cabin wall.

"Wow! What are you; some kind of millionaire?" she asked in awe.

Alex laughed, remembering how many times they had come close to being unable to pay the dock fee each month as well as the upkeep and utilities. "Sorry, no! My brother and a friend and I live here and use it as our office."

They boarded the Baby and Bo looked around the sumptuous interior feeling out of place in her old jeans and t-shirt. A large beautifully decorated living area led into a large dining area. The entire living space was surrounded on three sides by huge windows giving several views of the harbor and the water beyond. Alex was busy taking the food out of the bag and putting it on the breakfast counter. Bo gave him her bag and looked through the cabinets for plates.

"Wait till you taste this crabmeat; Sam's is the best you'll ever have," he said eagerly. "Oh, I'm glad you remembered the lemon," he took it out.

Bo looked over casually as she put out plates and utensils, "I don't like lemon." She cut it in half for him, putting one half on his plate and the other face down on a small plate. She went through the archway into the small but well organized galley to put the plate in the fridge. "Thank you for inviting me, Alex. I haven't had a good sea food lunch since—" she stopped abruptly. "I don't know when," she finished lamely.

Alex sat down, squeezing the lemon on the crabmeat sitting on a lettuce leaf and took a bite. "Mmm. This is good!" he mumbled with his mouth full.

Bo smiled, picking up a forkful of her crabmeat and absently smelling it. She tasted it gingerly then smiled and nodded. As if in a dream, time seemed to slow down; she watched a strange look come over his face. He appeared to be struggling for breath as he stood up and staggered before falling to the floor with Bo staring in horror, still holding a forkful of crabmeat halfway to her mouth until suddenly she flung it down on the table and grabbed the phone.

"I need an ambulance. Poisoned! A boat—" she squeezed her eyes tight, trying to concentrate. "The Baby at Wally's pier 54," she said quickly and then listened. "I don't know what slip number. It's a big sailboat. Just get here," she hung up, looking fearfully at Alex lying still and pale on the floor as she backed to the door. She pulled it open and ran out sobbing, racing away as fast as she could.

John and Nick got out of the truck laughing and joking.

"Do you believe that guy?" Nick complained. As they rounded the fence separating the parking lot, Bo ran into them and John grabbed hold of her to steady them both. She pulled fiercely away and kept on running.

"Hey, watch it!" Nick yelled after her annoyed as he pushed himself off the fence.

"She was crying," John said quietly, staring after her. "Did you recognize her?"

"Never saw her before," Nick shrugged.

They were boarding Baby when they heard sirens coming towards them. Nick turned to look as John went into the cabin. Nick ran in when he heard John call out.

"Alex!" John ran to his brother, feeling quickly for a pulse and turning to Nick, "He's barely breathing! Call an ambulance."

Nick ran back outside, waving the EMT's over to the boat as three police cars pulled in right behind the ambulance.

"What the hell is going on?" Nick asked out loud, running behind the EMT's.

TWO

John stared balefully at Lt. Wylan as he and Nick sat in his office.

"You can be charged with harboring a fugitive, you know," Wylan said gleefully.

"What the hell are you talking about?" John demanded angrily.

"Alex is in the hospital because your people let a murderer go free and that's somehow *our* fault?" Nick interrupted angrily. "Why aren't you looking for this girl?"

"Of course, we're looking for her, Beach Boy!" Wylan shouted, jumping up and losing his temper. He threw an APB picture across the desk at them, "You're such great detectives, why don't you find her? Really show us how to do our jobs, huh?" he paused and sat down. "Just remember *your* genius partner invited a mass poisoner to *lunch*; and he's by far the brightest one of you!" he taunted. Nick quickly grabbed John's arm to keep him from punching the Lt. "After all, it's only been in the papers every day for the last six weeks!" Wylan added snidely. "Now get out!"

Nick pulled John with him out the door, clutching the APB picture and showed it to John, "That's the girl that ran into us, I think."

John was still very angry and snatched the paper from Nick. The girl in the picture had a surly expression looking out from under her eyebrows. The print under the picture labeled her as Dagmar Benjamin/Caucasian female/brown hair/ blue eyes/5'2"/95 lbs. /17 years old.

"I didn't even know Alex knew this girl," he muttered forlornly. "I never heard him discuss her when the case was on the news; did you?" he turned to Nick curiously.

"No, but you know your brother; he forgets to mention a lot of things when his mind is on his work," Nick reminded John gently.

"He's the only one who survived," John mused still following his train of thought. "Why was she crying?"

"Who cares?" Nick spit out angrily. "Let's go talk to Beverly." He stalked away with John following slowly.

They went to the local library where Alex spent a lot of his time. Beverly was an older woman who worked at the library and was a great friend of Alex's. Without Alex's computer expertise, the two men were at a loss how to get information on this girl but with Beverly's help they reviewed all the information from the newspapers on the case. They hadn't been too interested in it since they had been busy with several different cases. They read that the first four people to be poisoned had been Dagmar's foster family in the neighboring town of Somerdale.

"Wild mushroom poisoning," Nick shook his head as he read the paper. "Why can't you just buy them at the store like everyone else?"

Although tragic, it had been declared an accidental death. After that, the deaths had occurred randomly it seemed in three neighboring towns and because the murderer had changed poisons it had been hard to find a cause of death; several people had died of Yew seed poisoning and others had died of Mistletoe berry poisoning.

"Who knew Mistletoe was poisonous?" Nick complained; he had been astonished when the doctors had told them that Alex had been poisoned by Mistletoe.

The police from several different towns had been cooperating with one another but no leads had been found until the eleventh and twelfth victims were poisoned. A nosy neighbor had recognized Dagmar going into the house the evening before. Once they had a name, they easily found out that everyone who had died had had dinner with Dagmar the evening before. When they had searched her house, they found distillation equipment in the basement; Mistletoe berries and Yew seeds as well as poisonous mushrooms were found hidden away. John and Nick were surprised to read that the police hadn't found Dagmar at all. She had given herself up to the police and professed her innocence.

They stopped by the hospital to see Alex on their way back but there was no change in his condition.

Nick hit the bed rail with his hand, "I hate seeing him like this! I can't imagine how you must feel." He yelled angrily, knowing his normally cheerful friend had been very silent the last couple of days. "You stay here with Alex, John. I'm going to get her." John opened his mouth to argue but Nick left the room saying, "I'll be back. I'll keep in touch."

"Wake up, please! Alex, I'll never tell you to shut up again! Talk to me," John pleaded with his youngest brother. He turned as their mother came back into the room. She saw the anguish on his face and put her arm around his waist and laid her head on his chest. John grimly put his arms around her, not wanting to even imagine how she must feel.

*   *   *   *

Nick drove the black truck down a country road through endless fields with nothing in sight when it began pouring; a hard driving rain accompanied by thunder and lightning. Around a sharp curve he saw a very wet hitchhiker and stopped. The hiker ran up to the truck and got in with drops of water flying everywhere.

"Sorry! Thanks a lot, I thought I was going to drown," she said abruptly with no real emotion in her voice.

"Where are you going?" Nick asked as he got back on the road.

"Somerdale."

"So am I," he glanced at her now that she was settled. Her hair was darkened and plastered to her head but he caught a glimpse of blue eyes and a pouting mouth as she tossed her head impatiently trying to get her long bangs out of her eyes. "What are you doing out in a rain storm?"

She looked annoyed at his question, "Don't worry about it." She said insolently.

"What's your name?" Nick refused to be snubbed, noticing the odd, quilted coat she wore which fell below her knees.

"None of your business."

"You know, if someone is nice enough to give you a lift, you could at least be nice to them," he lectured irritably.

"It was your idea to stop. I don't owe you anything," she lifted her left hand to tuck a wayward strand of hair behind her ear. Nick caught a glimpse of her unusual bracelets and suddenly swung the truck off the road, turning around.

"What the hell are you doing?" she yelled, clinging to the door and the dashboard since she wasn't wearing a seatbelt.

"We're not going to Somerdale."

"Look, Mister, you go anywhere you like; *me*, I'm going to Somerdale!"

"You're coming back to Bridgeton with me, *Dagmar*," he emphasized her name.

She stared intently but didn't speak. Suddenly she lunged, grabbing the wheel, trying to step on the brakes as they struggled for control of the vehicle which careened into a field and stopped abruptly as Bo grabbed Nick's face with both hands, scratching him. He gave a roar of pain and anger.

Bo leaped out of the truck and ran across the huge field towards a large old tree as Nick turned the truck off but left the keys in the ignition and his door open trying to catch up to her. He ran through the heavy rainfall, managing to catch up to her and grabbed hold of her coat just as he slipped in the muddy grass pulling her off balance so she fell against him.

"Go away! Let go of me!" she screamed, flailing and kicking.

Nick was dragging her back to the truck when a bolt of lightning struck the huge old tree near them making Bo shriek and instinctively duck. They looked up as the tree exploded and came crashing down towards them as the ground beneath them suddenly gave way and they tumbled down with leaves and branches following them.

*   *   *   *

Bo moaned and woke; drenched in mud. She stared in disgust at her hands and spit mud from her lips, rolling stiffly onto her left side and lifting herself on her elbow. Looking around, she saw Nick nearby; plastered with mud, lying motionless on his back. Bo sat up slowly, taking a look around their prison. Slick mud walls with old timbers showing, encased them in a rough rectangular pit. The fallen tree closed off over half the opening with branches, leaves and the blackened trunk. Rain poured down one wall but they were pretty much sheltered from the deluge by the tree itself. The water flowed downward along the dirt wall, disappearing behind a rough board wall. Putting her eye against one of the large holes in the board wall and seeing complete darkness beyond; Bo realized they were in an old abandoned mine shaft.

Bo examined her companion, poking him gingerly, "Wake up." When there was no response, she frowned slightly, "Did you break something?" She skillfully ran her hands over him. "Ah ha," she said softly, feeling his lower left leg. She looked around, picking up a long piece of rotting wood; she put one end on the ground and stomped a muddy foot in the middle of it, snapping it in two. She suddenly noticed something against the wall to her left and crawled over. She gingerly picked up Nick's gun by the butt, putting it in the corner closest to her and farthest from him. She tore a piece of the lining from her coat and wrapped the gun in it then patted mud into place over it before going back to Nick.

She set and splinted his leg, using more lining from her coat and the wood, and laid him on her coat, wiping her muddy forehead with an equally muddy hand. She wrapped the ends of the coat over him as much as possible; breathing heavily from the exertion of moving him.

"God, you weigh a ton," she chided the still unconscious man. She pulled his hip towards her slightly using his belt loop and leaned over him, taking out his wallet. "Let's see who you are." she murmured, sitting beside him. She was perusing his wallet pictures when Nick cautiously opened an eye, slowly turning his head; he saw Bo with his wallet.

"Give me that!" He grabbed it, wincing in pain at the movement.

Bo slapped his chest, "Don't be so uppity," she ordered indignantly.

Nick tried moving again but quickly decided against any more moving. Bo watched calmly, waiting for his attention. He finally looked up at her with a grim expression.

"If you're not a cop, why are you following me?" she demanded suspiciously.

"Why do you poison people?" he snarled.

Even with the mud covering her face he could see her expression harden, "They bother me." She drawled insolently.

The slap took her completely by surprise; her hands came up but not before he grabbed her upper arms pulling her face to face.

"How did *Alex* bother you?" he roared inches from her frightened face.

Bo tore herself from his grasp to stand in the farthest corner, staring malevolently from behind the screen of leaves, resting her cold fingers against the burning red handprint.

*   *   *   *

Dooley entered Alex's hospital room, "Hey, John." He greeted him casually, walking to the bed to look at Alex, "How is he?"

"The same, I guess. Have you seen Nick?"

"Yeah, he stopped by the shop. He asked me where Alex had been, who he'd been with the last week," Dooley brushed his wild hair back from his forehead, frowning down at Alex.

"What did you tell him, Dooley?" John prompted impatiently.

Dooley shrugged, "Not much, just that Alex's been real excited over a 'secret case'." John stared in surprise.

"What case?" he asked confused; it wasn't like Alex to be secretive. John would have said his brother was an open book and had no secrets.

Dooley wasn't much help, "I don't know any details. He's just been smiling and talking to himself." He continued staring at Alex, "Why doesn't he wake up?" He reached down, shaking his shoulder vigorously.

"I don't think that'll work." John protested with a smile.

John started in surprise as he heard Alex mutter groggily, "No, no, let me sleep."

"Sleep! Alex, wake up! You've been asleep for three days," John shouted, staring at his brother joyfully as Alex stared back very perplexed.

THREE

After two long silent hours had passed; Nick looked at Bo who still stood under the low hanging branch. He stared searchingly into the leaves, feeling her eyes watching him.

"How long are you going to stand there sulking?" Nick demanded irritably but got no response. He painfully propped himself up against the wall, "You know, Dagmar—" He began. "Hey!" he yelled, putting up an arm to shield himself from the clump of mud she threw. "Stop that!" he ordered angrily as another clod of mud hit him, "Dagmar!" he yelled.

"Don't call me that!"

"That's your name!" he cried indignantly, brushing off the lumps of mud. There was no response from the girl. "Okay," he sighed heavily, "What's your name?"

After a short silence, he heard a whispered, "Bo."

"Bo." he repeated slowly, "Well, *Bo*, if you wanted to get away; why would you go back to your hometown? That's the first place everyone will look and people would recognize you right away." He was irritated when he got no response. "And if you were really smart," he paused for effect, "You'd have found a way to get rid of those handcuffs." He taunted. Silently the girl slipped the cuffs off her hand, one at a time, holding them daintily in the air in front of her. "You're wearing them on purpose?" Nick cried incredulously.

"Symbolic representation." She murmured.

"I don't understand." Nick complained and sighed wearily as she didn't respond once again. "Look, kid, we're going to be trapped here with each other for a while yet; maybe we can be polite to each other, huh?" he tossed her his jacket, "Here, put this on." She caught it and tossed it back.

"You need it to guard against shock." she replied, remaining partially hidden by the tree.

"What's a nice girl like you doing in a place like this?" He deadpanned, trying not to grin. Bo tried to stop her smile. "Hey, she can smile!" he teased; she tossed another small chunk of mud which he dodged as best he could and laughed.

*   *   *   *

Nick opened his eyes to see Bo dancing and watched her silently, cradling his head on his arm. She suddenly noticed he was awake and sat down, leaning against the muddy wall looking distastefully at her filthy hands. Both of them were caked from head to foot in partially dried mud.

"Why would you go back to Somerdale?" Nick asked curiously; this girl was driving him crazy. She made no response. "Where have you been hiding for a week?" Still no response; she stared expressionlessly. "What grade are you in?" he asked hopefully. "Why won't you talk to me?" he complained with a deep sigh.

"I'm willing to talk to you!" she protested, raising her eyebrows. "If you ever get around to talking, that is."

"What have I been doing if not talking?" Nick demanded, raising his eyebrows, mocking her.

"You're questioning me about highly personal information that you could care less about anyway."

"How do you know I don't care?" he shot back irritably.

"A couple hours ago, you were going to take me back and throw me in jail."

"Can you blame me?" Nick asked harshly, his thoughts flashing to Alex lying in a hospital bed.

"*Yes*!" she lifted her arm, letting the handcuffs clink and dangle, "That's why I wear these! Since I was arrested three weeks ago, I have talked to dozens of people I don't know and only two have bothered to ask me if I was innocent or guilty. Everyone else had already convicted me!" Again she spoke without any emotion, but Nick watched a tear run down her muddy cheek.

"Who were the two?"

"The first lawyer who came to see me."

"You have more than one lawyer?" he interrupted.

"I've had three different ones. Sandra, the one I liked, she was in a car accident. I hated the guy who replaced her, so they sent another one."

"Do you like the one you have now?"

"No!" she said vehemently, turning her head away, her face a wooden mask.

"Why not?"

"He's a jerk! Talks to me as if I was eight and he never listens to a word I say; besides he calls me Dagmar." she wrinkled her nose in distaste as she said the name.

"You signed a confession—" Nick began.

"I signed ten of them! I just signed it to get that bozo off my back. Then I wrote nine more, all different just to make it invalid. He was furious!" Bo smiled smugly at the memory.

"What bozo?" Nick asked for clarification although he had a feeling he knew what her answer would be.

"Some stupid cop named Wylan," she spit out and noticed his grin. "You know him?" she looked directly at him for the first time. She hadn't made eye contact since he slapped her. She'd been staring up at the leaves above her, aimlessly tossing a clod of dirt up and down.

"Yeah, I know the bozo." Nick nodded and smiled as she fell silent. "So, you're innocent?" He kept his voice casual. "You didn't poison thirteen people?" he watched her closely out of the corner of his eye.

"Yeah."

"You don't sound very sure."

She stared at him out of the corner of her eye, her face tightening as she reached into the pocket of her coat at his side and brought out a pretzel which she offered to him.

"Wanna bite?" she offered provocatively.

"Very funny," he snarled.

"Oh well," she said slyly, leaning towards him, "You don't have to eat, just the touch—" she placed a muddy finger against his muddy lips.

He roughly slapped her hand away, frowning deeply, "You're a wacko!" He shouted, suddenly angry again.

"Psycho," she corrected with a pout, moving back to sit against the far wall watching angrily as he kept a wary eye on her.

*   *   *   *

Nick was asleep again; Bo jumped up several times, trying to grab a lantern hanging on a nail on the boards above her head. Grabbing a cross board and putting a foot on the wood wall, she pulled herself up enough to reach the lantern. She examined it closely and a panel on the base opened to reveal wooden matches wrapped in plastic.

"Even some oil left. This must be my lucky day." She muttered sarcastically. After several tries, she lit the lantern and looked over at Nick, putting a hand on his forehead, "A slight fever but there's nothing more I can do for you." She frowned looking around their prison, "Water, water everywhere and not a drop to drink!"

Nick opened his eyes, staring at the lantern, "Where did you get that?" he asked groggily.

"It was just hanging around," she smiled archly, picking up another handful of mud and tossing it up and down, "How long have you been following me?"

"I haven't been following you. I never saw you before today." Nick answered, confused by the question.

"Oh," she said confused, too.

"Who was the other one?"

"What?" she asked baffled.

"You said two people believed you. Who was the second?"

A soft smile lit her face; it was the first real emotion Nick had seen, "Just someone I met," she replied with a light laugh, "He said he was a private eye but he couldn't be."

"Why not?"

"He believes everything you tell him and he's too nice. He was worried about me because I wouldn't tell him about myself," she looked at Nick completely at ease, no longer acting. "He insisted on making lunch for me; crabmeat, it's been so long since I had it," she smiled happily, recalling the memory.

"What was his name?" Nick asked softly not wanting to break the spell.

"Alex. He was so intelligent, it's too bad—" she stopped suddenly, frowning and shaking her head and put her hand up to her forehead. "Alex," she whispered in confusion and put both hands up clasping her head rocking back and forth moaning, "Alex, Alex, Alex."

"Bo!" Nick reached for her but she was out of reach and he fell back in pain as he twisted his broken leg. "Bo!" he called insistently but she continued to rock and moan.

"I'm cracking up!" she cried piteously, turning her face into the wet hanging leaves to hide from him.

FOUR

John strode into the hospital room, "Alex, no one has seen Nick for over ten hours and he doesn't answer his phone! Tell me everything you know about Dagmar!"

"Who's Dagmar?" Alex asked in confusion, blinking at his brother's sudden appearance.

John stared back just as confused, "The girl you had lunch with! You know; *the one who poisoned you?*" He questioned impatiently.

"I had lunch with Bo," Alex replied, struggling to remember.

"Bo Who?" John asked even more confused, "Wait a minute; wait a minute." He shushed Alex and pulled the APB photo from his pocket. He unfolded it and handed it to Alex, "Isn't this the girl you had lunch with?"

"Yes, this could be her but her name is Bo," he read the description, frowning in confusion. He looked at John, "She didn't poison me," he stated very positively, frowning to remember, "She ate some too." The thought made him even more perplexed.

"Alex," John patiently explained, "This girl escaped from the police over a week ago. She's wanted for poisoning twelve people. You were number thirteen and the only one to survive."

"John," Alex explained equally patiently, "Bo could not have poisoned anyone. The police are wrong. They've been wrong before you know!" Alex defended his friend heatedly.

"Well, Alex, Nick went looking for her and hasn't called in. Something's happened to him; now tell me everything you know about Dagmar, alright— *Bo!*" John insisted, bringing the conversation back to where he started.

"Well, if he's with Bo, he's not in any danger from her," Alex insisted.

*   *   *   *

Nick opened his eyes to see light reflecting off metal. He tried to focus his eyes and recognized his gun in Bo's hand; just when he thought his time had come, she put the barrel to her temple and pulled the trigger.

"Damn!" she cursed loudly when nothing happened.

She leaned closer to the lantern to examine the gun; putting herself within Nick's reach. He grabbed the wrist with the gun and her neck. She gave a small shriek of surprise and tried to get away but he pulled her closer with his left arm around her neck and holding her left wrist. Her left arm was now bent and powerless and he pulled the right hand holding the gun across his chest pulling it into a painful extension as he ordered, "Drop it!" When she let it go, he let her arm go back to a more normal position but kept holding it, "What the hell do you think you're doing?" he asked furiously.

"I wasn't going to shoot you, you big clod!" she shouted, struggling to get free. "Let go of me!" Bo twisted and turned fruitlessly, kicking her legs in frustration. "I'm a poisoner, remember!" she screamed.

"Shut up!" Nick ordered sternly, rolling his eyes and sighing. "I know you weren't going to shoot me. It's a good thing you don't know how to fire a gun! Stop struggling!"

"Let go or I'll kick your broken leg." Bo threatened breathlessly.

"You go near that leg and I'll break your neck." he retorted calmly but placed his right leg over the broken one, just in case. "Why would you want to kill yourself?"

She ignored him as he rearranged himself slightly to make them both a little more comfortable. She still struggled feebly but knew she couldn't get away.

"I'm not going to let go until you answer the question," he said quietly.

"You should be able to figure it out yourself." She snapped.

"Well, I can't! So tell me," he waited patiently.

"I'm crazy." It was a simple statement in a voice devoid of all emotion.

"Are you really?"

"I must be! Why else would I kill Alex?" she cried sorrowfully.

"He's not dead."

He heard her sharp intake of breath as she twisted herself painfully in his grasp to look back at him.

"He's *not* dead?" she asked joyfully.

He shook his head, "Why don't you know that? It's been on the news every night."

"I never listen to the news. It's too depressing."

"But you did poison him?" Nick asked, getting back to business. He felt her give that characteristic shrug.

"I must have, who else could have?" she whispered brokenly as a tear slid down her cheek.

"But, you don't actually remember doing it?"

"No, I don't remember poisoning any of them! I gave myself up when I heard they were looking for me because I thought I was innocent," she cried softly. She had been lying quietly in his grasp but now became very agitated and started struggling fiercely. "Let me go!" she demanded breathlessly.

"Why, all of a sudden, do you think you did it?" Nick asked incredulously, unable to understand her thinking. Nick was secretly relieved when she stopped struggling; she was a strong girl and he was feeling very weak, it took all his strength to keep hold of her.

"I don't know!" she cried in frustration. "*He* kept saying I did it! And all the dreams; I must be crazy!" she sobbed. "*He* said I was doing it subconsciously and the equipment was in the house and the poisons! I had dinner with all those people. Hell! I cooked the food!" she caught Nick off guard; twisting free in one quick motion. He reached for her but she was too quick and was back hiding under the branch in the corner in a moment.

"By *he* you mean, Wylan?" Nick continued questioning in a quiet calm voice, hoping she'd continue talking. The branches shook as she slowly nodded. "What do you mean you cooked the food? Didn't you eat it, too?"

Bo sadly shook her head, shrugging her shoulders; it was painful to remember. She had tried to block out all thoughts of it, "They were all friends of my mother's. They had read of the deaths of the Montez family."

"The foster family you were living with?" Nick questioned trying to recall everything that he had read at the library as she nodded. "Did you cook that food, too?"

"But I used food from the refrigerator that Mrs. Montez had bought!" she defended herself. "I don't like mushrooms so I didn't eat any of them," she sighed sadly and Nick watched a tear fall.

"Now I wish I did! The police said it was an accidental death," she turned her face away from his gaze, looking into the wet leaves to her left. She pulled one or two of the leaves off, "I was petitioning the court to let me live by myself in my own home. I was only seven months away from being eighteen and legal."

"Why did you cook the food?"

"Because I'm a great cook; just like my mother! They invited me out of sympathy, but I didn't want pity. I would only agree to come to dinner if I made it; they supplied dessert," she explained still looking away. She picked up a lump of dirt and tossed it absently up and down.

"How come you didn't eat it?"

She shrugged, "When you spend all day cooking something, you taste it along the way and you get kind of full."

The lantern hissed and they looked at it in surprise. It went out abruptly.

"Damn," Bo said quietly.

"Get some sleep." Nick said softly.

Bo gave a short humorless laugh, "I gave up sleeping." There was a pause of several minutes, "When they rescue *us*, they're going to put *me* in a mental hospital," she whispered.

Nick sighed loudly, knowing there wasn't anything he could say. He knew from newspaper accounts that the hearing she had escaped from had been to send her to a mental hospital for a thirty day evaluation.

$$* \qquad * \qquad * \qquad *$$

The day dawned cloudy and overcast. Alex arrived at the marina in a taxi as John was getting in a rental car.

"Alex, what are you doing here?" John demanded in surprise, staring at his brother.

"They released me early," Alex said grimly. "I'm going with you to find Nick and Bo," he told John, paying the taxi and walking slowly to the car. "Where are you going to look first?" John watched him in concern; Alex was still pale but he recognized the look on his face. He gave in and got in the car, starting it before answering Alex.

"Wylan is convinced she's still here in Bridgeton. I'm—
we're going to Somerdale."

*   *   *   *

Nick opened his eyes; pale and feverish, he looked for Bo. It
was very early morning and last night's cascade of water down the
wall was now a trickle. It seemed to be drizzling lightly if it was
raining at all but it was hard to tell since there was a steady drip from
the leaves and branches overhead. Bo was slumped in the far corner;
Nick saw her head fall forward and then she jerked awake once
more. She looked terrible; tired beyond measure with her cheeks
flushed with fever.

"Bo," he called hoarsely. It took her a moment to focus on
him, "Come here, I need you." He begged. She crawled slowly
over.

"Your leg?" she asked in an equally hoarse voice.

"No, I'm freezing, lay here next to me," he ordered, lifting
his light jacket up slightly to let her get under it. He was chilled to
the bone even though he was lying on her thicker coat and covered
with his own light jacket; he didn't want to think how cold she must
be. Bo shook her head and he reached out, gently pulling her down
into the curve of his arm so she was lying on the bottom coat with
her head resting on his shoulder. She still strained to stay awake and
he could feel her shaking with cold as he placed his jacket on top of
them. "Go to sleep," he whispered.

"No," she refused, "Nightmares."

"What kind of nightmares?" he asked gently but she shook
her head, sighing deeply. She couldn't even talk about them. He felt
her relax against him as she fell asleep in an instant. He curled his
arm protectively over her and fell back to sleep.

*   *   *   *

John and Alex drove down a deserted country road as a light
rain began to fall. They came around a curve to see a tow truck and
a police car. A third vehicle was partially hidden by the other two.
John slowed down, pulling off the road, making the cop turn to look.
They ran to the tow truck.

"Hey, don't take that truck away," John ordered.

"And why not?" the cop demanded, "It's been abandoned."

"Our friend was driving it and he's missing," Alex informed him.

"He wouldn't leave it unless something happened," John told the policeman, turning to survey the surrounding area. It was a large open field bordered by large beautiful trees. In the center of the field was a large tree obviously recently felled by lightning, Alex was already walking towards it.

*   *   *   *

Bo screamed in terror as the knife plunged into her heart! Her scream startled Nick who had been dozing; he woke instantly and tightened his arm around her.

"Hey, it's okay! It's okay," he murmured, holding her tightly. "It's just a nightmare," he soothed. She elbowed him away; sitting up trembling and breathing heavily. "You're ok, Bo." She directed an angry glance at him and slapped his chest. "Hey, it's not my fault! Everyone needs sleep," he defended himself as she scooted herself a little farther away. Suddenly, she looked up sharply, startled. "What?" Nick questioned quickly, looking up.

"John!" Alex called excitedly. John ran to where he stood very close to the fallen tree.

"What is it?"

"I heard a scream somewhere over in that direction," Alex pointed to where the leafy part of the tree lay on the ground and walked towards it. "Nick!" he cupped his hands around his mouth and yelled. John joined him.

Nick and Bo heard yelling and Bo covered Nick's mouth as he was about to shout.

"Sh. They'll find us," she said urgently.

Nick hastily removed her hand, "We want them to find us!" He exclaimed impatiently. "John. Alex." he yelled. "We're in a pit under the tree. Don't fall in," Nick warned.

By this time, the policeman and the tow truck owner had joined them and they carefully pulled branches back, exposing the sides of the pit. They peered into the gaping hole to see Nick lying on his back.

"Are you alright?" John called down.

"Broke my leg." Nick informed him ruefully.

"We'll get you out. Don't go anywhere." John said before disappearing once more.

"Smart ass." Nick muttered.

It seemed like an eternity to Nick before John rappelled down the sides of their slippery prison, landing with a squish beside Nick.

"You look a mess! Been having fun?" he teased while examining Nick's splinted leg. "You did this yourself?" he wondered. Nick grimaced and silently pointed to the far corner. John turned quickly, clearly puzzled. He saw two muddy legs and one eye staring balefully from behind the leafy screen. He turned quickly back to Nick, looking a little stunned. "Dagmar?" he whispered cautiously and spun back around as a lump of dirt hit him in the head. "Hey!" he objected loudly.

"Bo," Nick smiled broadly at his friend. John turned back to Nick, deciding to ignore the odd girl in the corner for the time being.

"Ok, buddy, this is not going to be fun for you," John told Nick truthfully. "First, you gotta stand up," he helped Nick get groggily and painfully to his feet. Nick grit his teeth with pain and effort and looked over John's shoulder to see Bo cringing with sympathy at his plight. He smiled gently at her as John strapped him into the harness. Nick felt as weak as a kitten; it took all his strength to remain leaning upright against the wall.

John looked at him searchingly, "Are you gonna make it up to the top?" Nick was ashen but nodded, slowly taking a deep breath. John gave the men up top, the signal and they began hoisting Nick up. He kept his good leg extended, keeping himself away from the wall, knowing if he bumped the broken leg against the wall, he'd pass out. He grabbed John's jacket as he passed by.

"She's not happy about going back to jail," he whispered urgently. "Take it easy with her; she's not a bad kid. Start bail proceedings—" he continued giving instructions as he lost his grip on John's coat and was hoisted out of the pit, leaving John staring at Bo.

"Hi," he paused uncomfortably. "Come here often?" he asked with a touch of humor, giving her his most charming smile. He got no response from the girl who stood hidden from view. He picked the coat off the ground; it used to be navy but now was covered in mud on both sides and the lining was ripped apart. He looked at the slim legs he saw. The coat was about ten sizes too big for her.

"Is this yours?" He held it out.

She snatched it out of his hand; it had belonged to her grandmother and was very precious to her although she wasn't about to tell him that. She put the coat on as the harness was lowered back down and sirens were heard driving away.

"Nick's off to the hospital. Are you ready?" John said with cheerfulness he didn't feel as she remained silently where she was. He sighed deeply, "Come on, kid. You can't want to stay here. At least you'll get a bath, a bed and a hot meal." He cajoled her. "Okay, fine," he said in resignation; she wasn't going to do this the easy way. He put the harness on and walked to her slowly and calmly as she tried to back away but there wasn't anywhere to go. She put out her arm to ward him off. He grabbed her arm with a lightning quick move and after a very brief struggle; he held her clasped to his chest. She was too exhausted to fight him; even too exhausted to kick her legs uselessly as she lay in his arms. She pushed weakly against him until John gave the signal to pull him up. As they started swinging in space, she shrieked, grabbing him in fright. She put her arm around his shoulders, burying her head against his neck afraid she'd fall. John was free to use his legs to walk up the walls although they were so slippery he couldn't get any traction. They had used the tow truck as an improvised hoist. They dangled in the air over the pit for a few moments turning in circles until the men on the ground grabbed and pull them to the side of the pit. When his feet were once more on solid ground, John put Bo on her feet. She staggered and almost fell as Alex rushed over.

"Bo! Bo!" he grabbed hold of her. "Are you alright?" he demanded, amazed to see her. Nick hadn't told anyone she was with him. Bo took one look and flung herself into his arms crying hysterically.

"Alex, Alex, Alex!" she repeated his name, clinging to him. John struggled to get out of the harness, almost completely covered with mud, when Lt. Wylan appeared suddenly from the crowd of people milling around the group.

"So, here you are," he said harshly, grabbing Bo's arm, pulling her away from Alex. She started shrieking, completely hysterical and John rushed over. He roughly pulled Wylan away.

"Cut it out, Wylan!" he yelled at the cop as Bo wrapped her arms around John, grabbing hold of his belt and refusing to let go. She moved in circles trying to stay away from Wylan who followed her around as she pulled John in circles with her. John tried to release his belt and not trip over her as he was being pulled in circles. Finally, he just planted his feet, refusing to budge, using his longer arms to keep Wylan from reaching the girl hiding behind him. "Alex, get over here and get Bo," he ordered.

Alex rushed over, putting his arms around Bo, calling her name. She stopped screaming and looked at him piteously before she suddenly went limp and both brothers reached to catch her. Alex shot a venomous look at the Lt. as he took Bo from John, cradling her in his arms.

"Leave her alone," he ordered the policeman. "She's been in a pit for two days. She doesn't need you dragging her off to jail." He carried her to the second ambulance saying, "She's going to the hospital."

FIVE

Nick walked down the hospital corridor with a walking cast on his leg as John and Alex kept pace.

"Of course, we've been to see her, Nick!" Alex replied defensively. "She's been delirious with fever; she didn't even know we'd been here."

They entered her hospital room to see Bo lying listlessly in bed; her hands loosely tied to the bed rails and she watched them approach with a deep frown. Her deep unhappiness was very apparent.

"Hi," they chorused but she remained stubbornly silent, glaring at John.

"What's the matter with you now?" John rebuked her. "You're clean and fed."

"I'd rather be in jail than tied up with people sticking needles into me," she groused.

Alex smiled gently, "You've been very sick, Bo. You kept trying to leave and pulling out your IV lines."

Nick untied her, "You can go home today," he informed her cheerfully.

She frowned, "I don't call jail *home*. Not yet, anyway!" she muttered darkly.

"We put up your bail. You'll stay with us until we find out who's doing this," Nick soothed.

Bo stared incredulously, "You— you believe I didn't do it?" She was so moved she could barely say the words. She looked at Alex wordlessly as he smiled and nodded confidently.

"Thanks," she mumbled, barely able to speak, lowering her head to try to hide the tears falling from her eyes. She didn't see the expression on John's face; he wasn't at all happy about this decision, his had been the one dissenting vote.

*   *   *   *

They got out of the truck at the dock. Bo was obviously nervous, starting as the door shut behind her. She was distracted and glancing nervously behind them. Nick and John noticed but said nothing. They kept their very different thoughts to themselves. They stowed her gear in Quark's bedroom, introducing her to the robot. Nick laughed at her expression when she saw the robot coming up the stairwell wall.

"He's using electro-magnets in his treads to stick to the metal plate you see on the wall. He also has a hook and hoist system in one of his arms, in case the electro-magnets fail or in rough seas," Alex explained, sounding like a proud papa. Bo gave him a small smile and nodded as if she understood. There was an awkward silence, as they stood in the main room. Bo stood edgily against the wall as they silently wondered why she was so uneasy.

"Anyone want some ice tea?" John looked around but everyone shook their heads. He went into the galley.

"Oh, Nick, I have the, uh, victims up on the computer," Alex reminded Nick, who had asked him to hack into the police computer. They disappeared down the stairs. Bo nervously looked around and headed out the door. She walked up the ladder to the top deck and then checked out the wheel house. John came back to the main room, putting the glass of tea and half a lemon on a plate on the table. He heard Nick and Alex talking in Alex's room and went outside to check on the girl. He came out the main door as Bo came down the wheelhouse steps with her back to him. She turned without seeing him, looking across the marina at the large fishing boat anchored across from the Baby. Suddenly, she ran towards the ramp as if to flee the boat.

"Running away again?" John asked sarcastically.

She stopped, turning around abruptly, "Don't do that!" she snapped, considerably startled. "You shouldn't sneak up on people."

"You're just mad because I caught you trying to get away." he leaned against the rail watching her.

"Oh, I'm sorry. I didn't know I was a prisoner!" she spit out.

"Listen, little girl, we've put everything we own on the line to bail you out of jail. Nick and Alex have put their trust in you—"

"I didn't ask them to do that!" she flared angrily.

"No, they did it because they want to help you—" he snapped back.

"I don't need anyone's help—"

John interrupted her with a loud laugh and she stared, taken aback.

"You need help more than anyone I've ever met, little girl." he replied bluntly. "And Nick and Alex want to help you because that's the kind of people they are," he paused, eyeing her intently. "What kind of a person are you?"

She turned her back looking over the water, "The kind of person who should be locked up." It was barely a whisper; if he hadn't come closer when she turned away, he wouldn't have heard her. She looked over her shoulder and flinched, not expecting him to be so close.

"You *want* to go to jail?" he wondered.

"Of course not!" she denied unconvincingly, moving farther away. She leaned over the rail, her hair hanging down hiding her face.

"Wow, you're really a *bad* liar." he observed. "What's going on, Bo?"

She startled him by swinging around and grabbing hold of his arm, making him pull back slightly in surprise.

"Rescind the bail, take me back to jail! I'll even go to the mental hospital!" she begged earnestly. John was taken completely by surprise and didn't know what to say. "I just don't want any more people to die!" she wailed, turning abruptly away.

John caught hold of her as she headed for the ramp. "No one is going to die, Bo," he said positively; up to now John hadn't believed in her innocence but suddenly he saw in her what Nick and Alex had seen.

"You don't understand," she shook her head, trying to push him away. "I'm crazy."

John slowly released her, staying close, "What makes you think you're crazy?"

Bo looked around nervously once more, "I'm seeing things that aren't there," she whispered fearfully.

"Oh, is that all." He replied cheerfully, turning her around and putting an arm around her shoulders, "Come in and sit down." He gently steered her back into the cabin where Nick and Alex sat at the table.

"We were wondering where you two went." Alex said concerned. Bo wouldn't look at him and she looked pale. He glanced suspiciously at John who gave him a brilliant smile as he gave Bo a slight push onto the bench beside Alex.

"Bo was just telling me that she's been seeing things that aren't there," he informed them happily, sitting down in front of his glass as Bo sat motionlessly, staring at the table. The two men stared at John as if he'd lost his mind and silence greeted his remark. John picked up the lemon and squeezed it into his glass, making a face, "This is a lousy lemon."

"What the hell do you mean by that last remark?" Alex finally found his voice and demanded angrily. John busily stirred his drink, ignoring Alex.

"The only connection between all the victims is you. Do you have any enemies?" John asked Bo casually. He had aroused her interest and she picked her head up, blinking in surprise.

"Well, I must have one," she replied with a hint of spirit returning. Her glance fell on the lemon on the plate and she gave an audible gasp before flinging herself at John and putting her hand over his mouth. Alex had followed her glance and the same thought occurred to him at the same moment. He leaped up, reaching across the table to take the glass from John's unresisting grasp.

"What the hell is wrong with all of you?" A disgusted Nick asked plaintively.

Alex and Bo released John and stared at the glass in Alex's hand, "Oh, please, Alex, don't even touch it! John, hurry up and wash your hands. Hurry, hurry!" she pulled on his shirt until he got up and went to the sink. Alex gingerly put the glass down on the table; he wasn't in the mood to take a chance on being poisoned again.

"The poison was in the lemon." Alex explained, slightly bewildered.

"And neither one of us bought that lemon," Bo added.

"Then who did?" Nick questioned as they looked at Bo who stared sightlessly ahead. John bent over, waving a hand in front of her face but got no response.

"It's him," she murmured after a long pause while the three men exchanged worried glances.

"Who's *him*?" Nick leaned on the counter staring intently.

She turned, staring blankly, "He's going to kill me, just like in my dream." she whispered in a daze.

John grabbed her by the arm giving her a small shake, "Who, Bo? Tell us who."

"My father."

"Bo, you're father's dead," Alex reminded her gently.

She nodded assent, "I know. He's come back to kill me, too," she insisted matter-of-factly.

"Why do you think it's him?" Nick asked curiously.

"I saw him."

"You saw your dead father?" Nick asked clearly unbelieving which made her suddenly come to life, jumping up abruptly.

"What are you saying, Nick?" she challenged belligerently. "That I'm crazy?" she asked aggressively, advancing towards him, giving him a hard shove backwards.

He obligingly retreated while denying her accusation, "No, Bo. I'm not saying that."

John came up behind Bo, pulling her away from Nick, "Why are you jumping all over him? You told me the same thing up on deck."

She hung her head, leaning back against John, "I'm sorry, Nick." She said instantly penitent. Once again, she wouldn't raise her head to look at them. Alex slid from behind the table and taking her hand, pulled her to the living area to sit on the couch beside her.

"Maybe it's someone who is dressing up like your father." He suggested rationally.

"No, it doesn't look like him," Bo denied irrationally. John put a hand to his forehead and Nick shook his head as if to clear it and rolled his eyes; only Alex understood what she meant.

"You know it's really him because it doesn't look like him," Alex mused thoughtfully. "Yes, yes. I see. That makes sense."

John stared, "That makes sense to you, Alex?"

"Sure, John. If you were impersonating someone, you'd make yourself exactly like them. You wouldn't disguise yourself if you *wanted* someone to recognize you, would you?" he patiently explained to his brother. Nick held up a restraining hand as John struggled to sort out the logic of Alex's explanation.

"Fine. Tell us where you saw this guy, Bo," Nick wanted to keep the conversation on a practical level.

"I've felt like someone is following me around a lot lately but I only saw him twice. The first time, I saw his face reflected in a store window right before Alex and I had lunch. He was standing right behind me; close enough to put the lemon in the bag I was carrying. When I turned around he was gone," she stopped speaking, looking at them expectantly.

"When was the second time?" John prompted as she stared, unwilling to continue.

"Is it a secret or what?" Nick demanded sarcastically; patience wasn't one of his virtues. Bo blinked several times and took a deep breath.

"I— I woke up this morning and he was standing by the bed. He was wearing full surgical garb, gloves, mask, and gown and cap with— a— a scalpel," she spoke hesitantly. They could hear the fear in her voice.

"What did he say?" Alex asked, touching her hand to comfort her as she shook her head sadly.

"Nothing. He just stared at me, waving the scalpel in the air. I was so terrified I couldn't move, couldn't scream," she said breathing heavily. "I must have fainted because I remember opening my eyes and he was gone then the nurse came in," she hung her head.

Nick put a hand on her shoulder, "Maybe it was just a nightmare?"

She gave an unpleasant laugh, "Oh, no! In my nightmares, he stabs me with an eight inch knife! This was real." She anxiously searched their faces to see if they believed her. "He's come back from the dead to kill me!" she grabbed Nick who was closest as she cried out in fear.

"You don't come back from the dead," he replied adamantly, trying to push her back on the couch.

"I saw him die and I saw him in my room this morning!" she insisted.

"You saw a man covered head to toe, who never spoke." John reminded her. "How can you be so sure it's him?"

"Wouldn't you know it was Alex if you saw him disguised?" she demanded.

"Well, there's one thing we can do," Alex stated positively; three pairs of eyes turned inquisitively.

"What's that Brain?" John asked suspiciously, using his family nickname.

"Check the grave," Alex replied, surprised by their ignorance.

John and Nick stared at one another in alarm.

*   *   *   *

The truck was stopped in the center of a dirt road; they gazed down on the tiny town of Harrisonville. The whole town consisted of one intersection and two stores with ten houses clustered around.

"What were you doing here?" John wondered why anyone would come here on purpose.

"I have no idea. We camped near here and came into town every day. It was weird because my father hated camping. He made friends with the store owner who is also a doctor of something," she shrugged. "We were having dinner in the café when he died," she stumbled on the word as John drove through the town to the little cemetery on the other side. The cemetery was several miles past the town limits and silent with no one in sight for miles. The only sound was the wind blowing over the fields.

Nick and John stood in the grave; the coffin was cleared of dirt. Both men were bare-chested and sweaty from the effort as they leaned their shovels against the walls, looking at one another unhappily. They glanced up to see Alex and Bo anxiously looking down.

Nick glanced at John, "Ready?"

"Not really," John replied truthfully as they lifted the lid quickly and dropped it just as suddenly as a man in a dark suit with his hands crossed was revealed. They leaned back against the walls in shock.

"There wasn't supposed to be anyone in there!" Nick complained loudly; John suddenly looked over the top of the grave wall to see Alex bending over something in the long grass. Bo was nowhere to be seen. John put a foot on the casket and jumped out of the hole. He ran to Bo, stretched out on the ground and knelt on one knee beside Alex. Nick stepped up, standing on the casket to see; it was too much trouble to get out and back in with the cast. Bo wasn't unconscious as John thought; her eyes were tightly shut with a deep grimace.

"Bo, I'm sorry," he apologized softly.

She startled them by sitting up abruptly, "I'm not crazy!" she exclaimed in relief.

"There's a body in that coffin," Nick reminded her grimly. "It's not supposed to be there!" he said bitterly. "Disturbing graves is a serious charge unless, of course, the grave is empty."

"But it's not him!"

"That's not your father?" Alex demanded in surprise and she shook her head.

John wasn't reassured, "It was only a glimpse. How can you be so sure?" he argued.

"My father didn't have a beard when he died," she scrambled to her feet with their assistance and walked to the grave. Nick handed the two shovels to Alex and John reached down to help Nick out. They started shoveling the dirt back in.

"Then who is it?" Alex asked the question they were all thinking.

"Why are we burying him again?" Bo inquired perplexed.

"Now that we know for sure it's not your father, we'll go through the regular channels to have him dug up nice and legal-like," Nick cheerfully explained.

"Oh," she nodded and helped shovel the dirt in.

Nick paused in his shoveling, "Please tell me because I have to know," he begged. "Why are you called Bo?"

"Dagmar *Beauregard* Benjamin," Bo made a face. "Pretty terrible, isn't it?"

Nick grimaced solemnly in agreement.

*   *   *   *

Alex and Bo sat on the back porch steps of her house in Somerdale and John laid flat in the overgrown grass as Nick came around the side of the house.

"Well, there's nothing here; the house is completely empty," he stared at the house balefully; his leg was hurting him now.

"George Fennel," Bo stated suddenly.

John lifted his head, staring at her over his feet, "Who's he?"

"The guy in the coffin;" Bo replied, "my father's business partner." She got up to pace.

Alex frowned, "Isn't he the guy who took off with the company funds? Over a million dollars?"

"How'd you know that, Alex?" Bo questioned in surprise.

"There's nothing that Alex and Quark can't find out," John told her proudly.

"He's very thorough," Nick added; it didn't sound like a compliment.

"What's this got to do with anything?" John propped himself up on one elbow and looked at Alex.

"He disappeared one week before my father's '*fatal*' heart attack," Bo supplied, sitting beside Alex again. "The coroner in Harrisonville said the stress of bankruptcy probably led to the attack."

"That tiny little town has its own coroner?" Nick asked suspiciously.

"He's dead, too," Alex informed them.

"Who?" All three asked.

"The doctor who declared your father dead; he died two months later of a stroke. He was comparatively young for a stroke," Alex mused.

"Very interesting! Don't you find that interesting, John?" Nick demanded excitedly. "A man supposedly disappears with a million dollars; the next week his partner fakes his own death and buries the missing partner in his grave."

"Your father stole the money, not his partner! He kills Fennel, fakes his own death and kills the only person who knows; the coroner." John chimed in full of energy. Bo and Alex watched them pacing back and forth.

"Why would a man who got away with a million dollars and two murders come back six months later and murder twelve people?" Alex demanded logically, making them stop pacing and look at him malevolently.

"Because he doesn't have the money?" Bo questioned softly as the three men turned to her.

"Of course," Nick said. "Something must have gone wrong. The question is; where is it and what does it have to do with you?"

"Where's he been hiding for half a year?" John suddenly asked.

Bo waved at the house behind her, "Right here."

"How could he?" Alex objected. "There have been three tenants since he died."

Bo looked at him in surprise, "You're amazing, Alex!" she laughed. "Do you know why they left?" she challenged. He shook his head in defeat. "They said it was *haunted*!" she crowed triumphantly. "He's been staying here in the secret room!"

"The secret room!" All three yelled indignantly.

"When we were searching the house from top to bottom, you never mentioned a secret room," Nick rebuked her.

"I'd forgotten all about it! It's really a bomb shelter with an entrance shaft in both second floor bedrooms," she explained breathlessly.

They ran into the house and upstairs. They opened the closet in the first bedroom and pulled back the rug revealing a trap door in the floor and John descended the ladder with Alex following. Nick had no choice but to stay with Bo in the empty bedroom. She walked to stand looking out the window as he stood looking down the narrow opening.

"I wish I could go down there," Nick moaned regretfully.

"I don't," Bo said flatly. "My father took me down there sometimes when I was a kid. He made us stay there for hours, telling me how the world had been destroyed and this is where we would have to live for years, hoping the food, water and air would support us. It scared me to death," she shivered as Nick put his hand on her shoulder.

"You're father sounds like a great guy." He quipped sarcastically.

"I'm going to wait downstairs," she said abruptly. "I don't like this house anymore," she ran downstairs.

John and Alex opened the door at the bottom of the shaft which opened into a pitch dark space. They found the light switch after a few minutes of fumbling along the right side wall. The light flared, momentarily blinding them. Wall to ceiling shelves lined all the walls. Food supplies, candles, books and some clothing were in neat stacks. Bedrolls were neatly rolled against one wall. They went to the desk in the center of the room. Newspaper clippings were neatly piled in sequence and John read through them. CAMCO BANKRUPT, ACCOUNTANT FLEES WITH MILLION,

NICKATARRY STAMP SOLD FOR 1 MILLION TO UNKNOWN BUYER. He read them out loud to Alex who read a separate pile of clippings.

"These are all about the poisonings," Alex reported. He spied a picture on the bottom of the pile. It was a wedding photo but the woman had a big red X over her. Alex passed it to John, "That's Bo's mother."

"Wylan should see this," John said. They looked over their shoulders as they heard a strange clunk to see the door was now closed. They exchanged a look and Alex tried the door which remained firmly closed.

"We're locked in," he informed John unnecessarily.

*   *   *   *

Bo went downstairs, wandering into a room that was partially shuttered with one shutter open and hanging lopsidedly.

"Poor house," she murmured as she heard a step behind her and turned, "Nick—" She was face to face with a tall man with a beard. She couldn't move; couldn't even scream as she stared in terror at the large knife he held.

"You've been expecting me, Dagmar?" he questioned smoothly, sure of himself and his ability to instill terror as Bo looked from side to side seeking escape. "You won't get away from me this time, Dagmar. I'm tired of being nice. I've tried to poison you thirty-seven times!" his voice rose almost to a scream. "I had to kill your mother when she found out," he gloated. "This time you are going to give it to me and then I will kill you."

"Give—? Give you what?" she stammered perplexed, "And why do you want to kill me?"

"Give me the envelope," he explained, "Then I will kill you because you are not my daughter." He snorted as Bo's eyes opened wide, "Oh, yes, your mother thought she could fool me but I've known all along!" He laughed gleefully, "Why do you think I ran over your father?" He chuckled. "Where's the envelope?" he repeated becoming serious once more. Bo had been turning in a slow circle trying to get past him while he'd been talking.

"I don't know what you're talking about," she replied truthfully.

"Where is it?" he shouted. He had her cornered and advanced with the knife raised. Bo found her voice; she was still terrified but no longer mesmerized.

"Nick! Alex! John! Help me! Help!" she shrieked as loudly as she could. Nick was already halfway downstairs, walking slowly trying not to make any noise with his cast, his gun ready. When Bo started screaming, he thumped down the stairs as fast as he could, rounding the corner to see Bo trying to push her father away.

"Freeze, Benjamin," Nick yelled, firing the gun above her father's head. Her father never turned; he continued to force the knife down towards Bo who used both hands on his wrist to keep it away.

"No! No!" she screamed in terror. Nick couldn't shoot because her father was standing directly in front of Bo and he was afraid of hitting her, too. Suddenly, Bo slumped to the floor and Nick fired. Jacob Benjamin fell to the floor two feet from Bo as Nick ran to her and John and Alex raced into the room.

"Where the hell were you?" Nick challenged them.

"He locked us in," Alex explained as they knelt beside Bo who was returning to consciousness. Nick suddenly noticed the ax lying on the floor beside John.

"A well-stocked bomb shelter," John said sarcastically and turned to Bo. "Are you alright?" he asked solicitously as she slowly opened her eyes.

She looked at the three men in confusion. She put her hand out to Alex who helped her up. She glanced down at her father's body for a moment before turning away; walking outside with Alex supporting her with his arm around her shoulders. John checked to make sure Benjamin was dead then helped Nick to his feet. They followed the other two outside and called the police and sat in the truck waiting for the police.

"You'll be cleared of all charges, now," Nick comforted a silent Bo.

"He hated me," she murmured quietly, sitting in the back with Alex's arm around her.

"He wasn't in his right mind," Alex gently consoled her.

"He was a psycho! He killed sixteen people." John said aggressively before he could stop himself. Alex and Nick glared at him. "Sorry." he shrugged apologetically at Bo who hid her face against Alex, crying softly.

SIX

They sat at the table on the Baby, two days later, staring at a large manila envelope in the center of the table.

"This came in the mail about five months after he died. It had been lost and misdirected while I was placed in foster care. As far as I can tell it's a bunch of contracts that were never signed because of the bankruptcy and my— father's death," Bo stumbled over the word.

"My friend from the lab called," Alex interrupted. "He said it's true, he wasn't your biological father!"

Bo's face lit up, "How wonderful!" she enthused. "I don't have to worry about my children inheriting insanity! Or me!" she added happily, looking at Alex and blushing for no apparent reason as he grinned foolishly at her. John looked sharply at her and then at his brother as they hastily looked away from each other.

"We investigated the death of the only single man in Somerdale the year you were born. Josh Carpenter was a hit and run victim early one morning when he was out running. He rented an apartment on your block and he died three months before you were born," Nick added.

Bo nodded, "That was the name on the back of the picture in my mother's drawer." Bo sighed, "I never knew why she had a picture of a strange man in her drawer."

John picked up the envelope musing, "One of the articles on the desk was about a rare million dollar stamp." He reminded them, "But these are three everyday stamps and they're canceled." He finished sadly; putting it in Alex's outstretched hand.

"That's the only envelope I've seen," Bo objected. "Besides, it's his handwriting. He sent it to himself."

"What are you going to do now, Bo?" John asked to distract her.

"My Aunt Rachel is coming here to live with me!" Bo said excitedly. "I've never met her; she's my mother's sister! Alex traced her for me! I've talked to her on the phone and she sounds so nice!"

"Why didn't you know about her?" Nick asked curiously.

"She's ten years younger than my mother," Bo explained. "Their parents died in a car accident when Rachel was just a baby and they were adopted separately. My mother tried for years to find out what happened to her baby sister," she smiled at John. "I already have a buyer for the house," she shook her head in disbelief. "He's thrilled to buy a house with a bomb shelter and a famous criminal getting killed there," she grimaced.

"People are strange." Nick agreed, shaking his head and rolling his eyes.

"Hmm," Alex captured everyone's attention with the sound as he picked at the corner of the envelope.

"What is it, Brain?" John asked impatiently.

"I'm wondering why these stamps are taped on instead of glued," he gently pulled back on them revealing a small stamp encased in thin plastic underneath.

"The Nickatarry!" They exclaimed as Alex handed it to Bo.

"I don't believe it," she whispered, beaming at Alex, "Now all those people who lost money in the bankruptcy will be repaid." She flung her arms around Alex's neck and kissed him, "You're wonderful!" She jumped up to hug and kiss Nick and John, too. "You guys are great." She put the stamp on the table and told Nick, "I want to sign your cast."

He obligingly propped his cast up on the table. John took the opportunity to pull Alex aside; Nick watched them curiously.

"What do you think you're doing, little brother?" John ground out angrily.

"What are you talking about?" Alex inquired in real surprise.

"I've seen the way the two of you look at each other!" John hissed, "Are you crazy? She's jailbait!"

"I don't know what you're talking about," Alex denied hotly, "And anyway in five months, she'll be legal!" he retorted with a grin and turned to join Nick and Bo.

"You're twenty-six and she's seventeen!" John grabbed his arm, not letting him leave.

"Our father is eleven years older than our mother," Alex reminded his older brother, "And they are still very happy." He shook John's hand off his arm and walked to the table looking over Bo's shoulder, laughing as Nick looked down to see what she wrote.

"Hey!" he objected. Bo had drawn a skull and crossbones with the words DANGER: POISON underneath. She laughed loudly at Nick's pained expression. John came to look and had to laugh. Alex put his arm around her shoulders, smiling down at her as she happily smiled up at him.

CASE FILE: JENNY

ONE

A pretty fifteen year old girl sat on the beach engrossed in a book oblivious to her surroundings, close to Nick and John who were playing Frisbee. She glanced at her watch and jumped to her feet, hurriedly packing her things as John ran and made a leap for a wild throw; he bumped into her, knocking them both to the sand. He was charming and apologetic, helping her up as Nick came running over.

"I'm fine! I don't need your help." She shook off their helping hands; her tone sharp with annoyance.

"I'm very sorry. I didn't see you." John apologized once more.

"If you watched where you're going, you wouldn't have to be sorry!" she snapped, stalking away leaving John and Nick staring after her silently.

"Some people are very touchy." Nick shrugged, looking around for the Frisbee to continue their game.

The girl walked down the street, stopping at the corner for the light when someone bumped into her making her trip off the curb. She turned angrily to see Alex peering over the top of his book.

"Alex!" she cried in exasperation. "You can't read when you're walking down the street!"

"Oh, I'm sorry, Jenny. Did I hurt you?" he asked solicitously.

She frowned. "No, but that's the fourth time someone has run into me this week! I'm beginning to think I'm invisible or something." she grumbled. She looked at his book as the light changed and they crossed the street. "What's so interesting?"

"Oh, it's really fractal cool!" Alex began eagerly as Jenny linked her arm through his with a laugh and they continued down the street.

*   *   *   *

Jenny woke suddenly, lifting her head to listen intently, not sure what woke her. She threw back the covers and slid out of bed, creeping quietly out of the room to stand at the top of the stairs listening. She went downstairs, her bare feet making no sound and paused at the bottom of the staircase. Muted sounds came from her father's study off to her left. He often worked late at night and she peeked in the open door to check on him. She was rooted to the spot in horror as she saw a man with his back to her, strangling her father!

"Jase!" she shrieked.

The man turned quickly, letting her father fall to the ground and she shrieked again louder; seeing the stranger's face in the weak light! She ran out the front door which stood open and ran screaming across the street to pound on her friend Elizabeth's door.

"Help! Police! Help!" she screamed hysterically over and over.

The murderer slipped away into the shadows as the door opened for Jenny.

*   *   *   *

Everything was quiet aboard the Baby; everyone slept peacefully until the peace was shattered by loud pounding and shouting. Alex got to the door first and let the police in. Two uniformed officers and Lt. Wylan pushed past him.

"Get out of the way, genius." Officer Duncan ordered nastily.

"Lt., what the hell do you want at three am?" Nick asked Wylan angrily as he and John came upstairs. Wylan grinned at John, motioning the officers forward.

"I'm here to arrest you, pretty boy." he crowed triumphantly, placing a handcuff on John's wrist but John pulled away; truly startled.

"Arrest me?" John questioned, shoving Duncan away.

"Arrest him?" Nick got in front of the other officer attempting to help Duncan.

"For what?" Alex demanded angrily. "Now, wait a minute, Lt." he blocked Duncan.

Wylan angrily pushed him aside and grabbed John's arm. The two officers got the cuffs on him.

"I'm gonna add resisting arrest and interfering with an officer doing his duty if you don't knock it off!" he snapped angrily as he swung John around to face the door.

Nick planted himself in front of them. "You can't arrest someone without telling him the charges."

"John Colby, you're under arrest for the first degree murder of Joseph Laurence." Lt. Wylan said, taking great satisfaction in saying it aloud.

"Murder?" All three protested at once.

"Get him out of here!" Wylan barked belligerently to his men.

"At least, let me get dressed!" John argued, dragging his feet.

"Alright!" Wylan agreed grudgingly, noticing he wore cutoff sweatpants and nothing else. "Go with him." he ordered both officers.

"What's going on, Wylan?" Nick asked while they waited.

"Look, bum, you want answers, you get a lawyer. I'm the one who's asking the questions here." he snarled, poking Nick in the chest with one finger.

"You haven't asked any questions," Alex calmly pointed out.

Wylan was about to retort when he saw John coming up the steps dressed and handcuffed.

"This is a good one, Wylan." he told the cop. "You'll be facing false arrest charges by morning."

Wylan smiled broadly, "Oh, I got you this time, beach boy." Wylan laughed, leading him off the boat.

*   *   *   *

Nick and Alex paced the corridor. Nick wasn't waiting patiently, muttering and pounding the walls until a tall, lovely, dark haired woman came down the hall. Nick eagerly took her arm, propelling her to Alex and sitting her down.

"Calm down, Nick." She whispered urgently, eyeing the policemen passing in the halls.

"What's this all about, Mary?" Alex asked eagerly. "The police won't tell us anything."

"It's pretty bad, guys. They have an eye witness who saw John shoot and strangle a man last night around ten thirty. I just talked with John and he has no alibi for that time; he was walking on the beach by himself."

"Shoot *and* strangle a man?" Alex questioned; unable to believe anyone could think John would do that.

"I don't believe this! An eye witness?" Nick shook his head angrily. "Why, tell me, why is he supposed to have killed this guy?" he yelled.

Mary pulled him down beside her. "Nick, getting crazy isn't going to help John." she admonished sternly. "The motive is the weakest part of the case so far," she looked up at Alex. "I got the bail reduced to something I hope you can handle."

"We'll handle it," he replied grimly.

"John insists he doesn't know Joseph Laurence. He didn't recognize the picture of him. He's pretty confused right now."

"Can we arrange bail now?" Nick asked quietly.

"Yes." Mary took Alex down the corridor, leaving Nick sitting deep in thought.

Alex waited outside the office for Mary to rejoin him when he saw a girl with her head bent and her hands over her eyes, leaning against the wall.

"Jenny, what are you doing here?" he asked in surprise.

She looked up startled. "Oh, Alex!" she cried, wiping her tears away. "I— I had to identify a man who— who broke into our house," she sobbed.

"Oh, that's terrible," he sympathized. "Are you alright?"

She shook her head, "I don't know," she replied honestly. "I have to go, Alex. I'm very upset," she turned away, almost running down the hall.

"Are you alone?" he asked solicitously, following her.

"No, a friend is with me," she continued walking rapidly away.

He reluctantly watched her go as Mary came out of the office with John. They collected Nick and went back to the Baby.

*   *   *   *

Nick parked the truck, still peppering John with questions as he got out and slammed the door.

"Get off my case, Nick! You're worse than Wylan!" he yelled. "I'm tired. I didn't get much sleep and I just spent six hours in police custody. I don't want any more questions!"

"We haven't been partying for the last six hours either, you know buddy!" Nick snapped irritably and loudly.

"Guys," Alex pleaded very quietly.

They abruptly stopped shouting and silently boarded the Baby.

"Listen, guys, I really appreciate your concern. It's just that I have no answers to give you." John explained dejectedly.

"Let's not talk about it anymore," Alex said reasonably. "We can all use some sleep."

"Sorry," Nick apologized quietly, putting his hand on John's shoulder.

TWO

Alex was standing in the supermarket checkout line when he saw Jenny.

"Jenny," he called. "How are you doing?"

"Hi Alex," she sighed sadly. "Not too bad I guess," she hurriedly looked away and turned to leave.

Alex followed her with a worried frown, begging her to talk to him. They walked to her house around the corner with Alex carrying her small bag of groceries. After she unpacked the groceries, they sat at the kitchen table. Jenny was very quiet and Alex had been doing most of the talking.

"Did he steal anything?"

"Who?" she asked blankly.

"The man who broke in." he replied confused.

She looked flustered, "Oh, Alex! I didn't tell you what really happened. I just couldn't say it all again." She got more ice tea from the fridge, "A man broke in and— killed my father." She still had trouble saying it and began to cry again. "It was so awful."

Alex put his arm around her, "Oh, Jenny, I'm so sorry." he murmured sympathetically, not wanting to ask her any questions.

"I was in bed when I heard a noise so I went down to see what it was," she explained.

"Jenny, if you hear someone breaking into the house at night, you should just call the police. You should never investigate by yourself," he advised, shocked and horrified. "What if he had killed you too?"

Jenny stared in confusion. "I didn't hear anyone breaking in, Alex; something woke me up and I heard people talking loudly. My father keeps—" she stopped herself, "Kept late hours sometimes. My brother Jason visits at odd times, too; that's who I thought it was until I saw the man."

"Did he see you?" Alex asked worriedly. She nodded frightened. "What did you do?"

She gave a shaky laugh, "I started screaming my head off and ran out the front door that he had left open. I ran across the street to my friend's house. He didn't follow me, he just ran away." she jumped as the phone beside her rang and smiled slightly in embarrassment. "Hello? Yes. That's alright. I understand. It doesn't matter." she hung up and looked at Alex. "He's being buried tomorrow. The lawyer was going to read the will tomorrow but his office was broken into last night. He just postponed it a day."

Alex nodded in sympathy, "You were at the police station last night, because the police caught the man already?" Alex asked casually. "That's pretty quick."

"I went to the station and gave a description of the man. They put it on the computer and made a picture of him," she looked at Alex, refilling his glass. "The Lt. was very strange. When he saw the picture, he started smiling. He knew him right away and they went to pick him up and I identified him."

Alex asked worriedly, "Jenny, do you have any idea why this man would kill your father?"

"I don't know exactly why, Alex but I've been thinking about it. I overheard a conversation a couple of weeks ago. I had picked up the phone to make a call and I heard a man's voice say, '*If you don't give me the money, you'll be sorry*'. My father laughed and told him, 'What are you going to do? Tell the police? Stealing government secrets is a federal offense. You're slime, kid. I never want to hear from you again.' Then my father hung up but I heard the man say '*I'll kill you, old man*' very softly before he hung up." Jenny looked unhappily at Alex. "I asked my father what it was all about but he refused to tell me anything. I read in the paper a few days later that the military base was investigating the 'disappearance' of certain documents." She sighed deeply. "I was afraid to mention it to the police last night," she looked at Alex with a worried frown. "Do you think I should tell them?"

Alex thought quickly, "I would wait a couple of days, see what they come up with," he advised cautiously. "It may have nothing to do with the theft or his death."

She nodded, not entirely happy with the answer. "I just don't know what to do anymore, Alex." she said sounding lost and very young.

"What can I do to help, Jenny?" he asked gently.

She looked at him sadly, "Would you come with me to the funeral tomorrow?" she asked hesitantly.

"Of course!" he agreed eagerly, wanting to do whatever he could. He left after asking one more question. "Jenny, what's your last name?"

She smiled, "Laurence."

He smiled a little stiffly, "I'll be here tomorrow."

She watched him go down the steps before locking the door.

*   *   *   *

Nick and John were drinking coffee and discussing the case.

"I don't know this Laurence guy; I never heard of him, I told you!" John snapped testily.

"Alright, who would want to frame you for this?" Nick questioned.

John shrugged his shoulders helplessly. "What about this eye witness? We have to find out who he is! Oh, hi Alex."

Alex didn't return the greeting, walking past them to open the laptop sitting on the table.

"I've got bad news, guys. Whatever this is, it's good," he started typing in commands as the two men stared without understanding.

"What are you talking about?" Nick asked irritably.

"Where have you been, Alex?" John asked curiously.

Alex was still engrossed with his computer screen. "I went to the grocery store," he interrupted himself to say wearily, "Damn; I left the food in the truck."

John and Nick both waved the forgotten food aside.

"Alex," John implored his brother to get to the important information.

"I met a friend of mine last night at the police station. I met her again at the store this afternoon," again he stopped talking to pay attention to his computer.

"What does this have to do with me?" John shouted impatiently.

"Her name is Jenny Laurence; she's your eye witness. Joseph Laurence was her father."

"What's her game, Alex?" Nick asked eagerly.

"She doesn't have a game, Nick. She's young and confused," he paused to give the computer a few more commands. "She probably gave me the motive, though."

"Why would she tell you?" John asked skeptically.

"Obviously, she doesn't know I'm related to you. She doesn't even know your name," he paused, looking at them for the first time. "I didn't ask her, of course, and she didn't tell me how her father died but I put two and two together and I am rather—"

"Okay, okay," Nick hastened to stop him from explaining his thought processes for the umpteenth time. "What's the motive?"

"Espionage."

"What?" Both men gasped.

"Jenny overheard a phone conversation her father had with a mystery man. The mystery man stole the documents for her father who then refused to pay him. Jenny heard the mystery man threaten to kill her father before he hung up."

"Alex," Nick asked quietly, "how does any of that tie in with John?"

"Well, Quark and I just checked the base guest list and John is on it," he nodded at their unspoken question. "The same day the papers were stolen."

"You're kidding me!" John slapped his forehead suddenly, "That's right! You remember, Thursday two weeks ago, Ted Downs left me a message to come see him. When I got there, he asked me what I wanted to see him about. He told me I had left *him* a message."

Nick and Alex nodded remembering the incident; at the time it had only seemed very odd, now it seemed ominous.

Nick sat down suddenly, "This is a very good frame, John." He looked thoughtful, "Not air tight, though."

"No, that's what makes it work so well," John said bitterly. "Someone gets me on a military base at the same time documents are stolen. An eye witness sees me strangling a man but the gun is missing; that's weird, it should have been left with my prints on it."

"You were wearing gloves," Alex informed him.

"What?" Nick asked quickly.

"I tapped the police records. It says the murderer wore gloves."

"But why not leave my gun?" John asked. "The police searched the boat and didn't find it. Nick's gun is here but not mine."

"Why?" Nick asked no one in particular. "It's suspicious but not conclusive. Why not draw the noose as tight as possible?"

"This crime is half-premeditated and half-passion," Alex said thoughtfully.

"What are you talking about, Alex?" John asked puzzled.

"Well, you're set up for the robbery weeks in advance. The witness saw you but the victim was shot and then strangled. The shot killed him instantly, why strangle a dead man?" he got up to pace. "And how did he know the girl would wake up? He used a silencer." The men stared in fascination; it always amazed them how much information Alex could gather in a very short span of time.

"Why use a silencer when he wanted her to see someone who looked just like me," John added. "It is weird." He petulantly threw himself on the couch.

"If this man is involved in espionage, how come the government is letting the local police handle this case?" Nick asked curiously. "We should have the Feds all over us by now."

"They don't know about the espionage angle yet," Alex informed them calmly, as they stared. He glanced up noticing their blank expressions. "Jenny, didn't tell the police about the phone call."

"So, what do we do now?" John questioned.

Nick looked at him sharply, "*We* do nothing. *I'm* going to talk to Ted and find out what those stolen papers were. *You* stay here with Alex."

"Alright." John made a face but grudgingly agreed as Nick left.

Alex went down to his room to search for more information. John waited for Nick to get out of sight and checked on Alex before silently leaving the boat.

*   *   *   *

Jenny walked off the beach and John unobtrusively followed her down the street as the sun began its descent. Jenny looked before crossing the nearly empty street but as she neared the other side, a car pulled away from the curb heading straight for her. She heard it racing towards her and turned with a scream, staring at the driver. John ran, knocking her down with a flying tackle and they both landed hard on the pavement as the car sped away. He picked himself up and helped her up; she was dazed and not looking at him, watching the car disappear from view.

"Are you alright?" John asked. She gazed up at the man who saved her life and began to scream in panic. The growing crowd stared in fascination as Jenny pulled away from John and quickly ran out of sight. John suddenly realized he should not be hanging around and left just as quickly.

*   *   *   *

Jenny had been home for less than an hour after the car incident and was in the kitchen washing dishes, trying to steady her nerves when the phone rang making her jump nervously.

"Jase, where are you?" she begged desperately. "Why haven't you come?" she listened for a moment. "But I need you," she whispered, close to tears. "I'm scared. He's being buried tomorrow," she dropped the dish she was holding in her wet slippery hand. It smashed on the floor and as she bent to pick it up, a bullet shattered the window and slammed into the wall where she had been standing. She shrieked and crouched on the floor, clutching the phone. "Jason, someone is shooting at me!" when she didn't hear any response, she dialed 911 and remained crouching on the floor until the police sirens were heard out front.

Jenny sat on the couch in the living room; beyond frightened. "It's the second time today someone has tried to kill me," she told the policeman in an expressionless voice, staring straight ahead.

"Did you see anyone this time?" he asked but she shook her head. "What happened the first time?"

"A car tried to run me over on Fourth Ave. That man saved me."

"What man?" Lt. Wylan asked confused.

Jenny looked at him accusingly, "You didn't tell me you let him go."

"We didn't let him go; they arranged bail!" Wylan retorted angrily. "You're saying he pulled you out of the way?" he demanded, not quite understanding. Jenny silently nodded.

"Did you see the driver of the car?" The other cop asked; again she nodded silently.

"Good, come down to the station and we'll make a picture of him, too." Wylan seemed overjoyed; thinking he knew who the driver was.

"No," she stated emphatically, startling them.

"What?" he asked incredulously.

"No, I'm not going anywhere. I want you all to leave," she walked to the door.

"Miss Laurence, you can't stay here alone."

"This is my home. Please leave."

They reluctantly left after fruitlessly arguing for fifteen minutes.

Wylan was angry enough to make a late night call on the Baby.

"Where's your friend?" he asked Nick as he boarded the Baby, ignoring Alex as usual.

"What am I, his mother?" Nick asked angrily. "Unless you have a search warrant, get off my boat."

"Don't play the tough guy with me, bum! Your friend is in big trouble; someone took a pot shot at my witness."

"At Jenny? Is she alright?" Alex asked urgently, sitting bolt upright.

The Lt. smiled nastily, "So, you do know who she is! And I'm willing to bet that the bullet matches the one in the old man."

"Is she alright, Lt.?" Alex insisted.

"She'll be fine once we get Colby behind bars; be sure to tell him we're looking for him, ok?" Wylan shouted over his shoulder as he left chuckling to himself.

"I don't understand that man, Alex." Nick said when he was out of ear shot. "We've been a thorn in his side for years. But murder? He's enjoying this way too much!"

"Don't worry about him, Nick," Alex said sharply. "What's happened to John?" Alex had tried to reach his brother by phone several times since he disappeared.

"Right, you put up the flag and I'll put the ladder down. I'm sure Wylan's having the boat watched," Nick said ruefully, getting up from the chair. "I should have known he wouldn't stay put," he grumbled to himself.

THREE

Very early in the morning, Alex picked up a very silent Jenny and took her to the funeral. As soon as it was over, she asked him to take her home, politely refusing his pleas to take her to a park or the beach, explaining that she needed to be alone. Alex didn't like it but he did as she asked.

As soon as he got back to the boat, he and Nick left to search for John.

"It's very strange he hasn't called us," Alex worried. "Something must have happened to him."

"Something's going to happen to him," Nick threatened under his breath.

Two pairs of binoculars were trained on them as they left. One pair was lowered as soon as they were out of sight and a slight figure walked non-chalantly down to the dock. She hurriedly looked around and boarded the Baby. Once inside the main cabin, she unfolded a piece of paper, studying it carefully and went to Alex's cluttered room, opening a panel hidden in the wall. She reached in and tentatively pulled out a gun.

"He was right," she whispered sadly.

On the bay side of the boat, a man emerged out of the water wearing a wet suit and climbed up the ladder. He crouched down behind the bulkhead, removing his scuba gear before looking around and entering the side door into the galley. He was in the main cabin when he heard a noise downstairs and was on the bottom step when Jenny came out of Alex's room. She was shocked to see him but fearfully leveled the pistol at him.

"Get out of my way," she ordered.

John was more than shocked, "Where did you get that?" He asked curiously, not moving.

"Right where you hid it; now move!"

He moved in a circle around her, "You're not going to shoot me."

She stared angrily, "You killed my father! Don't try to stop me. I'll shoot you in the leg or arm, if you're lucky." She nervously backed up the steps; scared but determined, holding the gun steady.

John kept his expression carefully blank as Nick appeared at the top of the stairs.

"I didn't kill anyone," he informed her calmly.

She was on the top step when Nick reached over her shoulder and grabbed the gun, pulling it up. She hung on to it desperately, shrieking at the top of her lungs as John rushed forward up the stairs. Nick held onto the gun and put his hand over her mouth to stop the ear splitting racket. She twisted around and recognized the man who had driven the car that tried to kill her. She struggled even harder; keeping John at bay with her flailing feet and yanking out Nick's thick wavy hair. She bit Nick and let go of the gun so she could use both hands to scratch and pinch him.

Nick let go of her mouth when she bit his hand and dropped her completely when she let go of the gun. She fell into John, knocking them both down the steps to land on the deck in a heap. Nick flung the gun behind him onto the main cabin floor and leaped downstairs to help John. It took both of them over ten minutes to get her under control. John sat on her legs, holding one hand as Nick sat on the floor behind her with her torso clasped between his legs. He held her other hand while keeping her mouth covered. She still struggled against them, glaring furiously.

"Hey! Don't you dare bite me *again!*" Nick hissed angrily. He was in a very awkward position and tried to release her slightly but she instantly tried to wriggle free. He looked at John helplessly, "Now what do we do with her?"

"Look kid, we're not going to hurt you! Just settle down," John commanded reasonably. She stopped struggling, panting heavily.

"That's better." Nick sighed, "If you promise not to scream, I'll take my hand away. Promise?" She nodded and he gingerly removed his hand. She remained quiet, glaring at John malevolently. Very slowly, in stages they released her and got to their feet, pulling her with them, each keeping hold of one wrist. They remained awkwardly staring at one another.

"Okay, let's go in here and talk." John said quietly, motioning them back into Alex's room. He didn't want to take her upstairs in the main room yet. When she crossed in front of John, Nick released her arm and Jenny seized her chance. She stomped hard on John's foot and belted him in the mouth before shoving him into Nick. She ran towards the steps, screaming at the top of her lungs once more.

"Help! Murder! Help!" she yelled and made it to the top step once again.

Nick jumped over John and grabbed her ankle, yanking her hard towards him. She hit the main deck floor hard and he yanked her backward down the stairs. John regained his feet and rushed to help Nick as Jenny hung on to the rung-like stairs with all her might, still shrieking. John reached up yanking her hand off the rung, flipped her over and put his hand over her mouth. He could only grab one hand and her free hand scratched him and pulled his ears since his crew cut was too short to grab. Nick was getting well kicked but he finally got both legs locked in his grasp.

"Stop kicking me, you little witch," he hissed furiously.

"Stop complaining!" John snapped. "You've got the good end," he could only grab one hand at a time; whichever one was free scratched, pinched and grabbed his face as she wiggled around. They staggered into the guest room with their burden and John collapsed on the bed, pinning her free hand under him. Nick plopped down beside him with Jenny lying across them both. They took a few moments to catch their breath and exchanged a glance.

"We've got a little tiger here, John," Nick grimaced. "What the hell are we going to do with her?"

"If she won't cooperate, we'll have to tie her up," John replied fiercely.

Nick clearly didn't like that idea and sighed unhappily but he had no other ideas, "Alright, you sit on her. I'll get something to use." It took them several minutes to change positions. Finally, John straddled her legs and held both her hands in one of his. He still had one hand covering her mouth.

Nick paused at the door, "Think you can handle her?"

"Just hurry up, funny man." He growled.

Nick was gone for several minutes which seemed like an eternity to John. He said nothing to the girl and didn't look at her. She tried to struggle every few minutes but she could barely move. John saw her eyes dilate in fright as Nick came in the room with a length of chain and handcuffs; she started to struggle again, making muffled sounds.

*   *   *   *

Jenny anxiously lay on the bed with one hand cuffed to the chain attached to the bed post. The windows were locked tight and the door was closed. She couldn't reach the door and the porthole windows didn't break; she had tried several times! Looking out the windows, she could only see water; there was no one to see her. John and Nick morosely sat next door in John's stateroom; silently drinking coffee and trying to find some solution to their dilemma. Nick looked over the rim of his cup at John.

"This is kidnapping, you know," he mused sourly.

John shook his head in disagreement, "She broke into our boat."

"So, call the cops."

"This is just protective custody!" John snapped. "There have been two attempts on her life, remember. If anything happens to her, I'm in big trouble."

"Not to mention the girl," Nick reminded him sarcastically.

"What did Alex say her name is?"

"Jenny," Nick got up to pace again. "I wish there was some way to convince her, this is for her own good," he said for the twenty-eighth time.

"We'll just have to wait for Alex to get back and hope he can convince her," John said impatiently. "Where the hell is he?"

"Out looking for you," Nick reminded him nastily. "He's not answering his phone."

"Probably lost it again."

They both lifted their heads as they heard someone board the boat and bolted into the hallway. Alex ran into them as he leaped downstairs in his usual way.

"Alex—" John began only to be interrupted by Alex.

"John! Where the hell have you been?" he demanded irately. "I've been looking for you all afternoon. Why the hell don't you ever answer your phone?" he berated him angrily.

"I could ask you the same thing, little brother," John retorted.

Alex put his hand in his pants pocket, "I don't have it with me." He walked down the hall to his room. "I probably left it in my room," he opened the spare room door as he passed. "You'll get a better breeze if you open this, the wind is from the—" he stopped dead in the doorway.

"No!" John and Nick yelled but it was already too late; Alex stared at Jenny with his mouth hanging open.

"Jenny, I've been trying to call you all day! What are you doing here?" he asked before noticing the handcuff and the chain trailing on the floor. Jenny was startled and unmoving for a moment then backed away, standing on the bed in the corner as far away as she could get.

"Oh, Alex! I can't believe you're behind this!" her face crumpled and she began to cry.

Alex looked completely bewildered, "What the hell is going on?" He demanded, turning to stare accusingly at John and Nick. They dragged him out of the room; he struggled as they pulled him into John's room and closed the door.

"Now, Alex, it isn't what you think!" John denied sharply standing in front of the door.

"I think you have a girl chained to a bed in the guest room!" Alex shouted, trying to get past them but they pushed him back.

"Alright, it is what you think but we had no choice, Alex!" Nick said wearily as they continued to block the door, not letting him leave. He put out a hand to prevent Alex from leaving, "Listen to us for a minute, Alex." Alex stopped struggling, glaring at him balefully.

"I found her on the boat when I got back," John began hastily. "She was coming out of your room with *my gun*."

"The gun!" Nick yelled, flinging himself out the door. He ran back into the room in a few seconds, "It's gone!"

John ran back up to the main deck with him and made a careful search of the cabin and galley, checking that it didn't fall through the stair rungs in the struggle. They looked at one another mystified; it was gone. They turned to Alex who stood in the hall, staring as if they had lost their minds.

"You didn't pick up a gun when you came in did you, Alex?" Nick grabbed his arm and shook it.

"A gun? No. I thought you couldn't find your gun, John?" Alex asked suspiciously.

"I couldn't but *she* did," John retorted pointedly, going into Alex's stateroom. The secret compartment in the wall was still open. He turned suspiciously to Alex, "How does she know about that compartment?"

"Did you put John's gun in there, Alex?" Nick asked in confusion as Alex put up his hands and shook his head.

"Why the hell do you have Jenny chained up?" he insisted on knowing immediately.

"Because she keeps yelling for the police and trying to get away and she keeps attacking us," John replied irritably.

"She *attacked* you?" Alex scoffed, clearly unbelieving.

"Yeah, it took both of us to get her under control. Now, go in there and explain to her that she has to stay here for her own good, so we can protect her!" Nick ordered sharply, showing Alex his scratches.

"*And for me*! Alex, I don't have to tell you what will happen to me if someone kills her," John added urgently.

Alex looked at them unhappily, "I'll try, guys but I don't think she's going to believe me now." He looked doubtful, "Remember she saw John killing her father," he added as he opened the door.

"Watch it, she's dangerous," Nick hissed in his ear as he went in.

"Go away, Alex," Jenny ordered petulantly. "I *thought* you were my friend!"

"I am your friend, Jenny. I only want to help you and so do John and Nick," he said quietly, sitting on the opposite bed. She refused to look at him.

"Are they the names of the two men who kidnapped me and chained me up?" she raised her head to glare at him. "Of course, the blond guy is the one I saw killing my father. The dark haired man is the one who tried to run me over with the car. So I guess you're the one who took a shot at me through the window in my own house, eh?"

"Jenny, I know it's hard for you to believe me but John is my brother; he wouldn't kill your father. He doesn't even know your father—"

Jenny gave a short humorless laugh, "I'll tell you about brothers, Alex. You want to believe them but sometimes brothers do really bad things and then lie to your face." she muttered bitterly.

"I know you've been through a lot with your brother, Jenny," Alex sighed heavily. "But John isn't like that. Please believe me! Nick would never run you over and I would certainly never shoot at you," he spoke quietly and persuasively. "Answer a few questions for me, Jenny." He pleaded as she looked away. He knew she was frightened, angry and confused all at the same time. "If *we* wanted you dead, why aren't you dead now? We could easily take your body out to sea and dump you. Obviously, no one knows you're here." Jenny looked startled and fearful. "If Nick *was* trying to kill you with the car, why would John save you?"

Jenny stood up angrily, advancing towards him, standing over him, "Go away, Alex. Leave me alone!" She shouted. "Isn't it enough that you're keeping me a prisoner?"

"What were you doing on the boat, Jenny?" Alex continued relentlessly, standing up. "How did you know where to find the gun?" She pushed him towards the door. "Why didn't you go directly to the police and tell them where it was?" Jenny gave an anguished wail and flung herself on the bed, pulling the pillow over her head. Alex opened the windows and left the door open, "Please trust me, Jenny." He walked into the hall to see John and Nick hovering nearby and knew they had heard everything through the open door. He waved them up the steps. They didn't speak until they were in the main room.

"There's something missing here," Nick mused.

"Yeah, my gun!" John spit out. "Someone had to take it out from under our noses and put it back. It might have been her but she didn't take it this time."

"Someone set this up. But where do they fit in?" Nick continued. "What's their angle?"

"What does anyone gain from this?" Alex asked confused.

"If it works, I go to jail for the rest of my life," John grumbled.

"Okay. That's a revenge motive. But why kill Jenny?" Alex interjected.

"It just draws the noose tighter around my neck."

"Yes but that's overkill, don't you think?" Alex objected. "I don't think anyone could have a reason to kill Jenny."

They made dinner and John delivered it to Jenny who refused even to look at him, lying tightly curled on the bed, facing the wall. He left the tray on the opposite bed and Alex checked on her after they finished eating, on his way to his room to do some research on the computer. She hadn't touched the food.

"Jenny, please eat. It'll make you feel better," he begged but she ignored him and he went sadly to his room.

Two hours later they got ready for bed, having decided that the most obvious time for an attack would be during the night. John took the first watch and stayed in the main cabin. Nick would sleep in the room with the girl during John's watch then they'd switch positions. They refused to let Alex take the watch.

"What do you mean I can't take watch?" he demanded highly insulted.

"You are not staying with her; you're too soft hearted. You are not getting this key." Nick adamantly refused. Everyone remained fully dressed and went to their positions.

"Good luck with the dragon," John whispered as Nick left to go downstairs.

Nick went into the bedroom and unlocked Jenny's cuff to take her to the bathroom. While she was in there, he handed the untouched tray up the steps to John. Jenny was absolutely silent; refusing to look at anyone. Alex wished her goodnight as Nick locked the cuff on her wrist and lay down on the opposite bed.

"What are you doing?" she was startled into asking.

"Protecting you," he answered evenly. "Go to sleep," he turned out the light.

*　　　*　　　*　　　*

John dozed lightly on the couch upstairs. Jenny sat in the dark on the edge of the bed staring at Nick sleeping on his stomach.

"What?" he cried, sitting up startled after she kicked him lightly in the leg. He looked at her groggily.

"I have to go to the bathroom."

"Again?" he complained sleepily. He sighed deeply and unlocked her, walking her to the bathroom where he stood with his head leaning against his arm on the wall, moaning softly.

Nick was asleep once more, on his back, snoring softly with the sheet over him. Jenny stared intently before slowly turning her head to look at the chain attached to the top of the bed. She twisted the cuff, fruitlessly trying to get it off, jiggling the chain and watching Nick for a reaction. When there was none, she got a calculating look in her eye and smiled wickedly. She picked up her pillow and stood over Nick; in one swift movement she straddled his chest, pressing the pillow over his face. Nick began struggling but her weight pinned his arms to his side and his yells were muffled. He kicked his legs which were tangled in the sheet but finally got them free and pushed against the wall using leverage to roll off the bed. He and Jenny landed on the floor tangled in the sheet and each other; Jenny was still half sitting on top of him with Nick breathing heavily, holding one wrist and the other forearm.

"Now you know how my father felt when your friend strangled him." She hissed softly, calmly bending towards him.

The door flew open and the light snapped on revealing John in the doorway. He strode forward, lifting Jenny off Nick and dumping her on the bed in one smooth motion.

"Nick, what the hell are you doing?" he demanded irritably.

"Me!" Nick shouted, struggling to his feet and pointing a finger at Jenny who sat on the bed smiling smugly, "She just tried to smother me!" He sat on his bed and put his head in his hands, running his fingers through his hair, "It's a hell of a way to wake up." he complained.

"I wasn't going to kill you! *I'm* not a murderer," she snapped, looking spitefully at John.

"Shut up, kid!" He growled, barely controlling the urge to slap her. "I'll stay with her. It's almost time to switch anyway." He assured Nick angrily.

"No. She's gotten me up four times already," Nick replied, settling himself on the bed with his back against the wall. "I'll just sit here and keep an eye on her."

John reluctantly left the room as Jenny stared defiantly at Nick. She was the first to look away as she got up to pace the length of the chain, staring out the window at the darkness. After several minutes, she sat back down.

"Having fun?" she taunted Nick who continued to stare silently with an unfriendly expression. She looked at the clock, two-thirty am, before looking back at Nick. "If you're having trouble sleeping, why don't you go sleep under the stars? I hear it's very soothing," she gave a small humorless laugh. "I'd love to go but I can't," she daintily lifted the chain. Nick continued to stare so she gave him a tight little smile and turned out the light.

He turned it back on and moved the lamp out of her reach.

"You can't take a hint, can you? Okay!" she hollered, standing up. "If you're going to chain people up, the least you can do is not force your unwanted company on them," she yelled; a day in captivity was beginning to get to her. "Take your obnoxious self and get out!" she screamed when he made no response. When he still ignored her, she turned, grabbing things off the shelves lining her side of the room; throwing everything and anything she could get her hands on. She had good aim and a good arm and she began shrieking hysterically, "Get out! Get out! Get out!"

Nick leaped up as she threw things with both hands; breaking glass shattered over and around him and several wooden objects painfully bounced off him as he closed with her.

"Cut it out!" he yelled furiously, grabbing one arm. She leaned down to get something off the bed to throw while screaming in a high pitch but he pulled her back towards him. She cracked him in the head with a wooden statue which he ripped out of her hand and flung from him. He had a good grip on her upper arm with his left hand and grabbed hold of her hair bringing her face to face with him with a sharp yank. "Stop it!" he bellowed inches from her face, giving her a hard shake.

She was silenced at once, blinking rapidly several times as they remained standing inches apart. Jenny looked dazed and put a hand up to her mouth.

"I'm alright now," she said quietly, breathing heavily. "I went a little crazy."

Nick released her at once. The door was flung open once more as John rushed into the room, looking in surprise at the mess as Jenny silently watched him. She abruptly lay down on the bed and rolled on her side facing the wall, curled up in a tight ball. Nick pushed John out of the room and turned out the light.

*   *   *   *

Morning dawned in Bridgeton, gorgeous as usual as the marina hummed with activity. Inside the Baby, John and Nick sat at the table falling asleep over their coffee.

"Hello, guys," Alex's cheery greeting startled them awake.

"Hey, Alex," they returned his greeting with no enthusiasm whatsoever.

"Wow, you guys look terrible. Didn't you sleep well?"

Nick dropped his head to the table with a loud clunk as John looked balefully at Alex.

"You slept through all that noise?"

"What noise?" Alex asked, starting breakfast. "What happened?"

"Never mind," John snapped sourly, leaning back and stretching.

"Is Jenny still sleeping?" Alex asked.

"No," Nick picked his head up and rubbed his eyes, "I looked in on her a while ago. She was staring out the window. I wonder if she got any sleep." He said ruefully, feeling guilty about the incident last night; he had lost his temper when she had tried to smother him.

John volunteered to take her a breakfast tray; a bowl of cereal and a glass of orange juice.

"Try to get her to eat something. She didn't eat anything yesterday," Alex implored.

John found Jenny sitting on the edge of the bed.

"Take it away, I don't want it," she directed flatly the minute he stepped into the room.

"It won't kill you to eat something," he replied calmly. "Alex is worried about you."

He set the tray on the bed beside her but she angrily picked up the bowl and threw it at him. He took a step towards her, enraged and she quickly picked up the glass of juice.

"Don't you dare throw that!" he ordered, dripping milk and cereal.

"Get out!" she ordered warningly.

He left, slamming the door and heard the glass shatter against the door.

"Damn brat!" he muttered as Alex came downstairs trying unsuccessfully to hide a smile.

"She does have spunk John."

"Don't you laugh Alex," John demanded testily, reaching into the bathroom and pulling a towel off the rack to dry his face and hair. "She has no manners, is what she has! Now I have to get another shower and change. I smell like—" he pulled his shirt over his head, "milk!"

Nick leaped downstairs, "Quick, Wylan's on his way here!" He cried pushing Alex out of the way, "Hide John and the girl."

Nick and John abruptly ran into the guest room as Jenny warily turned towards them. They raced to her and Nick unlocked the cuff, throwing the chain behind the headboard where it wouldn't be noticed.

"What are you doing?" she demanded, startled and relieved to be unchained but their sense of urgency frightened her. John hastily put a hand over her mouth and wrapped his other arm around her pinning both arms down as Nick scooped up both her legs; they carried her across the hall to Alex's room.

"We're hiding you," John answered tersely.

They had been so quick she hadn't had a chance to react but now she began to struggle. They placed her on her feet with John's hand over her mouth, still pinning her arms down. Alex had the secret compartment in the couch open and John stepped in; lying down with Nick's help, still holding onto her. As they closed the lid, the last thing Nick saw was Jenny's frightened face; her eyes wide and panicked.

"Stay here and cover up any noise she might make," he ordered as Alex put the cushions back on the couch. Nick ran upstairs and was serving the rest of breakfast when Wylan came barging through the door.

"It's too early in the morning to deal with you," Nick snorted rudely. "You got a warrant?"

"Here's your warrant, smart ass." Wylan shoved a paper under Nick's nose and slapped it on the table. Two uniformed cops were with him and they spread out to search the boat. The Lt. went downstairs, leaving the main rooms for one of the junior officers. The first man came out of Nick's room, shaking his head.

"Nothing," he said, going into the guest room. "Both beds are messed up. There's a tray on the bed; cereal and milk are spilled on the floor and a glass of juice is broken," he reported looking at Wylan with a shrug.

"Someone leave in a hurry?" Wylan accused Nick.

"Alex and I had a little food fight, that's all! That's not against the law is it?" Nick grinned smoothly as pounding was heard from Alex's room. The Lt. was quick to get to the door, flinging it open to hear Alex yelling.

"No, Quark, no! Stop!" he manipulated a remote control box in his hand. Quark was repeatedly running into the wooden base of the couch where Jenny and John were hidden.

"Hey, Alex," Nick rudely pushed past Wylan. "That damn robot is going to damage the wood," he scolded.

"I'm sorry, Nick. I was trying to program a new relay. It must have shorted him out. He's not responding to the control box," Alex leaped to the computer console and frantically hit buttons while Quark continued to run into the seat. Suddenly lights blinked and loud siren noises came from the robot. "Oh no! Oh, my gosh!" Alex shouted frantically.

Nick rolled his eyes and left the room with Lt. Wylan following him and closing the door on the noise.

"Some genius," Wylan snorted in disgust. "Listen Duffy, we've got Colby dead to rights; we found his gun! The bullets match the murder and the attempt on the girl. When we find him, he's *mine*."

Nick moved away from the Lt., going upstairs and Wylan followed.

"Whose prints were on the gun, Lt.?"

"It was wiped clean, of course," he replied as if Nick was an idiot.

"Well, if I see John, I'll be sure to tell him," he smiled at Wylan. The Lt. looked none too happy as he left the boat empty handed and Nick followed them out to the deck, watching until the car left before walking slowly into the main cabin. Once inside, he bolted for Alex's room. He flung open the door, nodding at Alex who switched off Quark before he picked the robot up and put him on the desk.

"She started kicking," he explained as they quickly removed the cushions and opened the box. Nick nodded as they lifted the heavy lid. John and Jenny both struggled to get out first. Nick grabbed Jenny around the waist, lifting her out bodily and held her against him. John struggled out right behind her and grabbed her arm.

"Don't you touch me, you big ape!" she screamed. John's bare chest and back were marked with long, angry red scratches.

"Touch you!" he snarled. "I'm gonna break those little fingers." John threatened, trying to pull her away from Nick. Nick pulled her closer, turning so his opposite shoulder was towards John who was still gripping her arm.

"John, let go!" Nick ordered loudly, trying to push John out of the room. John was out for blood and tried to get Nick out of his way with his free arm while holding onto Jenny with his other hand while she struggled fiercely to get free from them both.

"After I break all her fingers," he yelled adamantly. Nick almost had John to the door when Jenny suddenly broke free of both men and ran to hide behind Alex.

"I'll bite you again if you come near me!" Jenny screamed hysterically.

John gave Nick a hard shove, renewing his efforts to get to Jenny. Alex joined Nick in shoving John out the door; they each had hold of an arm.

"John!" Nick yelled. "Cut it out! Get out of here!"

As they finally shoved him out into the hall, Jenny slammed the door and they heard it lock. In the hall, John easily swung Alex away from him and turned to find Nick standing in front of the closed door.

"Get out of my way, Nick!" he ordered warningly.

"John, if you think I'm going to let you break a little girl's fingers, you're crazier than I thought," Nick refused flatly.

John appeared to consider this for a second, "Okay, I'll just give her the spanking she deserves; she won't sit down for a week." He tried to shove Nick aside.

Nick stood firm, "John, you're not going to lay a finger on her!"

"Alright, I'll use a belt!" John agreed belligerently, calming down somewhat but still excited and breathing heavily.

"Now, John, I know you're upset, but she's just a little girl," Alex said reasonably.

John swung around, "Upset? I'm not upset! I'm *furious*!" He yelled in Alex's face, "She's not a girl; she's a demon!" He shoved Alex back against the wall, "She's kicked me, pinched me, bit me, scratched me, she tried to smother Nick last night and she threw her food all over me!" He indicated the bleeding marks on his chest, "Look, what she did to me!"

"Why are you yelling at Alex?" Nick asked quietly, standing behind him.

John looked over his shoulder at Nick in surprise and then shrugged, confused.

"Because you won't let me yell at her," he turned back to where Alex was backed against the wall. "Sorry Alex."

Nick cut him off, taking him by the arm and leading him into his room.

"Sit down and shut up, John. I've never seen you act like such a big baby," he told his friend harshly. John opened his mouth to protest in shocked surprise as Nick pushed him into a chair. "Stop thinking about yourself for a minute and think about her."

"I—" John began angrily only to be cut off again.

"Barely a week ago, she saw *you* murder her father. Someone's tried to kill her twice. We chained her to a bed. She hasn't had any sleep or food for two days, and we just threw her in a box with the murderer."

"I am not the murderer!" John interrupted angrily.

"I know that and Alex knows that but *she* doesn't know that!" Nick sighed. "She's fifteen and all alone in the world now. And she's trapped here with you," he looked at John. "How do you expect her to act?" John looked sullen and unrepentant.

"Well, not all alone," Alex mused.

Nick turned in irritation; he was trying to make a point and Alex wasn't helping, "What?" he snapped.

"Oh, well, you said she was all alone in the world. She's not *all* alone."

"Alex, you told me no one attended her father's funeral except you and the girl. You said she was the sole beneficiary of her father's will."

"Well, yes, I know, Nick and that's all true but she does have a brother," Alex clarified.

"Where is he, Alex?" John asked urgently; his anger at the girl evaporating.

"Oh, he's around here somewhere," Alex replied airily. "You see, she told me the night of the murder, she didn't hear a gunshot, just some noise. She went down stairs because she thought it was her brother, um, Jason. She said he visited at odd hours." He was startled as Nick grabbed his arms and shook him.

"Alex, why didn't you tell us this before? It's the missing piece!" Nick shouted excitedly. "How did she know where to find John's gun, if she didn't hide it? He told her! And he's the one who picked it up and sent it to the police."

"But Nick, if he did that he'd know where Jenny is. Why wouldn't he go to the police?" Alex objected.

"Because *he's* the killer, Alex," John explained, exasperated. He paused and looked up thinking hard. "Jason Laurence. That name sounds familiar but I can't place it." He frowned in concentration as he took a shirt out of his drawer and put it on.

Alex leaned back thinking out loud, "Joseph, Jason, Jenny, I wonder what her mother's name was? Probably Joan or maybe Jill." Alex was perfectly engrossed as Nick rolled his eyes.

"Joelle, she was from the south," John replied absently, making them turn in surprise. John realized what he said, "Of course! Jason Laurence!" He turned to Nick, "You remember him, Nick."

"No, I don't," Nick denied, shaking his head, perplexed.

"He received a dishonorable discharge for his involvement with drugs in the Caiber affair. He always blamed me for turning him in."

"Did you?" Alex asked curiously.

John shook his head, "No. I had nothing to do with it. But he insisted I did." He snapped his fingers, "He knew Ted Downs at the time, too. This has to be the guy."

"Great, now all we have to do is find him," Nick muttered sarcastically, looking at Alex, "You wouldn't know where he is, would you, Alex?"

"No. But if he's around, you know Quark and I can find him," he turned to the closed door.

"She locked us out," John reminded them.

"Quark, unlock!" Alex shouted through the door and they heard it unlocking. Jenny fearfully jumped to her feet as they rushed in. They ignored her and Alex sat at the computer; in a very few minutes an address flashed across the screen. 765 N. Umber Rd.; they read it silently aware that Jenny was watching them.

"Let's go!" John cried eagerly, turning to leave.

Nick grabbed his arm on the way past, "Where do you think you're going?"

John smacked his hand away, "I'm going with you to get this creep."

Nick shook his head, "There's a warrant out for your arrest."

"I'll go with you Nick." Alex volunteered.

"You need to stay here so these two don't kill each other." Nick replied only half-jokingly.

Alex reluctantly nodded in agreement and Nick went out the door but returned in a few seconds to take Alex's arm, "On second thought, Alex, you come with me." He looked at John who glared at Nick malevolently, "I remember what happened the last time! Look at him; he was planning to leave as soon as I was out of sight! With you gone, he has to stay to protect Jenny; anything happens to her and he's dog meat." Nick pushed Alex out the door in front of him and turned to a smoldering John. "Stay away from her and you won't get beat up," he advised with a smile and a cheerful wave.

John threw a statue at him, "Smart ass," he muttered and turned to Jenny who was standing fearfully in the farthest corner. He sighed, wondering what the hell he was supposed to do with her. He pondered leaving her in Alex's room. He looked around and changed his mind when he saw the computer, much too dangerous to leave her here! He suddenly wondered why she hadn't used the computer to alert the police and hit the button. A logo flashed on saying it was locked. Good old Alex, he thought.

He looked again toward Jenny who hadn't moved and realized he was blocking her access to the door. He walked out the door, wondering what she would do and saw a man standing in the hallway pointing a gun at him.

"Jason." John said matter-of-factly.

"Jenny!" Jason shouted, smiling smugly.

"Jason!" she ran out the door amazed and relieved to see him.

John could hear the relief in her voice. She cried out as he reached out, snaring her around the waist as she ran past.

"No Jenny, stay away from him," he ordered quietly as she struggled to break free.

"Let her go," Jason ordered angrily.

John ignored him, "Jenny, listen to me! He's the one who killed your father. He's the one who's trying to kill you!" She bit his restraining hand on her wrist, "Yeow!" He yelled, losing his grip and she ran toward her brother.

"Don't listen to him, Jenny. Go start the boat," Jason ordered. Jenny had to walk past John to go upstairs. John rushed forward, shoving her into Jason. Jenny and the gun fell to the floor as the two men grappled with each other. Jenny picked up the gun, aiming it at the two men.

"Stop it!" she cried.

When they ignored her, she fired the gun into the ceiling and they quickly separated, watching each other warily. Jenny had her back to the stairs, facing the two men.

"Good girl, Jenny," Jason said confidently walking towards her, holding out his hand for the gun but John grabbed Jason's shirt and pulled him back.

"Jenny, listen to me, he's going to take us out to sea and kill us both," John implored her to believe him.

Jason laughed unpleasantly. "Why would I kill my little sister?" he demanded scornfully, shaking off John's hand and holding out his hand for the gun as Jenny hesitated.

"For one hundred thousand dollars inheri—" John began.

"It's my money!" Jason shrieked hysterically, "Mine! Mine!"

Jenny stared sadly, silently handing John the gun as he blocked Jason from attacking her. "I thought you were the only person in the world who loved me!" she cried. He was still saying 'mine' over and over as she ran upstairs.

"Jenny, come back!" John called but she didn't return. John kept a wary eye on Jason as he flipped open his phone, calling the police before calling Nick and Alex. He looked down at Jason who lay on the floor weeping.

*   *   *   *

Jenny stood on the rocks on a deserted beach in the bright moonlight; John walked up behind her and nervously stopped a foot away as she ignored him.

"Jenny," he called tentatively.

"Come to break my fingers?" she asked sarcastically.

He flushed slightly, "I'm sorry. I was mad!" John apologized, moving forward to touch her shoulder lightly. She moved away, turning sharply and climbing down the rocks to her left. He followed her slowly.

"I thought you would be glad to get rid of me," she walked quickly down the beach. "What do you want now?"

"We've been looking for you for hours. We were worried."

She continued walking up the beach, heading for the parking area, "I'm fine. You can leave now." She replied rudely.

John stopped in disgust and stood still, looking after her. He sighed, running his hand through his hair, thinking morosely that he would have to be the one to find her first. He had called Nick as soon as he had seen her on the beach. He didn't know whether to keep talking to her or wait for Alex to get there. Suddenly he ran after her, grabbed her arm and pulled her around to face him.

"You want me to go!" he finally understood she was deliberately trying to make him angry to get rid of him.

"Yes, I do. So leave," she shook his hand off her arm and walked away but he followed at her shoulder.

"Well, I'm not leaving. Why won't you let us help you?" he demanded helplessly.

She spun around abruptly, "Why would *you* want to help me?" She stared suspiciously, "I accused you of murder, scratched every inch of skin you own, bit you, punch—"

John put his hand gently over her mouth, "I remember." He winced at the memory. "I also remember what we did to you," he removed his hand. "Let's forget it and start over."

Jenny turned towards the water with a sob, "Maybe you can forget, but I can't forget what Jason did to *all of us*." She started to run but John quickly grabbed her hand and didn't let go. She resisted him, turning her head away, "He killed my father and tried to frame you. I don't even know how."

John tried to put his arm around her shoulders but she wouldn't let him, pulling away.

"He used rubber masks he had made at work."

She looked at him sharply, "Where was he working?"

"In one of the movie studios," John informed her. "I remember he was always good at imitating people's voices. He made masks of me and Nick. He didn't count on me saving you from the car," he stopped abruptly, not wanting to remind her that Jason had tried to kill her.

Jenny didn't need to be reminded; tears fell from her eyes, "He tried to kill me for money. I had already signed half of it over to him. If he had asked, I would have given it all to him." She choked on the words, hanging her head.

John took her chin, lifting her face, forcing her to look at him, "Jason was over the edge, Jenny." He said very gently, "While we waited for the police to come, he told me the whole story. He stole the documents because your father told him he'd pay him a quarter of a million dollars. When he refused to pay, Jason killed him; thinking he'd get the money from the inheritance. He kept saying '*That money is mine. I need it to take care of Momma and Jenny*'. When he realized he was going to jail, he asked me to give you this." John reached into his pocket, bringing out a necklace. It dangled from his hand, sparkling in the moonlight.

Jenny took it hesitantly, "It was the only thing my mother owned. She gave it to Jason when she was dying. She died because my father wouldn't pay for the treatments to keep her alive and we had no insurance. Jason took care of her every day; she was the only person he ever loved. When she died, he just went to pieces." She cried and hid her face in her hands, "I tried to help him but he was drinking heavily and using drugs." She held the necklace up to the light. "I guess he loved me in his own way," she said softly and suddenly crumpled to the sand, sobbing, alarming John who went down on his knees beside her, putting his arm around her. "I don't know what to do! I don't want to think anymore. I'm so tired!" she wailed, crying heavily against his shoulder.

"Everything will look better in the morning, Jenny." he soothed softly, cradling her in his arms. She curled into him, putting her arm around his neck. He carried her to the parking lot and saw Nick just turning the truck in. Alex got out and ran towards them.

"Sh, she's asleep," John whispered.

Nick helped John get in the truck without waking Jenny. Alex and Nick both got in closing the doors quietly.

"Maybe we'll all get some sleep tonight." Nick turned the truck around and headed for the Baby.

CASE FILE: BO PART 2

ONE

"Uh, guys," Alex stammered, coming out of the main cabin as Nick and John were watching TV under the deck awning. John looked up absently to see Alex with a duffel bag slung over his shoulder.

"Going somewhere little brother?" he asked mocking Alex's habit of asking the obvious.

"Um, yes, I thought I'd take a little trip," Alex was curiously hesitant to explain. "I'll be back in a couple of days." He hastily headed for the boarding ramp.

"Where are you going?" John called innocently.

"Uh, nowhere special." Alex hedged and kept walking.

Nick laughed loudly. "You wouldn't be going to Baltimore by any chance, would you?" he called making Alex flush a brick red.

"Possibly. Anything wrong with Baltimore?" he demanded aggressively, turning to glare at Nick as he hiked the heavy bag higher.

"Not a thing," Nick smiled. "I hear it's beautiful this time of year," he smirked.

"Chasing after your little girlfriend?" John snorted in disgust. "Really, Alex, she's only been gone five days!"

"Tomorrow is her birthday. I'm going to spend it with her," he informed his brother coldly; John had been down on his friendship with Bo for months.

"Does she know you're coming?" John asked snidely. "Because apparently she doesn't want to spend it with you since she left the state."

"I told you; her Aunt Rachel moved back to Baltimore this week because Bo is now eighteen. She's settled in her new place and going to college," Alex protested angrily. "She doesn't know I'm coming. I want to surprise her," he snapped, walking off the boat still fuming at John.

"Maybe if I'm lucky, Bo will decide to live with her aunt in Baltimore," John said to no one in particular.

"Why are you so down on her?" Nick demanded curiously, unable to understand his friend. "I like her and they're obviously crazy about each other! I've never seen Alex so happy."

"She's just too young," John snapped and stalked inside, his interest in the game forgotten.

"At least she's legal now!" Nick called after him cheerfully. He drank his beer, unable to see a problem. Bo seemed very mature to him and Nick knew that Alex had been extremely careful these past few months to keep their relationship on the friendship level because of Bo's age. Nick knew their relationship would deepen now that she was older but he was happy for Alex and just couldn't understand why John was so upset by the relationship. He shrugged, focusing his attention once more on the game.

*   *   *   *

Alex's relatives raised a royal ruckus when they came back from Baltimore and announced their engagement. They told a stunned Nick and John first as Bo held out her hand to show them her ring.

"Oh, my God! She's pregnant!" John blurted.

Alex punched him in the mouth as Bo's mouth dropped open in surprise and she sighed with a roll of her eyes. Nick stared at John in surprise before separating the brothers.

Alex and Bo remained cool and detached through all the hullaballoo until the family gradually came to accept the engagement. Alex's mother and father liked Bo a lot and she liked most of her prospective in-laws, too.

*   *   *   *

Five months had passed since Bo's birthday and she had been a frequent visitor on board the Baby although she never spent the night on board. Alex had been a frequent overnight guest at her apartment. Nick was warm and friendly; John was cool, barely polite. Bo tried to be friendly, ignoring his attitude as much as possible, knowing it upset Alex much more than it upset her.

Bo stood behind Alex in his room on the Baby with her arms around his neck, staring at the computer screen in front of them.

"I don't think they appreciate you enough Alex." she said lightly, making him laugh in delight.

"Hey, little girl," John's harsh tone startled them; Alex quickly closed the computer window as John came further into the room. He had been passing by and heard her remark. "Don't be making trouble between us. We appreciate Alex plenty!"

"Look, *old man*, I've told you before about calling me *little girl*," Bo kept her tone light as she straightened up.

Alex laughed knowing it was true; for the past couple months, every time John called her 'little girl' she would call him 'old man' but Bo was getting a little tired of the game now.

"She wasn't making trouble, John!" Alex defended her, turning his chair to face John.

Bo put a gentle hand on Alex's shoulder and he sighed deeply. She had asked him before not to protect her, wanting to fight her own battles with John. Bo just didn't want Alex to be in the middle. Nick came down the ladder stairs and poked his head in the room.

"What's going on?" he asked curiously, seeing everyone standing around.

"Bo doesn't think we appreciate Alex enough," John snapped sharply.

"Oh," Nick smiled and walked to Alex, clapping him heartily on the back. "Thanks, Buddy for all you do," he left the room grinning.

Alex and Bo laughed and turned back to the computer as John grimly stalked out of the room. Bo quickly shut the door behind him making a small grimace at Alex.

"Whew! That was close! When are you going to tell them?"

"If all goes well— *never*."

She rolled her eyes, "I can't believe you've kept it a secret this long."

"It's been a lot easier than I would have believed possible," he agreed, amazed.

Later that same day, everyone was seated around the table as Bo put the last serving dish on the table and sat beside Alex. Nick dug in with obvious enjoyment. All three men could cook but their repertoire was seriously limited; Nick got tired of their cooking and was appreciative of a good cook. Bo was an excellent cook and Nick had been enjoying this added benefit of Alex's new relationship very much. He looked up in annoyance as John interrupted Alex and Bo's intimate conversation. She sat close to him as they stared into each other's eyes, whispering in his ear, making him grin widely.

"So Bo, tell me," John began, putting meatloaf on his plate; Nick got a bad feeling in the pit of his stomach. "Exactly what do you think Alex does for us that we don't appreciate?"

Bo looked up and smiled, "Well, he is the brains of the outfit, you have to admit." She picked up a roll and buttered it. "He takes care of *all* the financial aspects, too," she continued, ignoring the light kick from Alex. "He's the one who makes sure all your bills are paid on time and keeps you out of debtor's prison," she put the roll in her mouth, challenging John with her eyes.

"He pays those bills with money that *we* all earn," John returned fiercely. "He sits at a computer all day while Nick and I do all the grunt work. Do you know how many times he's been punched in the face?" Bo raised her eyebrows inquisitively as Nick continued shoveling food in his mouth, studiously ignoring them. "Three! Do you know how many times I've been punched in the face?" he demanded harshly.

"Not enough," she replied sweetly, smiling archly at him.

"What is your problem, John? Leave her alone!" Alex ordered angrily.

"She's trying to get you to leave us."

"She is not," Alex denied wearily.

"Yes, she is! You're just too love-sick to see it!" John snapped, glaring at Bo who sat blankly staring, wondering what he was talking about. "I overheard her the other day telling you, you're wasting your talent working here."

"Your eavesdropping skills need a little work, John." Bo smiled sarcastically. "That's not what that conversation was about," she remembered the conversation; she had been urging Alex to investigate and work on some of the projects that he had put on hold.

Alex suddenly stood up, throwing his napkin down on the table. "I've had enough of this," he said quietly. "Bo has done nothing but encourage me to stay here with you guys." He moved around the table, "I'm moving in with Bo!"

Bo's mouth dropped open, "I don't want you to move in with me!"

A shocked Alex turned, "What do you mean; we're ma— engaged!" he caught himself.

John leaped to his feet, throwing his napkin down. "Oh, my God, you're married!" he shouted, shocked. Nick stopped eating to gape at Bo and Alex.

"What of it?" she challenged John.

Alex still stared at Bo; confused and hurt and silently left the cabin, going outside to stand on deck. Nick looked down curiously at her hand to see the lovely diamond ring she'd worn since she returned from Baltimore; she wasn't wearing any other jewelry. She ran after Alex.

"Can you tell me one good reason I shouldn't move in with you?" he asked turning sad eyes to her.

She stood very close; leaning against him, resting both hands on his chest and kissed him. "Quark won't have his own room and if you leave him here, he'll pine for you," she whispered sweetly in his ear, Alex smiled in spite of himself. "It isn't time, Alex."

Bo had no family and she couldn't bear to be the reason Alex was alienated from his family. Alex knew they had discussed this but he was at war with himself at the moment; every fiber of his being wanted to be with Bo every moment of every day. He knew how unhappy she would be if there was a breach between he and John but at the moment Alex didn't care if he ever saw John again. He put his arms around Bo holding her tightly, kissing her deeply.

"Okay," he agreed unwillingly. "We'll do it your way." They walked back into the cabin holding hands. Alex didn't even look at John.

"You'll have to get an annulment," John stopped pacing, continuing the argument the minute he saw them.

Alex laughed, "Who died and left you the boss of me?" he asked mildly. "I'll make all my own decisions, thank-you." He sat down to eat his still slightly warm meal.

"She can't live here," John stayed on the attack.

"Hey, whoa, buddy," Nick jumped in. "It's Alex's room and he can share it with anyone he wants! I think you have lost your mind," he shook his head at John. "I for one would be thrilled to have Bo live here," he grinned at her.

"You just want a full time cook," John complained with a grimace.

"What's wrong with that?" Nick asked still grinning.

"I'm not moving in here."

"I'm not officially moving out of here," Alex said quietly. "I am not officially moving in with you either," he smiled at Bo. "But you're going to be seeing a lot more of me now that the secret is out." She returned his smile in delight, leaning forward to kiss him. John abruptly left and they heard him thumping angrily down the ramp.

Nick looked at Bo apologetically. "Give him time," he advised philosophically. She nodded sadly.

"I'm glad you're on our side Nick," Alex said gratefully.

"Oh, I'm not on your side," Nick replied quickly, catching them off guard. "I think you're both nuts," he replied, cheerfully helping himself to more meatloaf.

They ruefully shook their heads at him but they were smiling.

*   *   *   *

Several months had passed since the secret marriage had been exposed with Bo and Alex resisting all his relative's efforts to have a big wedding and renew their vows. Although Alex's family secretly had strong misgivings about how long the marriage would last, they accepted it as a done deal. Alex and Bo also resisted everyone's efforts to rearrange their odd living arrangements. Alex stayed at her apartment almost every night. However, he was very busy with his inventions and research and sometimes spent several nights in a row on the Baby to complete whatever he was working on.

John still couldn't accept this marriage even though he could see how incredibly happy Alex was. John couldn't find anything to complain about since Alex did his fair share of the detective work. He backed off baiting Bo and was always very polite to her. Bo and Alex noticed that he usually made some excuse to leave either the boat or the room when she was around so Bo limited her time on the boat. She was busy with college and happier than she had ever been in her life.

She parked her little blue car in her parking space at the small apartment complex. There were only two buildings and both faced the ocean so they all had balconies facing the sea. As she got out, carrying a book bag and a bag of groceries, she looked but didn't see Alex's motorcycle and felt slightly disappointed. The guys had been working on a hard case and she hadn't seen very much of him this week. Bo only knew that a woman had hired them to find her missing son who had disappeared several weeks ago; the police had been unable to find him and were of the opinion that he had left on his own.

She walked to the front of the building and stopped in surprise; the black truck was parked in a visitor space. She secretly hoped it was Alex or Nick. She couldn't imagine any good reason John would come if he knew Alex wasn't here. She walked to her door shifting her burdens to get her keys in her hand when she noticed the door slightly ajar and sighed in relief; it was Alex. She kicked the door open all the way and entered calling Alex.

She put her bags down on the kitchen counter and turned towards the living room and balcony and gasped as she saw John lying face down on the living room floor with the back of his head bloody. She ran and knelt beside his body, fearfully touching his hand; it was still warm. She had the phone in her hand when a pad was pressed against her face. She tried to scream and twist free to see who was behind her but he was holding her head. She pressed 911, praying silently as she felt woozy before everything went black.

TWO

Bo woke lying face down on a hard concrete floor and groggily opened her eyes as she rolled over, looking fearfully around her. She was in a small room with no windows and steel walls with a drain in the center of the floor. Against the wall, facing her was a large wooden table with very nasty looking tools lying on it. She looked hastily away from the table, over her shoulder and gasped as she saw John shackled to the wall!

He was still unconscious and hung limply from shackles on his wrists. She stiffly turned around, wanting to run to him but her legs wouldn't respond. She felt the familiar sensation of terror creeping up her body. As she sat there unable to scream or speak, John began moaning. He moved his head, slowly opening his eyes. It took him several moments to be able to move his feet and stand up. He looked dazedly at his outstretched arms, staring at the shackles as if in a dream, suffering from concussion and shock. His thought processes seemed incredibly slow and he couldn't remember what happened. He slowly gazed around the room, focusing on a girl sitting in the middle of the room gaping at him. *She looks frightened to death,* he thought; it took several minutes before he recognized Bo.

"Bo," her name came out more like a grunt. He licked his dry lips and tried again, "Bo."

Hearing her name seemed to release Bo from a spell and she struggled to her feet, running clumsily to him, falling down as she reached him. She wrapped her arms convulsively around his legs. "John," she gasped, horribly frightened. "John!"

At that moment, the steel door opened and a man came in. Bo stared, not really sure she was awake, after all. He was tall with a full beard and had long black hair falling below his shoulders. He wore a long, very dirty white robe with full sleeves made of a rough homespun cloth. Around his waist he wore a rough, loosely braided rope belt and a large wooden cross hung from the belt; on his head he wore a crown of thorns. John stared at him as if in a dream. *This can't be good,* he thought groggily.

"Don't touch him!" the man ordered in a harsh tone, striding across the room and grabbing Bo's hair. He pulled her away from John as she shrieked in pain and terror. She grabbed her hair as the man flung her down on the floor, standing over her, staring intently. He suddenly crouched down, his face only inches from hers as Bo fearfully flinched away.

"I have prayed to God to send me someone to help me do his work. Are you the one?" his eyes searched her face intently.

The chloroform was wearing off and Bo was able to think again.

"What happens if I say no?" she asked hesitantly.

"Then you die; like that one," he waved his hand dismissively at John.

"Yes, I'm the one he sent to help you," she nodded quickly. He smiled and took her arm, pulling her to her feet. He pulled her to the table, handing her a pair of large scissors.

"Remove his shirt," he directed curtly before turning to the table to pick up another instrument. Bo stood uncertainly by the table. "Quickly girl," he gave her a push in John's direction.

She walked towards John in a daze as he struggled to stay conscious and follow the conversation. Bo reached for his shirt hesitantly and John saw the scissors. He kicked her hard and Bo landed painfully several feet away with the scissors clattering to the floor as she started to cry. The nut ran over to straddle her legs, grabbing her hair once again as he pressed the blade of a large knife to her throat as Bo screamed in terror.

"I told you to remove his shirt," he shouted in a rage; foaming at the mouth.

"He kicked me!" Bo screamed, feeling blood trickling down her neck. The man suddenly sat back on his heels completely calm.

"Oh," he calmly stood up, releasing Bo who remained on the floor staring in terror. He walked to the table, picked up a crowbar and turned to stare at John. "The problem is he's too tall," he gazed at John sadly; his other victims had been of medium height or less and their feet had not been able to reach the ground. "I shall have to break his legs; like the criminals that hung with our Lord."

"No!" John shouted and winced. "I'll let her do it!" he told the nut quietly.

John was furious with himself; he had lost his one opportunity to knock out his kidnapper. Now his life was in the hands of a girl who looked like she might pass out any minute. The man nodded sagely and walked to Bo, picking her up from the ground once more. He dragged her to the scissors and put them in her hands as he gave her a little push in John's direction.

"There you go, my dear," he said cheerfully.

Bo walked to John in a haze of dread. She cut his shirt straight up the front from hem to collar and across the shoulders on each side from neck to sleeve hem and the pieces of John's shirt fell to the ground.

"Stab him with the scissors!" John hissed in her ear, making her jump back in panic and then wheel around in fright when the man reached over her shoulder, taking the scissors.

"Very nice, my child," he nodded approvingly.

He turned and left the room, leaving the door slightly ajar. Bo raced through it as John strained to hear. He heard nothing and they came back into the room, each carrying two metal pails of water. The man carried his easily but Bo struggled with the weight. John was vainly trying to figure out the purpose of the pails when the nut threw the buckets of near scalding soapy water on him. John barely had time to hold his breath before soap was running down his body from his head to the floor.

"Now yours," the man told Bo kindly and she obediently threw the buckets of cold water on him, making John again spit soap and water from his mouth.

"God dammit!" he cursed irritably; the man slapped Bo hard across the face, knocking her to the ground with a cry.

"You mustn't take the name of the Lord in vain," he told John quietly as John looked shocked at Bo lying on the floor crying. The man pulled Bo to her feet as she cringed from him. He handed her a robe like the one he wore and she looked at it in confusion. "Dry him off."

Bo tried her best to dry the water dripping off John.

"You have to get one of those tools. Hit him with the crowbar!" he whispered urgently but Bo wouldn't look at him.

When she dried John's upper body, the man called, "Come here, my child."

Bo looked over fearfully; he held out a can of red paint and a wide paint brush.

"Put the mark of God him."

She reached for the can and brush without understanding. The nut advanced on her and she backed up until she stood pressed against John. The man whipped his hand up so suddenly Bo cried out and turned her head in fear. The cross was in his hand and he shoved it in her face.

"Paint it over his heart!" he thundered. She nodded and began painting a small red cross on John's chest. "Let the world see it, my child!" the nut roared and Bo looked at him startled. "Make it big; so Satan knows we mean business!" he yelled gleefully.

Bo obediently began painting a large cross on John who watched helplessly. Her face began to twitch, alarming him considerably as she painted the cross. She giggled; John didn't like the giggle at all.

"Bo," he whispered.

She looked at him giggling again as she painted his chest with big swipes of the brush using large amounts of paint. John felt the paint dripping. Bo looked like she was enjoying herself, staring at him and giggling before turning to their captor.

"Now what?" she asked gleefully.

He took the paint and brush, turning his back to her, placing them carefully on the end of the table. Bo stood within reach of the crowbar as John mouthed words at her. *Get the crowbar* but she wasn't looking at him. He kicked out his leg trying to get her attention and she turned her head. He mouthed them again pointing with a motion of his head to the table. John felt shocked when Bo turned her head away. The phrase '*She has gone over to the dark side.*' passed through his mind; he felt all was lost now. The man turned, answering Bo's question solemnly.

"Now we kill him." he said solemnly, reaching into the pocket of his robe and bringing out a gun. Bo beamed, inching closer to him, gazing rapturously at the gleaming silver gun. She put her hand on the nut's arm.

"Let me do it," she begged in a whisper, shocking John again. The man looked at her as Bo looked at John and the expression on her face changed to one of malice. "He never liked me," she spit the words out. The man placed his hand over Bo's hand which was still on his arm.

"We do not kill for personal reasons, my child. This one must die because he wishes to stop us from performing God's work," he spoke softly, pompously. Bo looked at him with a wicked grin.

"There's no law that says we can't enjoy doing God's work is there?" she asked with a soft laugh. He smiled benevolently down upon her and put the gun into her right hand. "How do you turn it on?" she asked, making him smile widely. He stood behind her, slightly to her left. He had his arms around her, holding the gun with his left hand as she held it with her right.

"You take the safety off," he showed her. "Then you simply aim at the heart."

John had spent the last few minutes wondering how many bullets he could dodge before they killed him; but he suddenly looked Bo directly in the eye as she aimed the gun at his heart.

"I'm gonna come back and haunt you every day for the rest of your life for doing this to Alex," he promised in a hard voice.

Bo gave a wild laugh, startling her companion into looking at her. He took his hand off the gun for a fraction of a second and Bo quickly turned her wrist as far to the left as she could and fired. The gun went flying out of her hand as the man beside her uttered one short grunt then fell slowly to the ground dragging Bo with him. She untangled herself from him and ran to the gun, picking it up and running out the door. John had been too startled up to this point to even make a sound but now he yelled as she bolted out the door.

"Bo!"

She ran back before he could call again with the key to the shackles in her hand. She reached up; unlocking him and his arms fell uselessly to his sides. Bo had to help him out of the room before locking the door behind them. They were in another steel walled room; this one had freezers lining both walls. She helped him slowly upstairs as the blood from his head wound ran down his back and chest mingling with the red paint that still dripped from the cross on his chest.

Upstairs, they found themselves in a regular house. Bo stood with John leaning heavily against her in the living room as she picked up the phone. She dialed 911 and unexpectedly handed the phone to John; she couldn't bring herself to speak about what happened. John plopped quickly down on the couch as he talked to the operator.

Bo stood beside him, '*I've killed a man,*' repeated itself in her mind as she turned the gun over and over in her hands. John worriedly jerked the gun out of her hands and she looked at him in shock before she gave a cry and ran out of the house. The black truck was parked there and she got in the back seat and saw John's phone on the floor. She called Alex; the sound of his voice released all her emotions.

"Alex!   Alex!" she cried over and over sobbing heartbrokenly, "I need you." Tears ran down her face, "Find me, Alex, please, find me!" she begged.

Alex threw the phone to Nick, "Keep her talking!" He rushed downstairs calling loudly, "Quark, locate John's phone."

He heard the computer log into the desktop with a location and he scribbled it on a piece of paper, snatching up Quark. He raced up the stairs past Nick, who quickly followed. They got on their motorcycles and drove twenty miles away using the computer screen in the back of Quark's head as a GPS.

*   *   *   *

They arrived at an isolated house on a hill to find three police cars and two ambulances in the yard. They found John strapped to a stretcher, unconscious once more. They stared deeply alarmed until they realized most of the red stuff was paint. They looked for Bo but she saw them first and ran from the truck, flinging herself into Alex's arms, sobbing hysterically and clinging to him as he gently led her to a waiting stretcher and sat on it with his arms around her.

"It's alright now, darling! It's over," he repeated over and over to soothe her, holding her as tightly as he could. She clung to him convulsively as the EMT, who had been sitting beside her in the truck, waited for several minutes before he approached Alex.

"She's in shock," he murmured quietly. Alex nodded to let the EMT know he understood and continued using his voice to soothe her. The EMT wrapped a blanket around them. Alex tried to put it around her on his side but she clung to him, crying out when he moved away.

"It's alright, darling, I'm here," he said again, knowing there wasn't anything else he could do for the moment.

Nick spoke to one of the police officers, who told him what John had reported by phone while they were tracing the call. When they had arrived, the policeman told Nick, John was passed out on the couch inside and the young woman was sitting in the back of the truck talking on the phone with someone. She wouldn't look at anyone or respond in any way. Nick gave the officer his name and address and walked back to Alex and Bo as she slumped against Alex. The three men immediately laid her on the stretcher and strapped her in.

The EMT looked at Alex, "You'd better come with us. If she wakes up again, she should see you." Alex looked at Nick anxiously.

Nick put his hand on Alex's shoulder, "I'll finish up here," he assured him and watched the ambulance leave. He waited for them to bring out the body; the policeman walking beside the stretcher came up to him.

"You know him?"

Nick shook his head; the man's face was unfamiliar, "No, but I think you'll find the bodies of the four missing men somewhere around here. My partners and I were looking for Darryl Mites."

The policeman nodded, "The freezers downstairs are filled with cut up body parts. It's going to take some time to identify them all." He shook his head, "People are sick."

He let Nick take a quick walk through the building before the detectives came. Nick came out of the house to see the detectives pulling into the yard. He loaded the motorcycles onto the truck and left for the hospital.

Bo was released from the hospital after one night of heavy sedation and went home to the apartment with Alex. Nick came and went; keeping them updated on the case and John's condition. Bo wrote everything down for the police after they sent someone out to the apartment to take her deposition but she still couldn't talk about it. Alex and Nick read her report. In the end, the dead man was identified and the bodies were identified as the remains of eight men. Some of the corpses had been killed over ten years earlier.

*   *   *   *

Alex worried about Bo; she was so very quiet and sad. He shared his concerns with Nick.

"It was a terrible experience. It's going to take time." Nick tried to reassure his friend as they sat on the beach in front of Bo's apartment while she stood by the water's edge, looking out to sea. "I think she's doing better; she doesn't jump when I come in the room anymore!" Nick laughed lightly. "Oh, I forgot, John is asking for you; he wants to see you in person," he added as Alex pulled out his phone.

"I really don't want to leave Bo alone," Alex replied honestly.

"I'll stay here with her," Nick assured him as Bo walked towards them. When she reached them, Alex took her hand.

"John wants to see me. Will you be alright here with Nick?" he asked nervously.

Bo smiled tenderly, "I'm fine, Alex." Alex reluctantly left and Bo waited till she heard the motorcycle leave before turning to Nick with a smile, "You don't have to stay. I don't need a babysitter."

"How do you feel?"

"I'm just very sad," she answered, sitting beside him, rubbing her fingers in the warm sand.

"Does it have anything to do with John?" Nick asked cautiously. Bo looked at him sharply and then quickly away without saying anything. "He's getting out of the hospital tomorrow." She nodded; Alex had already told her. "He wants to see you too."

She jumped to her feet, "Well, I don't want to see him!" she shouted, running into the apartment building.

Nick stayed on the beach for a few minutes before he followed, trying to puzzle it out. He had read both their accounts of what had happened in that basement. The accounts had agreed in every respect; Bo had saved John's life by killing their captor. He knew she was upset about killing the man even though there had been no choice but he was sure it was more than that. What would make her so sad, he wondered for the hundredth time? What had John said or done that had upset her so terribly?

Alex was asking John the same thing at the hospital.

"I swear to you, Alex, I don't know what I did!   But obviously, she won't come to see me, so I must have done something," he paused thoughtfully.   "I want to talk to her tomorrow when I get out of here."

"No.   She's been through enough!   She doesn't want to see you; you haven't exactly been nice to her, you know, maybe she blames you for getting her involved with that nut.   Which by the way, I do blame you for!" Alex finished excitedly.   "What the hell were you doing at her apartment, anyway?"

"I was looking for you!" John defended himself heatedly. "The bartender, Marco, called and left a message.   He said you were talking to a strange man at the bar.   Marco remembered seeing three of the missing men talking to the same man.   I was trying to find you to warn you.   When I got to the apartment, he was already there waiting for you," John sighed.   "We struggled and he hit me with the crowbar."

Alex was immediately contrite, putting his hand on John's arm, "I'm sorry; I almost got both of you killed!   I should never have given him the address; I wasn't thinking like a detective."   Alex muttered sadly, thinking back to the night he had been hanging out at the gay bar trying to get information on the missing man, Darryl Mites.   The detectives had found out that the police *were* looking for Darryl.   He was one of four gay men that had been reported missing in the last two years but like the police, the detectives had found very few clues.   Alex had hung out at the bar pretending to be gay.   One night a man had struck up a conversation with him about computers; Alex had been very interested and had invited the man over to the apartment.

"Everybody makes mistakes, little brother," John replied wearily, lying back against the pillows, his anger had given him a headache.   "I know I did," he said softly.   "I wanted to see you both because I wanted to ask you to have a wedding and a reception when I get back on my feet," he reached out to Alex.   "I don't know what has been wrong with me these past months, Alex, really I don't! Maybe I was jealous; maybe I *was* afraid you'd leave the agency.   I don't know what we'd do without you." Alex took his brother's hand, deeply moved.   He never thought he'd hear John speak like this and wished Bo could hear him. "I wanted to tell you both how sorry I am."

"I'm very glad to hear you say that, John! I wish Bo was here to hear it; but as far as she's concerned we're already married and she doesn't see any need to do it again. I think maybe she feels that everyone doesn't believe we're serious because we eloped. She doesn't have to prove anything to you all," Alex explained bluntly.

"No, it's not like that, Alex!" John pleaded. "We just want to be there and celebrate with you; we feel like it's our fault you ran away together."

"Well, it was!" Alex snapped. "If everyone hadn't been so busy telling us we were making some kind of terrible mistake, we'd have invited you all." He sighed, "You all made such a fuss when we got engaged, I could only imagine how much fuss you'd make when we got married less than two months later."

"Two months!" John cried. "You've been married for ten months?"

"See?" Alex muttered.

John sat up abruptly, waving his hands, "Okay, okay. I'm just surprised, that's all!" He paused, "Listen, put in a good word for me with your bride, will you?" he pleaded.

"I'll try," Alex sounded less than confident. He left without telling John he had no intention of upsetting Bo. If it came to a choice between Bo and John; Bo won hands down.

Alex came home to find Bo curled up on the couch watching the ocean. He looked around in surprise.

"Where's Nick? He said—?" he stopped reluctant to finish.

"I sent him home, Alex. I don't need a babysitter!" she smiled to soften her words. "I like being alone." She pulled him down beside her and curled up to him, "Except at night." Alex smiled in delight. "I need you for the nightmares!" she teased.

"I don't care why you need me, just so you do," he grinned.

She snuggled closer. "I love you, Alex!" she kissed him.

"I love you more," he kissed her. *Sorry, John*, he apologized in his mind, noting that Bo didn't even ask him how John was. John was a taboo subject until Bo brought him up.

THREE

Nick got out of the truck, walking around the fence to the marina ramp and stopped suddenly seeing Bo leaning against Wally's shed staring at the Baby below.

"Hi, stranger." he kissed her cheek.

"Hey, Nick," she hugged him warmly.

"What are you doing up here?"

"I'm waiting for Alex to get finished; I'm taking him out to dinner. Go hurry him up, will you?"

"Why don't you come hurry him up?" he asked quietly.

She looked away, "You know why, Nick."

He nodded slowly, "Oh, I know why." He stared sadly. "I just don't know *why*!" he complained. "What did he do, kid?" She didn't answer and Nick was angered to see tears spring into her eyes. "Want me to beat him up?" he asked only half kidding.

Bo laughed lightly, holding onto the top bar of the fence, "No, just go hurry Alex up." She glanced down at the boat, "Oh, here he comes, *finally*!"

Nick passed Alex on his way down and turned to watch them leave hand in hand. He boarded the Baby to find John watching TV in the main room and stood in front of the set.

"Hey, what are you doing?" John irritably complained.

"You'd better do something about her," Nick ordered cryptically.

John didn't pretend to misunderstand, "What the hell can I do?" he shouted angrily. "I'm open to suggestions," he continued more calmly; the situation had been driving him crazy.

"I don't know! Just mentioning your name made the girl cry," Nick replied angry and frustrated. "You still have no idea why?" he questioned John for the hundredth time.

"No, I lie in bed every night going over and over it in my mind," John said desperately.

"You're just going to have to have it out with her," Nick sighed.

"Alex will flip out," John said unhappily. "It could be the last straw between us."

"You have to chance it," Nick urged. "Fortune favors the bold."

John sighed deeply, "How am I gonna get near her?" he asked practically. "She avoids me like the plague and won't come near the boat! Besides, Alex guards her like a tiger."

"Where there is a will, there is a way, grasshopper," Nick replied solemnly, adopting an Asian accent and the two of them laid their plans.

*   *   *   *

"I still say you're a better chef than Henri," Alex complimented Bo as they entered the apartment after their dinner. "I think you should drop business and change your major to Culinary Arts."

Bo laughed delightedly but stopped dead as she came around the corner and saw John standing in the center of the living room. Alex walked into her before noticing.

"John!" Alex shouted, stunned and angry. "What the hell do you think you're doing?"

John didn't answer, staring intently at Bo who quickly turned her head and was equally startled to see Nick standing in front of the bedroom door.

"We're here to do an intervention," Nick said quietly and Alex turned to frown at him in surprise.

"I have to know Bo!" John begged softly. "What did I do that was so terrible?" He took a few steps towards her as the tears coursed down her cheeks, "I know I did something but I swear I don't know what."

Alex was torn; wanting to throw them out but feeling the need to know, too. Nick walked over and put his hand reassuringly on Alex's arm. John moved closer to Bo, his eyes pleading with her. It hurt so much; Bo wasn't sure she could say the words and looked at her feet as the silence lengthened.

"You thought I was really going to kill you," she barely whispered the words.

"Of course, he knew you wouldn't—" Alex denied quickly but John interrupted him.

"God help me, Alex, she's right! I really thought she *was* going to kill me." he admitted sadly, walking up to Bo and folding her into his arms. "I'm so sorry! So very sorry! I didn't realize you knew that. I didn't know it would hurt you so much," he whispered hoarsely, tears falling from his eyes as Bo stood stiffly in the circle of his arms. "Please, please try to forgive me," he begged. "I'm an idiot! You know that Alex got all the brains in the family! I got the good looks and the brawn." Bo smiled slightly although tears still dripped from her eyes.

"You should go into acting, honey! I still remember how you scared the hell out of me with a pretzel," Nick added, trying to lighten the moment but Bo didn't reply.

"You grabbed the gun away from me when we got upstairs," Bo said accusingly in the same tight little voice.

John cast his mind back. He remembered taking the gun from her and remembered how she had looked at him strangely and run out. John suddenly realized that Bo thought he had grabbed it because he still didn't trust her not to shoot him!

"You were twisting it so convulsively in your hands; I was afraid you would accidentally shoot yourself!" He quickly explained.

She looked up in surprise, still standing in the circle of his arms. "Is that true?" she searched his face, afraid of the answer.

"Absolutely!" he truthfully assured her. "I already knew by that time what an idiot I was!" he looked at her with hope in his eyes. "Can you ever forgive me?" He took a deep breath, "Because, I really want to dance with you at your wedding." Bo looked very puzzled and he released her, looking at Alex, "You didn't tell her?"

Alex flushed as he ruefully shook his head and John turned back to Bo.

"Tell me what?" she directed her question to Alex who related the conversation he had with John in the hospital; there was a long pause when he finished.

"Well, we can get married again next month. We might as well do it on our first year anniversary 'cause we're only having one wedding date!" she smiled as Nick and John let out a loud whoop. She only flinched slightly when John picked her up off her feet to give her a huge hug and she noticed the strange look on Nick's face.

"Next month is your one year anniversary?" She smiled and nodded. "So, you got married two months after your eighteenth birthday?" She nodded again. "Hey, wait! That means you just had another birthday! You didn't tell us." He sounded aggrieved.

She grinned, reaching for Alex's hand, "You weren't invited." Alex grinned smugly.

"Well, see if I dance with you at your wedding!" Nick teased.

* * * *

The weather cooperated and the wedding was a lovely affair. They had decided to get married at sea on the Baby under full sail with the bride wearing a simple Grecian gown decorated with small flowers and an old lace veil that had been in her family for years with a crown of fresh flowers. John was the best man and Nick escorted her down the aisle; Quark was the ring bearer. The guests were happy, the wedding couple was blissful. Quark had to give up his room to the pile of presents and the day passed in a haze of bliss.

The Baby was once more safely anchored to her dock as the sun set and most of the guests had left. Bo relaxed on one of the deck chairs, tired after dancing with all the male members of Alex's family, young and old. An old woman, whose face was both strange and yet familiar came up to Bo and sat beside her.

"It's nice to see you so happy, my dear. Your mother would be thrilled for you," the woman smiled happily at Bo.

Bo smiled, "I was just thinking the same thing." She said softly, unable to place the old woman for a moment until memory came flooding back. "Oh, of course, Mrs. Payne!" Bo said out loud and then looked puzzled. "I don't remember inviting you." She said more to herself than the woman.

Mrs. Payne gave a rich chuckle, "That's because you didn't. I saw the announcement in the paper. So, I invited myself." She explained as Bo put her hand on the old woman's arm.

"I'm so glad you did," Bo replied warmly. "How have you been?"

"Not bad for eighty," Mrs. Payne grinned smugly.

Bo explained to a curious Alex sitting nearby, "Mrs. Payne was a friend of my mother's. She lived two houses down from us."

Alex nodded and introduced himself, solemnly shaking the old lady's hand.

The old lady continued staring at Bo, "You're the spitting image of your father, my dear. He was a wonderful man! It's a shame the bastard had to go and kill him."

John and Nick had joined them in the last few minutes and four stunned faces turned to Mrs. Payne. Bo found her voice first.

"You knew Josh Carpenter was my real father and— and that the bastard killed him?" she used the old lady's word for the man she had always thought was her father.

"Well, of course, dear; John was my nephew and lived in my house. Where do you think you were conceived?" Mrs. Payne stated matter-of-factly.

"He was your nephew?" Bo was again stunned.

Mrs. Payne nodded gravely, "My sister Emma's boy. His father died when he was ten. Emma brought him to me when she was dying of the cancer; he was sixteen," she looked off into the sunset. "Everyone loved Josh."

"You knew the bastard killed him?" Bo watched her intently. "Why didn't you do anything?"

"We both knew, your mother and me." Mrs. Payne nodded. "Nothing we could do. No evidence," she made a move to get up.

"But that means you're my great-aunt!" Bo realized excitedly.

Mrs. Payne nodded slowly, "Of course, girl! Why do you think I've left everything I own to you?" Mrs. Payne gathered her many shawls around her. "See that you come to visit me sometimes," she winked at Bo. "Bring that handsome husband of yours, too."

Bo jumped up to hug her. "Oh, I will! How are you getting home?"

"I have my own transportation, Dearie." Mrs. Payne waved Bo away as a young man came and took her arm. Bo sat down abruptly on the chaise next to Alex.

There were several moments of silence as everyone digested the sudden turn of events and they noticed they were now the only ones left on deck. John moved a large box wrapped in red heart paper out of his way as he perched on the table.

"Who gave you this?" he asked curiously; all the other wedding gifts were downstairs and wrapped in white or silver paper.

Bo blushed, "My anniversary present from my husband," she grinned widely as John nervously leaped away from the box.

"Wait till you see it!" Alex said eagerly.

Nick and John both backed away, afraid of what they might see as Alex took the lid off. He pulled out a robot almost identical to Quark except this one had a female mannequin head looking very much like a doll and the middle section was two separate pieces with nine arms. Bo laughed at their dismayed expressions.

"Mrs. Quark!" she shouted, choking on laughter. "She vacuums, dusts and does the dishes," Bo told them proudly putting her hand on the hair and twisting it out of the way to show them the computer screen.

"Great, now we'll have two of them following us around," Nick complained.

"Are you and Alex going to stay on the boat now?" John asked hopefully.

"No, we bought that house," Alex pointed across the street to a lovely house tucked into the hillside with a magnificent view of the bay.

"How are you going to afford that?" Nick always practical, asked skeptically. "Bo has another two years of school."

There was a strange silence as Bo looked at Alex with a grin, "You have to tell them."

"Well, I guess it's safe now," he agreed, looking speculatively at the two men staring at him. "Well, you see guys; you left all the financial arrangements in my hands. And I thought it best to split our portfolio, you know, not keep all our eggs in one basket. So I thought it would be good if we—"

"Bo, what's he trying to tell us?" Nick interrupted, cutting to the chase.

"You have lots of money," she grinned at him over her glass of water.

"We don't have *any* money," John disagreed making Bo shake her head and grin even more broadly.

"You and Nick are each worth two hundred fifty thousand dollars," Alex informed them quietly.

"What?" Both men shouted looking at one another incredulously. "How?"

"I just took half of everything we earned and invested it," he replied coolly.

"Wisely invested it," his loyal wife added.

"Wait a minute," John said catching on, "Do you mean to tell me that you've made us live on *half* of what we've been earning?" he roared.

"That's all we needed," Alex reminded him calmly.

"Hey, Alex," Nick demanded his attention. "What are you worth?" he asked suspiciously.

"Well, Nick, before my marriage I was worth the same as you two."

"And now?" John insisted curiously.

"The wife and I are worth two million," Alex replied smugly.

"How can you be worth that much more after only one year?" Nick demanded.

"Well, my wife brought two hundred fifty thousand in assets into the deal and lucky for me; I'm married to a financial wizard!" he boasted, grinning broadly. "Of course, we couldn't take the chances with your money that we take with our own."

"The hell you can't!" Nick yelled. "Give me something to sign. Play with my money! Have a ball!" he offered magnanimously. "Damn! I can retire tomorrow."

"That's just what you can't do!" Alex laughed. "That's why I kept it a secret," he shook his head. "You guys would spend it all in one year."

John came and sat between Alex and Bo making them move apart to make room for him as Alex frowned and John raised his glass.

"Here's to many happy years together for all of us," he said sincerely and they clinked glasses and drank. John reached over and picked up Bo who squealed in surprise before he put her down on Alex's lap. "But especially for the two of you," he said gruffly as they clinked glasses once more. Alex and Bo kissed as the sun sank below the horizon in a magnificent sunset and the lights strung on Baby shone brightly. The photographer came out of the main cabin and took one last picture before he left silently followed by John and Nick. Alex and Bo didn't even notice.

CASE FILE: JULIA

ONE

On the second floor of a warehouse, a young man crouched behind a large carton taking pictures of a group of men below when he suddenly heard a footstep behind him. He turned to see a pistol pointing at him and the camera was taken from him.

*   *   *   *

A young woman leaned on the fence staring blankly out over the water as Nick, John and Alex walked towards her, arguing over a ball game. She glanced at them without interest as they passed by; suddenly her entire body was alert. She looked out over the water until they walked on before turning to stare malevolently at their retreating backs. She looked around indecisively and then followed.

"Hey," Alex hit John lightly on the arm after noticing the woman following them. They ignored him, continuing to argue. "Guys!" he pushed between them, grabbing Nick's arm to interrupt him.

"What?" Nick snapped.

"I think we're being followed!"

"By who?" John looked around skeptically.

"A woman." Alex whispered.

"Is she cute?" Nick chimed in, interested now.

"Let's stop and see," Alex urged.

They sat on the next available bench and watched people pass by. Alex's suspect passed them with no show of interest but sat on a bench farther down.

"Hm— interesting," John concluded. "Alex!" he hissed as Alex walked towards her.

"Hello." Alex ignored him to sit beside the woman with a smile.

She looked up startled by his cheery greeting and stared grimly. Nick rolled his eyes, looking away as John went to rescue Alex by sitting on the other side of the woman who turned an expressionless face towards him.

"How are you?" he smiled his most charming smile.

Her frosty stare threw him off, "Is this your idea of a joke?" She growled, standing up.

John and Alex exchanged a startled glance as she stalked towards Nick, who sat with his elbows resting on his knees, staring out over the water, pretending he didn't know them. Alex and John followed as she planted herself in front of Nick.

"I'm Paul Tyler's wife! I know who you are. I'm not going to let you get away with it! Try and stop me!" she spit the words at him as Nick stared in confusion. She tossed her head and glared at him before stalking away. Nick hadn't said a word, just stared after her totally mystified. He glanced at Alex and John staring at him expectantly.

"Who's Paul Tyler?" John demanded when Nick didn't offer any information.

"Beats me," Nick said mildly. "She obviously has me confused with someone else," he added without interest.

Nick and John walked away, picking up the argument where they had been interrupted. Alex remained staring after the woman for several minutes before running to catch them.

Later that same afternoon, the three men were back on the Baby and Nick leaned against the wall near the stairwell with John and Alex watching him from the couch.

"No, no, that's not what happened, Alex." Nick objected.

"Yes, it is, Nick." John replied, supporting his brother.

"No, Wylan said the money was in the *second* briefcase and then he—" Nick broke off as Lt. Wylan appeared in the cabin doorway. "Speak of the devil," he quipped. The Lt. was followed by two uniformed officers.

"Nicholas Duffy, it's my great pleasure to place you under arrest," he smiled at a startled Nick. "Place both hands on top of your head and turn around."

"What's this about?" Nick demanded, continuing to lean against the wall with a frown.

Alex and John got to their feet but the two officers blocked them from approaching closer to Nick as Wylan gave Nick's shoulder a push.

"You heard me. Assume the position or I'll add resisting arrest to the other charges!"

Nick turned his back to Wylan, wearily placing both hands on top of his head with a heavy sigh of exasperation. "You're really enjoying yourself, aren't you Wylan?" he questioned sourly as Wylan put the cuffs on.

"What *are* the charges?" John asked impatiently, standing in Wylan's way as he turned Nick around to take him out the door. The two cops moved Alex and John out of the Lt.'s way.

"What's the matter, Lt.; haven't you made them up yet?" Alex demanded sarcastically, following the entourage out on deck. Wylan refused to answer and the two uniformed officers continued pushing them back.

"Call Mary," Nick ordered over his shoulder, walking calmly up the marina ramp to the parking lot where a marked police car was parked beside the Lt.'s car. As Nick reached the parking lot fence, he saw the woman from the morning and pulled away from Wylan. She fearfully backed up to the fence when Nick ran over. The two officers had been so busy keeping Alex and John away from Wylan, they didn't see Nick break away until it was too late.

"You've got something to do with this, don't you?" He shouted angrily. She stared silently as the officers and Wylan dragged him back to the police car. Nick resisted them slightly to turn and yell, "I don't even know Paul Tyler!"

The woman had been cautiously following them but suddenly ran to Nick, pounding his chest with her clenched fists.

"What have you done with him?" she screamed.

John and Alex ran to the group and one officer pushed them roughly away as Wylan pulled the woman away from Nick who had been backed up against the car. The second cop pushed Nick into the back of the marked car while Wylan pulled the woman to his car and put her in the back seat, crying and covering her face with her hands.

Nick sat in a questioning room with Wylan and another detective with a picture of a young man lying on the table.

"I told you, Wylan, I don't know Paul Tyler. I've never seen him before!" Nick's voice was hard but calm. "I wasn't even in the vicinity the night he disappeared. John, Alex and I were out fishing; for two days!" he said in a monotone.

"Then why was Paul watching you?" the other detective asked.

"I have no idea. That's your problem." Nick shrugged unconcerned and stood up. "Come on, Wylan, you know you can't hold me if I have the perfect alibi. If you try to hold me here any longer, Mary will slap you with a false arrest suit. You've already wasted enough of my time; you could have found this out without dragging me here!"

Wylan perched on the edge of the table watching Nick pace. "Why won't you take a lie detector test?"

Nick turned abruptly, "I don't have to prove I'm innocent, you have to prove me guilty! And you can't!" he told Wylan forcefully.

Wylan stared impassively. "I'm going to be keeping my eye on you, Duffy; I smell something and it ain't pretty."

Nick stared him down, "You do that, Lt.!" he replied aggressively.

*   *   *   *

Alex and John were waiting impatiently on the boat when they saw Mary coming down the marina ramp and ran to meet her on the dock.

"Where's Nick?" John questioned.

"I thought you said the charges had to be dropped?" Alex inquired suspiciously, not letting her answer John's question.

Mary put her hands up, "Whoa, guys, relax; he's out! He just said he wanted to be alone for a while." She explained as they led her onto the boat. She sat in one of the soft chairs. "Wylan is furious that Nick has an alibi; he said he wouldn't bother asking you to corroborate his story because you would lie for him any day of the week. But lucky for you guys, you logged your fishing trip in with the Coast Guard," Mary smiled. "So, the United States government gave him his alibi." John handed her a cold glass of ice tea. "Thanks," she took a sip before continuing. "What gives with this Paul Tyler?"

"We don't have any idea," John answered tersely, sitting beside her.

"He runs a halfway house for teenage drug abusers. He and his wife Julia take them off the street. Two months ago, they got into a hassle with the police over a kid's death. John Wells was fifteen years old when he overdosed; he was one of their people and the police were a little callous and not interested in investigating his death. Mrs. Tyler is saying that Paul started investigating some drug syndicate on his own. Three days ago, he went to spy out a big drug buy and never came home," Alex informed them blithely as Mary and John looked amazed. He shrugged, "I looked him up while we were waiting. Read the police reports, too," he added as Mary took a picture from her briefcase.

"This is Paul Tyler. Recognize him?" she asked hopefully but they both shook their heads at the handsome dark haired, dark eyed young man pictured.

"How does Nick get involved in this?" John asked still not understanding.

"Apparently, Paul has been following Nick around. There are about a hundred photos of him in the Tyler house. Now the police and his wife suspect that Nick is the drug dealer that Paul was investigating."

"Nick?" John cried shocked. "You know how much he hates drugs and drug pushers!"

"Boy, something is really screwy here," Alex shook his head in disbelief.

John looked at Alex, "Let's go talk to Mrs. Tyler."

Mary almost choked on her ice tea and sat up straight, putting her hand on John's arm, "No, no, that's not a good idea." She appealed to Alex, "It could be construed as harassment. The lady is already very nervous and worried; and pregnant!"

"We'll be very nice, won't we, Alex?" John assured her, pulling Alex to his feet as Mary sighed deeply, seeing another phone call looming.

"Alright, call me when you get arrested," she snapped, getting to her feet as John laughed.

"Thanks, Mary, send us your bill!" Alex called after her as she left.

She waved a hand over head without turning around, "I'll send it; maybe they'll even pay this one on time." she said resignedly before giving a short laugh. "Silly me!" she shook her head as she got in her car.

*   *   *   *

Nick got out of a taxi across the street from a large, ugly, old blue house with brown shutters. The taxi pulled away and Nick looked around the deserted street, strolling towards the house.

*   *   *   *

Julia came in the right side of the double doors leaving the heavy door open as the screen door banged closed behind her. She tossed her purse and keys on the chair, heading for the kitchen when she noticed the pictures strewn on the living room coffee table. She walked in the room picking up one of the pictures which were all of Nick. She frowned and turned to reach the phone when she saw Nick standing right behind her looking grim. Julia straightened with a scream and jumped back, recovering lost ground quickly by going on the attack.

"What are you doing in my house? Get out!" she ordered, her voice only shaking slightly.

"You've caused me a lot of trouble," Nick said impassively without moving.

"Good! I'm glad!" she retorted angrily. "I'm not afraid of you. Get out of here before I call the police!" she threatened, picking up the phone. Nick grabbed her wrist, effortlessly yanking the phone away, staring intently as Julia gave a frightened squeak and tried to pull free. "Let go of me!" she demanded breathlessly as he continued to grip her wrist.

"Just sit down, Mrs. Tyler," he moved her backwards to the couch, giving her a little push to sit. "I don't want to hurt you."

"No, of course, you don't!" she snapped sarcastically, resisting him.

Nick gave her a slightly harder shove and she plopped onto the couch as he stared down at her for a moment then waved his hand at the photos scattered on the table.

"Why was your husband following me?"

She glared defiantly, "You tell me!"

"Who do you think I am?"

"I think you're the man who killed John Wells; or had him killed! I think you're a drug pusher. I think you're the one who killed my husband!" she suddenly screamed, leaping up to attack him but Nick easily pushed her back on the couch.

"I don't have anything to do with drugs or pushers! *Paul* is the drug addict! He has a record longer than my arm." Nick replied caustically.

"He was fourteen! He did a lot of things he regrets when he was hooked on drugs. He was busted for pushing and went to jail at eighteen and was in jail for four years. He earned his BS in Social Work and his Masters in Psychology while he was there!" Julia defended her husband hotly. "We came out here and started the halfway house to keep other kids from going the same way." She narrowed her eyes at Nick. "I think you're the one who got him hooked on drugs when he was fourteen; he must have recognized you and that's why you killed him!"

Nick frowned angrily but didn't respond to her accusation; he bent forward and took her arm, pulling her resisting to the table. He moved several pictures aside and held up an old photograph; it was a picture of Nick with a smiling young woman.

"Who is this?"

She looked at the picture then stared at Nick, "That's a picture of Paul's mother and father," she faltered; the resemblance to Nick was uncanny.

"That's a picture of *my father*," Nick said grimly, letting go of her arm and walking away to stand in the middle of the room.

"You're Paul's half-brother," Julia barely breathed the words staring at Nick, wondering what this meant.

Nick suddenly walked away without another word. Julia followed him to the door. He was walking towards the sidewalk when she saw a black truck drive up and his two friends get out and run after him. They appeared to be arguing as she shut the door and locked it.

John and Alex drove up to the Tyler house in time to see Nick coming down the walk. He turned right, walking away from them as John pulled to the curb.

"What's he doing? He had to see us!" Alex demanded in surprise as they got out of the truck to run after him.

"Nick, what are you doing?" John demanded; grabbing his arm.

Nick shook him off, "Go home, guys. I'll see you later." He continued to walk away without looking at them as John and Alex stared after him helplessly, not sure what to do. John turned to look at the old house.

Alex grabbed his arm, steering him towards the truck, "No, John! Nick will tell us when he's ready."

John didn't want to let it go but sighed deeply and grudgingly got back into the truck.

*   *   *   *

It was dark when Nick came back to the boat looking tired and drawn as John and Alex were just finishing dinner.

"Want something to eat?" Alex asked quietly.

Nick shook his head, going to the fridge to get a beer and sat on the couch as they waited expectantly.

"Paul is my half-brother."

They were both stunned; whatever they might have expected, it wasn't that!

"I didn't know you had any brothers, Nick." Alex spoke first.

Nick gave a short humorless laugh, "Knowing my father, I probably have a dozen or more half siblings around the country," he said angrily as Alex looked confused. "My father was an actor in New York when he met my mother; as soon as she told him she was pregnant, he took off, never to show his face again!" he explained harshly. "Paul had a picture of his father with his mother." He looked away, "I only saw my father's picture once but it was him."

"Is that why Paul's been following you around?" John changed the subject.

"It's only a guess; we'll probably never know. He's been missing for three days; odds are he's dead," Nick replied dejectedly, standing up. "I'm going to my room."

TWO

Nick answered the knock on the door while they were eating breakfast, amazed to see Julia. She didn't speak and didn't look directly at him; she was the picture of misery, he thought as he stepped back.

"Won't you come in?" he invited quietly.

John and Alex stopped eating in mid-motion as Julia stood awkwardly in the middle of the room, unable to look them in the eye until the men suddenly snapped out of their stupor.

"Won't you sit down, Mrs. Tyler?" Alex suggested kindly. "Would you like something to eat?" She shook her head. "Coffee?" he questioned and she slowly nodded.

"I don't know what to do!" she murmured piteously. "I don't know what's going on; I don't know who to trust!" she looked at the three men standing in front of her with tears in her eyes. Julia Tyler was five foot seven with long dark hair, looking much younger than her twenty-seven years. Alex handed her a steaming cup of coffee, noticing how pale and tired she looked. She wrapped her hands around it as if seeking warmth. She wore jeans and the same man's pullover sweater she wore yesterday.

"What do you know?" John asked, more for something to say than a genuine request for information.

She gave him a wan smile, taking a sip of her coffee before saying, "I know Paul is missing and everyone assumes he's dead. I know John Wells was killed. I know you're his half-brother." She gave a small shrug as she took another sip. "This is actually very good," she said in a more natural tone looking at Alex in surprise.

"Why was Paul following Nick?" John asked.

She looked uncertain, "I thought it was because Nick was the drug pusher but it looks like I was wrong. Why else would he be following you?" She begged, looking expectantly at Nick.

"The most logical assumption would be that Paul saw Nick and immediately knew he was related," Alex suggested.

"Yes, Paul would recognize him, I think!" she replied eagerly. "Paul has been looking for his father for years," she turned eagerly to Nick. "Where is your father?"

Nick had been silently leaning against the counter, "Don't know, don't care!" he barked abruptly.

She looked surprised, "Why not?"

"My mother raised me by herself after he left when he found out she was pregnant. Why would I care where he is?" Nick explained reluctantly, not wanting to discuss his father with anyone but knowing he was part of the whole picture.

Julia made a small grimace of understanding, "You were lucky. Paul's mother put him up for adoption. He was adopted by a very nice older couple. Everything was fine until he found out he was adopted when he was thirteen; it was a terrible shock for him. He started getting into trouble and ran away a couple times trying to find his parents. When he was sent to prison, he used the computer to search and found out his parent's names. He also found out his mother died of an overdose two years after he was born and that he was born addicted. He's been searching for his father for several years," she sighed heavily. "The saddest part is that he knows he broke his adopted parent's hearts. They never saw him after he went to prison and they both died several months apart when he was in jail."

"You don't believe he's dead," Alex made it a statement not a question.

She looked startled and shook her head, "I know he's still alive; that's why I came. I want to hire you to find him!" She begged them to understand.

They were all suddenly uncomfortable, unable to look her in the eye, exchanging glances with one another, knowing that there was no hope when it came to drug lords; they had no mercy. She hung her head and stood up slowly.

"Well, it was worth asking." She smiled stiffly and moved towards the door.

Nick reached out to touch her arm, "Don't go." he pleaded as he led her to the table. "Have something to eat," he pulled out the chair for her. "We'll help you find him, dead or alive!" he promised grimly.

*   *   *   *

They entered the silent house after following Julia back to the halfway house.

"Where is everyone?" John asked curiously.

Julia glanced over as Nick helped her open the heavy door, "They're all in school." She explained, "That's one of the rules to stay here. You get good grades. You graduate."

"They do that?" John was curious.

She nodded, "Oh, yes, we have very few problems with them. Most of them have run away from intolerable home lives. They have all decided to change their lives. The ones who aren't ready to give up the drugs are soon gone."

Once inside the house, she took off the bulky sweater; as she pulled it over her head they could see for the first time that she was obviously pregnant. She walked into the dining room where half the table was covered with file boxes and pictures were neatly contained in a shoe box.

"We have three boys and three girls right now," she explained and looked at the men with a heavy sigh. "I wish you weren't all so handsome. You're going to have to be very careful with the girls," she said cryptically but they didn't understand. "They have no self-esteem and are terribly boy crazy; they're going to fall in love with you the minute they lay eyes on you."

While she talked, the men looked through the files and pictures.

"Where are the other pictures?" Alex asked curiously.

"Pictures of what?" Julia looked confused.

"These are all of Nick and the Baby." Alex pointed to the box of pictures on the table and she nodded in agreement. "Well, *we* know that Nick isn't the drug runner. So where are all the pictures he's been taking of *him*?"

"I don't know; these are the only pictures I've seen." She stared at the table blankly and then at Alex as understanding slowly dawned. "You mean he let me see these because they're not incriminating or important."

"Paul doesn't sound like a man who would leave documentation of illegal drug running lying about the house where anyone could see it or steal it." Alex agreed with a nod.

"No, you're absolutely right! He wouldn't," she agreed wholeheartedly. "How could I be so stupid not to see that?" she asked angrily.

John and Nick hurriedly assured her that she had other things on her mind while inwardly wondering why they hadn't thought of it.

"Do you think any of the kids know anything about this?" John asked.

"They might," she guessed. "I'm glad you're here to talk to them because they wouldn't tell me anything."

"Why not?" Nick looked intrigued.

"They've all been very protective of me since Paul—" she didn't finish and Nick suddenly understood.

They conducted a search of the house but didn't find any more pictures. They would read through the files later. They made a search of the neighborhood, speaking with some of the neighbors. They were back inside waiting for the kids to come home when Nick looked at Julia.

"How careful do we have to be with the girls?" he asked curiously.

Julia grinned, "*Very* careful!" She emphasized, "Don't be too friendly or too nice." She laughed, "One day Paul came home from work when I was at the store and found Sheila waiting for him—" She stopped and waited until they looked expectantly at her. "Naked in our bed," she dropped the bombshell. Nick laughed but she shook her head grimly, "Not funny, Nick."

"What did he do?" he asked looking properly chastised.

"He read her the riot act," she replied with a warm smile. "She's still a little miffed with him for turning her down."

They noticed once again that she spoke of Paul as if he might walk through the door any minute. They heard steps on the porch outside and turned to meet the returning students.

*   *   *   *

The three men sat in the main room on the Baby, silently musing over what they learned from talking with the kids. They knew now that Julia wasn't kidding about the girls. The three girls had entered chatting excitedly with each other until they had seen the three men standing in the hall. They had immediately attached themselves to the men, smiling and asking thousands of personal questions, appearing to hang on their every word and were very, very affectionate. Julia had shooed them up to their rooms to do homework so that the guys could actually talk to the kids. It had been Julia's idea to start with the three boys, Jeff, Mark, and Tony. They had interviewed them one at a time without Julia in the room.

They interviewed the girls separately as well. Debra was a tall, well built, serious black girl who smiled at them a lot but otherwise was well behaved.

Gigi was a short, vivacious red head with short, incredibly curly hair. She tried to sidetrack them into answering personal questions but they had persevered with charm and persistence.

On Julia's advice they had left Sheila for last. She practically threw herself in their arms anytime they were near her and managed to touch them constantly; stroking their hands, arms, back, shoulders and faces with an adoring look on her face.

Julia almost broke into a laugh when she came into the room to ask if they were staying to dinner to find all three men standing behind the large pieces of furniture to keep Sheila at bay. They refused the dinner invitation as politely as possible, wanting to get as far from Sheila as they could.

"She's very good," Alex observed thoughtfully making both John and Nick look over.

"Who, Julia?" Nick clarified.

"Sheila."

John nervously jumped to his feet at the mention of her name.

"Sheila!" they both hollered.

"What was so good about her?" John wondered.

"You notice that she's the only one who managed to avoid answering a single question." Alex informed them, surprising them because they hadn't noticed.

Nick suddenly jumped to his feet, "I don't like this case!" he muttered fiercely, running from the room leaving John and Alex looking at one another, shaking their heads ruefully before they went their separate ways.

Several hours later Alex came up from his room, looking very serious. John was watching TV in the main room and looked at Alex curiously.

"Where's Nick?"

"He's on deck." John shut off the TV and followed Alex outside to find Nick in a chair on the foredeck staring out over the water.

"He's here," Alex said without preamble.

"Who?" Nick asked without interest, not even turning his head.

"Martin Freeman. He's here in this city."

Nick jumped to his feet, grabbing the front of Alex's shirt, startling him. Alex protested, struggling to get free.

"How the hell do you know his name?" Nick demanded harshly, refusing to release him.

"Back off, Nick." John made Nick release Alex and then joined him; staring expectantly at Alex.

Alex was flustered and had the grace to look embarrassed. "I— I read your birth certificate," he explained hesitantly, he hadn't thought Nick would be this upset.

"Why didn't you just ask me his name?" Nick questioned angrily.

"I didn't want to upset you," Alex explained nervously.

"Way to go, Alex," John chided his brother gently. "What difference does it make where he is, Alex?" John asked unable to understand why Alex would take the time to research the man after Nick had made it clear that he had no interest in finding his father.

"Because he's the drug pusher," Alex explained eagerly.

Once again, Nick grabbed the front of his shirt but more aggressively this time, pulling Alex face to face with him in one smooth motion.

"What?" Nick roared. "How the hell did you come to that conclusion?" he yelled angrily.

John had more trouble separating Nick from Alex this time and Alex pushed away from both of them.

"I found the other pictures!" he snapped equally angry as John stood between them with his arms outstretched, one hand against each of them, keeping them apart.

"Knock it off!" John yelled and they turned away from each other at the same time and took a deep breath. Alex walked to the back of the boat to sit in one of the chairs under the awning. John waited for Nick to get himself under control before following him back to Alex.

"I'm sorry, Alex," Nick apologized quietly, sitting down facing him. John seated himself beside Alex.

"Begin at the beginning Alex," John begged.

Alex cleared his throat, "I'm sorry, Nick. I didn't realize that— well, he is your father."

"It's not that, Alex! I've never wanted to see that horrible excuse for a man. Now you tell me he's even worse than I ever imagined. You can't imagine how much I hate being related to that man," he sighed deeply. "Never mind me, what have you found? Where did you find the pictures?" he asked wearily.

"On his computer."

John frowned, interrupting Alex, "You told me you didn't find anything on the computer in the dining room."

Alex nodded, "Mark told us today that Paul never let his laptop out of his sight. It's on his laptop."

Nick interrupted this time, "No one knows where his laptop is. Where did you find it?" he asked curiously, knowing Alex hadn't left the boat.

Alex smiled, "His laptop is in the trunk of his car which is in the impound lot of the police station. They found it on Hampton Rd.," he reminded them. "He stored the pictures on the web. I hacked into his files. It wasn't easy; they're pretty well safeguarded but I found his password."

"Julia?" they both asked curiously.

Alex shook his head, "Nicholas Duffy spelled backwards," he smiled at Nick. "It's all there. Martin Freeman is using a boat, a trawler, the 'Patricia'—"

Nick jumped angrily to his feet, "Damn him! It's got to be her name, right?" He shouted, pounding the deck rail. They looked away, knowing Patricia was his mother's name. "When we find this guy, I'm gonna kill him!" he stated emphatically and sat down while Alex paused for several minutes to let Nick get himself under control.

"Quark has scanned the information from Paul and has found a pattern. Based on previous information, he says they're going to make another run tomorrow," again he paused.

"Where and when, Alex?" John asked very interested now.

"I'm not sure where the trawler will be. Paul didn't have that information," Alex said sadly.

"Then how did he find it?" Nick inquired.

"He followed Sheila; she's using again and has some connection with Martin." Alex looked even sadder.

They felt it, too, as disappointment washed over them. They had liked the kids they had met this afternoon and they liked Julia. They knew this information would hurt her very much. They talked quietly and seriously planning strategy and went to bed early; tomorrow would be a busy day.

THREE

They parked in front of Julia's house, knocking on the door before seven am. Julia opened the door looking very frightened but she was relieved to see them if not a little surprised.

"Give me a minute to get everyone off to school, will you?" she asked and was gone before they could answer. The kids ran up and down the stairs, yelling and collecting their things. The boys were the first to leave; the girls were slower since they stopped their preparations to flirt with the men. John and Nick courteously helped Debra and Gigi find their things and sent them on their way. Alex slowed Sheila down by *not* helping her get her things together. He asked her all sorts of questions and flirted with her. He looked up to see Julia staring at him in consternation and quickly turned Sheila around, steering her into the living room. He sat her down on the couch, sitting very close and staring into her eyes. Sheila enjoyed every minute until Julia came into the room.

"You're going to be late," Julia admonished her as Nick and John came from upstairs to stand in front of her, suddenly looking very stern. Sheila immediately sensed something was wrong and got to her feet.

"Oh, you're right, Julia, I'd better—" she didn't finish her sentence as Nick gave a sharp push to her shoulder and she fell back onto the couch with her mouth hanging open.

"She isn't going to school right now," Nick informed Julia in a no-nonsense voice as she stared at them as if they had lost their minds.

"What do you mean?" she asked fearfully. "What's wrong?"

Alex looked at Sheila who looked away, "Do you want to tell her or shall I?"

"I don't know what you're talking about," she lied angrily. "I want to go to school, Julia."

"Did you sell Paul to them because he refused to have sex with you?" Nick asked harshly.

"Or did you sell him out for drugs?" John asked before she could answer.

"What are you talking about?" Julia looked at them, not sure what to do or believe. She looked at the girl sitting silently on the couch staring at her feet. "Sheila, you had something to do with Paul's disappearance?" Julia demanded incredulously.

Sheila leaped to her feet trying to push past the two men. "No! No!" she cried. "They're lying."

John pushed her back down on the couch, "You're using again!"

She shook her head, "No, no, I'm not!" she protested, staring directly at Julia.

Nick took his hand out of his pocket and Sheila paled visibly seeing the small packet of white powder lying in his palm. "Then why was this in your room?"

"Oh," Julia looked away sharply with a sudden gasp.

"One of the other kids put it there—" Sheila began lying but looked at Julia and bit her lip and started to cry. Again, she tried to push past them.

This time John and Nick each grabbed an arm, stretching it out straight and pulling up her sleeves. The scars of her old habit ran up and down both arms but on her right arm, a fresh needle mark could be seen.

"I didn't do it. I swear I didn't do it!" she screamed hysterically and went limp in their grasp. They swung her back onto the couch. "At least I didn't mean to," she sobbed, hanging her head, "He made me do it."

"Who?" John demanded.

"Marty," she whispered, gazing at them pleadingly. "He wanted me to tell him where Paul was. He paid me to follow him around but I wouldn't; I told him lies. But I guess he knew. He had his thugs hold me down and gave me the stuff," she shook her head, sobbing harder. "I don't know what I told him!" she wailed, looking at Julia mournfully.

"What were you doing with him in the first place?" Nick asked scathingly.

"I met him downtown. He liked me; he took me out and gave me presents!"

"Oh, dear God," Julia barely breathed the words. "This is the new *boy* you've been telling us about?" Sheila nodded. "Who is he?" Julia asked Nick.

"Martin Freeman, drug pusher," he looked directly into Julia's eyes. "He's the *man* in the old photograph you showed me," he said meaningfully, not wanting Sheila to know Marty was Paul's father; or his for that matter.

Julia turned her head sharply to Sheila, "How old is this man?"

"Fifty, I guess; although he pretends to be forty!" Sheila rolled her eyes. She suddenly reached for the packet in Nick's hand but he pushed her abruptly away. "I bought that the day after he gave me the stuff but I haven't taken it! I want to be clean! I swear!" she implored Julia to believe her.

Julia stared at her intently before putting her hand on Sheila's shoulder, "I believe you." Julia looked at Nick warningly when he snorted rudely in disbelief.

"Tell us where we can find the Patricia." Alex urged Sheila, bringing the conversation back on track.

Sheila told them the three locations where the trawler had been when Paul had followed her; they decided to split up to check out the locations and contact each other by phone if any of the locations looked active or if the trawler was there.

They drove to the boat to get the motorcycles and were ready to split up when Nick's phone rang; he saw Julia's number on the screen but she was crying so hard, he couldn't understand anything she said.

"What? Julia, I can't understand you. Stop crying," he implored. He listened intently for a minute, "Call the police!" He ordered snapping his phone shut, "Julia sent Sheila to school with an excuse note for being late. She stood on the porch watching her walk down the street and saw a car drive up and two men grabbed Sheila, pulling her into the car."

They looked at one another wordlessly. Nick and John put on their helmets as Alex got in the truck and drove off, wondering if they could find Sheila in time.

*   *   *   *

Nick was almost to the farthest location when a car deliberately ran him off the road onto the gravel shoulder. The bike went skidding in one direction and Nick in the other. He was barely conscious but grabbed his phone. He saw the license plate of the black car pulling onto the shoulder ahead of him; he speed dialed Alex and quickly told him the plate number.

"They've got me; you know what to do!" He shouted as the man grabbed the phone out of his hand, flinging it into the underbrush.

"Hey!" Nick objected loudly as the other man backhanded him across the face before dragging him unconscious into the car and driving off.

*   *   *   *

When Nick woke, he was being carried on board a ship and immediately started struggling. He held his own with the two men until a third man ran to their aid. The three of them subdued Nick and dragged him, still struggling down three decks even though Nick gave them a really hard time getting him down the three ladders. Nick hated drug pushers with a passion and enjoyed himself immensely even though he got rather lumped up in the process.

The men finally opened a massive door and threw him in. He hit the hard steel deck with a sickening thud and heard them locking the compartment. A warm body threw itself on top of him as soon as the door closed; leaving them in total darkness.

"Nick! Nick! I knew you would rescue me!" Sheila cried, lying on top of him, pressing herself against him; kissing him feverishly. Nick roughly shoved her off, grabbed her upper arm and extended his arm straight out from his side to keep her away. He took a deep breath and winced as his ribs protested.

"Sheila, let me explain two things to you. I'm thirty-three and you're fifteen. There isn't going to be anything happening between us. Come back when you're eighteen and we'll talk," he told her flippantly. Nick felt her settle on the floor beside him and tentatively released her arm, "And people who come to rescue you don't get thrown through the door by three men."

He lay on the cold floor trying not to slide into unconsciousness. He didn't bother explaining that men who have just been beaten to a pulp don't want someone kissing their bruised and bloody face and bumping into their possibly broken nose.

"Turn on the light," he murmured vaguely.

"There isn't one," Sheila whispered in his ear, stroking his hair.

He irritably pushed her hand away and painfully sat up. "There has to be," he argued. "You don't load a ship in pitch blackness." He got slowly and painfully to his feet while Sheila did her best to help him. He walked cautiously forward with his one hand extended; his other hand was keeping pressure against his ribs.

"Damn!" he cursed, walking into a hanging wire cage. He reached up recognizing it as a bulb protector. It took them many minutes to locate the switch near the door. When he finally found it, he turned to see their prison. It was a storeroom with pallets stacked floor to ceiling in a line around all the walls. There were two wire cages guarding light bulbs. The center of the room was filled with four pallets stacked floor to ceiling in a square. The end of the room where they were standing was bare of cartons. Nick weakly leaned against the door with Sheila close by his side, gripping his arm convulsively. Nick knew she was truly scared as she anxiously looked towards the middle square of pallets.

"What are you looking at?"

"Before you got here, I kept hearing strange noises from over there," she whispered. "I was afraid to move away from the door." She looked at him and cried out, "Oh, your face! Your beautiful face!" she reached up to touch his face as he flinched away. He moved purposefully toward the square of pallets as Sheila held onto him, trying to drag him back, "No, no, don't go over there!" she begged fearfully.

He roughly pulled his arm away, instantly regretting his action and had to lean against the nearest stack, cursing under his breath until the blackness receded. He started forward again and rounded the corner to stop completely shocked. A man was tightly wrapped in a blanket with only his head visible; he was very pale and his eyes were open and glassy. Nick gingerly knelt beside him on one knee, putting his hand down the blanket feeling for a pulse; it was there but weak. Sheila followed close behind looking over his shoulder.

"Paul!" she shouted joyfully, trying to fling herself on the prostrate man as Nick painfully held her back.

"Leave him alone," he ordered bluntly.

She sat back on her heels chastised, "I didn't mean to hurt him." she cried softly.

"I didn't mean it like that; he's very sick!" He pulled the blanket from around Paul who was drenched with sweat and stunk. Nick looked at his arm; among the scars were fresh marks. "They've been drugging him," he slapped Paul's face a couple of times but he didn't respond in anyway. Nick looked at Sheila, "Help me pull him over to the door."

Sheila was young and strong and with only a little help from Nick they slid Paul to the other side of the room. Nick wanted to get Paul up and moving, but with his own injuries he couldn't hold him up. With Sheila's help, he got Paul into a sitting position and slapped his face a few more times. Paul began to respond; drunkenly flopping his arms around, trying to knock Nick's hands away. With a lot of help from Sheila and the wall, Nick got Paul to his feet and they both took an arm, putting it around their shoulders. They staggered up and down the length of the compartment twice before Nick collapsed, dropping Paul. Both men sprawled onto their backs unconscious, leaving Sheila paralyzed with fear, grabbing their shirts and shaking them one after the other.

"Wake up, wake up!" She sat between them crying softly when Nick regained consciousness, staring around him, hazily aware that the ship was moving at a good speed.

He realized they must have modified the engines and found Sheila staring at him hopefully. Beyond her, he saw Paul lying motionless and rolled over, getting stiffly to his knees. He crawled over and slapped Paul a couple of times before his eyes opened. He appeared to be focusing on Nick when his expression suddenly darkened and he grabbed Nick by the throat.

"Marty, you miserable—" he began but ended in a cough and his hand fell back to his side.

"I'm Nick!" Nick said loudly as Paul stared, unable to fully comprehend at first but then he grabbed Nick's shirt.

"Brother— Julia— take care Julia— my son—" he trailed off, sinking back into oblivion.

*   *   *   *

Nick estimated two hours had passed since they knocked him off his bike. Paul woke up for only a few minutes at a time. Sheila had been by his side and very quiet. Nick gave her credit, after all she could be hysterical; she was obviously scared to death and being very brave. Nick heard the compartment door being opened and hastily stood up with Sheila's help. He leaned against the wall as Martin Freeman walked in. Sheila slid behind Nick, staring nervously at Marty who held a gun on them.

"Well, well, my two sons!" he said in a hearty voice, ignoring Nick's expression of distaste. "I could never deny you, could I?" he asked jovially, startling Sheila who glanced from Marty to Nick to Paul on the floor suddenly noticing the resemblance and wondering why she hadn't see it before. "I wonder how many more of you there are?" he said making a wry face. "I know you have a sister somewhere in South Carolina," he shrugged. "I tried to talk him into coming into business with me," he nodded his head at the prostrate man on the floor. "He spit in my face," he told Nick angrily. *'Good for you, little brother'* Nick thought but said nothing to the man facing him. "I'm not even going to ask you," he informed Nick nastily. "It's a shame. I really didn't want to kill my own flesh and blood, but what can I do?" he laughed suddenly. "Besides, there's probably plenty more where you came from; stupid gullible women are a dime a dozen," he laughed again as Nick grimaced in pain, grabbed his side and leaned to his right, away from the wall.

He lashed out with a karate kick to Marty's jaw in one smooth motion and Marty lay unconscious on the floor before he even knew what hit him.

"Get his gun," Nick calmly ordered the startled Sheila who stared at Marty with her mouth open; it was so quick she hadn't even seen it happen. Nick used his pocket knife to rip the blanket into strips and tied Marty up and gagged him. He and Sheila dragged him behind the center pallets where he wouldn't be seen. Nick looked cautiously out the door, unable to believe Martin was stupid enough to come alone. Sheila was behind him, pulling on his shirt, thinking he was leaving.

"What about Paul?" she asked nervously.

"What about him?" Nick turned back to her.

"We can't leave him here," she begged.

"We're not going anywhere," he closed the door, sitting beside Paul.

"What do you mean? We have to get away!"

Nick looked at her curiously, "Sheila, we're on a ship heading out to sea. Where do you think we can go?" he smiled.

She stared in horror, "You mean we're gonna die?" she screamed, getting hysterical.

Nick grabbed her hand, pulling her down beside him, "Do you hear that?"

She heard a noise that grew louder. "What is it?" she asked unable to identify it.

"Dolly!" Nick replied with a grin.

Outside, the crew on the deck of the trawler saw a huge purple and yellow helicopter gaining on them. They fired their rifles but the helicopter stayed out of range and in a few minutes, on the horizon, they saw several Coast Guard vessels speeding towards them.

Several crewmen on the trawler were killed resisting the Coast Guard but the trawler was surrounded and it was only a question of time until they were released.

Nick waited patiently. He pushed Sheila behind the door when he heard someone opening the compartment and saw one of the crew come in with a gun in his hand. Nick shot him from behind the first row of crates and the man fell silently to the ground. Nick left the door open, motioning Sheila to stay where she was. The next sound they heard was Alex yelling their names and Nick went into the corridor to meet him.

John flew the helicopter back to the mainland after he saw the Coast Guard board the ship. Alex had come on the Coast Guard vessel. Nick felt great satisfaction handing Martin Freeman, still tied, gagged and glaring at Nick malevolently, over to the senior Coast Guard officer. Paul was airlifted to the hospital by the Coast Guard helicopter.

John was at the Coast Guard dock to greet them and took Nick to the hospital against his objections. Alex drove Sheila home and took Julia to the hospital to see Paul.

*   *   *   *

Martin Freeman was held without bail on kidnapping charges, drug running and attempted murder and Nick attended his arraignment hearing. Martin stood before the court at his most suave and charming as his lawyer argued to get the charges reduced and requested bail. Nick sat directly behind Martin staring at the back of his head. He had glared at the man as he entered the courtroom and Martin had looked directly at Nick and smiled before he sat down.

"If there was a God, you would be dead." Nick kept thinking over and over until finally the court denied all the requests and sent Martin back to prison to await trial. As Martin rose to leave, he suddenly turned to Nick.

"You're a chip off the old block, son," he said between teeth wired shut from the broken jaw Nick had given him and smiled nastily.

Nick clenched his fists; needing every ounce of self-control he possessed to resist the urge to hit him again and remained silent, staring balefully at Martin. The courtroom guards took Martin's arm, pulling him away as he threw back his head laughing. Suddenly a strange expression crossed his face as he gave a strangled gurgle and dropped dead. Nick stared in shock at Martin lying sprawled on the courtroom floor for several moments then turned silently and walked quickly out of the courtroom as people ran to and fro to deal with the sudden collapse.

FOUR

Two weeks later, everyone gathered on the Baby to celebrate Paul's release from the hospital. He had almost died from the drug overdose they had given him but now lay on a chaise lounge in the sun, pale but happy. He and Julia sat close, holding hands. Bo, Alex and John and his current girlfriend, Sally enjoyed the party. The kids from the halfway house were there. Nick sat quietly near his half-brother. He had spent a lot of time at the hospital talking with Paul.

Bo, Alex and John were worried about Nick who had been very quiet and unlike his usual self since he had returned from the courtroom. Nick had avoided all conversation about Martin and what had happened. They had learned what happened in the hold from Sheila.

Nick had volunteered for the job of chef and had spent most of the day barbequing on the dock but joined them now for a while after everyone had eaten. *Joined us in body only,* Bo thought as she watched him staring out over the water. Bo glanced at Julia and Paul and saw him shiver slightly in the breeze.

"Are you chilly, Paul? Do you want me to get you a sweater?"

"No," Paul denied with a gentle smile.

"Yes, please," Julia overruled.

Nick leaped up, "I'll get you one." He ran into the cabin.

The conversation flowed on as everyone laughed and talked; Nick was back in less than a minute without a sweater.

"Jul— ia!" he yelled, coming out the cabin door.

He rushed to her, taking the startled woman by the arm, practically dragging her to her feet and with his arm around her, rushed her into the cabin making everyone stop in mid-sentence to stare. Nick leaped down the stairs and lifted Julia down, pulling her to his bedroom door where he released her to point into his room. Julia peeked in the slightly open door to see Sheila in Nick's bed and smiled broadly.

"Not so funny now, eh, Nick?" she teased softly before flinging the door open. "Get out of that bed young woman and put your clothes on!" she ordered Sheila sternly as John and Alex were coming down the stairwell.

When they heard Julia, they turned and ran back to the deck. When they got outside Paul eyed them curiously.

"Sheila?" he guessed after one look at their expressions.

They nodded with broad grins and tried not to look at Nick as he followed them out of the main cabin. Nick walked solemnly to Paul, sticking out his hand. Paul shook Nick's hand looking somewhat confused.

"You're a braver man than I am, brother," he said sincerely, clapping Paul on the back.

Paul grinned, "I have Julia to protect me."

*   *   *   *

Their guests had left and Sally had gone home when Bo got up and kissed Alex.

"Don't stay too late, darling," she whispered as she turned to leave.

"Yes, darling," John and Nick both mocked Alex, making Bo grin. When she was gone the three men sat in companionable silence watching the sun just beginning to set.

"I've been thinking about what your fa— Martin said," Alex began and continued; oblivious to the warning look from John and the frown on Nick's face, "You know, about your sister in South Carolina."

John saw danger looming ahead; Nick hadn't even mentioned that, Sheila had told them.

"Anyone want another beer?" He got up, giving Alex a shove in the process.

Alex didn't take the hint, "You don't think Carly could have been your sister, do you?" Alex asked, referring to Nick's girlfriend of six months ago as John abruptly changed direction. Instead of going in the cabin, he headed off the boat.

"Al— ex!" Nick roared, dragging out the two syllables separately.

Alex looked over calmly, following his own train of thought, "You remember, Nick, how I said the two of you looked so much alike."

Nick jumped to his feet, advanced on the unsuspecting Alex and lifted him bodily out of the chair.

"Nick, what are you doing?" Alex struggled to get free as Nick silently walked to the rail. He threw Alex over the rail; his face set in a grimace. "Nick!" Alex yelled as he fell into the water.

Nick smiled grimly and went back to his seat; draining his beer with gusto. Alex swam to the dock ladder and got out of the water, dripping wet and mad. He saw John walking down the dock away from the boat.

"Where are you going?" Alex yelled but John just raised both hands over his head in the traditional surrender position and kept walking; and laughing! Alex stood on the dock, staring up at the boat expecting to see Nick looking down. Nick wasn't there so Alex walked up the ramp until he saw Nick. "Alright for you, Nick Duffy!" he said in a huff. "Just wait till the next time you want me to get you the number for some little chickie!" he threatened.

Nick just smiled cheerfully and it struck Alex that it was the first time in weeks he'd seen Nick smile. Alex turned and walked away with what dignity he could muster. He went home to Bo, leaving Nick staring at the sunset still smiling. He knew Alex was so easy going he couldn't hold a grudge for an hour, let alone a day.

CASE FILE: LAURA

ONE

Laura walked into the lobby of her high-rise apartment building, tired after a tough day of teaching. The elevator doors opened as she approached and she walked in with a grateful sigh, pushing the eighth floor button.

"Great." She groaned, noticing the basement button was already lit and stood in the corner, wearily leaning her head against the walls.

Nick was so furious he drove his motorcycle into the apartment house garage like a maniac, driving right up to the elevator doors, coming to an abrupt stop beside them. He parked the bike and tore off his helmet, throwing it on the ground. He and the bike were plastered with mud. The door opened as soon as he punched the elevator button, dripping mud all over. He stalked in turning to his left and hit the tenth floor button, flinging mud as he furiously waved his arms, cursing a blue streak.

"If she thinks she's getting away with this, she's crazier than I am. I'm gonna kill the bitch!" he yelled turning around and stopped dead seeing a woman standing in the opposite corner, splattered with mud from head to toe and clutching a briefcase to her chest, staring with wide eyes.

"Oh my God!" Nick shouted, instantly appalled. "I am so sorry! I didn't know you were there." She nodded with a tight little fake smile and he could only imagine what he must look like, covered in stinking mud. When the elevator doors opened on the eighth floor; the woman slid along the wall, keeping her eyes glued on him as he followed her to the door not knowing what to do or say. He stood helplessly in the opening, watching her bolt down the hall. "Let me pay to have your clothes dry cleaned," he called after her.

"No thanks, Nick." She disappeared into the second doorway. He heard her quickly lock the door and moved back into the elevator, angrily hitting the close door button. He noticed the once elegant elevator was now covered in mud and continued his journey angrier than ever. When he pounded on the door of 1016, it was opened by a gorgeous blonde, whose eyes widened, seeing Nick drenched with mud. She unsuccessfully tried to hide a smile.

"That's right, Lillian. Laugh. You sent us on a wild goose chase. Told us a bunch of lies to get us to beat up your 'ex-boyfriend'. Well, woman, write me a check for six hundred dollars right now or this place and *you* are going to be covered in *manure mud*," he waved his arm threateningly making Lillian back hurriedly away.

"Now, Nick—" she began, trying to think of something to placate him. She couldn't think of anything; she could smell him from ten feet away and knew he was dead serious about his threat. She ran to a small desk, wrote a check and silently handed it to him. He snatched it from her and turned with a grimace.

"It better not bounce," he warned as he left. He heard her laughing as she hurriedly shut the door and locked it.

Back at the marina, he stood under the cold water of the outside shower to rinse as much dried mud off as he could before going into the shack at the marina entrance, stripping down to his black silk boxers and throwing everything into the washing machine. He boarded the Baby in a black mood. Working on his laptop under the awning, Alex casually glanced up and stared open-mouthed as Nick handed him a check.

"Take it to *her* bank right away, Alex," he ordered tersely. "And call me immediately if it bounces," he continued into the cabin. Alex gazed after him with raised eyebrows, intensely curious and dying to ask what had happened but knowing it was better not to speak to Nick when he was angry. John came upstairs, doing a double take when he saw Nick, mud still dripping from his hair down his bare chest and back.

"Did you lose a bet?" he grinned cheerfully.

"I've lost my damn mind." Nick replied grimly going downstairs without another word. John stared after him with a frown for several seconds before going outside.

*   *   *   *

Nick had a hot shower and lay on his bed staring up at the ceiling with his hands behind his head. He sighed deeply; he couldn't seem to shake his bad mood or relax enough to fall asleep. He'd been having a hard time getting to sleep lately. He restlessly slid his feet into his sneakers and went upstairs.

Alex and John were relaxing on deck and Nick joined them, petulantly flinging himself down into a chair.

"The check cleared without a problem," Alex hoped the good news would cheer him up.

"Swell!" Nick snapped bitterly.

"What's up with Lillian?" John asked curiously.

Nick had been very sympathetic toward Lillian Danes when she hired them to find an ex-boyfriend who had run off with several very expensive pieces of jewelry; wanting them to get the jewelry back because she didn't want to press charges.

"The damn bitch lied to us!" he shouted explosively, leaping out of his chair, startling them and making Alex stare in surprise knowing Nick wasn't one for cursing. "Robertson wasn't her ex-boyfriend! He didn't steal any jewelry from her!"

"Then why would she want us to find him?" Alex demanded in surprise.

Nick laughed humorlessly, "He's the guy who stole her latest *girlfriend* away from her. She just wanted us to beat him up!" He paced angrily.

"How'd you find that out?" John inquired mildly.

Nick swung around to face him, "Because *I* went out to the ranch to find him while you were playing with Suzie."

"Sally." John corrected automatically.

"Suzie, Sally, what difference does it make?" Nick yelled in annoyance. "You should have been with me!"

"All you had to do was call me, buddy. Don't get uppity with me!" John yelled back.

"What happened at the ranch?" Alex interrupted quietly.

Nick threw up his hands, "Robertson and his little friends sprayed me with liquid manure and then told me the truth; laughing their asses off the whole time!" He was furious all over again just thinking about it. John laughed loudly and Nick shoved him making him fall backward into a chair; Alex tried hard not to laugh. "I didn't find it funny at all," he growled harshly. "I'm getting tired of being the only one around here who does any work," he added nastily.

"Hey!" Alex objected in surprise.

John interrupted him, "Don't listen to him, Alex. He's just cranky because he hasn't been getting any." John told Alex snidely, staring straight at Nick.

Alex looked perplexed, "Getting any what?"

Nick jumped over Alex in the lounge chair to punch John in the mouth.

"Guys," Alex sighed in resignation and went back to working on his computer. He had learned the hard way not to get between John and Nick.

The fist fight quickly turned into a wrestling match. The two men were pretty evenly matched; John had a three inch height advantage but Nick had a ten pound weight advantage. They didn't fight often. Nick had a much shorter temper than the easy going John but John was angry now and that anger evened them out. Even so, the fight was short lived. They rolled around the deck for several minutes until John's anger abated slightly and he shoved Nick one way while he rolled the other. They got to their feet glaring at one another angrily.

By this time, Alex had figured out what John was talking about. He knew Nick had been very different since they had the run in with his father about a month ago. Alex had been home with Bo and hadn't really noticed Nick hadn't been with any women lately.

"Can't we talk about this?" Alex asked reasonably as the silence lengthened.

"No, we can't!" John snapped sharply. "You get to go home to a smiling Bo. I get to stay here with a morose moron who hasn't put two words together in two weeks," John said in disgust, challenging Nick. Nick had been standing silently but suddenly turned on his heel and left the boat as John frowned darkly. "Damn!" he yelled when Nick was out of earshot. He looked down as Alex opened his mouth to speak. "You should shut up," John advised. Alex closed his mouth and went back to work.

Bo came down the marina ramp, stopping when she saw Nick walking towards her with his head down.

"Hey, Nick!" she called when he was about three feet away. He gave an angry grunt, brushing past her in such a hurry he actually bumped into her making her fall back against the chain link fence on her side of the ramp, staring after him in amazement. He turned around immediately, grabbing her hand and pulling her upright.

"I'm sorry, Bo! Are you alright?" he asked quietly not meeting her eyes.

"I'm fine. How are you?" she asked pointedly, bending her head to look up into his averted face. He gave her a small smile.

"I just had a fight with John," he turned to leave.

"Nick, I'm worried about you." She grabbed his arm. "Something is really bothering you. Won't you please tell me what it is?"

He looked at her sadly, "I don't know what it is." He replied honestly, pulling away roughly. "It's tearing me apart and I don't even know what it is," he cried angrily as he left.

Bo sadly watched him go. She turned to look at the Baby before she walked slowly down the ramp.

John left the ship when Alex went home with Bo and didn't return until two am. As he boarded the Baby, he saw Nick sitting on the foredeck with his feet on the rail. He hesitated but didn't know what to do or say to his friend anymore. Sighing deeply, he went inside to bed.

*   *   *   *

Nick woke early and couldn't get back to sleep, so he washed the motorcycle and took a long ride in the country. He was riding back through town when he suddenly remembered the woman in the elevator.

He had been falling asleep last night when he saw again in his mind, the woman running out of the elevator. He heard her voice saying, '*No thanks, Nick*' and had instantly been wide awake. He had irritably gotten up and gone on deck to watch the stars and think. At the time, he hadn't noticed she had called him by name. He couldn't remember ever seeing her before. Even now, what he remembered most was a pair of wide, beautiful dark blue eyes staring at him. She hadn't seemed frightened or angry, he mused as he stopped for a light. She was about five foot four, he guessed and had been wearing a skirt and blouse, he screwed his eyes up in concentration, in blue or green, he remembered. He couldn't see too much because she had been holding a soft sided briefcase in her crossed arms. She had short, dark, wavy hair and he guessed her to be twenty-two or twenty-three years old.

Nick suddenly decided to stop and talk to her; the least he could do was apologize. He entered the building, going to the eighth floor, stepped off the now spotless elevator and glanced down the hall. He remembered her going in the second door so he knocked. There was no immediate answer and he began to think she wasn't home when he heard noise inside. The apartments were well made but he could just hear some kind of commotion. He leaned towards the door straining to hear when the door was jerked open very suddenly. She stood there holding a crying baby on her hip, talking angrily on the phone.

"I'm hanging up now! I'm taking every phone off the hook so don't bother calling me again. Do you hear me?" she pressed the end button and angrily threw the phone over her shoulder back into the apartment. Nick was startled, *husband*, he thought. He hadn't even thought she might be married. The baby boy cried loudly and Nick guessed he was about six months old. As the woman moved the baby to her other hip, Nick looked quickly; no ring on either hand. Boyfriend, he decided, feeling relieved. Nick tried to charm her with a smile. She stared blankly at Nick then suddenly recognized him without the mud. "Oh, it's you!" she said petulantly. "What do *you* want, mud man?"

Nick was taken completely off guard, shaking his head helplessly and stammering, "I— um, I just—" as the woman slammed the door in his face. Nick let out his breath. "Whew!" he left; inexplicably smiling.

When Nick got back to the Baby, Bo and Alex were sitting on the deck. As always, they sat right beside one another speaking quietly into each other's ear.

"Hey, Alex," Nick cheerfully interrupted them. "I need you to get me the name and phone number of a woman who lives in apartment eight-twelve of the Westmont Towers over on Trenton Drive," he was surprised to see Alex's slowly widening grin.

Alex said nothing, just made a wide arc with his right arm pointing over to the side of the boat. Nick was flabbergasted, suddenly realizing Alex had been waiting weeks for him to ask for a woman's phone number. Nick remembered, very clearly, tossing Alex over the rail; the memory still made him smile. He stared at Alex noticing Bo grinning, too. "It's all your fault, woman. Being married to you, he's beginning to grow a backbone," Nick turned away deeply disappointed. "I'll be damned if I'm going to jump into the water for any woman!" He went into the cabin thinking, '*I'll do it myself. I am a private investigator, for God's sake.*' He suddenly realized how much he and John depended on Alex's miraculous ability to uncover even the most obscure facts about everyone and everything in the shortest time imaginable.

*   *   *   *

Nick sat disconsolately on the sand near the edge of the water staring at the horizon and the waves while people enjoyed the beach all round him. He barely noticed anything; the blue funk he had been in for weeks was worse than ever. He and John had barely spoken to one another this past week. Nick admitted it was mostly his fault but he couldn't bring himself to apologize; wanting to keep everyone at arm's length for some unfathomable reason.

He gradually became aware he had been staring at the rear end of a short, dark haired young woman standing in the water almost directly in front of him. She wore black swim shorts which Nick liked, *she has nice legs*, he thought. She also wore a long sleeve, black surfer shirt. He admired the back view of her curvaceous figure as she turned to look towards the lifeguard stand and Nick was startled to recognize the elevator woman. He got up cautiously and walked over wondering what he was going to say.

Laura stood up to her knees at the water's edge, staring out to sea, letting her mind roam when the lifeguard's whistle brought her back to the present and she looked towards the stand. The current had been steadily covering her feet with layers of sand and a big wave snuck up, hitting her hard above the knees. She spread her arms out suddenly, flailing the air to regain her balance but couldn't move her feet. As someone standing slightly behind her lightly grabbed her left elbow, steadying her, she quickly turned with a laughing smile to thank them. She saw Nick smiling at her and he heard her quick intake of breath as she quickly turned away.

"Oh, thank-you, Nick."   She murmured, her smile inexplicably gone.

"How's the baby?" he smiled, releasing her elbow.

She laughed, "Back with his mother, thank God," she replied with heartfelt feeling.

Nick perked up at once, "Oh, he's not yours?" he asked very casually.

The woman turned and walked up the beach, "He's my nephew; the first grandchild in the family. His insane parents left him with me when they went on a trip and then called me every fifteen minutes for eight hours until I just took the phone off the hook and turned off the cell." She laughingly explained. "Oh!" she made a small exclamation and turned. "I'm sorry I shut the door on you," she giggled in embarrassment, remembering her abrupt and rude action.

"That's okay, it was just bad timing," Nick watched her pack up her stuff. "You're done with the beach already?"

"Actually, this is late for me; I'm usually off the beach by ten. It's already eleven; I guess I just lost track of the time," she explained. He helped her close the umbrella in the wind. She straightened up, looking directly at him. "I'm not a sun worshipper like you. I'm a moon child," she bent to pick up her chair and bag but Nick beat her to it and picked them up. He smiled lightly, holding them and motioning her to precede him up the beach. She glanced at him curiously before turning towards the street.

"Actually, I just stopped by the other day to apologize for the mud," he smiled confidently. "Your clothes must have been ruined—" he began.

She laughed, "They're fine. Wash and wear. I only buy from the clearance rack so if anything happens to it, I can easily replace it."

"I'd still like to apologize. I'm not usually that bad tempered. How about I buy you some lunch?"

"That's okay, you don't have to," she stared with an odd smile.

"But I want to," he assured her. "How about Donnelly's?" he raised the hand with her bag, pointing to his left at a small restaurant with tables outside under umbrellas.

She looked uncertain before shrugging and smiled, "Okay."

She walked to one of the tables in the shade. They seated themselves and a waitress took their orders. Nick ordered his usual seafood while Laura ordered a cheeseburger.

"You should try the crab cakes, they're the best," Nick advised.

She shook her head with a grimace, "I'll take beef any day of the week." He grimaced at her mention of beef, suddenly remembering the ranch. "Don't tell me you're a 'no red meat' kind of guy?" she demanded incredulously, staring at his well-muscled physique.

He laughed, "No, it just reminded me of why I was covered in manu— mud," he replied ruefully.

She immediately looked interested, "Why were you covered in manure?" Nick hesitated, unsure what to say. "I'd rather know why than have a free lunch," she added with a twinkle in her eye.

Nick grinned, "One of our clients told us a bunch of lies to get us to beat up a guy for her. I was outnumbered on a farm and got sprayed with liquid manure for my trouble," he explained succinctly; for the first time, it didn't make him mad to remember it.

She sipped her soda and nodded her head, "Lillian."

Nick was considerably startled. Is that how she knew my name, he wondered. He was instantly disappointed to think she might be one of Lillian's lovers. He didn't know what to say but luckily their food arrived.

"I heard through the grapevine that Lillian had hired a bunch of toughs to beat up her ex-lover's new boyfriend," Laura made a face; realizing what she had just implied about Nick. "Sorry," she smiled apologetically.

She has a nice smile, Nick thought smiling back. It frustrated him that he still didn't know her name. She obviously knew him so he didn't want her to know he had no idea who she was. He tried vainly to think of someway to find out her name. He was surprised to see her frowning.

"What color would you say her suit is?" she asked curiously, nodding her head in the direction of a woman sitting at the table behind him. Nick looked at the reflection in the sunglasses on top of her head again.

"Pink," he replied confused by the question since the woman at the table behind him wore a fluorescent pink bikini. His companion nodded with a strange expression.

"What about the man; what color is he wearing?" the woman asked with a bigger grin.

Again, Nick was confused, "She's sitting with another woman, not a man." He stared as she grinned widely. "What's so funny?" he asked mystified.

She laughed openly at him, "Not a thing," she assured him, still grinning. She suddenly looked over his left shoulder. "Oh, there's my friend Rachel; she's a model," she waved at someone behind him.

Nick grinned eagerly; he knew lots of models and if he knew Rachel he could pump her for information about his nameless woman! Nick quickly turned but didn't see anyone over his left shoulder; all the tables were empty. He turned back unsure what was happening and gaped in amazement. She was gone and so were her things. He looked around in a daze but she was nowhere in sight. Where could she have gone so quickly, he wondered, and why did she leave like that; her food only half eaten? The waitress came back and Nick asked for the check.

He walked slowly back to the Baby. John was lying in the sun when he got back and looked up as Nick passed him. "Where've you been?" He asked just to say something.

"In the twilight zone," Nick replied, dazed.

John turned over on the lounge with a sigh, afraid Nick was really cracking up.

TWO

Several days had passed and Nick was determined to forget the strange woman from the elevator since she had shown no interest in him. He was still having trouble sleeping at night but before he was having trouble getting to sleep now he couldn't stay asleep. He refused to acknowledge the dreams that woke him in the middle of the night just as he refused to admit why he couldn't go back to sleep; why he had to go for a run in the middle of the night. In the daylight, he refused to think of the face that haunted his dreams; the blue eyes that twinkled at him before disappearing.

Nick got out of the truck at the store in the early evening looking at the dark clouds that had been threatening to rain all day. The parking lot was crowded and he had to park way back along the side of the store.

"You'd think they were giving stuff away," he groused, walking to the entrance taking out his wallet to get the note Alex had given him. Nick walked swiftly along the side wall of the store as it started to pour and quickly shoved his wallet in his jacket pocket; it was raining like the end of the world. "Damn!" he shouted and ran.

He turned the corner and ran full force into someone. They hit hard and fell to the ground. Nick knew it was a woman so he wrapped his arms around her, twisting himself around so she landed on him when they fell. He hit the ground hard as his face was pressed into soft cleavage. It was raining so hard he could barely see the woman above him. She raised herself by straightening both elbows and looked down.

"Get your hand off my ass." A frosty voice ordered.

He didn't realize until she spoke that he was still clutching her to him; one hand across her back, the other hand cupping her butt. He released both hands immediately.

"Sorry," he said less than apologetically as he recognized the elevator woman getting off him. *It would have to be her;* he thought wearily, getting slowly to his feet. They were both soaked to the skin by now. "Are you alright?"

"I'm fine!" she snapped, bending down to retrieve her cloth shopping bag; everything had fallen out. Nick politely helped her scoop things up and shoved them into the bag. "Thanks," she mumbled and walked away, there wasn't any reason to run now.

Nick continued into the store to get Alex's things. When he got back to the boat, he was still soaked but the rain had stopped.

*   *   *   *

The next day dawned clear and the three men went to lunch for the first time in over two months. John and Alex were both glad to see Nick acting more like his old self. He was actually chatty for the first time, telling them what happened at the store.

"I almost kill myself to make sure she lands on top and she isn't even the least bit grateful!" he complained. "I mean, sure, my face was in her cleavage and my hand was on her butt but really I didn't even get a chance to enjoy it!" he grinned broadly. "I wish I had realized where my hand was because she has a very nice as— Ow!" he cried out as they both kicked him under the table. It took him only a second to realize they were staring at someone standing behind him; he didn't have to turn his head to guess who it was. He grit his teeth and made a face as Alex stood up, smiling at the woman.

"Hi, I'm Alex."

"I know." Laura smiled calmly. She had heard the conversation but wasn't going to be sidetracked. She held a wallet out to Nick. "You must have dropped this last night. It was in my bag. I just found it this morning."

He took it silently; he hadn't noticed it was missing until this morning since Alex had given him cash last night. He hadn't even bothered to look for it yet.

"Would you like to join us?" Alex invited eagerly.

She smiled again, "No, thanks. I was on my way to the marina when I saw your truck out front so I stopped. I have to go. Bye." She quickly walked away.

The three men watched her leave before John looked at Nick, "She's the one from last night?" he asked unnecessarily.

"Yep," Nick nodded. "Thanks for the kick. How'd you know?"

"The look on her face when you were talking," Alex and John both answered.

"Who is she?" Alex asked.

"How'd you meet her?" John wanted to know.

Nick felt curiously reluctant to tell them about his mystery woman. "She's just someone I keep bumping into," he answered evasively, putting money down on the table and walking away. He was dying of curiosity to find out who this woman was and how she knew so much about him.

John and Alex followed more slowly. John was very intrigued; if this had happened three months ago, he and Alex wouldn't have rested until they wormed the truth out of Nick. But, Nick had been so touchy lately, John was afraid to ask any questions. He'd have to wait for Nick to tell him. John sighed deeply; patience was not his forte.

*   *   *   *

Two days later, Nick was in a hurry to leave the mall. He hated the mall so much he'd rather be in a fight than go there but Bo had begged him to pick up a washer for her. *It would be quick in and out;* he thought and reluctantly agreed.

He backed out in the crowded parking lot and heard a crunching sound. *That can't be good,* he thought irritably. He looked in his rear view mirror but didn't see anything. He pulled forward, putting the truck in park and walked around to see his bumper had dented the rear side panel of a little white car. He sighed in exasperation, running a hand through his hair and looked towards the driver of the car standing beside the driver's door, staring at him ruefully, and sucked in his breath sharply as he recognized her.

"Shit, shit and double shit," he muttered under his breath, walking towards his mystery woman, when a sudden thought perked him up. They'd have to exchange insurance information; he'd finally know her name.

"I'm really sorry," he apologized quietly.

She shook her head, "That's all right—" she began.

He whipped out his wallet. "No, it's my fault!" he said happily, handing her his cards.

She backed away, "No, really, Nick. You don't even have a dent in your bumper." She opened her car door, "I'll just get it fixed."

"No, wait!" he begged. "Here, just take it to Duke's Auto Body on Marshall. Have him send me the bill," Nick scribbled the name of the body shop on the back of one of his business cards and handed it to her with his most charming smile.

"Oh, well, thanks," she smiled shyly as she took it.

He stared at her until she disappeared into the car. He moved out of the way as she backed out and watched as she drove away.

Laura drove straight to the auto body shop.

Duke examined the dent, telling her cheerfully, "I can make it as good as new for three hundred dollars."

Laura looked deeply disappointed, "Nick said you had the best price in town," she lied convincingly.

"Nick Duffy?" Duke asked suddenly interested as she nodded with a hopeful smile. "For a friend of Nick's, I'll do it for a hundred," he grinned.

"Great," she returned his smile.

                    *   *   *   *

"Hey, Duke, did a friend of mine bring in her car? A little white KIA® with a dent in the passenger rear panel?" Nick asked eagerly when he bumped into Duke a couple of days later in town.

Duke nodded, "Yep, did it in one day for a hundred bucks, Buddy," Duke heartily slapped him on the back.

"Did you mail me the bill?" Nick asked curiously knowing Duke usually delivered them in person, hoping to meet some gorgeous women on the Baby.

Duke looked confused before grinning. "No, *she* paid me. In cash! Not like your usual little friends, eh?" Duke waved goodbye and continued down the street.

Nick stood in the middle of the sidewalk, frowning.

"She's really getting on my nerves, now!" he blurted out loud. He made up his mind and went to an ATM machine; getting the cash before heading over to Westmont Towers.

As he walked up to her door, it opened and Laura backed out. She locked it before turning around and jumped back with a small shriek seeing Nick behind her.

"Oh, you scared me!" she cried, heading for the elevator. "What are you doing here?"

Nick had had the whole conversation planned out in his head, now, everything was going wrong again. *Of course, the elevator has to be right there waiting for her*, he complained silently as he got in with her. "I want to give you the money for the car," he held out the cash.

She made no effort to take it, looking surprised, "Why?"

"It was my fault; I backed into you," he replied getting annoyed; he was used to women taking money from him gladly.

"It wasn't anyone's fault, Nick," she got off the elevator in the garage. He silently cursed the quickness of the elevator as he followed her to her car. "It was the classic parking lot accident." He looked confused. "We were both in each other's blind spot, that's all. I've seen it happen lots of times," she got in the car.

Nick held onto her door so she couldn't shut it. "But it didn't cost me anything; at least let me pay half," he insisted.

"It isn't necessary," she refused. "I'm late for the dentist. I have to go," she tried to close her door.

He released the door reluctantly, moving out of her way. He walked to the motorcycle feeling stupidly disappointed and angry with himself for caring so much about a woman who obviously didn't like him. *And why should she like you*, he asked himself angrily, *every time you're near her, something stupid happens*, he argued with himself driving back to the Baby. As he drove, he pondered the lunch conversation again but he still couldn't understand the point of her questions, what was so funny or why she disappeared. He arrived at the Baby so cranky and miserable, John and Alex stayed out of his way. They were glad they had so many cases right now to keep them all busy.

THREE

Nick took Samson for a walk in the park on a beautiful Sunday morning that was especially welcome since it had been raining for three days. Samson was a huge Saint Bernard dog belonging to John's latest girlfriend, Melanie. She was a stewardess who was unexpectedly assigned back to back long distance flights when one of the other girls got sick, making her beg John to take care of Samson while she was gone. Alex immediately fell madly in love with the huge beast but Bo told him in no uncertain terms they would not be getting a Saint Bernard, ever!

Nick didn't mind walking Samson as long as he walked but Samson was a very badly behaved dog who usually pulled Nick and John anywhere he wanted to go. He had dragged Nick through a huge bush yesterday chasing a squirrel and Nick was determined Samson would walk where Nick wanted today. Everything went well until Samson saw another squirrel and lunged for the creature. Nick was ready for him this time and pulled back hard on the leash. Samson fell back before he lunged again in the direction of the squirrel and the thick chain collar snapped in two, leaving Nick holding a leash firmly attached to a broken collar as Samson raced away.

Nick spent the next hour chasing the dog which was having the time of his life running through the huge puddles left by the torrential rains. Nick was just about to give up and go home without the stupid creature when he saw him just ahead. Nick was almost close enough to catch the dog when Samson saw a woman walking towards him. He raced over and jumped up on the woman who was dressed as if she had just come from church; wearing a dress that reminded Nick of daffodils in the spring. Samson knocked her down into a huge mud puddle and leaped from one side to the other over her as she tried to protect her face with her arms. Nick was cursing the beast as he ran to them. He tried to help the woman up but Samson kept knocking them both down, making them fall over one another multiple times until he tired of the game and stood still, dripping mud and happily panting.

Nick finally got to his feet and held the muddy woman up by the arm, fully expecting to get cursed out or kicked. He was amazed to hear her laughing. He looked at her in surprise, recognizing his mystery woman through all the mud. A policeman ran up to them; Nick groaned, recognizing Officer Duncan. Duncan yelled at Nick as Samson turned to meet him.

"Duffy, that beast belongs on a leash!" Duncan shouted, running away from Samson at the same time. Nick couldn't help laughing until his nameless friend suddenly snatched the leash out of his hand. Nick flinched; not exactly sure she wasn't going to use it on him. She walked to the dog, slipping the clip end through the hand loop making a lasso which she slipped over the dog's head and pulled up on the leash.

"Samson, sit," she ordered firmly and to Nick's utter astonishment the dog instantly obeyed.

"Whose animal is this?" Duncan demanded angrily, running over. Samson didn't like his tone of voice and growled, making Duncan quickly retreat.

"Oh, shut up and go away, Duncan, before I push *you* in this mud!" Nick threatened irritably. "Everything's under control now." Duncan retreated unwillingly; he had always been afraid of Nick and he wasn't willing to risk being humiliated. Nick turned back to his mystery woman; he couldn't help smiling, glad to see her grinning back at him.

"I am so sorry about your dress," Nick apologized ruefully. "This is not my dog," he hurriedly explained. "We're just dog sitting for a friend." She walked towards the parking lot as he talked with Samson, the traitor, walking beside her like a well-trained dog. "Please, let me pay to have your dress dry cleaned. Or better yet, get a new one," he looked at the dress which was silk and looked completely ruined. It was strapless with a high waist and straight lines and had a yellow floral pattern. It looked deceptively simple but Nick knew it was a very expensive dress. It was a dress that would have been described as a summer frock; having dated so many models over the years, Nick had picked up the garment industry lingo and knew prices fairly well. He had spent way too much time attending fashion shows to placate his current lover. The only thing he liked was looking at all the gorgeous women.

Laura looked down at her muddy dress and shrugged, "We'll see if it can be cleaned." She stopped beside the black truck.

Nick was desperate to keep her talking, "What do you do?" He pointed to Samson, lying quietly on the pavement, "Lion tamer?"

She laughed, "Special Education Teacher."

That stumped Nick; he didn't know anything about that. He looked around the parking lot. "Where's your car?"

"I walked here," she replied ruefully. "But you can give me a ride home." She said delighting him. "I'll sit in the bed with Samson."

"Oh, no, you won't!" he insisted, opening the passenger door.

"I'll get it filthy," she protested and he raised his eyebrows, motioning to himself covered in mud. Samson attempted to jump in the open door. "Samson, no!" The dog obediently sat down again. Laura smiled at Nick and walked Samson back to the truck bed. Nick let down the gate and Samson leaped in. She hooked the clip end of the leash to the hook on the side of the truck bed. "Be a good boy," she patted his head.

"Fat chance," Nick couldn't help muttering as he helped her in.

*   *   *   *

Nick ran up the ramp to the Baby with Samson loping beside him. He threw the leash at Alex, who was sitting on the deck finishing breakfast with Bo and John.

"Give him a bath, will you?" he called happily to Alex. He stopped for a moment to strip; throwing his wet muddy clothes in a pile on the deck.

"Hey!" Alex objected heatedly, glancing at Bo who was grinning. Alex was relieved Nick stopped at his underwear. Nick grinned and ran into the cabin to get a shower. The three exchanged looks, wondering what had made him so excited and happy. They ran for cover as Samson shook himself, spraying them with a shower of mud.

"If only you could talk," John told the muddy dog, unable to understand why Nick would come back from the park covered in mud and be so happy.

Nick showered and changed in record time. He stopped hurrying to get ready, telling himself to slow down. He was so amazed he had able to talk his still nameless friend into having lunch with him that he had forgotten she had to get showered and changed, too. He didn't want to rush her. On the other hand, he reminded himself, if he got there early maybe he could sneak a peek at her wallet and ID. He smiled at the thought and rushed upstairs.

John met him at the top of the stairs. He had waited for Nick to come out but got impatient.

"What's going on?" he demanded impatiently as Nick tried to brush past him, equally impatient. John grabbed his arm; he wasn't going to let him get away without some kind of answer.

"I've got a hot date."

Thank God, John thought to himself, following Nick out on deck. Bo and Alex were bathing the dog in the shower by the marina gate.

"What's her name?" John ran to keep up with Nick.

"I don't know!" Nick grinned like an idiot; running down the ramp, leaving John standing at the entrance to the boat.

"Damn!" John growled. *Her again*, he turned away in disgust. "I'll lay odds you're going to come back a morose moron again," he called out but Nick was too far away to hear.

*   *   *   *

Unfortunately for Nick's plan, Laura was standing on the curb waiting for him. He glanced at her uncertainly as he opened the door for her.

"Isn't that the dress that got muddy?" he asked, helping her climb in.

"Yes," she grinned. "I just got in the shower with it on; the mud came out and it's already dry," she laughed at the expression on his face. He went around the front of the truck and got in.

Nick had decided in the shower to take her to La Chat Noir. It was the most elegant and expensive restaurant in town and his usual first date restaurant. The ladies were always impressed. He also wanted a place she couldn't just fade away from. She hadn't said a word since she got in and he looked over; almost telling her he didn't know her name but changed his mind again. It would make him look too stupid, he decided nervously. He couldn't ever remember being nervous on a date. It wasn't a long drive; when he came to help her out, Laura was staring at the restaurant.

"Wow. The full treatment," she said mysteriously.

"What?" he asked; not understanding why she seemed slightly antagonistic.

"I love French food." She smiled and he took her arm, walking in to be greeted by name by the Maitre'd.

"Ah, Monsieur Nick. We have not seen you in quite a long time."

Laura looked at Nick slightly surprised.

"It's good to be back, Andrew." Nick said as the Maitre'd led them to Nick's usual table.

When the waiter came to take their order, Nick was surprised to hear her speak fluent French. They had a long conversation which Nick couldn't understand and he gave the man his order in English. Now that business was taken care of, she turned to Nick expectantly. Nick always felt at a loss with this woman, feeling an undercurrent he couldn't explain. He had wanted to get her alone so badly and now he couldn't think of anything to say.

"Tell me about your job."

"I teach autistic children."

Nick had no experience with handicapped children to help him. "That sounds hard," he smiled encouragingly.

She gave him a mysterious look he didn't understand. No woman had ever looked at him like that.

"You don't have any idea what Autistic children are like, do you?" she challenged.

"Not a clue," he replied honestly. "I don't know anyone with a handicapped child."

"Really?" she asked mockingly. "Do you even know anyone who has children?"

"No," Nick felt surprised, having never really thought about it. At the moment, he couldn't remember anyone he knew having kids.

She nodded her head slowly giving him a hard stare, "Have you ever read a book?"

"Of course, I've read a book. I'm not illiterate!" he retorted angrily, getting a little tired of her attitude.

She waved his protest aside, "I'm not saying you *can't* read. What book have you read in the past— two years?" She paused to pick a random number. The waiter arrived with the salads and Nick waited until he left.

"So, I don't like to read. What's your point?" he demanded, taking the offensive.

"What do you like to do?" she ignored his question.

Nick tried his best to get the conversation back on track, "I like sports, all kinds. I like to watch sports and play sports." He looked across at her, "How about you?"

She shook her head, "I'm not big on sports. I don't mind watching a game now and then except basketball. I hate basketball."

"What's wrong with basketball?"

She waved her fork in the air at him, "That horrible squeaking noise their shoes make drives me up the wall!"

Nick laughed out loud, "That's a new one." He felt more relaxed.

"Why did you want to have lunch with me?" she asked point blank, startling him.

"I want to get to know you better," he replied truthfully.

She stared intently, "Why?" she could tell by his expression that he didn't understand. "I mean, I'm hardly your type."

"What is my type?" Nick tried to laugh off her question.

"Tall, leggy, skinny, busty, bleach blonde, blue eyed models," she answered immediately without taking a breath.

"How do you know?" he challenged, unsure if he felt irritated because she was right or because she was so smug about it.

"Brenda told me."

Nick wracked his brain for any Brenda he knew but he couldn't think of one. "I didn't know you knew Brenda," he stalled.

She smiled that smug smile once more, "I know a lot of your girlfriends, Nick."

"How do you know so many models?" he felt in over his head again.

"Both my sisters were models." She shrugged as he hoped against hope that he hadn't dated either sister.

"Tell me why you left the restaurant the last time," Nick decided to go on the offensive again and steer the conversation away from this dangerous area but she didn't answer; instead she watched a customer come into the restaurant following him with her eyes as he passed by their table, turning her head to see where he sat. "Do you know him?" Nick asked curiously.

"No," she watched two new men enter and walk past. She made eye contact and smiled at them.

"Friends of yours?" Nick demanded angrily.

She grinned, "No." she paused, looking at him with both eyebrows raised, "Now, do you know why I left?"

Nick stared, thinking maybe she was a nut before he suddenly understood her little stunt. "I do not stare at women like that!" he protested vehemently but even as he said it, a lovely woman walked past them to the front of the restaurant and his eyes followed her. "Damn," he muttered, turning to see that smug look on her face.

"Face it, Nicholas Duffy, you are a pig!"

"If I'm such a pig, why did you come out with me?" Nick demanded indignantly.

"Because I wanted to tell you to your face that you're a pig," she grinned cheerfully.

"Stop saying that," he ordered irritably. "I like women; that doesn't make me a pig!" he countered defensively.

"Oh, you're a pig, just ask Brenda."

The waiter interrupted to serve the main course and Nick waited till he left, boiling inside.

"Who the hell is Brenda?" he exploded, tired of pretending and suddenly realized she'd been playing him all along. "You've known all along I don't know your name!" She laughed out loud as he took a deep breath, "Why didn't you just tell me your name?"

"Why bother?" she replied cuttingly. "You'll never remember it, anyway." She looked directly at him, "What do you call everyone, baby or honey or something?"

Nick frowned, uncertain what to do so he went on the offensive again; now he *had* to know things.

"How come you know so much about me?" he asked snidely. "Could it be you're interested in me yourself and jealous because

I've never noticed you?" he took a shot in the dark. Her laugh rang out making several people look over.

"Once a pig, always a pig," she replied smugly. "I've been places you've been. I've seen you picking up and discarding women. I've known a lot of them. What's the longest relationship you've ever had with a woman?"

"What's Brenda's last name?" Nick demanded suspiciously.

"Don't worry about it, Nick. You're just one of the 'dog people' of this world," she said shrugging her shoulders.

"What the hell are 'dog people'?" he asked completely mystified.

"People who have the same three rules for sex as dogs," she replied calmly, sipping her water. She had been eating her meal during the entire conversation while Nick hadn't even touched his.

"And they are?" he asked just as calmly; now he had to know.

"Anyone, anywhere, anytime," she stared balefully.

"You have a lot of nerve; do you know that?" he asked icily. "What the hell have I ever done to you?"

"You broke my friend's heart." She added anticipating his next question, "Brenda Mills." She stood up suddenly. "She lived in Westmont Towers and you dated the woman for over three months, less than a year ago and you can't even remember her name!" she said accusingly. He stood up, too, desperately trying to remember Brenda.

"What did she look like?" he asked but saw her expression and held up his hand. "I know; tall, leggy, skinny, busty bleach blonde with blue eyes," he mimicked her earlier recital.

"She's a natural blonde with green eyes," she stared angrily. "She came home from work one day and found you in her bed with her *friend* Tina," she snapped since he obviously couldn't remember. She spoke loudly and the other diners were staring at them. "You would think you'd remember a woman who fired three bullets at you!" she muttered in disgust.

Nick remembered Brenda very clearly, all of a sudden. "Tina *begged* me to have sex with her! I just couldn't say no!" he defended himself flippantly.

Laura slapped his face hard and ran out of the restaurant. He fell back against the table before turning to run after her but a very large young man, dressed in white, who had come out of the kitchen at the noise, blocked him.

"Don't you dare," he ordered Nick menacingly. The other patrons, who had stood up and clapped when she had slapped him, sat back down and Nick shook off the large man's hands and threw money on the table. He left the restaurant with her hand print burning his face.

*   *   *   *

Bo and Alex were still on the deck when Nick marched up the ramp to the Baby. He stalked up to Alex reclining on the chaise lounge reading and ripped the book out of his hands, throwing it on the deck before grabbing Alex's shirt with both hands and lifting him partially out of the chair.

"I want her name and phone number and I want it now!" he bellowed ferociously.

Alex merely looked over to the side of the boat. Nick released Alex, hanging his head. He went to the rail and jumped over as a stunned Alex and Bo watched. Bo ran to the rail to see Nick swimming around the back of the boat towards the ladder. A dripping Nick marched up the ramp once again to stand in front of Alex with his hand out. Bo looked away with her lips tightly clenched.

Alex grinned wickedly at Nick, "It's on your bureau."

Nick jerked his fist back with a grimace. Alex flinched, not sure Nick wasn't going to deck him. He could still see the outline of a hand print on his cheek but Nick just walked into the cabin.

The leap into the water had helped. He had been so furious driving home he wanted to kill someone. The shock of the cold water after the twenty foot fall brought him back to reality. The cold water made his face hurt less. He looked at the name on the paper on his bureau; Laura Nelson, her phone number was printed plainly under her name followed by her cell phone number. He crumpled it up, throwing it across the room and got his third shower, changing yet again. He went up on deck, feeling the need to get away and decided to take a bike ride.

As he came out the main cabin door, he saw the moose from the restaurant coming up the ramp.

John was on the deck and greeted him cheerfully, "Hi, can I help—"

"What the hell do you think you're doing here? Get off my boat!" Nick angrily challenged the bigger man.

John turned to Nick in consternation as Bo grabbed Nick's arm.

"Nick!" she hissed in warning even as Nick shook her off.

The man ignored everyone, heading straight for Nick; grabbing the front of his shirt and pushing him back against the cabin wall. The newcomer was about six feet six and well-muscled.

"I want you to stay away from my sister," he ordered Nick menacingly.

Nick struggled to get free, "Who the hell is your sister?"

The man pulled him away from the wall only to push him back against it hard. They all heard Nick's head hit the wall.

"Laura Nelson," the man replied through gritted teeth. John came up beside the man and put a hand on his arm.

"I've never touched your damn sister, you big lummox!" Nick's shouted, pushing uselessly against the younger man.

"You made her cry," the man said quietly. "Stay away from her," he warned, letting go of Nick and turned to leave.

John stepped in and grabbed Nick as he was about to jump on the man. John kept Nick pushed against the wall until the man was almost out of the marina gates.

"What the hell happened now?" John demanded angrily, releasing Nick.

Nick shoved him away. "Go to hell, all of you!" he shouted, leaving the boat. They watched him get on the motorcycle and drive away.

FOUR

John was sound asleep when something woke him. He listened carefully, not sure what woke him. He heard only the usual sounds of the boat as he rolled onto his back and noticed a shadow in his room darker than the darkness. He quickly hit the light switch.

"Damn, Nick," he muttered grumpily, seeing him on the couch. "What the hell are you doing?" he asked when Nick remained silent.

"Do you remember Brenda Mills?"

"How the hell could I forget her?" John retorted immediately.

"I did," Nick admitted wearily.

"You forgot a woman who took three shots at you?" John demanded incredulously.

"She called me a pig," Nick said in the same monotone.

"Brenda?" John asked slightly confused.

"Laura."

"That's the new one, right?" John tried desperately to understand this confusing conversation at two in the morning.

Nick gave a short humorless laugh, "Laura Nelson, friend of Brenda Mills, sister to the big moose. She hates my guts." Nick hung his head morosely.

"Why do you care so much?"

"God only knows," he replied throwing himself backwards on the couch. He told John the strange saga of his unplanned meetings with Laura Nelson.

"If you ask me, you should avoid her like the plague."

Nick laughed, "I tried that; it didn't work. I tried to be friends with her; that was a big flop." He sat up running both hands through his hair, "She's driving me crazy."

"Just find another girl!" John urged. "You haven't been out with anyone since—" he hesitated.

"I can't!" Nick cried helplessly. "Ever since I saw that man, all I can think about is how much I'm like him and I hate it!"

"Nick, you're nothing like that man!" John replied truly shocked. "How can you say that?" He sat up looking at his friend, "You look like him, true. You have a way with women like him, true. But that's all." John swung his legs from under the sheet, sitting on the edge of the bed, "You haven't left a trail of fatherless children behind you! You've never had sex with a woman without wearing protection. I know! I've seen you turn down the most beautiful woman because you didn't have a condom with you." John said sincerely, "You're not involved in drug running, for God's sake."

"She's right; I am a pig!" Nick shook his head sadly. "The incident with Brenda was the lowest point of my life; I was really disappointed in myself. I promised myself I wouldn't sink that low again."

"And you haven't," John couldn't remain silent, remembering how upset Nick had been with himself; he had refused to press charges against Brenda.

"What's the longest relationship you've had?" Nick asked suddenly.

"I don't know, maybe five months," John replied irritably. "Then they start talking about getting married." He looked at Nick, "You?"

"Three months," he sighed. "Then the same thing happens; 'When are we getting married?' all the time." he glanced warily at John, "Maybe something is wrong with us?"

"And maybe we just like being bachelors," John retorted sharply.

"Do I?" Nick paused, "I wonder."

"Nick, you have to stop beating yourself up about this! You're a great guy; she would be lucky to get you," John said honestly. "I don't get what you see in her, after all, she's not even your type."

Nick groaned, burying his face in the couch pillow, "Don't you start." he muttered. "I don't want to have a type," he complained. "I don't see anything in her; she just bugs me, maybe it's because she isn't interested in me." He moaned again, "Maybe it's just because I keep running into her." He was reluctant to tell John that Laura haunted his dreams every night.

John was puzzled by something, "This woman slaps you, humiliating you in public and you rush back here and attack Alex for her name and number. You even jumped in the bay for it! Why in God's name would you want it?" he felt compelled to ask.

"I guess because I'm crazy as a loon," Nick brushed it off. "Listen, sorry, I woke you up. Thanks for listening," he made a quick exit.

Nick couldn't bring himself to talk about it with anyone. He didn't want to tell John he went into his room and crumpled up the paper and threw it from him so he wouldn't call Laura and beg her to forgive him. He couldn't tell John he still couldn't bring himself to throw her number away.

John wasn't fooled; he knew Nick was crazy about this woman. If someone had told him a year ago that Nick would act this way over a woman, John would have laughed in their face.

*   *   *   *

Nick lay in bed fully awake; he'd been awake, arguing with himself for hours. He looked at the clock, it was seven am and emotion defeated common sense.

"Damn!" he muttered, leaping out of bed, searching the room for the crumpled paper. He dialed her home phone pacing nervously, waiting for her to answer.

"Hello?" her voice answered, disappointing Nick because she didn't sound sleepy.

He had hoped he could wake her up and catch her a little off guard, "Hi, Laura. How are you?" He said in a normal tone of voice.

"Who is this?" she asked in a brisk business-like voice.

"Nick," he said calmly as if he called her every day and his heart wasn't pounding.

"Nick who?" she asked curiously; there was a slight pause. "Nick Duffy?" her whole tone of voice changed, she said his name as if it was a challenge. "You mean you actually know my name?" she said spitefully.

"I just wanted to thank you for sending your brother over to beat me up," Nick replied in a falsely sweet voice; he was surprised to hear her sharp intake of breath.

"Oh, no!"

Nick was shocked that she actually sounded horrified.

"Are you alright? Was it Eddie or George?" she questioned unhappily.

"I thought you had two sisters," Nick demanded accusingly.

"I do. I also have six brothers!" She replied making him grimace. "Who was it?" she begged.

"He didn't tell me his name! He's a big moose about six foot six."

"They're all at least six feet six inches tall," she informed him making him roll his eyes in horror.

"It was the guy from the restaurant," Nick suddenly remembered she had run out before the man had come over. He heard her gasp again.

"Danny!" she moaned. "I forgot he worked there!" Another slight pause, "Did he hurt you?"

"Not as much as you did," Nick replied honestly.

"I'm sorry, Nick. He won't bother you again," she promised brusquely and hung up as Nick threw himself on the bed smiling; that had gone better than he had hoped.

For a woman who had been furious with him yesterday, she sounded very concerned. He couldn't stop smiling as he pondered his next move carefully.

John, Alex and Bo were perplexed; Nick had been in a good mood all day. They worried about him; one day he was happy, the next distraught. They'd been discussing him; trying to find a way to help him. They knew he'd been dealing with feelings brought up by meeting his father. They weren't sure if that issue was affecting Nick's interest in this woman. Nick had always been intensely private about his personal life and although he had never been easy-going he was as prickly as a pear lately. His usually short temper was noticeably shorter and they didn't want to upset him anymore than he already was. Alex wanted to confront this woman but Bo and John negated that idea.

"But why?" Alex protested plaintively when they once again vetoed his proposal.

"Because Nick would kill you," Bo replied sharply. *Not to mention the six brothers*, she thought ruefully. Bo hadn't mentioned to any of the three men that she knew Laura slightly from the library.

*   *   *   *

The next morning, Alex ran into the cabin, yelling their names while they were still in bed.

"Get up, get up! You have to help me find Samson!" He yelled, jumping on the bed to wake up John.

"So help me, Alex, I'm gonna kill you if you don't knock it off," John growled in a surly voice, trying to shove Alex off the bed. Alex leaped off his bed to go wake Nick.

"Nick, Samson's run away! Get up, help us look for him!" He shook Nick by the shoulder. He didn't dare do more as Nick growled and shoved him backwards. Alex ran back to John who was buried once more under the covers.

"John, get up! The dog is missing!" Alex shouted.

"Good!" John hollered. "He's a pain in my ass!" He tried to kick Alex who jumped back in time, "And so are you!"

"Melanie is coming back today. What are you going to tell her?" Alex asked snidely. John responded with a string of curses, throwing off the covers as Alex left laughing.

Forty minutes later, the three men were dressed and fed and unwillingly going to search for Samson. The dog had been spending the nights with Alex and Bo because they had a fenced yard. They were walking down the ramp when Nick saw Laura's white car pull into the marina parking lot.

"Sorry, guys, I can't help you!" he shouted; eagerly running up the ramp as Alex and John rolled their eyes in disgust, following him slowly. Laura got out of her car and opened the back door; Samson jumped out with his tail wagging furiously. He stayed by Laura's side as she turned to see Nick walking towards her. He smiled but she couldn't look at him.

"Lose someone, did you?" she kept her tone light. "He was waiting beside my car in the parking garage," she explained, bending down to rub his head.

Nick reached her side, greeting Samson effusively; *good dog*, he praised him silently. He noticed Laura stood stiffly and wouldn't meet his eye.

Bo came running from the other side of the street. She was coming to help them look when she saw Samson get out of the car. She had his leash in her hand and put it on him, before she noticed the driver was Laura.

"Hi, Bo," Laura greeted her in surprise, glancing at the two men running to meet them.

"Hi, Laura," Bo greeted her warmly, avoiding the maniacal look in Nick's eye.

"Is this *your* Alex?" Laura asked Bo quizzically.

Bo linked her arm in Alex's, "Yes, he is." She smiled fondly at her husband.

Nick wished them all away in his mind while he stood in front of Laura's door. At the moment, he was behind Laura and motioned with his head at Bo. Bo wickedly ignored his obvious command to leave. "Would you like to come onboard and have some coffee?" she asked Laura sweetly making Nick look daggers at her.

Laura appeared flustered, "No thank-you, Bo! I have to go!" she hurriedly turned, bumping into Nick. "Oh, sorry," she stepped back, unable to escape because he was in her way.

"Where are you going?" he asked casually.

Laura said the first thing that came into her head, "The post office."

Nick was thrilled; this was the first time he'd seen Laura flustered and not in command of the situation. "I was just on my way there; can you give me a lift?"

Laura hesitated, not knowing what to say.

"Why don't you take the truck, Nick?" John asked, oh, so casually. Nick walked past him around the front of the car to get in the passenger side and saw Laura's face brighten.

"Alex needs it to drive you to the hospital," Nick looked him in the eye as he got in Laura's car. He heard John chuckle as Laura got slowly in the car.

She drove rapidly and silently to the post office, parked right in front and looked at Nick, "Here you go." As usual, Nick couldn't think of anything to say; he had gambled and lost. He turned to get out but Laura put her hand on his arm, "Wait." He turned curiously to see her looking straight ahead.

"I want to apologize for yesterday."

"You mean your brother?" he asked hesitantly.

"No, I mean me." she said surprised and looked over, "It wasn't fair to blame you."

Nick had no idea what she was talking about and he wondered silently why this happened so frequently to him with this particular woman.

"I don't understand," he said quietly, having decided in one of his many long hours of sleeplessness that honesty was the only way to deal with Laura. She looked at him quickly and then away.

"Brenda was my friend; she wasn't very bright but she was very nice. After you broke her heart, she moved back home but we kept in touch," Laura paused for several minutes. She seemed to be trying not to cry. Nick was very curious and immediately sympathetic and put his hand over hers but she snatched it away. "Her mother called me last week and told me Brenda killed herself."

Nick was shocked, "My God! Why?" he asked as a chill ran down his spine.

"In her note she said she didn't want to live without you anymore."

"Oh, God!" Nick threw his head back and practically yelled it. He turned swiftly to the door, yanked it open and rushed out of the car. He slammed the door and walked swiftly down the street.

Laura scrambled after him, "Nick!" She called, running to grab his arm, pulling him to a stop, "It wasn't your fault! I told you, I was wrong to blame you."

Nick can hardly bear to listen. He pulled his arm away and took a deep breath but he couldn't look at Laura.

"Don't get me wrong, you were a pig!" she said with a little grimace. "But we are all responsible for our own actions. Brenda killed herself because of her own problems, not yours."

Nick appreciated Laura talking to him like this, but he was terribly upset by the news and felt he just had to get away. "I've got to go," he turned and walked rapidly away; breaking into a run.

Laura didn't know what to do; staring after him until he was out of sight before walking slowly to her car.

Nick ran all the way to the Baby only stopping at the top of the marina parking lot. He bent over with his hands on his knees, breathing hard. He stood up and shook his legs and swung his arms to loosen them up before he walked down the ramp. John was on the cabin roof checking the ropes on the main sail and saw him running down the road. John wasn't surprised to see Nick walking down the ramp with his head down, the all too familiar droop in his shoulders.

Alex and Bo were in town and Samson had gone home with Melanie so John had Nick to himself. He wasn't going to let this opportunity pass by; he climbed down the ladder and met Nick as he boarded.

"I knew it!" he said belligerently, standing in front of Nick. "Every time you're near this woman, you come back looking like you just lost your best friend." Nick glanced at him sharply and tried to brush past but John shoved him back. "What is this hold she has over you?" he demanded nastily.

"Get away from me!" Nick ordered harshly, trying to go around him.

"No! I'm sick of you moping over 'Daddy' and now over this woman!" John refused angrily.

Nick threw a punch to his face but John blocked it, throwing one of his own. They punched one another for several minutes before knocking each other down and continued wrestling.

"Oh, no! Not again!" Alex complained as he and Bo boarded the Baby; he grabbed Bo's arm as she started to run to the two men. "Do not go near them!" he ordered, reaching into the cabin and bringing out the fire extinguisher. He sprayed the two men until they broke apart and rolled to their feet, spitting out foam.

"Damn you, Alex!" they both hollered, dripping foam.

"What happened?" Bo asked Nick in concern.

Nick gave her an angry look before sighing deeply, "Brenda killed herself last week! She didn't want to live without me," he said dejectedly as John's mouth dropped open.

"Oh, please!" Bo retorted scornfully. The three men looked at her considerably startled and she returned the stare. "If Alex did to me what you did to her, I'd shoot him too but I wouldn't miss! There's no way I'd kill myself over a man like that," she explained pointedly.

Nick was shocked Bo knew about the Brenda incident and looked accusingly at John and Alex who both guiltily looked away.

"The girl was obviously not wrapped too tight to begin with. I mean, look at Laura. She's crazy about you, but she knows your history and isn't about to get mixed up with you!" Bo continued making Alex nervous as Nick stared murderously. "She's only interested in a serious relationship but she knows she'll never get that with you. Brenda couldn't possibly have thought you would settle down with her unless she had a screw loose to begin with."

Nick was so flabbergasted; he didn't even know where to begin to answer Bo. He opened and closed his mouth several times without saying anything.

"What the hell do you mean, she's crazy about him? She won't give him the time of day!" John objected angrily.

Nick stared at Bo and suddenly grinned. "She is?" he asked; afraid to believe it.

Bo smiled and nodded, "She's scared to death." Bo suddenly realized Nick was too. "But I'd be careful if I were you," she warned a grinning Nick, confusing him. "If you break her heart, she won't miss," she grinned. "And the six large brothers will beat you to a bloody pulp, *many times*."

Nick looked at John who was still angry and slapped him on the back. "Thanks buddy!" he grinned before running into the cabin. John looked at the other two grinning.

"You're all nuts," he said gloomily and went to shower and change, shaking his head.

FIVE

John gave Nick an odd look as he came upstairs into the main cabin dressed in a black suit and a black silk shirt with his hair neatly combed.

"Where are you going all dressed up at four in the afternoon?" John asked curiously.

"I'm going to pick up our check from Joe Lange."

"You have to dress up for that?" John demanded suspiciously.

"He invited us to come to that high society cocktail party his wife is throwing, remember?" Nick reminded, using the mirror over the breakfast counter to tie his tie.

"And you're going?" John demanded incredulously, knowing how much Nick hated getting dressed up; even now he took the tie off and threw it on the counter.

"The hell with it," he said cheerfully. "*Laura* likes to dress up," he informed John with a smile.

John rolled his eyes, *I should have known*, he thought. Nick was thrilled to death; he had called Laura last night several hours after the fight with John had revealed Bo's opinion that Laura was crazy about him. He had talked her into going to this cocktail party.

"Maybe I'll come with you," John said slowly, considering it.

"Only if you want me to break your legs," Nick threatened with a smile as he left.

John threw himself back on the couch, "I can't wait to see what happens today," he muttered under his breath.

Nick picked Laura up at her apartment. He knocked on the door which she opened immediately wearing a short, strapless electric blue dress. Her shining hair waved softly around her face and she wore make up for the first time since they met.

"Wow! You look beautiful," he murmured sincerely as she blushed; flashing that smile he loved. Nick had never been out with a woman who blushed at a compliment.

"You look very GQ® yourself," she complimented, pulling the door shut and locking it. Nick wasn't used to a woman being ready on time and wondered if he was ever going to see the inside of her apartment. She had a matching scarf hanging over her arm and a small beaded purse. The top of her head reached his shoulder with the black strappy high heels.

"You should be getting into a limo looking like that," he complimented her as he helped her up into the truck; she turned anxiously.

"Do you think I'm over-dressed?" she asked quickly.

"No, you look lovely." He assured her, unable to take his eyes off her.

The drive to the house in the hills was uneventful. It was a lovely house tucked into the hillside in one of the canyons with the city and the ocean spread below them. The valet parked the truck.

"Wow. This is really posh," Laura whispered nervously, putting her hand in his. Nick congratulated himself on one of his best brainstorms as they entered the house which was crowded with guests but their host stood by the door as they entered.

"Nick!" Joe Lange came forward greeting Nick effusively. "I'm so glad you've come," he shook his hand, pulling him forward. "Let's conduct business first then you can party!" he laughed heartily and Nick turned to Laura, taking her hand again. Lange chuckled, "My wife will look after the little lady till you get back." he said quickly and didn't give Nick a chance to speak or escape as he drew him from the room, looking at Laura helplessly until she was lost from sight.

Laura walked farther into the room noticing how beautifully the house was decorated. She rounded a corner and stared slightly startled at a man smoking a huge hookah. He saw her gaping and offered her the pipe; she smiled slightly, shaking her head. Laura noticed most of the people were couples standing in groups and she felt very out of place until she saw a teenage girl sitting on the couch by herself and decided to join her. As she got closer, Laura noticed the couple on the other end of the couch snorting a white powder and she stopped, deeply shocked. A lovely middle aged woman came up to her smiling broadly.

"Hello dear! Here have some!" she chirped, offering a gallon size freezer bag full of every color pill to Laura. "Color your world!" the woman said gleefully. When Laura refused with a shake of her head, the woman made a face, "You're not a *square*, are you?" she asked brightly.

"Honey, I'm so square, I'm a cube!" Laura replied cheerfully. "You can color me gone," she turned abruptly. The young girl on the couch jumped up, grabbing Laura's arm, looking frightened to death.

"I'm with you," she walked out the door with Laura. Laura fumed as she walked down the path to the sidewalk. She took out her phone, looking at it angrily; the canyon blocked reception. She turned to her new friend.

"Does your phone have any service?"

The girl shook her head mutely, "I was so scared!" She sounded as if she might cry. "I don't know how I'm going to get home," she wailed still clinging to Laura's arm as Laura patted her hand.

"I can't believe I put on high heels for this!" Laura complained angrily; privately wondering how far they'd have to walk to get a taxi. She was furious with Nick and was wondering what the hell kind of business they did for this man when she heard someone running after them. *Yeah, you can run; you're not wearing four inch heels*, she thought angrily.

"Laura, wait!" he called breathlessly but she kept walking. He caught up with them, running in front and putting both hands out, blocking their path when they were about ten houses away. Nick panted lightly, staring curiously at the teenage girl who stared fearfully at him.

"Who's your friend?" he asked Laura curiously.

"She's just a new passenger on the square train," she muttered repressively without looking at him.

"What's your name, honey?" Nick asked gently.

"Amy!" she started to cry. "I want to go home," she sobbed. "My father's going to kill me!" she wailed.

"Only if you tell him," Laura replied cheerfully, making Nick look at her quickly.

"Laura, I swear to you, I didn't know it would be a drug party!" Nick begged her to believe him. "We did a job for him," he saw her frown, "Nothing illegal!" he snapped. "He invited us to pick up the check and stay for the party." He ruefully shook his head, "I didn't notice everyone was doing drugs until I came out of the office." He put his arm around her and turned her around but Laura refused to walk. "When I was looking for you; little Mary Sunshine told me to *'color you gone'*," he said in a disgusted voice with a deep sigh as Laura still refused to budge. "Why won't you believe me?" he asked in frustration.

"I believe you," she said quietly and he again tried to lead her back but she stood firm.

"Then come back to the truck," he insisted irritably. She picked up a small foot and held it out for him to see.

"You go get the truck and bring it here," she insisted grimly, winking at Amy, who gave a watery giggle. Nick ran back to get the truck not quite trusting her not to disappear again.

Nick returned home at two am; entering the main cabin to see John asleep on the couch with the TV still on. John sat up when Nick turned off the TV and was astonished to see him smiling.

"You're not muddy." He observed as Nick grinned. "You're happy!" John smiled suddenly. "Wow, a real date and nothing happened?"

Nick grinned even more broadly, "We saved a teenage girl from the drug underworld, went to dinner, went dancing and had a great time." Nick replied clearly elated.

"Yeah but is she any good in bed?" John asked crudely.

Nick gave him a hard shove, "Don't be a pig!" he admonished sharply but even John's sarcasm couldn't dim his happiness. He was smiling as he went downstairs with John closely following.

"Are you telling me you didn't have sex with her?" John demanded point blank, grabbing his arm.

Nick smiled, "I didn't even kiss her goodnight." He said cheerfully, shutting the door on John's astonished face.

"Then what the hell are you smiling about?" John asked the closed door before going to his own room. He was taking off his shirt off when he stopped suddenly, "The drug underworld?" he asked aloud, shaking his head.

*   *   *   *

Two days after the big date, Alex poked his head in Nick's room to see him lying on his back with his hands behind his head, staring grimly at the ceiling.

"What's wrong?"

Nick looked over and then away, "She won't return my calls." He muttered morosely and sat up on the edge of the bed, "We had a great time, Alex!" He insisted, looking at him, "I've left messages. I went over there; her car was there but she wouldn't answer the door." Alex didn't tell him that Bo had called Laura and she hadn't answered that call or called her back. "She had a great time, Alex. I know she did!"

"Well, if it's meant to be, it'll happen, Nick." Alex encouraged hopefully.

"Don't start with the fate stuff again," Nick begged and stood up, punching the wall. "I'm going for a drive," he ran out of the room, leaving Alex wishing there was something he could do.

Nick ran up the steps, colliding with John coming down; John held onto him to steady them both.

"What's up?"

Nick tried to twist away, "Go ahead say it."

"Say what?" John asked mystified.

"*I told you so*! You know you want to!" Nick challenged harshly.

"I'd like to go over there and slap her a couple times," John replied quietly, letting go.

Nick put a hand on John's shoulder, "Thanks, buddy." He said in a husky voice and turned away, "I gotta go for a ride. If Fate is kind, maybe I'll fall off a cliff!"

Fate had other ideas. Nick rode back on the old highway that ran beside the sea, passing through a multitude of little towns. He entered Bridgeton from the north; it wasn't the best part of town but it was pretty deserted at this hour. He was glad he'd be home in a few minutes, knowing it would be dark soon when he saw a car pulled to the side of the street with the trunk open and a jack under the rear end. A woman jumped up and down on a cross bar lug wrench with her hands leaning on the car. Nick grinned as he pulled up behind her; Fate was being kind to Nick Duffy today, he thought.

"Need some help?" he walked up behind Laura.

Laura whirled around and almost fell as she knocked the lug wrench off the tire. She rolled her eyes, "Do you have me Lojacked®?" she asked irritably.

Nick smiled; in no hurry to fix the tire now that she was a captive audience.

"Where are all the brothers?" he asked casually.

"Damn phone is dead!" she bent to pick up the lug wrench. Nick was quicker and got it first and stood toying with it, staring at her bemused. He was always amazed how just being near her affected him; he hadn't felt like this since he had a crush on his teacher way back in middle school. Laura looked up impatiently, "Are you going to help me or not?" she demanded, bringing him back to the present.

He smiled, "Why won't you take my calls?" he asked quietly as he squatted and put the lug wrench on the nut then stopped to look up at her. She leaned against the car staring off into the distance and he couldn't read her expression.

"Why didn't you kiss me?" she asked very quietly, not daring to look at him.

"You didn't want me to!" he protested, straightening up.

"What?" She looked shocked and nervously stepped back as he stepped towards her.

"You didn't give me any of the signals." He said softly as she gazed at him and laughed nervously, not quite understanding. "Have you ever tried to kiss a girl who didn't want you to?" he questioned, taking another step towards her.

She took another step back, making a face and looked away, "To tell you the truth, I've never really wanted to kiss a g—"

Her words were lost as Nick grabbed her and kissed her ardently. He released her saying, "Well, that was easier than I thought it would be," and smiled as she stood there blushing. "I wish you wouldn't do that," he folded her into his arms, kissing her again. He found a little slice of heaven and continued kissing her slowly and deeply. She kissed him, enjoying it very much but suddenly felt frightened and pulled away.

"Oh, my God! What am I doing?" she cried, trying to push him away.

"I like it; keep doing it," he whispered in her ear, keeping his arms around her as he bent his head to kiss her neck.

"Oh, it's just not fair!" she moaned cryptically, still trying to get out of the circle of his arms. "Just leave the damn car, I'll walk home!" she cried breathlessly, struggling to get free.

He let her slide an arm's length away but still held her wrists, grinning at her protests. He was just about to pull her back into his embrace when he was spun around to see a solid green wall in front of him before he was sucker punched; he went down hard, lying in the street behind Laura's car. When he could focus his eyes, he saw a man towering above him.

"George!" Laura yelled in protest, looking up at her brother aghast. "Nick!" she cried, quickly kneeling in the street next to Nick who was gratified to see tears. "Nick!" she cried again, putting her head down. Nick thought she was going to kiss him but she laid her head on his chest; putting her arms around him, hugging him tightly, "Are you alright?" Nick saw the giant move away, shaking his head in disgust as he began to change the tire. Nick raised his arm to put it across Laura.

"I'm alright," he murmured weakly, trying to sit up. Laura helped him, staring sadly into his face.

"Oh, your beautiful face," she moaned, touching his cheek below his injured eye lightly and bent forward to kiss him gently. He put both arms around her, kissing her passionately; laying back down on the street, pulling her with him and kissing her until the world was spinning. He didn't know if it was concussion or lack of oxygen because she was lying across him or just sheer pleasure and he didn't care. George bodily picked up Laura, pulling her off Nick and swinging her to his left while he kept hold of her upper arm.

"Leave the injured darling alone, *Sheila*," he ordered gruffly. "Stay away from her," he threatened Nick before he pulled Laura to her car, "Go home."

She angrily pulled her arm away as Nick got slowly to his feet. George was taller than Danny and had blond hair worn in a military crew cut like John's. He had bright blue eyes but Nick preferred Laura's deep blue eyes. Laura argued furiously with George.

"Go away! I'm twenty-eight years old. I'm not a child! I can do as I please!" she spit out the words, turning away from him.

"Why can't you just marry an accountant or doctor like your sisters?" George demanded irritably. "What the hell do you see in this pretty boy?"

Laura ignored him, running back to Nick. "Can you ride?" she asked in concern. Nick nodded carefully, knowing it was only a fifteen minute drive back to the Marina. "I'll follow you."

Nick watched warily as George angrily got in his truck parked across the street and drove off. Laura helped Nick get on his bike and followed him back to the marina. Nick rode slowly; he had one hell of a headache and he couldn't see out of his right eye.

Laura helped him off the bike, gasping as he took off his helmet and she saw how much his eye had swelled.

"Oh, Nick!" she cried, kissing him gently.

Nick had to restrain himself this time, knowing he had to lie down quickly and could barely walk. Laura put his arm around her shoulders and her arm around his waist. Alex came running off the Baby as they came down the marina ramp and got on Nick's other side. Bo was on the deck watching and called down to John. He came out on deck as they walked up the ramp and gave Laura a black look as he took over her spot. Nick wanted to protest but he knew he needed their help to get downstairs.

"What the hell have you done to him now?" John demanded accusingly.

"George hit him!" She wrung her hands but John didn't look any less confused. "My brother drove by and he saw us— never mind, it doesn't matter. He sucker punched him."

Nick was glad to hear her say it; it was never good to be decked in front of your lady love. They rolled him onto his bed. Laura took off his shoes and Bo brought him a cold, raw steak for his eye. He let Laura put it on his eye and then looked at them standing beside the bed woefully staring down at him.

"Go away." he ordered irritably. They all turned to leave and he reached out to take Laura's hand. "Not you!" he muttered rolling his eyes. *That was a mistake,* he thought as pain shot through his head and Laura sat on the bed beside him.

"Sheila?" he asked quietly, wanting to know why George called her by a different name.

"It's an Australian word for girl. My father is Australian."

"*Six* brothers?" he muttered unhappily. She shrugged her shoulders helplessly. "Are they *all* going to beat me up?" he teased.

"Probably," she replied grinning cheerfully.

He grinned and she sadly looked down at his hand as she held it in her lap in both of hers.

"I love you."

She looked at him in amazement before laying her head on his chest and putting her arms around him. "God, help me, I love you too," she whispered.

"Kiss me!" he begged.

She giggled, "I can't; you have meat on your face."

He could feel her laughing as he pulled it off.

She gave a small shriek, "Don't do that!" she gently put it back. "You have to get that swelling down."

"Kiss me," he demanded softly.

She turned her head to kiss him gently on the lips. He flipped the steak off, pulling her against him, kissing her fiercely. He wanted to kiss her forever but somewhere in the middle of the kiss oblivion took him. Laura put the steak back on his eye and sat gazing at him tenderly for several minutes. She finally had to admit to herself that she loved him madly. When he had fallen to the ground after George hit him, she had felt her heart stop beating. She leaned forward to kiss him gently.

"Please don't break my heart!" she whispered fearfully in his ear.

"Never!" he said very clearly, making her look at him startled. He was unconscious and she put her hand over his heart, smiling as tears gathered in her eyes.

*   *   *   *

Nick and Laura sat on her couch kissing slowly; his black eye almost healed. Laura stood up, taking him by the hand and he followed her into her bedroom as his heart started pounding. Laura sat on the edge of the bed, reaching up to pull his head down to her and kissing him. He put his knee on the bed beside her, leaning her back on the bed still kissing. He stretched out next to her pulling her higher and rolled her on top of him. She ran her fingers through his hair as she kissed him; loving the feel of his thick wavy hair. Nick pulled her shirt out of her skirt in the back and ran his hands up and down her spine. He caressed her buttocks; it was something he'd wanted to do ever since the day on the beach. He ran his hand up under her skirt, surprised to find that it had attached shorts underneath that interrupted his caress. He could feel Laura laugh lightly and he rolled them over so he leaned over her, kissing her while his hands explored under her shirt.

"Nick," she murmured, stroking his back under his shirt as he concentrated on unbuttoning her shirt.

"Yes?" he responded absently.

Laura knew the shirt buttons were sewn closed and she interrupted his hands to raise herself up slightly to pull the shirt off over her head. She heard Nick's quick intake of breath as she lay back down; his breath taken away by his first glimpse of her breasts cupped in a lovely lacy décolleté bra. He stared mesmerized.

"There's something I want to tell you," she said trying to get his attention.

"What is it, Love?" he whispered in her ear as he kissed it and continued kissing her neck down to her breasts.

"I'm a virgin," she said softly.

Nick lifted his head abruptly, "Oh my God!" He cried out suddenly, kneeling on the bed staring down at her. He backed off the bed, staring as if she had told him she was a man. He paced at the end of the bed, "Oh my God!" he said again; wringing her shirt in his hands as he paced.

"Nick—" Laura called gently, sitting up, reaching her hand out to him.

Nick took one look at her sitting there so invitingly and groaned loudly. "Oh my God," he muttered again as if in pain and ran from the room. She heard the apartment door open and slam shut.

"Well, that went well," she said sarcastically and sighed deeply. She put on another shirt since Nick had left still frenziedly clutching the one she had been wearing.

*   *   *   *

It was dark outside when Laura answered a knock on the door to find Nick standing there. He silently handed her the shirt and she took it without saying anything.

"Can I come in?"

Laura moved aside, gesturing him in, closed the door and followed him into the living room. She sat on the couch watching him expectantly, waiting for him to say something.

"There's something I want you to understand," he began quietly. "I'm not a wolf preying on helpless little sheep, you know," he began anxiously watching her. He sat on the couch turning to face her, "I've never had sex with a virgin," he begged her to understand. "I don't know what to do."

"I don't see why it should be any different than sex with the thousands of other women," she replied calmly.

He wasn't sure how she felt but she didn't sound angry. "It's very different! Everything about my relationship with you is different. I've never had to work so hard to— woo a woman," he used an old fashioned term. "All the women I've dated have thrown themselves in my arms the minute I look at them. They hunted *me* down." He smiled ruefully, "Don't get me wrong, I've enjoyed every minute of the chase with you. But everything about you is a new experience for me." He looked at her tenderly, "Before I met you, I thought of them as women. But since I've fallen in love with you, I think of them in my own mind as vultures. They planned every move. They want you to move in with them but the longer you're with them, the more strings they attach to sex." He ran his hands through his hair in frustration. "Do you know how many women have begged me to marry them?" he stood up pacing across the room. "When I had sex with them, they told me what they wanted. Nick move a little to the left, Nick work a little harder, Nick—" he stopped imitating them and turned abruptly. "I'm scared to death of doing the wrong thing."

Laura smiled as she stood up and walked to him. She reached up, putting her arms around his neck, pulling his head down to kiss him.

"Well, now you get to do what comes naturally. If I don't like something you're doing, I'll tell you," she whispered against his ear.

He kissed her feverishly and bent to pick her up in his arms; carrying her into the bedroom. "It hasn't been thousands," he denied firmly as she laughed and looked deep into his beautiful dark brown eyes.

Nick lay on his back with Laura against him; her head on his chest. Nick was truly amazed; he didn't know sex could be this good. He had enjoyed himself more than he had for a long time and silently hoped it has been that good for Laura. She seemed happy but he was a little afraid to break the spell. Laura broke it for him.

"Nick," she whispered.

"Hmm?" he murmured cautiously.

"Do it again."

He laughed happily; his question answered, "I don't think I can," he replied honestly. Laura slowly slid her hand down the length of his torso making him groan deeply. "Maybe I can!" he said hoarsely as she laughed softly and encouraged him some more.

SIX

Nick sat on the deck of the Baby using binoculars to stare at the house across the street on the hill. He saw the front door open as Bo left the house. He ran across the parking lot to the street. When he saw her car drive away, he ran up to the house.

Alex came out of the bathroom with rumpled hair, wearing pajama bottoms and yawning widely. He opened his eyes and jumped back when he saw Nick standing directly in front of him.

"Geez, Nick!" Alex yelled, falling back against the wall. "What the hell are you doing?" he groused as Nick took his arm trying to hustle him into the bedroom but Alex resisted him.

"I wanted to talk to you alone," Nick said mysteriously, pushing him toward the bedroom.

"You know that key is for emergencies only," Alex lectured, pushing him back. "I don't want you two busting in here at the wrong time."

"I waited until Bo left," Nick snapped, getting annoyed.

"Well, is there any reason you couldn't just knock on the door like normal people?" Alex questioned irritably; he could tell by Nick's expression it had never occurred to him and shook his head. Nick was still trying to push him into the bedroom but Alex broke away.

"I want to talk to you," Nick insisted.

"Fine! We have the whole house to ourselves. We can talk in the kitchen so I can have a cup of coffee. I can't really deal with you before my coffee," Alex replied grumpily.

"Were you always this grumpy in the morning?" Nick asked cheerfully, following him into the kitchen. The coffee was already made and Alex poured some for Nick. Alex sipped his hot coffee and looked expectantly at Nick.

"You've been married about three years now, right?" Alex nodded and yawned again. "Is the sex less exciting?" Nick asked unexpectedly.

"Nick!" Alex yelled shocked. "Of course not!" he looked at Nick in disgust. "Oh, my God, you're thinking of breaking up with Laura!" Alex shouted horrified.

"No. No, I'm not!" Nick protested vehemently. "I'm crazy about her."

"Then why are you asking me this?" Alex asked clearly confused. Nick sighed and tried to explain.

"Laura and I have been together for four months now; that's longer than any other woman I've ever known. The sex is still unbelievably good," Nick shrugged apologetically. "I just wondered how long it stays good."

Alex laughed, "Nick, it's the relationship you have with the woman that makes sex interesting. Maybe you got bored so quickly with all your lovelies because you had no relationship other than sex with them."

Nick thought about it, "You may be right about that." Nick mused, "All Laura has to do is give me that look and I'm hers to command."

"The person you should be talking to is my father," Alex startled him.

"Why?" Nick stared, completely clueless.

"He's been married for thirty-five years. When I was over there the other day, I happened to see my mother give him that look. He hustled me out the door in a minute flat," Alex laughed at Nick's pained expression. "Oh, what? Are you planning to stop having sex when you're fifty or sixty?" he asked sarcastically.

"No!" Nick objected loudly. "That's just too much information for me! I'll never be able to look your mother in the eye again!" Nick complained and Alex laughed loudly as Nick beat a swift retreat.

*   *   *   *

Laura had her head on Nick's chest and sighed contentedly.

"I'm so happy," she murmured softly, knowing she had to admit Nick had surpassed all her expectations. He was a wonderful lover as she suspected he would be but he was warm, caring and romantic in ways she never imagined he could be. He was attentive and appreciative of the things she did for him. She sighed softly; sometimes she was still afraid it was all a dream and would come crashing to a halt. Her biggest fear was that he'd get tired of her, she thought as Nick ran his fingers through her hair.

"Hey," he said getting her attention. "What's the matter?" he had felt her tense up. She laughed, rolling on her back.

"Nothing," she watched him get out of bed and go to the bureau. She loved the way he moved. He came back to the bed with his hand behind his back smiling at her. He brought his hand from behind him, showing her an open ring box with a beautiful diamond sparkling in the sunlight.

"Will you marry me?" he asked eagerly.

Laura stared, appalled as a thousand emotions poured over her in a single moment. "I— I can't," she stammered, confused and terribly upset. She couldn't say yes; it upset her terribly but that was the answer in her head and her heart.

It upset Nick even more as he gaped in shock. He simply couldn't believe she said no and a thousand emotions poured over him, none of them good, as he shut the box with a snap. He backed off the bed and shoved the box in his pants pockets and pulled on his pants and shoes. He turned and left the room as Laura rushed to get up, pulling on a robe as she ran after him.

"Nick, please don't leave!" she begged, grabbing his arm. "Let's talk about it."

He shrugged her off and walked out the door. She sobbed as the door closed behind him; the dream had just come crashing down in a way she had never imagined in her wildest fantasies.

Alex and John were at the dining table when Nick walked through the cabin. They stopped their argument to greet him but he walked past them like a man possessed.

"Uh oh!" John looked at Alex. "I recognize that look." He hadn't seen that look on Nick's face for five months, "Trouble in paradise!"

The brothers stared at one another wondering if they should go talk to him or let him cool off for a while. They decided to talk to him and walked into his room, surprised to see him packing.

"Nick, where are you going?" Alex asked cautiously.

"Don't know! I'm going to the airport and get on a plane! I'll call you when I get somewhere," he spoke in a monotone.

"Why are you leaving? What happened?" John demanded.

Nick zipped the case closed before turning to them, "I asked her to marry me." Both their faces registered astonishment. "She said no," he snapped harshly, pushing past them, heading up the stairs with Alex right behind him.

"You asked her to marry you and she said she wanted to break up?" He asked incredulously.

"She just said no," Nick replied ominously as John grabbed Alex's arm but he didn't take the hint.

"Maybe she just needs more time."

"She can have the rest of her life!" Nick retorted angrily. "Drive me to the airport?" he asked looking directly at John.

"Sure," John said quickly, shoving Alex back as he was about to speak again. *Shut up*, John mouthed the words at him as he followed Nick.

*   *   *   *

Nick sat on the beach near the water's edge. It was six am but he'd been there since four, staring mournfully at the waves. It'd been four days of torture since he left; his body ached for her. He didn't know what he was going to do, every fiber of his being told him to run back to her but he couldn't. Her rejection of his marriage proposal had hurt him more than anything in his life.

Someone sat down near him and he didn't have to turn his head to know who it was. The sudden pounding of his heart was enough to tell him but he didn't look at her and his face remained grim.

"What are you doing here?" he asked in a hard voice, hoping she wouldn't know how absolutely astounded he was that she had followed him across the entire country to Cape May, NJ. His heart was doing flip flops and other parts of him were equally excited.

Laura sat about a foot away without looking at him. She too stared out over the water and kept her tone light.

"I got lonely."

Nick gave her a quick glance, "How'd you find me?" He looked at her again when she didn't answer to find her running her hand through the cool dry sand. "Bo," he made a good guess.

She glanced at him with a wry smile, "We girls have to stick together, you know."

He quickly looked away, not knowing what to say; afraid she'd see the pain in his eyes.

Laura looked out to sea again, "Have you ever been in the middle of a black cloud so big, you can't begin to understand it?" she asked softly. "I was shocked by my own reaction. I still don't understand it," she said, her voice cracking slightly. "I just know that I can't get married right now." Tears ran down her face, "I don't even know why."

Nick looked over and saw her tears and something inside him snapped; he pulled her to him roughly, kissing her passionately. He lay back on the sand, pulling her with him. He was breathing hard when he released her mouth as she lay across his chest.

"Do you believe in fate?"

Laura was bemused by his passion and stared down at him for several seconds trying to find words. She nodded slowly, "I do believe in fate. But I'm surprised to hear that you do."

"I'm not sure I ever really believed in God. I certainly never thought about him. I never asked him for any favors," he paused, looking up at the sky as Laura waited for him to continue "Until I ran into my— Martin," Nick still couldn't bear to use the word father in connection with Martin. "I stood in that courtroom and I thought to myself, if there really was a God, Martin Freeman would be dead. The man dropped dead in front of my eyes. It scared the shit out of me!" he murmured with a deep sigh. "When I looked at him, it was like looking in a mirror. I hated what I saw. I didn't want to be anything like him." Laura shook her head with a grimace, she started to speak but Nick cut her off. "I had that same feeling; being stuck inside a big, black cloud. I knew something was wrong but I didn't know what it was. I didn't know what to do. I had the strangest feeling I was waiting for something to happen."

Laura got a strange look on her face, "That's exactly how I feel!" she cried in amazement. "Like I'm waiting for something to happen but I don't know what," she looked down into Nick's eyes as he grinned up at her. "Did something happen?"

His grin got wider, "I ran into you. Again and again and again! No matter how hard I tried to stay away from you; there you were."

Laura laughed lightly, putting her head down on his chest in the now familiar gesture.

"I tried to run as far away from you as I could. And every time I turned around; there you were."

"Fate," Nick kissed her again, amazed that he was suddenly happy again. He tried desperately to think of somewhere he could take her to be alone.

"Nick," she murmured against his mouth.

"Hmm?" he mumbled but didn't stop kissing her.

"I want to meet your mother."

Nick made a sound like someone punched him in the stomach and sat bolt upright. Laura fell back onto the sand. He looked down to see her laughing at him.

"You are a cruel woman," he stood up, reaching for her hand to help her up. He might as well take her home to meet his mother; it would take him awhile to get that image out of his head. They walked up the beach arm in arm to the street.

*   *   *   *

Pat looked up from the couch to see her son returning from the beach, immediately noticing the change in him. He looked a totally different man than the one she had found standing on her porch four days ago. She understood as soon as she saw whose hand he held as a petite brunette followed him nervously through the door. She has lovely blue eyes, Pat thought, liking her instantly.

"You must be Laura!" Pat exclaimed, rushing to give her a big hug.

Laura was a little startled; she had expected Nick's mother to be mad at her. Pat was a lovely woman in her early fifties, taller than Laura, with the same dark wavy hair and deep brown eyes as Nick. Laura nervously looked at Nick, wondering if he had even told his mother what had happened. Pat correctly interpreted her look and took Laura's hand, drawing her to the couch.

"Oh, yes, he told me you turned him down," she said cheerfully, patting Laura's hand. "Don't you worry about it! It was just the shock. It's good for him; ever since he's been fourteen, women have been throwing themselves at him. He's used to women begging *him* to marry them. You just dented his pride a little bit," Pat smiled fondly at her son as he gave her a martyred look.

"Mother," he muttered warningly.

"I'm so glad you came out here so I could meet you," Pat obligingly changed the topic. "Has Nick met your family?"

Laura smiled, "Yes, he's met them all."

"Some of them rather painfully," Nick teased.

"Yes, I understand you have six very large brothers," Pat replied with a twinkle in her eye; obviously, Nick had told her everything.

"They don't like me very much," Nick told his mother cheerfully.

"My mother and sisters like Nick a lot," Laura hastened to explain. "The male members of my family are very overprotective. They don't like other men until after we marry them," she gave a small laugh.

"So, why don't you want to marry my son?"

Laura blushed and stammered. "I— I don't really know— It's a lot of little things.   I'm sorry," she dropped her head in embarrassment.

Pat patted her hand gently, "Oh, I'm not upset, darling." She looked at Nick, "Do you love him?"

Nick's face reddened, "Mother!" he cried out horrified.

Laura picked up her head instantly, "Oh, I do! Really!" she assured his mother.

Pat studied her, "You don't trust him." Laura quickly looked away.   "Well, it's only to be expected," Pat sighed deeply and walked towards an annoyed Nick. She swatted the back of his head. "I always told him, it would come back to bite him in the ass," she said cryptically.

Nick was about to say *mother* again when he realized it was no use. His mother was going to have her say anyway and he grinned at an equally embarrassed Laura.

"I don't know if it's that really," Laura replied sincerely. "When we're out, he hardly even looks at other women anymore."

"How'd you accomplish that?" Pat asked, impressed.

Laura grinned, "I hit him upside the head every time he did it."

Nick grimaced, knowing she wasn't kidding but he didn't tell either one it was actually the fact that every time his eyes strayed to follow another woman, he would turn back to find Laura flirting with a handsome man nearby who returned her interest.

"It's his job," Pat murmured with a knowing nod.

"It's a lot of things. I don't like him being an investigator and getting beat up all the time," Laura said as they both ignored Nick's protest. "I don't want him to move in with me, I don't want to live on the boat," Laura sighed. "We have a lot to talk about and I just never thought about marrying him before."

"You *never* thought of marrying me?" Nick cried, astounded.

"Yes, you do," Pat agreed, ignoring Nick's interruption. "What is your family like?"

"Everyone in my family is blond and tall. My mother and two sisters are six feet tall and were all models. My brothers and brother-in-laws are all doctors or accountants, except for my youngest brother Danny, who's a chef. My father is Australian, he used to be a cowboy but now he owns cattle ranches. I have one nephew," Laura rushed out nervously.

"How old are you?" Pat asked curiously.

"Twenty-eight."

"Oh, good," Pat was relieved. "You look so young; I was worried Nick was robbing the cradle." Nick groaned loudly. "Where are your things?"

"I rented a hotel room down the street."

"Nonsense! You'll stay here," Pat insisted firmly.

Laura blushed furiously, "I'd rather not, if you don't mind," she murmured softly, unable to meet Pat's eye.

Nick agreed wholeheartedly on this one and immediately started thinking of how he could get her there as soon as possible.

"Do you want children?" Pat asked, embarrassing Laura once more. Nick opened his mouth to protest when he froze and a stunned look crossed his face as his mouth dropped open. The two women stared in concern. He looked at Laura, taking both her hands.

"What hotel and room number?" he demanded urgently. She answered, confused by his urgency. "Meet me there in fifteen minutes!" he shouted, running out of the house like a man possessed; leaving the two women staring at each other completely mystified. There was really nothing either of them could say.

"I guess I'll see you later," Laura said politely as Pat nodded. Laura walked down the street to her hotel, wondering what had happened.

*   *   *   *

Laura had only been in the hotel room a few minutes when Nick pounded on the door. She ran to open it and he rushed in, shoving a bag into her hands and turning her around, pushing her into the bathroom.

"Here take this," he ordered sternly.

She adroitly twisted away and closed the door. "Nick! Calm down. What is wrong?" She calmly looked in the bag. She took a pregnancy test out, looking at Nick clearly confused. "Do you know something I don't?" she smiled.

"Just take it, Laura, I have to know!" Nick begged turning and pushing her towards the bathroom again.

He was so distraught, she took the test. When she came out, Nick was pacing the floor.

"Well?" he demanded desperately.

"You have to wait three minutes," she said gently taking his hand and leading him to the couch. "I'm not pregnant, Nick!" She looked at him wonderingly, "Why do you think I am?"

Nick was unable to sit still and jumped up, running both hands through his hair, "Do you know that I've never had unprotected sex with any woman?" he asked, knowing by her expression that she was surprised. "I promised myself when I was fourteen that I would *never* be like him! I would never get anyone pregnant!" Laura put her arms around his neck, kissing him tenderly but he gently put her at arm's length. "I never even thought about it once with you!" He cried angry with himself, "We've been having unprotected sex for five months!"

Laura tried to put her arms around his neck again but he stood stiffly erect.

"I'm on the pill, Nick."

It didn't make him happy, "It can take two months to give you full protection." He replied unhappily.

Laura sighed and went into the bathroom. She came out; handing him the stick so he could see for himself that she wasn't pregnant. He flung himself down on the bed on his back with a huge sigh. She sat beside him with a slight frown.

"I've been on the pill for six years, Nick," she put her hand on his chest.

He lifted his head to look at her, "You said you were a virgin!"

She laughed out loud, "Virgins can take the pill, Nick." She lay beside him with an arm over him. "My doctor prescribed it to regulate my periods." She played with his hair, feeling the tension still in him. "Besides a girl never knows when she's going to fall madly in love and need back up." She teased lightly.

He laughed lightly and took a deep breath, finally able to relax slightly.

"Would it be so terrible if I was pregnant?" she asked wistfully.

He turned on his side to put his arms around her and squeezed her tightly. "No, of course not," he said quickly. "It was just the shock when I realized I hadn't been using condoms," he assured her, kissing her hungrily.

They continued to kiss deeply and Laura sighed with happiness.

Nick pulled away sharply, "Damn!" he cried irritably.

She laughed, "Now, what?" she looked at him questioningly.

"I was just at the damn store and I didn't buy any!"

She wrapped her arms tightly around him, "Must be a Freudian slip," she murmured, nuzzling his ear. "You secretly want me to get pregnant, so I'll have to marry you," she whispered, giggling.

Nick didn't find it funny; he tried to make himself get up and go to the store but it was no use. He couldn't tear himself away from her embrace.

Nick lay on his side looking over Laura's head, out the sliding doors of the hotel room letting him mind drift as Laura curled against him sleepily.

"Don't you want children?" she asked tentatively.

"I thought of having kids when I got married." he said softly, looking out at the sea. After a few moments of silence, he looked down and asked her, "Why were you a virgin?"

"It wasn't anything I planned." Laura sat up and leaned back against the headboard. "I just never fell in love with anyone."

"You've never been in love with anyone?" he asked in surprise.

"Talk about opposites attracting one another, huh?" she teased ruefully. "I've never been in love and you've fallen in love with every woman you've met."

"I've never been in love before." He denied softly, staring intently. "I didn't love any of those women!" he said fiercely, getting out of bed and putting on his pants to sit on the couch. "I'm very much like my father, I'm afraid! I just wanted to have a good time without any responsibility!" He jumped to his feet, unable to sit still, wrestling with his emotions as Laura stared shocked. "And don't fool yourself; those women weren't in love with me, either!" he said vehemently. "Lisa said she was in love with me! Begged me to marry her over and over until I broke up with her! She was *'heartbroken'* and called and wrote letters and stalked me. She was so upset she called John every day, begging him to help her! He felt sorry for her, I guess and before you know it they were dating! Two months after I dropped her, she was begging John to marry her!" He stood at the glass doors breathing heavily, angered by the memory. "They just want to be married! It doesn't matter who! Anyone will do!" He turned to see her kneeling on the bed, staring sadly. "You're right not to want to marry me!" he turned back to the view. "You're the only one who's honest! We're all a bunch of hypocrites!" he said angrily.

Laura got out of bed and put on her robe before taking him by the hand. She led him, resisting her slightly, to the couch. He sat down stiffly, not looking at her as she curled up on the couch beside him, gazing at him intently.

"You are *nothing* like your father, Nicholas Duffy!" she said softly. "You are a gentle, warm and caring man. You are the most romantic man I have ever met. And I love you very, very much." He turned with tears glistening in his eyes to see tears in her eyes as she kissed him tenderly. "*I'm* just not ready to get married, yet. And it scares me because I don't know why! I feel like I'm waiting for something but I have no idea what."

"I love you, Laura Nelson and I'm going to wait for you no matter how long it takes!" he promised in a husky voice as he put his arms around her and kissed her tenderly. They continued to kiss, wrapping their arms tightly around each other.

Nick lay beside Laura once again with her head on his chest and his arm around her as they both looked out at the ocean.

"Why don't you ask your mother to come live in California?" Laura asked suddenly, startling him.

"What?" he hedged to give himself time to think.

"You don't want her to live out there?" Laura made it half statement, half question.

"She wouldn't want to," he assured her. "She hates California."

"She'd like to be asked," Laura insisted. He looked at her uncertainly as she rolled onto her back, looking up at him. "What's the matter? Afraid she'd cramp your style?" she laughed.

"That's your job now," he grinned, thinking silently. "I'll ask her," he agreed suddenly, surprising Laura as well as himself; a year ago he wouldn't have dreamed of wanting his mother that close but now it suddenly sounded like a good idea.

SEVEN

It had been a month since Nick and Laura came back from New Jersey. Nick's mother had decided to join them in California and lived in an apartment in Laura's building.

Laura and Nick were taking a stroll through the town, walking down a beautiful tree lined street. All the houses were large, old and well maintained.

"Oh!" Laura made a cry of distress and stopped to stare at the house across the street where a sale sign announced an open house.

"They're selling my house!" she cried in despair.

"Your house?" he asked confused, looking down at her in the crook of his arm.

"Every time I walk down this street, I pretend that's my house. I always tell myself that the next time it's for sale I'm going to buy it," she explained as Nick stared at her strangely. "I know it's silly," she ducked her head. She made a move to keep walking but Nick didn't move.

"That's *my* favorite house," he said very quietly. "I tell myself the same thing," he looked down to meet her gaze and they stared into each other's eyes for a very long minute before grinning at one another as Nick pulled her quickly across the street.

Laura stood on the beautiful wrap-around porch looking very sad. "I love this house," she sounded as if she might cry; they had just toured the house. "We could never afford it," she murmured sadly, turning to leave.

Nick pulled her back into his arms and picked her up; joyfully lifting her up over his head. She looked down into his face with her hands on his shoulders wondering why he was so happy.

"*I* can afford this house!" he shouted ecstatically but she looked skeptical and he stared at her, willing her to believe him.

"Really?" she asked astonished and joyful at the same time.

They bought their house. Laura insisted it was in Nick's name since he was paying for it and he insisted on putting it in her name since it was a present for her. Alex settled the argument by insisting they put it in both names and no one went against Alex the genius' advice.

Nick wondered if Laura would say yes to him. He'd never brought the subject of marriage up again, but it was killing him still. He wanted to be married to her.

*   *   *   *

On a beautiful California Saturday, three weeks after Nick and Laura settled in their house, everyone gathered on the Baby for a barbeque.

"What's he doing?" John finally asked Laura the question that was on everyone's mind when Nick hadn't appeared by two pm.

"He's logging flight hours," she shrugged; he had told her he'd be back by one when he left in the morning.

Half an hour later, Nick boarded the Baby with a strangely blank look and he didn't return any of their greetings. He silently sat beside Laura as John looked suspiciously at her.

"That's how he looks when you upset him," he said accusingly.

"I haven't done a thing," she denied with a smile and a shrug. She put her hand on Nick's shoulder, "Honey, what's wrong?"

Nick turned his head, looking at her as if he'd never seen her before, "I just sold Dolly." He said in a dazed voice.

"What?" John objected loudly. "She isn't yours to sell, you know!"

"I agreed to sell her," he clarified, looking at the others as if suddenly noticing them.

"Why, Nick?" Alex wanted to know.

Nick still looked dazed but his power of speech was returning, "You remember Steve Fisher?" The men both nodded as the women shook their heads. "He owns two jets which he rents out to corporations and such," he explained for their benefit. "I bumped into him today. He said he's retiring and wanted to know if I was interested in taking over the business." Nick looked at the two men, "I said yes. Alex can do the reservations and the financial aspect and you and I can fly and maintain them." He looked first at John and then at Alex. John had been ready to say no to anything but he was clearly interested. "We could fly again," Nick said simply.

John smiled, "It sounds great." He sobered, "But we'd have to look over the planes."

"And I'd have to look over his books," Alex interjected.

"Why did you sell Dolly?" Laura questioned, knowing how much he loved the big ugly helicopter and wondering why anyone would want it.

Nick shrugged, "It was part of the deal; Steve's always wanted her. He wants to keep his hand in flying, just not all the time."

They all looked at one another a little stunned until the smell of burning meat brought everyone back to reality and they all started talking at once.

*   *   *   *

They started a new business while tying up the loose ends from the old business. John and Nick flew, letting Alex handle all the bookings and the financial aspects. It was unexpectedly a very good business and they became busier than they expected in a short period of time. Bo and Laura occasionally flew on the longer trips as stewardesses and sometimes they just went along for the ride.

Laura looked out over the lights of the city as she and Nick sat in a restaurant in the Eiffel Tower.

"Have you ever seen anything so beautiful?" she asked dreamily.

"Never," Nick agreed, never taking his eyes off her face.

She turned her head to find him staring and smiled tenderly, "This is the best part of the whole business." He smiled in agreement. "I am so happy, Nick!" she looked into his eyes. She suddenly looked away, blushing for no reason; he was making her feel shy. She looked up startled to see him standing beside her. He went down on one knee and heard her quick intake of breath; his heart pounded as he pulled out the ring box.

"Will you marry me?" he asked, holding his breath.

She looked at him with shining eyes and threw her arms around his neck crying, "Yes, yes I will!"

He stood up with her in his arms, kissing her passionately; unaware that the patrons in the restaurant were clapping and cheering for them. A waiter came to them and had to cough rather loudly to get their attention. Nick suddenly remembered where they were and released her and they sat down once more. The waiter offered them a complimentary bottle of champagne. Laura looked at him with tears in her eyes and Nick was so choked up he couldn't speak as they clinked their glasses.

A wedding was once more held on the Baby under full sail. The bride was radiant in an elegant white tulle gown with small bunches of tiny pink flowers. She wore a tiara and an off the face veil. Every one of her male relatives solemnly shook Nick's hand, telling him what would happen to him if he ever broke her heart. Every woman there was secretly envious of her handsome loving bridegroom who only had eyes for her.

CASE FILE: MARY

ONE

John lay in bed; he should be asleep but he wasn't. He wouldn't admit it to anyone, not even himself but he was lonely. He'd been living on the Baby alone for more than three months and it was the first time he'd ever lived alone. He had left home to join the Army at eighteen and met Nick in boot camp. They did two four year hitches and decided they had had enough of Army life. They had gotten a two bedroom apartment and rented an office to start a private investigator business. A year later his younger brother Alex had joined them and they had bought the Baby and moved in. The gorgeous three mast schooner became both home and office for them.

Six months ago, they had traded the investigator practice in for the flying business. Now Alex and Bo lived across the street and Nick and Laura lived three blocks away. John saw all of them almost every day. Although he and Nick usually flew different flights; they sometimes flew one plane on international flights. John was very happy for Alex and Nick, who had never been happier, but he sometimes felt like a fifth wheel. He usually had a girl with him but she wasn't part of the circle. Bo and Laura were great friends and he gave them a lot of credit; they always went out of their way to include his current girlfriend in the conversation. John had to admit that sometimes it wasn't easy; his dates were lovely but not all of them were very bright and they only wanted to be alone with him. To be honest, he sometimes found his dates very annoying when he was with the others.

He didn't miss their old business one bit; he really enjoyed flying again. He sighed heavily and rolled over, wondering what was wrong with him. He had never noticed before how quiet Wally's Marina 54 was at night.

In his younger days Wally had run a fleet of cargo ships and had built this private marina to dock his ships. Over time the huge supertankers had phased him out of business. Wally had retired and rented the marina out to people he knew. Nick, John and Alex had helped him find his daughter, from whom he had been estranged for many years, and had offered them a berth for Baby at a great price.

Once they had impulsively bought Baby, they couldn't find a marina that was deep enough for her draft.   Because the marina had originally been built for larger cargo ships, it was perfect for the hundred foot long schooner. They were the only boat owners who lived at the marina; most of the others were commercial fishermen.

John adored the Baby and he knew without them mentioning it that Nick and Alex were thinking maybe it was time to sell her.

He remembered his father, an ex-Navy man, taking all his sons, including Alex when he was home, out sailing.   John had always adored sailing and he was the undisputed Captain when they took Baby out to sea.   He treated Baby with kid gloves; he was the one who insisted they log all their trips with the Coast Guard, just in case, and at the first sign of heavy seas or rough weather, John made them take the sails down and use her powerful engines. He loved her and didn't want to sell her; he'd been seriously considering buying her from the other two. They hadn't taken her for a sail since Nick's wedding since it took three men to sail her and everyone had been too busy.

John groaned and rolled onto his back again, trying to make himself stop thinking! Everything kept going round and round in his head, driving him crazy!

He sat up suddenly, thinking he heard a scream. He listened intently and it came again. He leaped out of bed and ran upstairs when he heard a frenzied pounding on the door. A woman screamed and he thought he heard his name. He ran across the room and pulled the door open. He couldn't believe his eyes as their lawyer Mary threw herself into his arms looking scared to death.

"They're trying to kill me!" she gasped, clinging to him.

John looked out the door cautiously but saw no movement. Mary's car was sitting in the parking lot with the lights on and the door open.

"Stay here," he ordered, pushing her onto the couch. He ran downstairs to get Quark and put the amazing little robot down on the deck outside the front door.

"Perimeter check," John commanded.   Quark rolled out the door, patrolling the entire deck and stopped again in front of the main door.

"All secure." the mechanical voice told John.

"Stand guard." John ordered; Quark rolled to the back of the boat, going up a ramp leading to a raised platform. Quark positioned himself on top of the platform where he had a 360 degree view of the marina.

John took his gun out of the big teddy bear cookie jar one of the many girlfriends had made for them. He glanced at Mary who stared in amazement. He cautiously went out on deck and ordered Quark to scan the parking lot. When the robot gave the all clear, John ran up and shut off the engine. Mary's car was marked by long deep scrapes along the driver's side; someone had repeatedly sideswiped her and the driver's window was shattered. John ran back to the boat and locked the main cabin door. Mary flung herself into his arms as soon as he came in.

"Oh, John! Oh, John!" she kept repeating his name.

Mary had been their lawyer for over seven years. She was a tall, willowy, black haired beauty; very soft spoken with a lady like way about her. Bo, the little tigress, referred to Mary as a girlie-girl. In those seven years, John had never seen her with a hair out of place. She'd never been anything but calm and quiet and he stared at her now; shaking with fear, her face wet with tears and absolutely hysterical.

He held her tightly against his chest and sat down on the couch with her pressed against him. He didn't bother asking any questions, knowing she couldn't answer coherently if she tried.

"You're safe now. There's no one there now," he soothed quietly, stroking her long dark hair and patting her back. She still shook like a leaf but she wasn't crying as hard now as he glanced at the clock. It was two am and he couldn't imagine what she was doing out at this time of night. He waited about twenty minutes until her shaking lessened and she wasn't crying anymore. She still clung to him convulsively which John didn't mind at all. He'd always had a soft spot for Mary. If she had even shown him one little spark of interest, he would have asked her out. But she had always been all business even when he flirted with her.

"Tell me what happened, Mary."

She straightened up, releasing him and took the tissues he handed her, trying to fix her face. "I was at a party tonight; a bachelorette party for my friend. It was late when I left." She took a deep breath, "I was driving home. There was very little traffic. This black car came up behind me on the highway and ran into me from behind. I knew he had done it on purpose so I didn't stop. He came up beside me and tried to run me off the highway into the ocean! I slammed on the brakes. He kept going and now I was following him. Of course, I couldn't turn off anywhere, right there. I tried going slower but he went slower, too. I didn't dare try to pass him. He kept going slower and slower. I didn't know what to do. I couldn't reach my phone while I was driving. There wasn't anyone else on the road," she started to hyperventilate again so John took her hands and held them in his. "I tried to pass him but he swerved to the left each time. Then suddenly a truck came around the next curve and he had to swerve out of the way. I got past him and drove like a demon. He caught up to me and kept sideswiping me. I just kept driving. Then as I realized I was only about three miles from the marina, he pulled up next to me and fired a gun!" she stopped, closing her eyes; John worried she might faint, she was so pale. "I waited until the last minute to take the exit road," she sighed. "They missed it. I drove here like a maniac."

John patted her, "You did great, Mary." She looked at him doubtfully but was grateful for the compliment. "Any idea who it was? Or why?"

She shook her head, "The car had no plates on it, John. It wasn't just someone out for mischief. They were trying to kill me!"

"Well, we should call the police—" John started to get up.

"No!" Mary cried out, pulling him back down. "Please, not tonight," she begged, looking away. "I just can't do anything else tonight," she pleaded. "Please, can I just stay here tonight?"

John smiled; under other circumstances he would have been thrilled to hear her beg him to stay. "Of course, Mary, whatever you want." He agreed while privately wondering why a 'by the book' lawyer didn't want to report a serious crime to the police. He dug out a pair of pajamas he'd never used; another present from one of his many girlfriends and Mary slept in Nick's old room, next to his room. He left his door open and kept his gun on the table beside him. He left Alex's door open so he could hear any warning from Quark, still on guard outside, on the computer. The night remained quiet and peaceful and he went right to sleep.

*   *   *   *

In the morning, Alex pounded on the door. Mary looked fearfully out the bedroom door as John left his room.

"It's Alex," he said briefly, going up the steps to unbolt the door.

Alex rushed in, "Why is Mary's car smashed up in the parking lot? Why is Quark on guard? Where is Mary? Are you alright?" he threw the questions at John without letting him answer.

"Alex!" John complained. "It's seven am!" he tried to push Alex back out the door.

Alex eluded him, "I know! Mrs. Quark was flashing when I got up to go to the bathroom."

"Mrs. Quark?" Mary asked, coming up the steps in John's robe. Alex turned in surprise and stared even more shocked, seeing her attire making Mary blush deeply.

"Mrs. Quark is the female version of Quark and stays with Alex and Bo. Baby Quark stays with Nick and Laura," John grimaced as he said the last name. Baby Quark was a miniature version of Quark which Alex had given to Nick and Laura for a wedding present; that way all three of them could be instantly in touch.

Way too much in touch, John thought as Nick came rushing into the cabin asking the same questions as Alex. He stopped to stare at Mary with the exact same expression that Alex had. John sighed heavily; *so much for waking up late after a late night flight last night and Mary's dramatic entrance*, he thought grumpily. He had secretly been looking forward to having her alone and getting to know her better over breakfast. He went to the galley to make breakfast as Mary told them of her adventure.

He walked back into the main room with a platter full of pancakes when he heard her say, "Thank God, John was here last night! I know he saved my life. I wouldn't have gotten any sleep if it wasn't for him." She took the platter from him and put it on the table which Alex had set for four. Mary smiled gratefully at John and he felt himself redden under her gaze.

"I didn't really do anything," he protested.

She put her hand on his arm, "You were wonderful; so sweet and kind. You made me feel safe," she gazed soulfully into his eyes.

"That's John; sweet and kind," Nick teased. "Isn't that what we always say, Alex?" Nick pulled out a chair for Mary and sat right beside her.

Alex declined to tease his brother as he saw John frown, noticing he had to sit across from Mary since Nick was beside her.

"I didn't know you were such a good cook, John," Mary was very impressed after one bite. "The pancakes are great."

John smiled and was about to reply when Alex said dismissively, "Oh, we can all cook." John shot him an angry glare.

Breakfast was spent with the three men regaling Mary with funny stories from their private investigator days.

When breakfast was over John told her, "Get dressed and I'll call the police."

Mary looked upset, "Oh, I want to go home and change first. I'll call them from my apartment."

He looked at her suspiciously; last night and now again, this curious reluctance to report this to the police.

"Fine. I'll follow you home to make sure you get there safely." When she left to get dressed, John turned to Alex, "Get working on the body shops. See if you can find one that has a big black car with white paint on the passenger side." Alex nodded as he finished his breakfast.

When Mary and John were dressed, Nick followed them to the parking lot and took samples of the black paint scrapes on her car then followed John to the truck.

John waited until Mary got in her car to ask, "What are you doing?"

Nick looked surprised, "I'm going with you," he got in the truck.

"Shouldn't you be home with your wife?"

"My wife is at work. What's up with you?" he stared at John curiously.

John shrugged nonchalantly but Nick smiled knowingly as they silently followed Mary to her apartment.

When they arrived, both men insisted on walking her to her door. Mary wouldn't admit it but she was still scared and glad they were being so protective. She opened the door, turning to John.

"I can't thank you enough, John," she said gratefully, looking up at him as he stared over her head with a strange look on his face and she turned to look inside her apartment and gave a little shriek. Her apartment was a shambles; she tried to go inside but both men stopped her.

"Stay behind us!" Nick ordered curtly as they slowly opened the door and looked behind it before entering. John stood her almost behind the door once they got inside.

"Stay here."

The two men carefully checked out the apartment. The four rooms were all torn up but there was no one there. They went back to the living room and shut the door. John opened his cell phone and dialed 911.

"Please! Don't call the police," she requested quietly, startling them both.

"Pack a bag. You're coming back to the Baby with us," Nick ordered quietly.

Mary wordlessly sifted through the jumble in her bedroom and packed a bag. They escorted her out of the building and into the truck.

*   *   *   *

As they drove down the highway, John and Nick both kept an eye on the mirrors wishing they had brought their guns with them.

"What's going on, Mary?" John asked when they were halfway back to the marina.

"I'm not sure," she replied quietly, pushing her heavy hair back from her face in a familiar gesture. "It all started last week. I was assigned to represent a young man caught with five pounds of cocaine in his possession. He's charged with possession and selling. He says he's innocent and he's being framed. The police say he's part of an East Coast mob syndicate, who are out here trying to muscle their way in."

"Do you believe him?" Nick asked.

"I'm not sure. He's not telling me everything but there is one thing in his favor."

"What's that?" John asked curiously.

"How many mobsters do you know that need a Public Defender?" she quizzed drily.

John looked at her swiftly, sitting in the front seat tucked between them.

"You don't work for the city, do you?" he asked slightly startled; Mary had worked for a private law firm for the past seven years.

"No, but every once in a while, the public defender's office gets swamped and they contract out for lawyers. My company holds the contract this year. I was handed this case last Thursday. The man is still in jail, he can't raise bail."

"That is very strange; you can afford five pounds of pure cocaine but can't bail yourself out. Even if he's just one of their mules, they should bail him out," Nick agreed.

She nodded, "As soon as I had seen him in jail, the phone calls started; threatening me not to defend him." She looked at Nick as she heard his sharp intake of breath, "I reported it to the police." She looked at John, "They didn't do anything. They didn't tap my phone; nothing." She remained silent for several minutes, "The next set of phone calls warned me that the police wouldn't help me. They warned me not to do anything. They threatened me if I continued on this case. I asked George who could be doing this; he said he didn't know."

"George is the defendant?" John questioned as they pulled into the parking lot at the marina.

"Did you believe him?" Nick helped her out.

"No." She said quietly as Nick carried her bag. "I reported this to the state police," she stopped talking abruptly.

"What happened?" John helped her up the boarding ramp.

"A black car tried to run me off the road and took a shot at me."

They entered the main room on the Baby and Nick asked point blank, "Mary, who do you think is behind this?"

"The police."

They were unhappily startled; she sounded so positive.

"But, you're talking state as well as local police," Nick reminded her.

She nodded grimly, "Scary isn't it?"

Alex came upstairs, surprised to see Mary with them.

"Her apartment's been trashed," Nick answered his questioning look.

He nodded, "No one brought a black car in to any area body shop, yet. I asked them to keep me posted," he looked up. "There is one strange coincidence." They waited expectantly. "I've been reading the police files. The state police have a black car in their body shop. It was sideswiped while parked; the officer was on a dinner break. The paint was white," three pairs of eyes stared in shock as he looked at them.

"What?" he asked eagerly. "You think someone stole the car and hit Mary and then returned it?"

"Why would they take a chance on getting caught returning it?" John asked sarcastically as Alex looked perplexed. Light slowly dawned.

"You think the *State Police* attacked Mary?" he demanded incredulously. All three nodded their heads solemnly.

"Get the name of the officer, will you, Brain?" John requested; Alex immediately leaped downstairs.

*   *   *   *

Four hours later, John, Nick and Mary sat in the main cabin; they had discussed the case from every angle but still had no real clue why this was happening. An hour ago, Alex had gotten up looking pensive and gone to work on his computer.

Alex came upstairs and placed an eight by ten photo in front of John.

"Know him?" he asked casually.

Mary and Nick leaned in for a look at the photo. Mary looked up startled but Alex caught her eye and shook his head, warning her not to say anything.

"No," John looked at Alex curiously.

"I don't recognize him either," Nick added.

"You wouldn't know him, Nick. He was gone before you moved out here," Alex stared at John intently. "Doesn't he remind you of anyone?" John looked puzzled and looked again at the picture.

He sighed, "He looks a little like Brandon Kelly." He shrugged, not understanding what Alex wanted from him. He saw

Alex looking at him with an expectant nod. John suddenly frowned and looked again at the picture. He looked at Alex excitedly, "Brandon Kelly!"

Now Mary looked very puzzled; "Alex, that's the mug shot of my client, George Brent."

Nick and John looked from her to Alex. "That's Brandon Kelly; he used to live around here. His father was a cop who blew the whistle on organized crime in the police department. The whole family had to enter the witness relocation program." Alex explained to Nick and Mary.

"But what the hell is he doing back here?" John asked.

"And why haven't the Feds come in to get him out?" Nick asked skeptically.

"Because he hasn't called them," Alex explained. "I checked police records. He never made a phone call."

"That might explain why he won't tell me anything," Mary said quietly. "But why would the police be after him?"

"They're trying to flush his father out of hiding, I bet." John supplied. "There must be people who got away the last time but still want revenge."

"What are we going to do about it?" Nick brought them back to the problem at hand. "We're going to have to go to the Feds."

"Not necessarily," John said slowly. "Do you remember Franklin Werron?"

"The married man who was accused of murdering his pregnant girlfriend?" Nick wondered what it had to do with anything.

"Yes." John had three pair of perplexed eyes staring at him. "What was the name of the hard-nosed Captain we talked to at the state police?"

"Philip Hunter," Alex supplied immediately.

John nodded. "I think we should look him up and talk to him," he said positively.

Mary looked dismayed, "I'd feel safer going to the Feds," she laid her hand on his arm. "I don't have a shred of evidence but I feel like the police are behind this."

John put his hand over hers and looked into her lovely startling blue eyes which were the color of the summer sky.

"I'm certain they are but they can't all be in it," he consoled her. "This Captain Hunter is an internal affairs guy. He's straight as an arrow; I think we could trust him if we can find him."

"He's the only one who actually listened to us when we told them that Franklin Werron was innocent. He was being framed by his estranged wife," Alex informed her.

Mary sighed deeply, "I'll do whatever you feel is right," she looked directly at John. "I'm so scared; I don't know what to do."

"Um, guys, we have a flight in two hours. John, you were supposed to fly," Alex reminded him as John looked disturbed.

Nick put his hand on John's shoulder, "I'll take the flight."

John looked instantly relieved, "Great! Thanks Nick!" He glanced at Alex, "We'd better make sure this is Brandon. You go with Mary to the jail as her assistant so you can eyeball him and talk to him." He smiled at Mary as he put on his holster and gun, "I'm going as guard dog."

She tried to smile bravely at him but they all knew how scared she was.

*   *   *   *

John drove them to the jail with Alex dressed in a suit and glasses with his hair slicked back, looking every inch the lawyer. He went inside with Mary and John waited outside.

George Brent was brought to the small room by a guard and walked in looking very depressed. His face unexpectedly lit up when he saw Alex and he walked towards him with a big smile until he abruptly wiped all expression off his face. He looked down at the table, pale and scared.

"George, I need you to read these papers over and sign them," Mary said quietly. George took the papers without looking up and held out his hand for a pen. He looked at her curiously when she didn't give him one. She nodded at the papers, "Read them first." He was annoyed but started reading and looked up in shock. He looked quickly at Alex and then continued to read. He held out his hand for the pen again without looking up. Mary handed him the pen so he could write answers to the questions that Alex had written down along with the information they already knew.

In answer to the first question; why did you come back? He wrote; I read of the engagement of Betsy Connors in the paper. I came back to ask her to marry me; she got married yesterday.

The second question asked; does your father know you're here? No, he thinks I'm still at Syracuse University taking a summer course, George answered.

They didn't ask him where his family was but they asked who he thought was involved in this frame. George wrote down the names of three officers; one of them was Tom Duncan. Duncan was the officer who had pulled him over on a traffic charge and had kept him there waiting until two other units had come. They had searched his car and 'found' five pounds of cocaine in the trunk.

The final question asked why he hadn't contacted the Feds. George told them the whole family would have to be relocated again because he had been stupid. He had put them all in danger again. Relocating to a whole new identity and life had been very hard. He didn't want to make them go through it again. He handed the pen back to Mary keeping his head down, unable to look at them.

The last page told him they were going to help. He was to sit tight and do nothing. Alex thought George would be fairly safe as long as the cops thought they could to get to his father through him. Obviously, they thought George might tell Mary what was going on. They might even be worried she could get him out or get the charges dropped.

Alex locked the papers in the briefcase and they left the jail. John was waiting but didn't tell them the same police car had driven past him seven times while they were in the building and was now following them at a distance. They told John what George had written. Alex calmly informed them they were being bugged when they were "talking" to George.

TWO

Nick, meanwhile, flew a corporate group to New Orleans and called Captain Hunter while he waited to make the return trip but had to leave a message with the secretary. He gave her his name and cell phone number and the message, '*Urgent*'. He was pacing outside the hangar several hours later when his phone rang.

Captain Hunter remembered the Onboard Detective Agency and assured Nick he would be interested in state and local police who were on the take. Nick laid it out for him; telling him he had no proof. Hunter agreed to look into things from his end. They set up an e-mail contact system. Nick then went to an Internet café and sent an e-mail to the guys who e-mailed him George's information.

*   *   *   *

Captain Hunter worked closely with Alex; they both agreed the cocaine could only have come from a recent State Police bust. He sent an undercover officer to the State Police unit to investigate. He sent a senior Internal Affairs officer to the local police to investigate a charge of illegal conduct lodged by Mary Stevens, lawyer.

It was hard to keep the flights going and keep an eye on Mary at the same time for the next two days. John and Nick both called in favors from pilot friends. The two men took eight hour guard shifts. Bo and Laura wanted to keep Mary company but Alex and Nick refused to let them near the boat; with pressure coming from all sides they expected something to happen at any time.

Mary was holding up fairly well but the strain began to show by the fourth day so John decided to take her to the park. They had a nice lunch at a restaurant on the beach and Mary was laughing as they walked down a shady path.

She gave a scream and clung to John as a grey van drove over the grass and parked across the path in front of them. John stood still as two masked men got out of the back, pointing guns at them.

"Get in. No tricks," one of the masked men said harshly. John helped Mary get in the back; he could feel her shaking as she clung to him. He enjoyed holding her in his arms. They were taken to a warehouse on the docks and shoved in a small office with no windows or furniture.

"Oh my God!" Mary cried. "They're going to kill us." They sat on the floor leaning against the wall.

"No, they're not," John assured her positively.

She looked at him sorrowfully, "I'm so sorry I got you involved in this!" She sighed heavily, "Why didn't I just drop the case? Why?" She cried out.

John patted her hand, "Don't worry about me. We'll be fine," he reassured her.

"You're not wearing a gun," she murmured suddenly, looking at him strangely.

"They would have just taken it away," he replied calmly.

"You knew this would happen?" she demanded outraged. "You used me as bait?" She struggled to rise. He helped her to her feet as he stood up.

"Well, we had to bring them out of hiding somehow; the strain was getting too much for you. And apparently they're not stupid enough to attack us on our home base."

She stared in amazement, "I owe all of you an apology." He looked at her without understanding. "I've always thought of you as wild men. I had no idea how brave you all are!"

John felt himself flushing at her praise, "T'weren't nothing, ma'am," he gave his John Wayne impression and laughed.

Mary didn't laugh. "We're going to die!" she stared as if she'd never seen him before.

"We'll be rescued any minute now! Trust me, Mary," he felt an incredible urge to kiss her.

"I've always had a crush on you, John Colby," she admitted softly, considerably startling him. "Please hold me tight and kiss me before I die," she pleaded with tears in her eyes.

"You're not going to die!" he refuted roughly, pulling her to him and kissing her anyway. The door swung open with a bang; Duncan stood in the doorway with a gun pointed at them.

"You just can't keep your hands off any woman, can you Colby?" he sneered. John calmly turned towards him, keeping his arms around Mary.

"Give it up, Duncan. I always knew there was something wrong about you. You're going down this time!" John warned quietly.

"It's going to be a pleasure to kill you, Colby!" Duncan fired.

Mary screamed and shoved John with all her might. He fell; bringing her with him. John heard a second shot and saw Duncan fall as Captain Hunter came through the door. Hunter turned quickly and ran out.

John was still holding Mary against him but she was limp. He looked down horrified to see blood pulsing from a bullet wound in her chest. He was stretched out on the floor with her lying across him. He pulled her to him, frantically kissing her face and lips.

"Mary, Mary, no dear God! No!"

Captain Hunter and Nick ran back into the room followed by the EMT's with a stretcher. Nick had to tear John away so the men could put her on the stretcher, racing against time to save her life. The rescue helicopter arrived as they brought her out of the warehouse. Nick pulled John to the truck as he tried to follow Mary.

"We'll go to the hospital, John! Come on!" Nick cried, pushing him away from the helicopter. "You can't go with her!" he yelled over the roar of the helicopter. John's eyes followed the helicopter out of sight as Nick tried to push him into the truck.

"That should be me in there." John turned an anguished face to Nick. "Why did she have to do that?" he asked in despair. "Why didn't she let him shoot *me*?" he agonized as he finally let Nick shove him into the truck. They drove to the hospital in silence; there was nothing Nick could say. He had heard the EMT's talking; they weren't sure Mary would survive the trip to the hospital.

*   *   *   *

They'd been waiting hours with no news; Mary had been rushed into surgery as soon as the helicopter landed on the roof.

John stood up suddenly when he saw Mary's parents walking down the hall. Mr. Stevens had his arms around his wife who cried softly.

"Mr. Stevens?"

Mr. Stevens looked up startled, looking at John inquiringly.

"I'm John Colby. I was with Mary when she— it happened," he stammered unable to say the words. "They won't tell us anything because we're not relatives," he motioned to Alex, Bo, Nick and Laura behind him. "How is she?" he begged.

"She just got out of surgery. They're moving her to ICU now. We can see her for a few minutes in about an hour. They— they don't know if she's going to— live," his voice broke.

Mrs. Stevens put her hand on John's arm. "I want to thank you," she murmured softly.

John pulled his arm away as if she had burnt him, "For what?" he asked harshly. "*She* saved my life!" he cried bitterly.

"She called us every day and told us how all of you were protecting her," Mrs. Stevens continued, including all of them in her glance. "We're very grateful to all of you for taking care of our Mary."

Mr. Stevens moved his wife away, "We're going to wait in the chapel and pray."

*   *   *   *

John sat in church staring intently at the altar. It had been two days since the shooting and Mary was still in a coma in ICU. She was doing better; they said she would survive if no complications developed. Her parents had told the hospital John was a cousin so he could see her for five minutes at a time every couple of hours.

He had taken a flight yesterday over the protests of Alex and Nick who didn't think he was ready to fly. John had told them he had to fly to get his mind off Mary for a few hours, at least. He had awakened at three am today and couldn't get back to sleep so he had gone for a run and ended up in church.

He gradually realized someone stood beside him in the aisle. He turned his head to see an older woman gazing at him. It irritably crossed his mind that the whole church was empty, why did she have to sit in this particular row? It took him a full five seconds to realize he was looking at his mother; he blinked at her, unable to speak.

"John?" she put her hand on his shoulder and gave him a slight shake.

"What are you doing here?" he asked wonderingly.

"Father Barlow called me," she sat next to him, holding his hand. "He said you've been here since four am."

He nodded with a deep sigh, "What time is it?" he asked, not really interested.

"It's seven am," she continued, "Father Barlow is holding a special mass to pray for Mary." That got John's full attention.

"He is?" he asked happily. "Thanks, Mom!" he figured she had arranged it.

"Don't thank me; it was Father Barlow's idea. We've all been praying so hard for her lately. We just decided to get together and do it in church as a group. You know, they've done studies that show that people who are prayed for, get better more often and faster than people who don't have anyone praying for them."

John stared at his mother, deeply perplexed, "You *know* Mary?" he asked slowly, trying to comprehend all of this on only three hours of sleep.

"Well, of course, dear, Mary belongs to this church. I've seen her here every Sunday with her parents since she was born," Sara looked at him in deep concern. "How many hours of sleep have you been getting?" she asked in her mother voice.

"Enough," he said abruptly.

"Alex told me you flew yesterday," she rebuked him with a simple sentence.

"I'll have to thank him for that!" John snapped sarcastically.

He suddenly noticed people were entering the church and decided to stay for the mass. He sat silently listening to words he hadn't heard since he was fifteen and had told his parents he wasn't going to church anymore. He smiled, remembering his mother's reaction. She hadn't been surprised and had taken it well. She had tried to get him to continue going to the youth group events for about a year but John had vetoed that idea as well.

It was a shock to find out his mother was well acquainted with Mary and her family. He had surprised himself when he had recognized Mary's parents in the hospital. He had thought he recognized them because Mary resembled both of them. They were tall and dark haired with the same amazingly blue eyes. They were both lawyers but he never remembered actually meeting them. But now he realized he must have known Mary and her parents casually from childhood. Now that his mother had opened his mind to the past; he vaguely remembered seeing her parents in church. They had always seemed old to him. Mary had been born when her mother was in her forties. He barely remembered a dark haired, gangly girl hiding behind her parents because she had been so shy.

"I've always had a crush on you, John Colby." he heard her words again, haunting him. He had heard them over and over in his mind the last two days. He remembered again looking into her eyes, taking her in his arms and kissing her. He groaned out loud; causing his mother to glance over in concern and he tried to bring his mind back to the present.

Near the end of the service, John leaped to his feet; startling the priest who stopped talking. The little group of people stared at him oddly.

"Mary's awake!" he cried and bolted out of the church. The startled priest turned once again to his interrupted service as John ran back to the Baby to get his motorcycle.

*   *   *   *

John ran to the ICU unit and into her room against the protests of the staff. Mary's parents stood beside the bed looking at Mary who had been taken off the ventilator yesterday. Her eyes were unfocused but open as he ran to the bed and grabbed her hand.

"Mary!" he almost shouted breathlessly. He had stood beside this bed so often in the past three days holding her ice cold hand for his allotted five minutes. Her hand was still cold but gripped his lightly.

Mary slowly turned to see the man who had rushed into the room. She stared as if she didn't recognize him for another moment.

"John?" she murmured hesitantly, her voice barely a whisper. "What are you doing here?" she gazed around the room in confusion and turned to her parents. "What am I doing here?"

Her mother bent to caress her face, "There's been an accident, darling. You're going to be all right." She looked at John as if to caution him but he only had eyes for Mary. He grinned like an idiot, his eyes shining. Mary turned her head to John, looking perplexed. She smiled hesitantly before turning back to her parents and smiling at them.

THREE

John was in a quandary; he didn't know what to do. Mary had been moved out of ICU into a regular room and he had gone to see her everyday in-between flights. She had no memory of the last three days before being shot and was absolutely amazed when John told her what had happened. She had been slowly recovering and was going to rehab in two days to get her strength back and do some physical therapy.

Mary had no memory of her last words to him or of their kiss. She acted like the old Mary; friendly but not personally interested. John wanted to hold her in his arms and kiss her all day long. He wanted to tell her about the kiss and what she had said. He hadn't told anyone what happened between them in that office before Duncan came in.

Duncan and the other two local cops were dead. The State Trooper, who masterminded the deal and had attacked Mary on the road, had shot himself before the police came to arrest him. Brandon Kelly aka George Brent had had to go back into hiding with new identities for his family.

With Mary in the hospital and her parents and all the church people popping in and out all day long, John hadn't had a moment alone with her. He didn't really want to bring the subject up while she was in the hospital; even if she again admitted her true feelings for him, he couldn't really seduce her in the hospital.

John's friends were thankful that the business was so busy because John was acting suspiciously like Nick, a year ago; temperamental and not wanting to talk to anyone. He had trouble sleeping and abruptly came and went at all times of the day and night. They all reminded him when his flights were scheduled even though he yelled that he knew. He'd been late for three flights this week.

The five of them were hanging out on the Baby, enjoying a beautiful sunny day when Alex took John to task.

"You can't yell at the clients, John! These people are paying a lot of money and they want their pilots to be ready."

"Go to hell, Alex," he growled angrily, making Alex look at him in surprise.

Nick laughed. "Don't listen to him, Alex. He's just cranky because he hasn't been getting any lately." Nick said looking cheerfully at John. Alex, Laura and Bo look shocked but Nick grinned broadly; he'd waited a long time to say that to John. John jumped up with a roar, grabbing Nick who prevented John from punching him as they fell to the deck, wrestling.

Alex sighed; preventing Bo and Laura from going near them.

"Just let them go! It's a guy thing, you wouldn't understand." Alex shooed them away from the men rolling around on the deck, punching each other.

"Alex, stop them! They're going to hurt themselves!" Laura pleaded; trying to get past Alex's outstretched arms.

"No, no, they're fine!" he assured her.

They stared worriedly as the two men wrestled furiously but it crossed Laura's mind that they appeared to be enjoying themselves. They finally rolled in opposite directions and got to their feet, bruised, sweaty and bleeding slightly. John directed an angry look at them all before ducking into the main cabin. Nick grinned and nonchalantly sat at the table.

"He needed that!" he told Laura cheerfully before she even said anything. He drank his beer, wiping his sweaty face as Laura stared uncertainly. Bo had seen this scenario played out before. Nick waited ten minutes to catch his breath before he went inside to talk to John. Laura nervously grabbed his arm as he got up to enter the cabin.

"Nick, leave him alone," she begged, looking sadly at his fat lip. He took her hand off his arm and moved her gently out of his way, brushing her lips with a kiss.

"Don't worry; I know what I'm doing. I've been there," he replied confidently and went into the cabin. Laura turned uncertainly to Alex and Bo.

"Another one bites the dust!" Bo grinned over her glass.

"Poor John!" Laura shook her head as she sat in the shade.

"Poor John?" Bo retorted. "I'd say poor Mary. I don't think she's woman enough to handle John."

"Bo!" Alex rebuked her; he'd always had a soft spot for Mary. "She's a sweet and lovely woman."

Bo nodded in agreement, "Way too sweet for John; she's going to let him walk all over her," Bo predicted mischievously.

Laura wondered; knowing Mary had a reputation as an excellent lawyer. You didn't get that without a core of steel somewhere inside.

Nick found John lying on his bed, his hands behind his head, staring at the ceiling with a foul expression on his handsome face. Nick remembered that position well even though it had been almost a year. He stood silently in the doorway until John finally noticed him. He picked his head up, glaring angrily.

"Come to gloat?"

Nick shrugged, leaning against the doorjamb. "Remember a year ago, my friend?" he smiled. "I know where you're coming from," Nick turned his head to the side, pretending to think. "What was your advice to me?" he smiled wickedly. "Oh, yes, get myself another girl."

John leaped to his feet in a single bound, "I don't know what you're talking about!" he denied angrily. "I'm just worried about Mary," he came face to face with Nick, challenging him.

Nick pushed past to sit on the couch. "You've been bitten by the love bug, John and you've been bitten *bad*!" he laughed. "I should know! I recognize all the signs."

John ran his hands through his hair in despair, "I don't know what to do!" He told Nick what happened between he and Mary before Duncan came in.

Nick looked confused, "I don't understand the problem. You know she's crazy about you," he said slowly.

"Mary can't remember any of it!" he shouted, glaring at Nick. "She's back to treating me like a good friend," he sighed. "I can't do anything about it now, of course, but I don't know what to do when she gets out of the hospital."

"Grab her and kiss her!"

John groaned, throwing himself face down on the bed. "I want to do that every time I see her," he admitted truthfully, raising himself up on his elbows. "I didn't even know you could feel this way about a woman," he murmured in a daze.

Nick nodded sagely; "Tell me about it!" he still cringed when he remembered the agony he felt before he knew Laura loved him, too. "At least you know she's got it bad for you, too," he consoled his friend.

"If she's got it so bad, why didn't she ever say anything until she thought she was going to die?" John demanded morosely.

Nick laughed, "Because you're a *player*, you idiot! Women like Bo, Laura and Mary find that a real turn off!" Nick advised seriously. He had learned a lot about relationships when he fell in love with Laura. Nick leaned over the bed to slap John on the back, "I predict a happy ending if you can get your act together, my friend."

He went upstairs to collect his wife. "We have to go, darling," he gave her a kiss that made her blush. They bid Alex and Bo goodbye.

"I'm going to go check on John," Alex told Bo.

She collected her things, "Okay, but I'll be waiting for you at home," she kissed him goodbye, making him raise his eyebrows. She looked back at him at the entrance to the Baby; he knew that look.

John threw Alex out of his room after five minutes of pity.

*   *   *   *

John had to wait three more weeks while Mary was in rehab. He offered to drive her home and visited her every day, keeping their visits short and friendly. He ran errands for her and called every day; after a week at home, he couldn't wait any longer.

He pulled up in front of her apartment and saw a car parked in the visitor spot beside her car. He knocked on the door and it was opened immediately by Mary, who stood in the short entrance hall. Her ex-fiancée Ted stared at John dolefully.

"Oh, hi John!" Mary greeted him warmly. "You know Ted West, don't you? Ted was just leaving." John stepped into the hall, grasping Ted's hand, shaking it firmly.

"Nice to meet you, Ted," John said pushing Ted unceremoniously out the door. He closed the door in the surprised man's face and locked it before turning to an astonished Mary, taking her in his arms and kissing her. Mary stood stock still, she tried to resist him but she knew it was no use. She put her arms around his neck, kissing him back. They had no idea how long they stood in the hall kissing before John took his mouth from hers and looked down into her beautiful eyes.

"You're not a virgin, are you?" he asked calmly as a startled Mary shook her head.

"Why are you looking for one?" she asked impishly. He picked her up, carrying her into her bedroom and laid her gently on the bed.

"Is this okay with you?" he asked standing beside her. She smiled and held out her arms. He lay beside her, taking her in his arms. Mary pressed herself full length against him as he kissed her passionately, letting his hands explore her body.

He startled her when he stopped and moved back to stare at her anxiously.

"Do you think we should call the doctor?" he asked anxiously.

"Do you need medical advice?" she teased, pulling his head to her and kissing him. He pulled away once more.

"Are you sure you're well enough to do this?"

She smiled, "*I'm* well enough but I'm not so sure about you," she teased pointedly. "Here, let me help you," she pulled off her shirt. John barely noticed that she wasn't wearing a bra; he stared at her scar, after two months it was still red but healing nicely. Mary had forgotten all about it and searched his face anxiously, "Is it too ugly?"

John looked shocked, "Ugly? It's a beautiful scar! Wait till you see the one I got in a knife fight," he replied happily pulling off his shirt.

Mary laughed in delight and pulled him down, kissing him passionately.

*　　*　　*　　*

Mary was quickly accepted into the group and stayed on the Baby with John quite frequently. She loved the boat as much as he did and arranged several sails on the weekends with all six of them.

Life was good but John still felt a little restless. When Mary wasn't staying with him or he wasn't at her apartment, he felt something was missing. He'd talked to her several times about moving onto the Baby but she wasn't as receptive to the idea as he wanted. She just said it wasn't time. He admitted to himself that he wanted to be married to her; he wanted to know she was his forever. But if she wouldn't even move in with him, he was afraid to ask her to marry him. He planned how he was going to ask her.

They laid in bed on the Baby listening to the soothing creaking of the ship.

"Mary, why did you save my life?" John asked suddenly. He felt her tense up and she tried to roll away but he held on to her. "You remember that day, Mary, I know you do. The other day you were talking about our first kiss; you were talking about thinking you were going to die. Why did you sacrifice yourself to save me?" he looked down into her face.

She turned her face into his chest, "I didn't want to live without you." She mumbled reluctantly.

He held her very tightly to him, suddenly feeling desperately afraid. He felt disturbed, in a way he didn't understand, by this information. He held her for a while longer before getting up to dress.

"Where are you going?" she asked knowing something was wrong.

"I have to check the planes for tomorrow's flights," he said, forgetting to kiss her goodbye as he hurriedly left.

Mary got up and dressed slowly; she hadn't wanted him to know why she saved him. She still felt that she loved him so much more than he loved her and was afraid of losing him. She had never had any illusions about John; she never thought she would be more than a passing flirtation for him. She had been happier than she ever thought possible after she admitted to herself, the day he kissed her in the hall, that she was lost to him forever.

She had known she loved him since the day she had gotten him out on bail for the murder charge. When he had held her hand and looked into her eyes and thanked her for her help, she had felt chills. She had gone home and broken her engagement to Ted; in the four years she had been with Ted, he had never once made her feel the way she felt when John held her hand and looked into her eyes. She had known instantly that she could never marry Ted. When she had told her parents of the broken engagement, her father had been very disappointed and Mary realized she had stayed with Ted to make her father happy. Her mother hadn't been surprised.

"Did you marry Dad for love?" Mary had asked her mother.

"Of course, dear! What other reason is there to get married?" her mother had looked at her in surprise but Mary had just shrugged and let the conversation drop.

Mary looked around the familiar main cabin sadly and decided she needed to take most of her clothes with her to be cleaned. "Chicken." she chided herself aloud. She felt afraid as she got into her car, staring hard at the Baby before turning around and driving away.

John was at the hangar checking the planes. At the moment, he stared into space unable to decide what was bothering him. A large hand fell on his shoulder, startling him and he turned to see Mary's father. He hadn't even heard Mr. Stevens walk up to him.

"Well, son, how's it going?" Mr. Stevens asked; his tone falsely hearty. John had had several dinners with Mary's parents and had always gotten the impression they weren't too fond of him. They had been friendlier at the hospital.

"Fine, sir. How are you?" John replied stiffly, wondering why he was here.

"The Mrs. and I have been wondering when you were going to make an honest woman of our little girl," Mr. Stevens came directly to the point.

John stared flabbergasted; even though he had wanted to ask Mary to marry him, he couldn't believe her father was asking him about this. John simply couldn't find any words to answer him and felt unexpectedly pressured.

"Excuse me, sir?" he finally managed to gasp.

Mr. Stevens smiled apologetically, "I know you young people today don't consider marriage important but we do. Mary is a very special lady. We don't want anyone trifling with her affections," he told John stiffly. "You do plan on marrying her, don't you?"

"*Mary* and I haven't discussed marriage, yet," John replied, getting annoyed.

"Do you think you can afford a wife and children with this business you have?" Mr. Stevens continued, looking around him disparagingly. "Mary was raised with the best of everything. You'd have to sell that ridiculous boat, of course!" he continued, not noticing the anger growing in John's eyes. "Of course, her mother and I would be happy to help you turn these two planes into a proper airline fleet. Then you could give her everything she deserves and expects from a husband."

"If you'll excuse me, I have an appointment," John replied in a hard voice as he brushed past him. He threw the rag in his hand down on the table by the door as he left. He locked the door and turned to Mr. Stevens who was frowning. "Just close the door on your way out."

John didn't get back to the boat until late that night. He called Mary to tell her he wouldn't be around for the next two days because they were booked for flights. Mary heard a change in his voice; he sounded distant.

"John, what's wrong?" she asked softly.

"Nothing, I'm just tired! Goodnight," he hung up without saying 'I love you' for the first time since they'd been together. Mary looked at the phone in her hand and started to cry.

FOUR

Two weeks later Bo was in town and saw Mary coming out of the bookstore; Bo ran after her calling her name. Mary turned reluctantly.

"Hi, Bo, how are you?" Mary avoided looking her in the eye.

"Mary, what the hell happened with you and John?" Bo came right to the point.

"I don't know. John started avoiding me; I guess I was just too needy for him," she told Bo sadly. "I can take a hint," she turned to go.

Bo grabbed her arm, "Mary, I don't understand. John has been like a bear with a sore paw! We thought *you* broke up with him; especially when you wouldn't take our calls." She and Laura had both left several messages for Mary.

Mary hung her head. "I'm sorry, Bo! It's just too painful for me!" Mary replied with tears in her eyes.

Bo put her hand on Mary's arm in sympathy, "I'm sorry, Mary." She let Mary walk away but stared after her for a long time. "Damn that man!"

Bo went home and lit into Alex, "What is wrong with that brother of yours?" she demanded angrily. "*He* broke up with Mary!" She informed him as he turned a startled face towards her.

"You talked to Mary?"

"She's devastated," Bo told him. "What could have happened?" she asked, pacing. "I would have bet you money he was thinking of asking her to marry him. He's obviously miserable."

The next day Alex walked on the Baby to find Nick and John in the main cabin.

"I saw Mary yesterday—" Alex began. John abruptly got up and walked out of the room. They heard his bedroom door slam as Nick angrily looked at Alex.

"Why would you bring up that woman's name?"

"John broke up with her!"

"What are you talking about?" Nick was clearly unbelieving.

Alex nodded grimly and Nick jumped to his feet. He leaped down the stairs making Alex follow him with foreboding. Nick swung John's door open; John looked up angrily from the bed.

"*You* broke up with her?" Nick asked aggressively.

"What of it?" John replied just as aggressively.

Nick stared angrily, "You deserve to be miserable!" he told his friend and slammed the door. He turned quickly, running into Alex. He pushed past him and kept going.

*   *   *   *

It'd been over a month since they found out the truth about the break-up of John and Mary. John had been a mess; late for all his flights, missing some of them completely. Nick had been working double shifts to cover for him. John had been drinking heavily and they'd had several meetings but no one wanted to make the decision they had to make.

Laura silently boarded the Baby; John was supposed to fly in three hours and she wanted to give him plenty of notice, tired of Nick always being gone or tired out when he was home. She knocked on the door but received no answer. The door was unlocked so she went in. The main cabin was a mess; clothes, food and dishes were lying about everywhere and the place stunk. She walked downstairs and knocked on his bedroom door and again got no answer. She cautiously opened the door and was shocked by what she saw.

There were two blondes asleep in John's bed. She turned her head as she heard the bathroom door open. John came out and Laura was thankful he wore cutoff sweats. He looked like hell. He stopped when he saw her and his glance flew to the bed as Laura walked up and slapped him hard across the face. He staggered back as much from shock as from the force of her slap.

"Hey!" he yelled angrily as he straightened up.

"You have a flight in three hours, *pig*! Be there!" she shouted sternly, turning on her heel to leave the room.

John ran after her, "Laura!" he yelled, grabbing her arm and turning her around on the stairs even as she angrily pulled her arm away.

"Don't you touch me, pig!" she practically spit the words at him and turned to leave.

He grabbed her arm more forcefully this time and dragged her back to his room. She struggled and kicked him making him stumble and swear but he didn't let go. He kicked the bed on his way past, waking up the women.

"Go home, girls," he told them abruptly. They sleepily got out of bed. Laura stared at them angrily; relieved to see they were wearing bikinis.

They turned at the bedroom door, "Bye, John!" they both chorused, blowing him a kiss. Laura could see they were identical twins and she renewed her struggle to get away from John who shoved her down on the couch.

"Just sit down, you little spitfire!" he yelled and winced with pain as she kicked him hard in the shin. "Ow!" he shouted, jumping back. "It's not what you think!" he hollered but as soon as he released her arm, she jumped up and he shoved her back down, "Laura, knock it off!" He shouted and grabbed his aching head, sitting gingerly on the edge of the bed. "They brought me home last night. I slept face down on the living room floor all night," he vaguely remembered falling forward last night and that was the last thing he remembered before waking up a few minutes before Laura arrived. "I don't think I can fly today," he groaned.

Laura marched over and slapped him hard again, "Oh, yes, you are going to fly today, pig!" she shouted as he grabbed her wrist. "I'm sick and tired of this poor me act and it's going to stop right now! You broke Mary's heart. I saw her yesterday and she looks even worse than you!"

"That's pretty bad," John said slowly and caught her other hand as she was about to slap him again. He was being perfectly serious.

"You've let everyone down, John! You should be ashamed of yourself. I know I'm ashamed of you. Nick and Alex are at the end of their rope; they don't know what to do with you but I do! Throw you out of the corporation before you run this business into the ground." She shouted, struggling to get her wrists free. He felt incredibly weak and quickly turned her to face away from him. He pulled her towards him, wrapping his arms around her and covering her mouth.

"Will you shut up for one minute!" he begged in exasperation as she pushed her feet against the floor, pushing backwards against him to get away. She only succeeded in making him fall back on the bed still holding her on top of him. John heard Nick calling from upstairs.

"Laura?"

"Damn!" John tried to roll Laura off him quickly and stand up but he didn't quite make it before Nick came in the room.

Nick came leaping down the stairs and found his wife struggling with John on the bed and saw her handprint on his face. The pent up emotions of the past miserable month came boiling to the surface. Luckily for John, he wasn't wearing a shirt and his crew cut was too short to grab. It slowed Nick down a few seconds as he grabbed John by the arm, spinning him around. John managed to block the first punch and tried to close with him but Nick was a madman. John got punched several times but didn't hit Nick back or even try to block the punches. John body blocked Nick to the floor and lay on top of him, pinning him to the floor with his body. John was sweating profusely and panting with the exertion after a hard night drinking. Laura quickly sat on Nick's free arm.

"Nick! Nick!" Laura shouted, trying to get him to look at her instead of glaring at John with hatred in his eyes. "Stop it, please," she begged as he looked at her suddenly realizing she was there. He grunted with the exertion of getting John off so he could continue to beat him up.

"Laura, get out of my way, babe!" he ordered tenderly, completely serious. Laura put her head down on his chest as much as she could with John in the way and laughed lightly.

"Calm down, Nick," she pleaded as Alex and Bo appeared in the bedroom doorway.

"What the hell?" Bo said clearly. "Who's beating up whom?"

"I'm gonna kill him!" Nick ground out, trying to grab John.

"Why?" Alex asked cautiously, knowing the handprint on John's face must be Laura's.

"The filthy pig was attacking my wife!" Nick renewed his struggles to grab John who had one arm pinned to the floor while Laura was still sitting on the other one.

"I was not attacking her!" John protested wearily. "I was just trying to get her to shut up so I could talk to her!"

"Why did she slap you?" Alex asked curiously, sitting on the bed.

John sighed deeply, "She came in and saw the Mosley twins asleep in my bed. I came out of the bathroom and she slapped me and called me a pig. She slapped me and called me a pig *again* when she was reading me the riot act!" He wondered if it was safe to get off Nick now; he felt he might throw up any minute.

"Good girl, Babe." Nick praised her with a soft smile.

She smiled down at him, "Can we get up now? I'm getting a cramp."

He nodded slowly and John got up first, reaching down to help Laura to her feet. Nick sprang to his feet, roughly pushing John away from her.

"Don't touch her again!" he warned John menacingly as he led Laura to the couch.

John sighed deeply and sat on the edge of the bed beside Alex. Bo sat on the couch next to Nick and they all stared at John.

"I'm sorry! I know I owe all of you a huge apology. I'm an idiot! It was my fault Mary and I broke up. I got scared," he muttered looking at the floor. He looked up suddenly at Bo. "And I did not sleep with those women! They brought me home last night and I was passed out on the floor upstairs all night."

She raised her eyebrows, "Why were they sleeping in the same bed?" she had to ask, not quite believing him.

John sighed, "They're a little odd. Just ask Ni—" John pointed to Nick but stopped and grimaced as he realized Laura was now looking askance at her husband. Nick glared at John and if looks could kill, John would be dead. "Now, if you'll all excuse me, I'm going to throw up!" he ran into the bathroom.

Nick stood up to leave but Laura and Bo each grabbed an arm, pulling him back down to the couch.

"How odd are they, Nick?" Laura asked in a sugary sweet tone of voice.

"Yes, Nick, do tell us!" Bo added, supporting her friend.

A disgruntled Nick sighed loudly. "They're so weird that we've never had sex with them, if you must know," he replied truthfully. Three shocked pairs of eyes were glued to his face and he sighed deeply again, planning revenge on John. "They've never slept apart even one night in their entire life and they wanted the four of us to sleep together," he stood up decisively, "That's a little too weird for me!" he began walking out of the room.

"Wow, I can't believe there's actually something you and John wouldn't do!" Bo said, making Nick turn abruptly and glare menacingly as she grinned wickedly at him.

"One of these days, you're going to get spanked!" he threatened. He anxiously looked at his wife to see her eyes twinkling, enjoying his discomfort enormously. Nick growled and walked away.

They left John alone to shower and dress and went upstairs to make breakfast. Bo and Laura put all the dirty things into a big pile far from the table; they weren't going to clean up after John. They were just finishing breakfast when he came up. He still looked like hell, but he was clean and gratefully accepted the coffee Bo offered. He could feel Nick's eyes on him; he still looked angry. John looked at Laura apologetically.

"I didn't hurt you, did I?" he asked softly and she shook her head with a smile.

"You're in no condition to fly!" Nick said abruptly.

John sighed, "I'm sorry, Nick!" he hung his head.

"This has to stop or we're throwing you out of the corporation," Nick replied grimly, so Alex didn't have to say it.

John smiled, "I heard," he looked at Laura but she wasn't smiling. "It won't happen again. I promise!" They left him, wanting to believe it but they were afraid. Nick took the flight and John went back to bed.

Later that night, Nick was sleeping on his back, limbs stretched out across the whole bed. He woke suddenly, unsure why and stretched further. He used to love sleeping this way, he thought and then sat bolt upright. Now he knew what woke him; his bed partner was missing. He went to search for her.

He found Laura sitting on the porch in a rocker. She rocked slowly and didn't hear him until he knelt beside her, taking her hand.

"Don't think about them!" he begged softly.

Laura looked at him without understanding, "Who?" She ran her hand through his hair.

"You're thinking about those stupid women today! I could kill John! None of them meant anything to me, I swear—"

Laura put her fingers against his lips and then put her lips against his, "I wasn't thinking about them." She assured him gently.

He stared still worried, "Why are you out here? What's wrong?"

She smiled gently, "If you want to know the truth, I was thinking how incredibly, impossibly happy I am. Thanks to a former playboy, now a model husband," she said with a light laugh, kissing him again slowly.

"Come back to bed." he begged in a deep voice filled with emotion.

They walked upstairs arm in arm; at the top he stopped and turned towards her. She looked at him inquisitively.

"Laura, I want to have children."

She smiled and put her arms around his neck. He picked her up and carried her into the bedroom as she snuggled into his neck, smiling a secret smile.

*   *   *   *

John took the early morning flight the next day. He decided to stop and see Mary on his way home from the hangar. He had tried to call her yesterday evening when he woke but she didn't answer the phone. He had driven to the apartment but she didn't answer the door.

He was nervous and didn't know what to say. When he got there and saw her car wasn't there, he parked out of sight of her apartment and waited for her in the hall. She walked down the hallway carrying a briefcase. He felt the same shock when he saw her that Bo felt. Mary looked like she'd lost weight; she was pale and walking with her head down and her shoulders slumped. She looked so very sad; John's heart broke at the sight of her. He ran to her taking her in his arms.

"Mary! Mary!" he could only say her name over and over. "Please forgive me, Mary! I'm an idiot! I don't want to live without you, either!"

She dropped her briefcase when he put his arms around her but looked up at him with a strange look in her eye, holding herself away from him. He kissed her passionately pressing her against him. *She feels different somehow*, he thought. She hadn't said a word yet and he looked down into her eyes. Suddenly, he knew why she felt different.

"Oh my God!" he cried shocked. "You're pregnant!" his face lit up and he pulled her to him. "Mary! Mary! Will you marry me?" he shouted, excited and eager. He kissed her feverishly but she pushed roughly away from him.

"No, I won't marry you!" she retorted grimly. She unlocked her door as he stared in shocked disbelief. She picked up her briefcase, staring at him as she slowly entered the apartment. She closed the door and locked it and John felt a rush of sudden anger wash over him as he heard the lock turn.

"I have a key, you know!" he yelled through the door.

"I changed the locks!"

He pounded the wall angrily and left breathing as if someone just punched him.

Everyone was on board Baby waiting for him, wondering if anything had gone wrong. He should have been back forty-five minutes ago. They hadn't wanted to check on him this morning before the flight. They didn't want him to know they weren't sure they could trust him.

John stalked into the room in a black cloud of despair and rage. Laura put out a hand to stop his mad rush past them to get to his room.

"John, what's the matter?"

He looked at her silently for a few seconds before turning to see three more pairs of eyes staring in concern.

"Mary is pregnant!" he told them the stunning news and was shocked to see four pairs of eyes slide away as they looked at each other guiltily. "Oh my God! You knew!" John shouted; beside himself with rage. "You all knew and didn't tell me!" he turned to leave but Alex blocked him.

"We didn't *know*. I think we suspected but we didn't say anything to each other. We wanted to let Mary tell us," Alex took a deep breath.

"I asked her to marry me. She said no!" he said angrily, pushing past Alex and going downstairs.

"Ouch!" Nick muttered, "I know how that feels." Laura put her arm around Nick laying her head on his shoulder.

"You and me both!" Alex added with feeling.

Bo asked Alex curiously, "What do you mean? I said yes the minute you asked me."

"Yes, you did; and after we had been secretly married for three months, you told me you didn't want me to move in with you!" he reminded her indignantly.

Bo threw her arms around his neck, "Oh, my poor Alex!" She nuzzled him and looked at the others. "What are we going to do with these two?" she asked sadly.

"What can we do?" Nick and Laura both asked. Secretly, they all hoped John wouldn't go off the deep end again.

John threw himself into his work. If he wasn't flying or maintaining the jets, he ran and worked out. He spent the evenings with friends and never mentioned Mary. No one guessed that late at night he drove over and sat in the truck staring at her apartment windows.

FIVE

The situation continued for three weeks until Mary took her mother's jewelry to be cleaned by their family jeweler. She walked in and Mr. Anderson greeted her with a cheery hello, having known her almost her whole life.

"Ah, Mary, how are you?" he beamed. "I've been expecting you."

Mary looked surprised, "Did my mother call you?" she asked not understanding.

He shook his head smiling gleefully, "No, no my dear! I try to tell all the young men who come in here to buy diamonds for their lady loves to bring the lady with them. I can't tell you, my dear, how many of them bring the diamond back to exchange it. It isn't something they would have picked themselves, you understand." He smiled at Mary who didn't understand at all. "I told John; he should let you pick it out or at least shop around with you to get an idea what you would like. But he was positive you would love it! He said it called your name the minute he saw it," he smiled again but suddenly noticed Mary's wooden expression and added hastily, "Not that it isn't a lovely ring; the diamonds are flawless!" He smiled once more.

Mary stared as if turned to stone, "When was this, Mr. Anderson?" she asked in a strangled voice.

He tilted his head thinking, "Why it must be almost three months ago."

She continued to stare at him, utterly bewildered and then suddenly turned away, "I have to go!" She ran out of the store and down the street until she was out of breath. She leaned against a building, gasping for breath. She had a pain in her side and tears flowed down her cheeks. Several people stopped to ask her if she needed help but she shook her head and ran off. She finally found her car and drove to the marina.

She parked and ran onto the dock. When she got to the Baby, she could hardly speak. No one was on board and Mary became frantic. She ran back to her car but Bo had seen her from across the street and came running over.

"Mary! What's wrong?" she asked frightened by Mary's tears and her air of tragedy.

Mary clung to her breathlessly, "I need to talk to John!" she gasped through her tears.

"He and Nick are on a flight to Rio." Bo told her, "They won't be back until late tonight," she tried to lead Mary back to the Baby but Mary broke away, heading for her car, looking stricken. "Please, Mary, won't you tell me what's wrong?" Bo begged following her as Mary mutely shook her head. "Let me help you!"

"No one can help me except John!" Mary wailed and got in her car. She drove away leaving Bo staring after her frightened and helpless.

Bo called Alex at the airplane hangar. He too was upset but he didn't know what to do if Mary wouldn't tell them anything and advised her to wait until John was back.

Bo went to talk to Laura; both women were deeply upset by Mary's distress. Bo reached for her phone. "I left my phone at home!"

Laura wordlessly handed her phone to Bo, "Who are you calling?" she asked curiously.

"Nick!" Bo stated positively, knowing they should be in the air by now.

John was flying the first leg back and Nick was in the copilot seat. He answered his phone eagerly seeing Laura's name, feeling that little thrill he got when he knew he was going to see her or heard her voice.

"Hey, Babe! What's up?" he asked, his voice caressing.

"It's not babe, it's Bo!" Bo retorted sharply and heard him give a violent snort. Bo grinned as she glanced at Laura.

"What are you doing calling me on Laura's phone, brat?" he began, deeply annoyed. "Is she alright?" he asked suddenly fearful.

"She's fine, Nick. Will you shut up, please?" Bo said gently. "What time will you be getting back?"

"We'll land about eleven-thirty your time, just like we planned. Why?" he wondered what was going on.

"Don't say anything to your friend but Mary came looking for him at the boat. She's a mess; crying and terribly upset. She wouldn't tell me what was wrong, just that she needed John; only John could help her," Bo murmured in a low voice so John couldn't overhear.

"Oh!" was Nick's only response, "Okay, that's fine. Tell Laura I'll see her then." he lied, to say something.

"Make sure he goes right over to her when you get here," Bo added and hung up.

Nick put his phone away without saying anything to John.

"What's up?" John asked when he didn't speak.

Nick shrugged, "The girls are going out on the town tonight. They didn't want us to worry if they're not back when we get home." He lied glibly.

Fifteen minutes later, John glanced at Nick.

"You know I could fly this plane all the way home without your help, right?" He asked very seriously.

Nick looked at him oddly, "Yeah, buddy, I know that," he assured him solemnly.

John breathed a sigh of relief, "Good, because if you don't tell me what that phone call was about; I'm gonna kill you," John threatened angrily.

Nick grinned, "Alright, alright," he paused to think how best to tell him. "Mary came looking for you. She was very upset; something is wrong but she didn't tell them what. She needs to see you." He looked at John who stared straight ahead with a grim expression.

"Take the controls, will you?" He asked and they traded places.

John took out his phone, "Mary, what's wrong?" he asked as soon as he heard her voice.

"John, John, where are you?" Mary cried, bursting into tears again.

"Mary, I'm in the air! Are you sick? Is something wrong with the baby?" John asked desperately. He listened to Mary for a few minutes but she was crying and sobbing so hard he couldn't understand anything she said. "Mary, I can't understand you! Stop crying and tell me, please!" he begged. He was listening intently when the line went dead. He looked out the window; they were flying over mountains and he'd lost the connection.

"Damn!" he cursed despairingly as he snapped the phone shut, looking grimly at Nick. "I couldn't understand one word she said; she's hysterical!" He got up to change places with Nick again.

"I'll take it," Nick offered, not getting up.

John tapped him on the shoulder, motioning him to move, "I'd rather fly. It'll keep my mind off Mary for a little while."

*   *   *   *

It was a very long flight; John tried to call once they were closer to home but Mary wasn't answering the phone. They landed early due to a tail wind and the passengers were slightly startled when one of the pilots pushed past them to get off the plane first. John leaped down the stairs and kept running. The passengers looked at Nick slightly alarmed.

"Family emergency!" he explained with a small smile and did his best not to rush the passengers off the plane but he was dying to know what had been going on and if there was any news.

John drove like a maniac and arrived at Mary's apartment in ten minutes. He bounded up the steps, pounding on the door, shouting her name.

The door opened and a tearful Mary flung herself into his arms, clinging to him, crying and sobbing; several of her neighbors had poked their heads out of their doors by this time. John hustled her inside. He shut the door and picked her up, cradling her in his arms and sitting down on the couch with her on his lap.

"Mary, Mary, please tell me what's wrong!" he begged, holding her tight.

"No—thing!" she gasped, looking at him through her tears.

He looked completely mystified, "Then why all the tears?"

"I'm so happy!" she stammered, burying her face in his neck.

John was stunned, "Mary, I don't understand!" he cried helplessly.

Mary tried to stem the flow of tears and took several deep breaths, "You bought me an engagement ring!" she said with shining eyes.

"Yeah?" he agreed still confused.

"Three months ago!" she shouted joyfully and kissed him soundly. John kissed her back hungrily; he'd longed to be in this position so often he didn't want to say or do anything to upset it but he just didn't understand and decided to keep kissing her until she changed her mind.

"Why didn't you ask me to marry you three months ago?" she demanded, finally pulling back to gaze at him.

"I was afraid! You wouldn't even move in with me. I started to ask you a couple of times and then the phone rang or someone came to visit!" he remembered in disgust.

Mary laughed, "I was afraid if I moved in with you, you would get tired of me so much quicker and it would be over," she explained softly without looking at him.

"Mary, you are nothing like all the women I've dated. I will never get tired of you. I don't want to live without you!" he lifted her chin to make her look at him.

"When I told *you* that; it upset you!"

He nodded ruefully, "Yes, it did," he sighed. "I was so afraid that if I let you down, you would end up like Brenda and I couldn't stand that! And then your father had that little talk with me and I knew I wasn't really good enough for you. You'll get tired of me before I get tired of you."

Mary looked uncertain, "Who's Brenda?" she inquired suspiciously.

John couldn't believe there was actually someone who didn't know about Brenda.

"She was an old girlfriend of Nick's who was really in love with him. When she found him in bed with her friend, she took a couple of shots at him."

"Oh, yes, I remember that. I didn't remember her name," Mary nodded.

"She killed herself almost a year later and left a note saying she didn't want to live without Nick," John finished the story.

"Well, if I find you in bed with anyone else, I'll take a couple of shots at you, too!" she warned playfully. "But I won't miss!" she pulled his head down. "If you leave me, I will be devastated but I wouldn't kill myself," she promised seriously and kissed him.

John lost himself in her kisses, adjusting his position on the couch so she was lying back on the cushions and he was leaning over her.

"What talk did you have with my father?" Mary stopped kissing to ask curiously. John explained making Mary sit up suddenly. "My father said that?" she asked amazed and angry all at once.

John nodded, "He's not quite right. I *can* afford a wife and kids. I don't have any idea how well the business is actually doing but I have a nest egg thanks to my brainy brother. You can ask him how much money I'm worth at the moment," he tried to return to kissing.

Mary pushed him back, "We can't sell the Baby! I love that boat; I want to live on her!"

His face lit up and he held her tightly to his chest, "What about our baby?"

She grinned, "Oh, I want him to live with us, too," she took his hand and stood up, walking into the bedroom.

"Him?" John asked in a dazed voice.

"Him," she grinned as he lay on the bed and she lay beside him, kissing him.

"Damn!" he sat up and reached into his back pocket. He opened his phone, "Everything is fine. I'm going to be a daddy and a husband!" He glanced at Mary as he spoke; she was taking off her clothes. "Gotta go!" he snapped it shut and threw it out into the hall. He closed the door and came back to his fiancée; taking the ring out of his wallet. Mary noticed that he had carried it with him so long the wallet has shaped itself around the little bulge.

John knelt on one knee and placed the ring on her finger, "Mary Stevens, will you marry me?" he asked formally.

"I will, John Colby!" she answered equally formally before throwing her arms around his neck as he stood up. He tumbled them both back onto the bed.

Mary was enjoying herself very much when John gasped and stopped suddenly.

"What's the matter?"

"What about the baby?" he whispered making Mary giggle. "Is it okay to do this?"

"It's fine, darling," she murmured against his mouth. She decided this wasn't the time to tell him that her parents had sex the day she was born to induce labor. There was plenty of time for him to learn about babies.

*   *   *   *

No one saw John or Mary for two days after they became engaged but they appeared on the Baby the third day, both unable to stop smiling. Everyone was very happy for them and a party atmosphere prevailed as they had an impromptu barbeque on the deck in the sunshine.

"Mary, I just don't understand how an intelligent woman like you could let yourself get pregnant in the first place," Alex stated curiously, sitting in the lounge chair staring at Mary, sitting at the table beside John.

There was a moment of dead silence before John, looking like thunder, stepped toward his brother menacingly. Nick quickly got up to stand in front of Alex while Bo smacked the back of Alex's head.

"Well Alex, being shot and in a coma and on antibiotics for over a month really messes up the effectiveness of any contraceptive," Mary grinned, taking John's hand and smiling up into his face. He glanced at Alex balefully but sat down beside her.

"One of these days, Alex," he muttered fiercely.

*   *   *   *

The wedding took place one week later on the Baby since they had decided there wasn't any reason to wait. The bride was radiant in a satin dress that showed her long slim figure to its best advantage. She had lost so much weight when she was separated from John that she didn't look five months pregnant.

The guests were leaving and Mary's mother gave her a hug and kiss goodbye.

She leaned in closer, "I'll tell him tonight," she winked at her daughter.

Mary smiled gratefully at her mother as she kissed her father goodbye. He gave her a long hug while looking unhappily at John.

"Don't you break her heart again, you hear me?" he warned his new son-in-law. He had been very much against the wedding until John had sent Alex over to tell him how well situated John was financially. His fears were lessened considerably until they told him they were going to live on the Baby. Mary didn't know how he would take the news that she was pregnant when her mother told him tonight. Everyone kept a smile on their face until he turned away and John gave a deep sigh of escape.

"Whew!" he looked at Mary. "Think he's ever going to like me?"

"Hey, be happy you only have one hostile male relative!" Nick replied cheerfully with his arm around Laura. John got a picture of Laura's six huge brothers in his mind and suddenly didn't feel so bad.

"You can have Nick teach you his hiding skills; I saw him hiding from Eddie and George the last time they were here," Bo teased Nick with a broad grin. Nick advanced towards her pretending he was angry.

"You think it's funny, do you, little girl?" he asked, using John's old nick-name for her. "It's time for that spanking!"

Alex leaped up, stepping in front of Nick and giving him a hard shove backwards.

"Don't touch her!" he yelled angrily as Nick stepped back with his arms spread wide, completely taken aback by Alex's attitude. They all stared at Alex who stood behind Bo with his arms crossed protectively in front of her. Bo had a wide grin on her face while Alex looked distraught.

"Alex, you know I would never do anything to hurt Bo!" Nick murmured, very hurt.

Alex looked down at the ground, "She's— very fragile," he mumbled as Bo's grin got wider.

"Since when?" Nick asked mystified.

"Bo! You're pregnant!" Mary blurted suddenly, staring at Bo and Alex who grinned from ear to ear. Everyone was so surprised, there was total silence.

"God help us men," Nick said dolefully, "All three of them pregnant at the same time!" It took a minute to sink in.

"Laura, you're pregnant, too?" Bo asked for all of them.

Nick put his arm around her as they both grinned. The women jumped up for a group hug. The men hugged one another separately. They hugged each of the women in turn and ended with their own wife in their arms. They couldn't stop smiling and everyone talked at once. A sudden silence fell as the sun was setting.

"We're having a boy," John beamed proudly.

"We're having twins!" Nick said looking rather dazed.

"So are we!" Alex cried excitedly, standing beside Bo who had sat down again, as a strange expression crossed her face and she looked up at him.

"Actually, darling, that was the doctor on the phone this morning," she said and paused as Alex looked at her in concern. "She said the hormone levels are so high; we're having triplets!" she shrugged her shoulders apologetically. John shoved a chair under Alex as his knees sagged as he stared at Bo.

"I was worried about you having twins," he muttered faintly. "You can't have triplets!" he firmly shook his head.

"We can't send them back, honey," Bo calmly patted his hand.

"You're too small to carry triplets!" Alex insisted adamantly.

"Well, unless you know of another way, Alex, she'll have to," Laura replied with a laugh.

Alex groaned, "I don't think I can do this!" he moaned mournfully making them all laugh.

"Then it's a good thing *I'm* the one who has to do it!" Bo snapped sourly.

"Wow! From zero to six kids in seven months." Mary murmured, impressed.

"I'd better start inventing a Nanny Quark that can change diapers and give bottles." Alex cheered up just thinking about it and they laughed at him again.

They turned to watch the sun set over the ocean. The couples kissed as a new adventure began for all of them.

www.ingramcontent.com/pod-product-compliance
Lightning Source LLC
Chambersburg PA
CBHW071241170626
46809CB00001B/38